QUEST

QUEST

by Helen R. Hull

Afterword by Patricia McClelland Miller

THE FEMINIST PRESS
at The City University of New York
New York

Afterword © 1990 by Patricia McClelland Miller
All Rights Reserved
Published 1990 by The Feminist Press at The City University
of New York, 311 East 94 Street, New York, N.Y. 10128
Distributed by The Talman Company, Inc., 150 Fifth Avenue,
New York, N.Y. 10011

Quest was originally published in 1922.

94 93 92 91 90 6 5 4 3 2 1

Library of Congress Cataloging-in-Publication Data

Hull, Helen R. (Helen Rose), 1888–1971.
    Quest / by Helen R. Hull; afterword by Patricia McClelland
Miller.
        p. cm.
    Reprint. Originally published: New York: Macmillan, 1922.
    ISBN 1-55861-021-9: $11.95
    I. Miller, Patricia McClelland. II. Title.
PS3515.U363Q4   1990
813'.54—dc20   90-30445
                                                                      CIP

This publication is made possible, in part, by public funds from
the New York State Council on the Arts. The Feminist Press is
also grateful to Helene D. Goldfarb for her generosity.

Cover design: Lucinda Geist
Cover art: 03.180 American Painting: James McNeill Whistler,
1834–1903, *The Little Red Glove,* 1896–1902. Oil on canvas:
51.3 x 31.5 cm (20 1/4 x 12 3/8″). Courtesy of the Freer Gallery of
Art, Smithsonian Institution, Washington, D.C.
Back cover photo: Helen R. Hull, c. 1930. Courtesy of Frederick
C. Hull.

Printed in the United States of America on pH-neutral paper by
McNaughton & Gunn, Inc.

QUEST

PART I
THE SMALL SELF

QUEST

I

LIFE enclosed Jean as a drop of water holds an amœba. She felt it in its entirety; she could not as yet break it up into parts. Sometimes it was warm, pleasant, and the tiny nucleus of herself expanded, glowing. Sometimes it irritated her with harshness, coldness, and she contracted to shut away the pain from without. Later there were the sounds "good," and "bad." Good was when her self expanded. Bad was when she drew in tensely. Slowly she found that good and bad belonged to her. "Don't touch that, Jean." Her hands wanted to touch. Bad hands. If they touched, then the air around her lowered, difficult to breathe. She was no longer the amœba; she knew dimly a relation between herself and her world. Struggles between her hands, her feet, and the tiny inner self that craved warm pleasantness about it. Swift alternations in the tone of the enclosing world.

The world split into parts: Mamma. Papa. Baby. Other people. Things.

Mamma was always in the world. Papa went out of it. Presently Jean learned to sit on the steps when mother said, "Time for papa to come home now." Waiting hurt. It held her suspended, breathless. Then papa, at the corner,

3

and she could run, run, while her hair lifted from her head, until she reached him. Panic for a moment, lest he should be something else! Then she would be swung up in a shivering arc, up to his shoulder.

There was the house, and around it the yard. That was the world. Sometimes feet carried Jean running, running, through the wind, beyond the yard before she saw where she had gone. That was bad. Mamma's face was dark, her voice made something within Jean curl into a tight ball; until presently, mamma shone again.

Sometimes the air darkened, with the harsh, hard coldness from which Jean recoiled, and the child searched vaguely for the sense of cause.

"Jean bad, mamma?" she begged, clinging to her mother's dress.

"No, child. You've been a good girl to-day. Go away and play. Mamma feels bad."

That was difficult to comprehend. It drew the child from her own preoccupations to linger, baffled, on shores of strange adult seas, until, inexplicably, the feeling altered, and she was freed again.

II

Jean sat close to the big bed, her feet tucked against a round of the chair, her knees hunched up to her small square chin.

"An' then the Big Bear came to the middle-size bed, an' he said, 'Who's been a-sleeping here? It's all rumpled, and there's a dent in the pillow'——"

"That wasn't Big Bear," protested Roger fretfully. He twisted under the sheet, his blue eyes queer and hot.

"Lie still. You're sick." Jean patted his sheet. "It was the Middle-size Bear. It's so hot it's buzzing!" she said. "No, that's a fly. Lemme see——" She thought drowsily of last night, when she actually couldn't sleep, she was so warm, and papa had come in in his funny short nightshirt, to fan her with the sheet—long sweeps up and down, so the air came in waves against her face and legs. "Want me to fan you, Roger?"

But Roger had twisted away from her, and when she bent over him, she found his eyes shut and his hands buttoned up tight. She cried out and her mother came hurrying up the stairs.

"Run, Jean, and tell your father! It's another convulsion!" How white and damp her mother's forehead looked! Jean started to run down the stairs. "He's at the library."

Run! Run! The dust poofing under her feet, something pounding in her chest, the warm air moving past her face. Convulsion! White and stiff like a doll! Tears rolling down her cheeks, cool in the warm air. Jerk, jerk, went her knees. Mr. Thomas, a neighbor, wiping his face.

"You shouldn't run so, in this heat, Jean!"

"Convulsion!" Her heart swelled with panic and importance as she brushed off his plump, detaining hand. "Got to get my papa!" She heard his "Well, well!" float after her.

Two blocks straight, then a path across the campus. She couldn't run so fast. There! He was coming toward her, books under his arm. She flung herself at his knees, sobbing.

"What's the matter, Jean?" He dropped his books in the grass, and bent over her.

"Convulsion! Roger!" she gasped. Then she was left, to watch him, his long legs like swift black scissors, eating up the distance over which she had toiled. She had found him. She sat down on the grass, her soft dark hair hanging into her eyes. She'd run pretty fast! She'd prob'ly saved Roger's life. Her tears dried, sticky, on her cheeks, and she lifted the books her father had forgotten. She tried to spell out the title of the largest, but "Aes-the-tics" meant nothing. She tried to hang her arm around them as her father did, and failing, clasped them against her stomach and started slowly home. She looked hopefully for someone whom she could impress with her dread word, convulsion, but the street was deserted.

Home. Papa and mamma with tubs of hot water, Roger's thin little body held carefully in the water; presently his blue eyelids fluttering, the doctor coming, his portentous black case opened to show its neat rows of enticing vials. At length Roger in bed again, asleep, Jean, round-eyed, sober, sent downstairs. That was over.

At the end of the yard was a high fence, behind which rose the embankment of the railroad. Long tracks, running together in a solid gleam in the distance. Jean sat on the fence in the morning when the freight clattered and dragged past, waving to the engineer, envying the brakesman in blue who moved recklessly along the tops of the cars. Then, after the circus, papa put up a horizontal bar, one end on a fence post, one with a post of its own in the ground. Jean hung by her knees, her short skirts petaling about her head, and waved violently when the freight puffed along. She could skin the cat, but when Roger tried, urged by her, and landed on his head, mamma had the bar taken down. Jean ought not to hang upside down, anyway. Nice little girls didn't do things like that! Just because she could and Roger couldn't.

III

Jean pushed open the screen door into the kitchen. She was hunting for Primrose, her kitten. Suddenly her heart rose and pressed against her ribs, beating hard. That was their awful tone of voice! In the library. She crept to the door and listened.

"You had money enough to buy those books! You won't buy shoes for your child when he hasn't any fit for Sunday School!"

"He can stay home, then."

"Books, while your children run naked!"

"They aren't naked, Kitty. You know I've got to have books——"

"You've got to have what you want! You spend your

money and your time——" How shrill her mother's voice could sound!

"Do you want me to get that degree or not? You know I've got to if I'm going to get anywhere!"

"Do you want your family to be decent or not?"

A door closed. Behind it the voices mumbled and roared. Jean crept into the dining-room, the noise of her heart sounding louder than the indistinct voices. A shrill cry, and the door burst open. Her father stood an instant on the threshold, a vein in his forehead swollen, his face red.

"I tell you I've had enough of this! I'll kill myself! Won't stand it!"

He didn't see Jean, who had slumped down on her heels, trembling; he rushed through the hall. The slam of the front door died away, leaving only the terrible sound of sobbing in the library. Jean started with a cry as something touched her hand—Primrose, rubbing her arched back against Jean. Behind her in the kitchen stood Roger, his eyes horrified "O's."

Jean stumbled to her feet and ran through the kitchen, seizing Roger's hand.

"We got to get papa," she cried. "He's going to kill himself or something!" She was crying softly. Roger, padding beside her, sniffled companionably. As they came out of the yard to the street, he pulled back.

"Can't to go so fast," he grumbled.

"Got to!" sobbed Jean, dragging him along. Her father would go to his office, she knew. He always went there after a quarrel. But this was worse than most quarrels! Their voices had been worse.

She pulled Roger to the door of the white stone building, and then, desperately, left him at the bottom of the long stairway. Up she climbed; even in her distress her nostrils vibrated to the familiar odor, cool and damp, of the empty building.

Her father crouched behind his desk, his face white.

Jean stopped at the door, quivering.

"What do you want?" The question pounced at her.

"You got to come home." Her breath came with difficulty.
"You shouldn't kill yourself!"

"Did she send you?"

Jean hesitated.

"I won't come till she does!"

"She did." Jean felt the words drawn out of her by
his demand. "She says you come home."

She had her first murky glimpse of the twisted threads of
human feelings in that moment. Her father had raged off,
but he wanted to be sent for; he could believe he was summoned as easily as that! And secretly she knew her mother
was sobbing at home because he had gone, so that in reality
she hadn't lied.

Roger puffed up the stairs behind her. Her father looked
at the two, and dropped his head down on his desk. Was
he crying? Oh, she couldn't bear that!

"Tell your mother"—that was a crying voice!—"that I've
taken Roger down town for shoes. I'll be home by and by."

Jean entered the house cautiously, her ears pricked. Yes,
she was still crying, in long, gasping sobs. Jean dragged
her feet to the library.

"Mamma," she whispered. The crying continued. "Papa
says to tell you he's taken Roger down for shoes and he'll
be home——"

Then she fled, picking up Primrose on the way, to the
low apple tree behind the house. Later, hours it seemed,
she saw Roger and her father coming around the house.
Roger wore a new hat, white, with a sailor band, and he
walked stiffly in new brown shoes.

They did not see Jean. When they had closed the door,
Jean hung forward from her limb, holding her breath to
listen until things roared in her ears. She couldn't hear a
word. That was good, for their awful voices would have
reached the tree. Primrose stretched awake, kneaded white
paws against her arm, and then jumped down. White tail
curving from the funny black and yellow spot at its base,
she disappeared under the shed. Jean chanted softly to
herself,

This is Jeanie Me
In a napple tree
Myself Jean-ie
In a napple tree.

Herself. Papa himself. Mamma herself. Roger himself, only Roger didn't feel much himself, he was so little.
Voices in the kitchen: her father in a soft rumble, then her
mother clearer, "Don't be silly! Leave me alone!"

Jean slid from her tree. When her mother said it that
way, "Leave me alo-one," with the o-o-one sliding off, she
didn't really mean it. Jean stood at the door, her eyes
gravely observing. They were separate folks, not just
mamma and papa and Jean and Roger. Separate. She had
said, "She says to come home," and that had changed their
voices. That was not easy to think about. Her father was
making jokes, and her mother pretended not to laugh, but
her eyes smiled.

Jean felt tired. Dragged out too early from the hard
little shell of her growing self into confusing awareness of
these other selves.

IV

In the summer they visited Grandpa and Grandma Stevens,
and Grandpa and Grandma Winthrop. They waited at the
station for an endless time, with Jean rushing out of the
door at strange sounds to find the tracks still empty gleaming lines in the sun. Suddenly all the people in the seats
stirred at once, bending for their fat telescopes, and Jean
clung to Roger's hand, her heart coming up into her wind-
pipe; in the distance came the long vibration of the whistle,
and then, black, immense, a maze of sliding bars and shining
wheels, the engine thundered past, and while Jean held her
breath, the train ground to a standstill. Then, her nose
against the window, she saw the country run past, trees
and gleaming rivers, mysterious towns with people she had
never seen in her life before, and, if she was alert at the

right minute, a glimpse of a blue lake through trees. Finally
mamma said, "The next station!" and took down Jean's
hat and Roger's cap from the rack high overhead. A despairing moment lest the train forget to stop, a glimpse of Aunt
Mary in front of the green station, a scramble down the
steps, a wild flinging of self into Mamie's arms—Jean
called her Mamie always, for she was little and warm and
loving, and "Aunt Mary" was long to say. A long drive over
dusty streets in a hack which rattled lustily. The little house
back from the road, honeysuckle over the porch. Grandpa,
his hair silver, his face pink, wiping tears from his eyes while
he kissed Jean and said, "Well, well, little Jean's a big girl!"
Grandma Stevens, her eyes dark and fiery; Jean was afraid
of her, a little.

Jean waited always with eagerness for the first hour after
dinner. Mother and Mamie sat together in the sitting room,
Mamie rocking gently, while Jean curled up on the couch.
Then they talked. Fascinating and curious, that first hour
of talk. Jean never remembered what they said, but the
long domestic Odyssey held her, silent, wondering. Mamie
had quick little motions of her head, and between sentences
she made always a little "ts" sound. How the boy who took
down the sitting room stove almost broke the ashes door;
what had happened when William Stone, in the next house,
had the grippe in the spring. On and on, first Mamie, then
mamma.

When mamma talked, Jean listened in amazement. That
was the story of the hired girl, Ella. How strange it sounded,
with Ella's dirty aprons, her crying, her burning of the
chicken, all remembered and related. Other stories, of
Roger, of a church supper and the pans of scalloped oysters
mamma had made, on and on.

The fascination lay partly in the inevitability of that
hour, partly in the strange fact that after the hour was
gone, they never sat down again to talk. Sometimes by the
end of the visit, they didn't speak to each other at all, but
said, "Jean, tell your aunt the milkman is here," or, "Jean,
ask your mother if she wants tea for supper."

There was the garden to play in, with poppies for dolls, their petals tied back with grass for petticoats, and beautiful green heads with black hair. Nasturtium leaves for plates. A bush with brilliant red berries under which Jean spent long hours. A fence around the garden, of high boards with knotholes. On one side lived a strange man and his sister, and all their yard was planted in poppies, a marvelous sea of color with a heavy languorous perfume in the sun. Sometimes Jean, peering through a knothole, saw the man, heavy-bearded, slow, moving among the poppies. She never saw the sister except as a shadow against a drawn shade. He ate the poppy seeds. She heard Mamie talking about him, in one of the first hours.

Grandma stayed in her room, sometimes even for dinner. Jean hurried past the window of that room, although a beautiful bank of grass lay just beneath. Sometimes when she slipped past, she heard mamma in there, talking, but so low she never caught the words. Grandma's hair was sleek and dark, rolled down over her ears, and coiled at the base of her small head. Her chin thrust itself out beyond her mouth, and Jean was afraid of offending those shining eyes. Grandpa, gentle, sweet, shuffled about his garden, almost as if he hoped to find a weed somewhere in its long rows. He never talked.

Sometimes, after Jean had gone to bed in the tiny room where she slept with Mamie, she heard small feet creeping through the house. Mamie said, "Hush, child, that's only grandma." And once, a warm night, when Jean went barefooted through the long pantry in search of a cup for a drink of water, she ran straight into grandma, bent over the cracker jar, a cup in her hand. Jean smelled the clean aroma of fresh tea, even in her panic.

There was one secret terror in that visit to Grandpa Stevens. The road past the house came from the country straight into the village to the triangular park with the red stores along one side. Jean had almost forgotten the time when the terror began. She must have been very little, for the small latticed porch had seemed to her like a house. It was hot, so hot that the air pressed down heavily on the leaves and made pale, colorless waves over the grass. She sat on the floor of the porch, watching the bronze whir of a humming bird among the orange trumpets of the honey-suckle. Suddenly, as if the earth exploded, there came a terrifying noise. Jean, flinging herself in panic to the door-way saw something—was it a dragon?—huge, fiery coals dropping in its trail, smoke billowing above it, and then, toward her across the grass, plunged a horse, great nostrils dilated, enormous hoofs beating. Jean's fright brought Mamie from the house, and the child, gasping against her aunt's breast, heard, "See, dear, it's nothing but a threshing machine. The horse was scared, too. He's all right now. Look, Jean, there's nothing will hurt my pet. The machine whistles here so the farmers over town will take care of their horses, that's all."

Jean forgot. But in her dreams sometimes she lay, helpless, while great hoofs thundered down upon her, or an enormous black shape rolled toward her. And every summer she waited, not knowing for what, a fear curled in her heart. Once she was in the kitchen, watching Mamie roll out cookies, the morning-glory vines at the windows throwing a green gloom into the room. Suddenly she heard it, that dreadful noise, and hurled herself toward the door to the cellar. She tripped and fell. When Mamie picked her up, she had her hands tight against her ears.

"Is it gone?" she cried.

"It can't hurt you, Jeanie." Her aunt sat down on the step, the child's arms frantic about her neck. "You might have hurt yourself lots worse on these stairs. It's silly to be scared!"

Every summer it would come. Every summer there would sound that horrible shriek. Right at the very door. Nothing to hurt her. But something within her shriveled and died at the sound. Until the summer when Jean sat with Roger under the red berry bush. They were playing store, with berries for money. Jean lifted her head; that was the pre-liminary rumble and clatter and hissing—another instant!

The air thundered about her. But Roger puckered his face for a startled wail, and Jean, in a queer little voice, her hands shut into icy fists, said, "That's nothing but a threshing machine, Roger. Can't hurt you!" She heard Mamie running through the house to find them, and there were tears in her eyes when Mamie peered under the branches. Mamie knew; Jean saw that in her blue eyes. But she said only, "Having a nice time, children?"

Father went with them to Grandpa Winthrop's house. That was a longer journey, and they had to change trains at a junction. Grandpa Winthrop had a large house, but no garden. There was a turkey gobbler, and Jean discovered that if she poked a stick at him through the wire and scolded long enough, the hanging skin at his neck would swell mysteriously and turn a terrifying red. Mamma was very polite, always. She never sat down for a long, rocking-chair talk. Papa sometimes took Jean over to grandpa's office, a room up many stairs, from the windows of which she could see a dirty little river. Grandpa Winthrop had a square face, and his hair was streaked gray instead of silver. He never cried when he saw Jean. He always had round white peppermint candies in his pockets, mixed with bits of tobacco. Jean asked mamma why Grandpa Stevens had no office, with men coming up the stairs to ask him questions. She was sorry she had wondered when she saw her mother's face. Shimmering light on it, as if she were very angry. She said only, "Jean, my father is not a politician or a lawyer. He served his country in the Civil War, and since then he has not been strong." Jean wanted to find out why being a politician was bad, but she went away before that angry light flashed out upon her.

Grandma Winthrop wore a silk dress on Sunday, and never, never stayed in her room. Instead she moved quickly through the house, talking to anyone in a voice that seemed to laugh. On Sunday Jean went to church with grandma and mamma and Roger, sitting on a warm red cushion, and watching the sun through colored glass make queer patterns on the faces of people, sometimes even on the face of the minister. There were cousins, too, but no aunt like Mamie; and mamma had a little pursed-up tone when she talked to the aunts and uncles in that town. Father liked to talk to grandpa, and he made jokes with grandma. He and Grandpa Winthrop had long talks about "'lections," and sometimes grandma said, "Now stop discussing politics! I'm sick of hearing you!"

Finally Jean was home again, with Primrose purring about her ankles, and apples with red cheeks through the leaves of the tree. The first night Jean woke to hear voices from the next room, her father's and her mother's. After her first flurry of alarm—she never was sure what kind of talk they might be having—she wriggled comfortably back under her sheet. Quiet, not angry. Then, sleepily, she heard her mother's words sharpen.

"I'm not going there again, I tell you. Your mother does nothing but find fault with me, the children, everything!"

"Nonsense. She was nice——"

"She thinks your brothers' children are good enough, and look at them! Dirty little ragamuffins! She was careful not to say things when you were around. You ought to hear her! 'Katherine, do you let Jean read all the time? Think of her eyes! Katherine, do——'"

"Oh, what's the use? Just because she's old and her ideas are different——"

"You defend her against me every time! Look at her own boys——"

"Let's not start anything to-night, Kitty. I'm tired and so are you."

Jean thrust her head, turtle-wise, up from her bed. Was her mother crying? She heard nothing, and, with a sigh, dropped asleep.

V

Jean stood at the window, watching the rain. The house lay quiet about her; mother was upstairs, sewing; Roger was asleep. Silver beads on the window, clinging to the sash, clinging, slipping, other beads running to fill the place where the first had fallen. Beyond them threads of rain. No, long hairs, fine, straight, without end. Through them the houses across the street had a different look; farther away, mysterious. When she looked up against the gray sky she could scarcely see the rain-hairs, but against the dark maple they were distinct.

She turned back to her beautiful clutter on the floor. The new hired girl, Hulda, had let her choose among the shiny kitchen things, and she had carried in an armful—pancake turner, a long fork, a wooden spoon, a cup. She had been gardening among the flowers of the Brussels carpet. List-lessly she sat down to weed the third row. Rain stretched a day out hours long! Plump brown roses. The pancake turner made a good shovel. As she worked, the roses shaded into gorgeous pinks and reds, rising higher than her head. She smelled them! And strangely, she found a gravel path between the rows. Flinging down her shovel, she ran along the path, in quest of something she knew she would find. A wall, of rough stones. Beyond it a great stretch of water, moving in sunlight, and as she watched, breathless, a bird with strong white wings flew low over the water, swooped up in wide circles, dazzling white against the deep sky. She clambered on to the wall, the stones cool under her hands. Another bird, larger, whiter than she had ever seen. And the blue water, moving toward the shore, sending a strange pungent breath to mingle with the heavy rose fragrance. What was it? What were those birds?

"Jean! What are you up to now? Quickly, take those things out of the parlor. Mrs. Green is coming up the walk."

Jean, huddled against the old grandfather's clock in the corner, shivered as if the words bruised her. At her mother's second, "Hurry, Jean! This room was cleaned this morn-ing," she moved slowly, gathering the tools.

She tried many times to recapture that garden, with its stretch of water and its birds. It was real! She wanted it. But never, although she waited until the rain spun gray hairs past the maple leaves, could she find it.

VI

Jean went to school. She had a new apron, white with red dots and ruffles over the shoulders. The teacher had brown eyes, the softest brown Jean had ever seen. Jean was the smallest child in the room. Because she could read, and knew her tables up to the six's and even the nine's—they were easy, after papa taught her the trick about them, how they always made nine out of themselves—she was to try the third class. Her excitement blurred into dismay as she watched the sophistication of the boys and girls around her, and when at recess one girl said, "You're only a baby! Wearing a napron like that to school! What you doing in our grade?" Jean, with a desperate glance at the long red braids of her inquisitor, ran out of the sandy yard and home.

The next day she was back, apron and all, and presently she knew that if a boy yelled at you, "What's your name?" you should stick out your tongue and holler back, "Pudden tame! Ask me again and I'll tell you the same!"

She finished the stories in the green reader the second day, all but the thing about Columbus, which wasn't a story, and some of the poems. Then she squirmed in her place on the bench while the girl with the red braids struggled with words in the first story. It was funny, though, to hear how different the words sounded when she read them. At the end of the first week the teacher said, "Now we will have a spell-down." And Jean, her cheeks like peonies, her little square chin trembling, stood with her stubbed toes on the crack until "separate" floored her, next to the last man down.

The girls whispered secrets at recess. Jean heard some of them, obscure, cryptic sentences. One day she took home to her mother the sensation of that day. A girl in the seventh grade had left school to have a baby. Her mother, startled, said, "Nonsense! Who told you such a story?"

Jean, insisting gravely, added what the red-headed girl had whispered. "You could tell by her looks."

"Jean! What are you talking about? What do you mean?"

"Yes, her face was all twisted up."

"Don't you think of that bad story again, and don't you listen when the girls talk about such things!"

But Jean overheard her mother repeating the story to her father that night, and wondered about the way they both laughed in little soft noises, as if they didn't quite want to laugh. Then her mother sent a note to the teacher, and the next day the red-haired girl told her she was a great baby, running to her mother!

Jean deliberated on her way home from school. Perhaps you didn't tell things to your mother unless you were a baby. Anyhow, telling had no satisfaction in it. They had laughed about her.

Later she came home too excited not to tell. The girls had asked her who her beau was. When she admitted that she had no beau, they had commiseratingly agreed to find one. Percy Jones, a boy in the same grade, had consented to be her beau. Only he said Feller. He had freckles, but he could wriggle both ears at once.

"What does a beau do, mamma?" she finished.

"Jean, what will you do next!" her mother had cried out.

"I haven't done anything." Jean withdrew, puzzled, a little wistful. She had felt that the day marked a triumph, when the older girls had reached down to lift her to their level.

VII

She forgot that triumph in a new, disturbing excitement at home. Papa and mamma talked together, long talks, without ever lifting their voices into their awful tones. Mother's cheeks were pink and her eyes grew large and bright.

"What is it?" Jean begged. "Tell me, too! It can't be Christmas, yet."

Mamma laughed, and papa said, "Tell her!"

Papa wanted a new position at another college, farther away even than Grandpa Winthrop's. Jean had not known there was another college.

"Why do you want it?"

"More money to feed hungry little mouths, Jean." Her father rubbed his hand over her soft hair. "Better place. I'm in an awful rut here."

"When are we going?"

"It isn't decided. I may not get it. Now run away and play."

Jean went, slowly, listening with a little glow to the sound of their voices, talking. She knew what a rut was, in the road. How was papa in a rut? She stood under the apple tree, rubbing her toes through the grass. She knew! She would pray to God. She couldn't outdoors, of course. Perhaps it wouldn't work until bedtime. She would try it. She climbed to her room and knelt by her small bed, her eyes screwed shut.

"Dear God, Now I lay me down to sleep——No, I mean, Our Father who art, please make papa get the job at another college. For more money. Out of a rut. Amen." God would understand about ruts.

Ecstatic, she descended the stairs quietly. Voices, louder.

"If only I had that degree! That's what counts."

"If you'd paid less attention to books and more to people with influence, you'd stand more of a show."

"We can't change things now. What I've done, I've done."

Jean slipped out of the door, dancing across the porch. He'd get it! She wouldn't tell them she had prayed until he had it. Then they'd know why!

Saturday. Papa had gone away, to the other college. Mamma couldn't sit still. She looked out of the window, she told Roger to go and play and stop bothering her, she jumped when the bell rang.

Jean dusted the chairs and table slowly, that she might linger near the vortex of this exciting time. She did every round of the straight dining-room chairs. The bell rang again. Her mother in the hall, one hand over her lips, a yellow envelope shaking in the other. She sank down on the low seat of the hall rack. Jean saw in the mirror the fine curls at the base of her neck moving in the little breeze from

the door. How slowly her fingers pushed under the yellow
flap!

"Oh!" She crumpled the paper and began to cry—soft,
tender crying. Then she smoothed it again on her knee,
brushing away the tears. Jean read it.

"Am appointed. Home to-morrow. Love. James."

"What does it mean?" Jean pressed close to her mother.

"He's got it, Jean! Oh, he's——"

"Don't cry. I knew he would."

"You knew—you funny little girl." Her mother's arm
was tight around her.

"Yes. I prayed to God about it. More money, 'nevery-
thing."

"Why, Jean!" Her mother's tears stopped. "God doesn't
give you things just because you ask for them. You
shouldn't talk that way!"

But Jean knew better.

Moving was an adventure. Huge wagons at the door,
like mouths yawning, like dark caverns; men like giants
moving piano, desks, tables, as if they were playthings. The
house strange and empty, full of noises. A last night when
they slept at a neighbor's, in delighting formality. A last
search for Primrose, who scratched and struggled when Jean
thrust her into her basket.

They were going into another state. Jean watched eagerly
to see when they crossed the line, so black in her geography,
but somehow she missed it. A black hack, with doors shutting them into a little room, mamma and Jean opposite papa
and Roger. A strange house, very large, with wagons in
front of it, and the same identical furniture appearing out
of the yawning mouths. Different horses here, white.

Mamie came to see them to help settle. Jean led her on an
exploring tour through the house. Front stairs, a narrow
hall, and three rooms opening from that. Down again,
through the square dining-room into the kitchen, and—
wonderful!—rear stairs with a small room at the head.
Then, surprising, a door into a large open space, which
seemed not quite a room because it reached across the house.

Finally, while Jean tried to look as if she had not known it all the time, another door, and there they were, back in the front hall! Mamie said, "Well, I declare!" and Roger, puffing after them, laughed when he saw Mamie's eyes so wide and surprised.

School again, less terrifying now, although Jean was still the youngest child in the room. She had come from another state, and the knowledge fortified her, gave her distinction. She no longer wore an apron over her wool dress.

VIII

It was queer, about telling the truth. They told you lies were wicked. But when the lady in the rustly dress who came one afternoon before mamma had taken off her blue morning dress, said to Jean, "Do you like this new home, little girl?" and Jean replied, in her politest tone, "Oh, yes. Papa gets more money," mamma, who came in just then, looked at you with hard eyes. And later she said, "You must never say such things, Jean." Then, to Jean's protest she added, "Whether it's true or not, you mustn't talk about private affairs to strangers."

One morning papa took Jean to his new office. She sat on a hard chair near the window and watched the people who came in. Mamma asked her that noon what she had done, and when she said that she liked to hear papa talking to the girls, mamma pressed her lips tight. Later Jean heard her in the library.

"So that is what you do when you say you are studying! Talking to the girls!"

"If students come in about their work, don't I have to——"

"Even your little daughter notices it! You leave me alone in this strange city, while you amuse yourself——"

Jean slipped out to the front steps. She knew her father would rush away presently. He came out, the door banging after him, and she made a dart toward him.

"Papa!" Tears on her cheeks. "I didn't mean to tell on you!"

He stopped, looking down at her, his dark mustache twitching, his eyes harassed.

"You have to be careful what you say—oh, Lord! You're too little to know!" Halfway to the street he swung around. "Jean." She went to him, sobbing. "Don't cry, Jean." He wiped her cheeks gently. "It's all right." Then, after a moment, "You mustn't ever say anything to people about things your mother says or things I say—you understand?"

Jean flamed.

"I never did!" she cried. "I—I'd be too ashamed!"

His face moved so strangely that Jean feared he might cry. She rubbed her fists into her eyes and stood up sturdily. He muttered something she did not hear, stared up at the house with its blank door, and strode away down the street.

Jean sat on the steps, reflecting. If she hadn't told about the girls, her mother wouldn't have hollered and cried. The girls had come in. But she shouldn't have told about them. They had been nice girls, who giggled at papa's jokes. She sighed. The truth was troublesome. You kept it to yourself. You didn't always know what would happen.

IX

Jean had a friend, Anne Bishop. Long black hair in two smooth braids, and a little pale face with black eyes and red mouth. Her mother had called on Jean's mother, and had invited Jean to come over Saturday to play with her little girl. One of the best families in town, Jean heard her mother say. Best family—what was that? They lived in a brick house with oak trees in the yard. After Jean had looked at the books in Anne's white bookcase, many books, they had gone up to the attic to play. Trunks of old silk dresses, more beautiful than Jean had ever seen. They dressed up, and played Bluebeard. Jean was Sister Anne and called from the narrow, high window, "Nothing but a cloud of dust! Nothing but a flock of sheep!" Then she was Bluebeard himself. When Mrs. Bishop called them for

supper, Jean still wore the lovely yellow dress she had
selected for Sister Anne, and her fine, dark hair blew in a
mist about her face.

"Come on," said Fatima. "We'll wear these to supper.
Mother won't mind."

Mr. Bishop, tall, with an amazing black beard, said,
"Who's that little girl? Isn't she pretty?" and Jean's excited eyes had searched the room for some pretty little girl.
Did he mean her, Jean herself? With a sigh, she looked down
at the pale silk. It was only the dress. Her grandmother
Winthrop had said, "She has the Winthrop chin and forehead. Well, she'll make a fine-looking woman, perhaps."

Jean stayed all night with Anne. She had never stayed at
night with any girl. But Anne belonged to the best family.
Anne's older sister, Flora, who was darker and much larger,
made jokes about them at supper. When the two girls were
in bed, in Anne's big white and blue room, Anne said mysteriously, "Do you know things?"

"What things?"

"Oh, you know. About things. **Babies!**"

"Some," said Jean.

"What?"

Jean shrank away. But Anne went on talking, in her
soft, dark voice. Talking about things. Jean stared at the
unfamiliar outline of the windows. She was dragged in two.
Part of her was a curiosity, shy, sly-footed. Part of her
was fear, shrinking, hurting fear. At last Anne snuggled
warmly against her and slept.

Jean looked at her mother the next morning. Should she
tell her what Anne had said? Anne had said to her, before
breakfast, "Now don't tell your mother a word I said, or
she won't let you come again." That was true. Jean wished
to go again, and yet she didn't quite wish to. But she said,
when her mother asked, "Did you have a nice time, Jean?"
only, "Yes, mamma. Anne's got a whole bookcase full of
her very own books."

Roger went to school. The first day Jean took him, and
left him with the primary teacher. When she came home

at noon, mamma laughed and said, "What do you think? Roger ran home as soon as you left him!" Mamma took him the next day, and the next, and finally he decided he liked it well enough to stay. He walked so slowly, because his legs were still so short, that Jean was sure they would be late. Once they were a whole block away from school when the last bell began to toll. Its slow notes pounded on Jean, a fatal, ominous dirge. She raced up the block, dragging Roger behind her. When she had reached the sanctuary of her own seat, just as the last note droned into silence, she wondered whether Roger's feet had touched the sidewalk in all that block, or whether he had streamed behind her like a flag.

Then Jean skipped a grade. The teacher said she couldn't keep her busy.

Primrose had disappeared. Jean hunted for her, called her, left saucers of milk for her on the kitchen porch. No Primrose. She heard her father say, "I think I ought to tell the child. She's worrying." And mother, "You can't tell her that!" But papa found her crying, her hair powdered with cobwebs and dust from the woodshed floor, where she had crawled through in search of her kitty.

"Jean, she won't come back. She isn't lost."

"Where is she?"

"She won't ever be cold and hungry."

"You know where my kitty is!"

"Your mother thinks you aren't old enough to understand. Jean, she's dead. She had some little kittens. She didn't know how to take care of them. She thought they were mice, I guess. She ate them. So she's dead. Sometimes animals are like that—perverse. She did it before, but I thought maybe the second time——"

Jean felt sick, as if something turned over in her stomach.

"We'll find another kitty for you."

Her Primrose! With her cool pink nose and those funny spots. She didn't understand. But she didn't want to. She walked out of the woodshed without a word and down across the back yard. Suddenly she was homesick. She wanted the old apple tree, the fence, and the railroad gleaming beyond it. Nothing here but a silly bush.

X

Life was in three parts. One was school. One was home when papa and mamma felt nice. Sometimes they dressed up after supper and went away, leaving Jean and Roger with the hired girl. That was an adventure, seeing mamma in her blue silk dress, her eyes bright, her hair in little curls over her forehead; and papa shaved till when you rubbed your cheek on his you felt no stiff tickle. Sometimes Roger cried because mamma was going away, but Jean liked it. Sometimes there was company for supper; then they might have creamed potatoes, thin slices of pink ham, preserved strawberries, and cake with cocoanut sticking all over the frosting. There was a repressed adventure in company, too. Or there were quiet evenings, when mother read to Roger, and Jean listened. Sometimes she sang, in a sweet, hushed voice. Jean liked best "Sleep, baby sleep. Thy father watches the sheep———"

But when things were nice, Jean paid on the whole little attention to other people; instead, she read books, or sat down to weave part of the long story she carried on from day to day, or invented games.

The third part of life was home, with everything wrong. First, would be what papa called a scene. Sometimes it was late at night, and Jean woke to find the dark full of their awful voices. It always seemed wrong to go to sleep again until the voices ceased, although sometimes when the door was closed, and the sounds roared on for hours, her eyes seemed to stick together. Then the next day mamma would not come to the table. She ate after papa went away. Sometimes Jean heard her crying in her room. She went on tiptoe through the house, and it was difficult to think about her story or to read. She tried to play with Roger, to pour out love on his small head, but he, sedate and determined as always, went his own way. Then, one day, the feeling of dreadful tightness would be gone, usually in the morning, when Jean went down to breakfast, and she could take up her own life again.

XI

Jean skipped another grade. She was in the mixed grade now, half seventh and half eighth. She didn't like the teacher, who had red hair and eyes that looked too blue through sandy lashes; she was always reading letters behind her handkerchief and laughing to herself. The boys and girls were interesting, all strangers, and one boy in long pants! The girl in the next seat said he had been in that grade for three years.

Then Estelle Young was in this room. She was the richest little girl in town, and she wore silk dresses to school. One day her curly hair had a part as crooked as a geography river.

"The maid was sick," Estelle told the girls, lisping a little. "I had to comb my hair myself, all alone."

"Couldn't your mother comb it for you?" asked Jean.

"Oh, I couldn't bother mother. Who combs your hair?"

"Mamma parts it and then I do," confessed Jean, with a swift picture of herself at the hands of a maid. "Once our hired girl curled it, though," she added. She watched Estelle every day after that, her feelings mixed envy and derision. The other girls watched her, too, and the teacher smiled at her. At Christmas Estelle went away.

"To a private school," the girls said. "Away off! Say, her father's got more money even than he had. He got it making those horseless carriages. She's promised to write us a letter."

Jean had seen one of those horseless carriages, and had stopped to watch its trail of smoke up the street. It looked funny, too short, and the men looked as if they would fall out in front, without even a horse between them and the road. But Roger said he meant to have one for his own,

some day, and people took rides in them, although folks stood
and laughed when they went past.

Papa said, "I'm going to have her try the state examinations this spring."

Mamma said, "Why, she's much too young. She's not
eleven!"

But papa said, "It won't hurt her to try. She doesn't have
to work hard enough."

The examinations were in a huge white building where
Jean had never gone before. Lots of children, some of
them giggling, some of them scared. The inkwells filled.
Long sheets of ruled paper, a red line on one side. Men
passing lists of questions. Jean wrote and wrote until her
fingers ached under their smudge of ink. She liked to write,
but pens were a dreadful nuisance. What funny things
they asked! Physiology—that was her gray book. When
she shut her eyes she could see the page with the picture
of a heart, and read, halfway down the page, what the book
said. She wrote it down, word for word. Arithmetic, reading, geography. The man with the red, bald head pronounced
the words for spelling. "Separate." She knew that one!

A few days later her father and mother talked in low
tones about her. She heard her name. Then her father
said, "Come with me, Jean, to the office." She walked at his
side, stopping to peer at the tight purple knobs on the spires
of a lilac bush. In her father's office sat the man with the
red, bald head.

"So this is Jean Winthrop?" Jean felt accusation in his
oily voice, but she had to say yes.

"This is Professor Brown, Jean. He is one of the state
examiners. He wants to know——" How worried her
father looked! Almost like the face he wore when mamma
called him a selfish brute! What was the matter? "He
wants to know whether I helped you with your arithmetic."

"That's it, little girl. You got a hundred and you were
the only one to get a hundred on that test. You seem small

to get it alone. We wondered—since your father was on the committee."

The vein in her father's forehead stood out like a red slate pencil. What did they want her to say? Jean twisted one hand in the pocket of her dress, her eyes shrinking from the protuberant stare of Professor Brown, begging her father to give her some clue.

"Your papa helped you a little? Maybe he suggested that you look up compound interest?"

Jean plunged desperately.

"My father always helps me," she announced. "He helps me more'n the other girls' fathers. He knows a lot."

"And he helped you before the examination?" Professor Brown leaned back in his chair, one hand patting his watch pocket.

"Yes, he helped me." Jean's glance at her father was a swift, winged caress.

"Just what I feared, Winthrop." Professor Brown's voice snapped.

"Jean, what do you mean?" Her father jumped up from his chair. "Tell Mr. Brown just what you mean."

What did they want her to say! She struggled to pierce the inimical tenseness. Her father must have the credit he deserved.

"He showed me about compound interest," she hesitated. "I couldn't do it, first."

"When did I show you, Jean?"

Jean felt hot tears behind her eyelids.

"I don't remember."

"Last week?" suggested Professor Brown.

"Oh, no. It was in the winter, because I dropped my arithmetic and got it all snowy, and lost the problems we worked out. But then I could do them myself at school."

Her father settled back in his chair.

"Does that satisfy you, Brown?" he shouted.

"And he didn't give you a hint before you came to the examination the other day?"

"No. I asked him——" Jean floundered again. Would

it be wrong to say this? "I asked him what were state examinations, and he said, 'You'll find out. Just go and write what you're asked.' But he helps me lots!" She threw that out defiantly. The need to protect her father blazed in her eyes, the desire to say what was wished tormented her until the tears almost fell.

"That's all, Jean. Run along home."

In the hall, pausing to rub the tears away with an angry hand, she heard the horrid man.

"Well, I apologize, Winthrop. She must be an extraordinary child. Letter perfect!"

That night mamma said, "Why did you tell Professor Brown your father had helped you?"

"I didn't know what they wanted me to say." Jean had again that uncomfortable feeling, like a fist doubled at the pit of her stomach.

"They wanted you to tell the truth, of course. It was very serious, Jean."

Jean burrowed her cheek against the pillow and stared up at her mother with bright, remote eyes.

"If you always tell the truth, Jean, you save lots of trouble." Her mother kissed her good night and went away.

"No, you don't! No, you don't!" muttered Jean, softly. Truth. That meant saying something the way it had happened. But things happened so many ways. Sometimes telling was safe, and sometimes it was dangerous.

Jean wriggled farther down in bed, pulled up her knees till she made a drowsy crescent moon, and closed her eyes. She had to lie very still for a moment, and then, as if she was the jar in Sinbad the Sailor, out floated the beautiful and strange people of her night story. Somewhere the old day-Jean watched them, but among them moved the night-Jean, a princess with long golden hair. She was Jean Winthrop only in disguise. Some day everyone would know that. Now she was herself only in the softly radiant moments after she had been left alone in bed. Night after night the story unwound, and in the morning Jean did not know what she had visioned before she slept and what her dreams had built. At rare moments in the day she could slip into the rooms of that gold and crystal palace, but for the most part she waited for the dark.

XII

Mother was sick. Mamie had come to take care of her. The hired girl called Jean, "Poor lamb!" and clucked her tongue as if she had a secret.

Jean woke, late in the night. She heard the front door close softly and then creeping steps on the stairs. Her heart beating swiftly, she listened. Step. Creep. A burglar! No, that was her father's whisper, and Mamie.

She had slipped just over the edge of sleep again when a cry dragged her straight out of bed. Shivering in the doorway, she listened again.

"So you came home! Why did you bother to come home at all? I'm worn out and sick. Why come back here?"

"Kitty, it was just the lodge meeting. I told you I had to go."

"Lodge meeting!" Jean trembled at the acid laugh. "Lodge meetings last all night! Of course!"

"Don't argue with her, James." That was Mamie, hurried. "She's feverish——"

"What are you whispering? Get out of my room."

Jean was drawn, unwillingly, along the hall. Her feet stuck to the prickly carpet. She reached the door of her mother's room, and peered fearfuly within. Her mother sat up, away from the pillows, her hair straggling about her face, her eyes enormous. She held out her hands, the fingers twisting, writhing.

"See what you've done to me! Look at my hands! Worked to the bone. Look at them! Poor hands! And then you stay out all night. I'm worn out. I'm nothing but your old drudge."

Papa went over to the bed, trying to hold the writhing fingers.

"Lie down. You'll make yourself worse."

"Go away! Don't touch me! Go away!"

Mamie stood beyond the bed, in a gray bathrobe, her face queer and pinched. Suddenly she pushed mother against the pillows.

"You'd better go," she said to father, very low.

"Look at my poor hands!" They made dreadful, weaving gestures above the white counterpane. "Look at them! That's what I am! Slaving! Worn to the bone!"

"I'll stay here," said Mamie.

Jean crouched in the shadow of the corner as papa came out. He went heavily down the stairs.

"Has he gone? To another lodge meeting? Ah——"

"Now you just stop, Kitty." Mamie held a glass of water to mamma's lips. "I'm ashamed of you, if you are sick. Drink this."

Mother knocked away the glass. It splintered against the chair.

Jean felt tears rolling down her face. Holding her breath, she ran through the hall, back to her own bed, where she could bury her face under the blanket and let the sobs muffle themselves. Oh, what was the matter this time? What was it about her hands? When her sobs stopped, the voices were gone, too, and finally she slept.

She woke to find Mamie in her room, brushing her hair before the white dresser. Mamie had short, curly hair, which ran after the brush instead of lying smooth. Jean watched the quick fingers twist and pin, and then she remembered.

"Mamie!" she cried. "What's the matter with mamma's hands?"

Mamie spun about.

"Were you awake, child?"

Jean nodded, heavy-eyed. "What's the matter with them?" she begged.

Mamie sat down on the edge of the bed.

"She just meant she'd had to work hard, Jeanie. Her hands used to be real pretty, soft and white. She was sick last night. Your father ought not to stay away so late. She worried. She's had to work hard, with you children, and your father's position to keep up. She never was very strong." Mamie sighed. "Now you'd better hop up, Jeanie."

Jean threw her arms about her aunt's neck.

"I'm glad you're here!" she cried.

When she had dressed, she peered into her mother's room. Mother was asleep, her dark hair spread on the pillow. She looked like a little girl. Her hands were covered. Jean felt she must cry, if she stood there a second longer.

XIII

Jean was in high school. One of the big boys said, "Gee, look at the primary class!" She was excited, so that her face felt warm and her nose too large most of the time. But her legs had, over the summer, grown longer, and she didn't feel quite so little. The English class was fun. Jean had read "Rip Van Winkle." Latin was queer. Jean couldn't make sense of it. Mamma tried to help her, but when Jean had said over and over, *"Mensa,* nominative; *mensæ,* genitive," and still couldn't see what it meant, she cried. Mamma said, "She is too young. I thought so." Papa said, "Give her time. Latin's different, that's all." And after a few days Jean found she could remember *mensa* without knowing in the least what it was about. Algebra was like a game, like the cipher the pirates used. Anne Bishop's sister Flora was in the next room, and she laughed at Jean when she met her in the dark halls.

One day a strange woman came to the house with her suitcase. Jean had to sleep with Elsie, the hired girl. That was very uncomfortable, for Elsie made noises in her sleep and rolled over and over. One morning Elsie said, mysteriously,

"Did you hear it, last night?"

"What?" asked Jean, turning for Elsie to button her dress.

"D'yuh mean you slept right through it?"

She wouldn't say what.

When papa came down to breakfast he said, "Well, Jean, would you like another brother?"

Jean stared at him. Just then the woman came into the room, dressed in a stiff white dress and cap.

"Well, morning always comes, Mr. Winthrop," she said, breezily.

"Is Mrs. W. awake?" asked papa. "Then come, Jean."

Jean tiptoed into the room and peeked at her mother's white cheek when she said, faintly, "Kiss mother, Jean." But Jean's eyes were on the tiny, squirming bundle at her mother's side. Father lifted a corner of the blanket and Jean stared at the curious, crimson, puckered thing. Then she tiptoed away. She had again, within her, that strange, tight fist, fear and curiosity doubling together.

"Where did they get that?" she asked the nurse, who was coming upstairs with a tray.

"Doctor brought it in his satchel, of course." The nurse laughed at her.

Jean and Roger went out on the porch together.

"The doctor brought it in that shiny case he carries," said Jean solemnly. She didn't believe that story, but she had to tell it to Roger. She felt rather grown-up, repeating it to him. He nodded, his round face puzzled.

At school she met Flora Bishop, and told her proudly that she had another brother.

"Huh!" said Flora, "I knew you would, weeks and weeks ago."

That was a knife in Jean's pride. She went home at noon, still hurt. She couldn't talk to her mother, but when she found the nurse eating her dinner, she repeated Flora's words, tentatively.

"My, wasn't she a smart girl!" said the nurse, with her brisk laugh rustling like her dress.

Her mother must have told Flora. She told Flora and not Jean. Whenever Jean saw Flora she remembered that, and hated her.

Babies. Something strange about them. But Jean's fear held her aloof. She didn't want to know.

They named the baby James, after papa. When the nurse had gone, Jean could sit in the low wicker chair with the tiny bundle in her arms. She liked to lay one finger gently on the queer, soft spot on his head, where a mysterious throbbing reached through her finger into her very heart. He had funny dark fuzz on his head, and he would stare at her out of blue eyes until Jean shivered a little. Roger didn't like the baby.

"Put it away and play with me, Jean," he would say from the doorway.

They didn't go away that summer. Mamie came to stay with them for a while, and mamma was tired most of the time. Papa stayed at home, and sometimes on Sundays he would drive up to the house with a horse and surrey from the livery stable. Mamie would stay at home with the baby. Jean sat on the front seat with her father, her mother and Roger on the back seat. Then they drove through the streets out past the houses until they came to the country, where the road climbed over hills, wound through woods, sometimes crossed a river, the horse's hoofs plunking hollowly on the wooden bridge. Once mamma said, "It's going to storm. We'd better go home." Papa said, "Oh, I guess not. The horse is hired for the afternoon," and drove straight on.

The leaves on the trees along the road began to rustle sharply, and turned their pale under sides out to the wind; great clouds rushed along, dragging dark shadows over the meadows, and then piling over the sun. Papa said, "I'll turn at the next cross-road." A long rumble of thunder, and mamma, sharply, "If you'd ever listen to me! We'll be drenched!"

"Thunder won't hurt you, Kitty!"

Mother held Roger tight in her arms and wouldn't say another word, although father made jokes and larruped at the horse. Jean sung out, "Get ap!" More thunder and flashes of lightning. Then the rain was on them, so that the horse threw back his ears and the trees swayed over the road. Exciting! Jean huddled against her father's arm and exulted. But mother wouldn't go driving again for weeks.

XIV

Fall came, with hazel nuts bristling in the hedges and the crisp smell of burning leaves. School again. The second day Jean came home with a queer feeling in her head. "It floats away from my neck," she explained.

She was hurried into bed and the doctor came. Jean saw his eyes, like those of the owl she had seen on Saturday in the hazel hedge, but she seemed to fall asleep before he talked to her.

She woke later to hear her father and mother in the hall.

"He says if we can get the baby away at once, he'll let him go. Telegraph Mamie and you take him to-night. Roger will have to stay."

That was mother's excited tone. Not angry.

"If I get a nurse in, can you manage? I can't stay here and go to college too."

"Oh, James!" Even in her drowsiness Jean wondered. Had she ever heard her mother call her father that? Then she slept again.

She had scarlet fever. The nurse was not so brisk as Nurse Watts, who had come with little James. Mother sat by her bed. Then Roger was sick, too, in the next room. Light cases, they said. She felt hot all over, and covered with mosquito bites. She mustn't scratch them. The nurse cut off her hair, because it snarled.

One strange night, when terrible dreams chased her. A campfire above the bed, with Cæsar's cohorts massed about it. She had to get up, to carry the message——Mother's voice, "What is it, Jean?" The campfire dwindled into the gas light over her bed, swathed in something yellow to soften the light. The windows of the room were terrifying—lurid, orange, with dark shapes floating past! "What is that, mamma? Oh, what is it? The end of the world——"

Mamma held her hand tightly.

"No, child."

"Is it to-morrow? What are those flying things?"

"See, Jean. They are just leaves. I drew the shades. There's a big fire in town, a factory. That's what the light comes from."

Strange, confusing night.

After that, she felt more like the real Jean. At night she heard her father at the front door. He couldn't come in. Mamma cried sometimes, but never very loud.

Finally she could sit up, a pink shawl over her shoulders, her hair flat on her head like Roger's. After she had begged and begged, the doctor said she could read, if she didn't read too much. Mamma brought her a fat gray book from the library, "David Copperfield." When at last she was out of bed, and the nurse had stopped saying, "Here, Jean of Arc, take your medicine like a lady!" she found the shelf full of fat gray books—Barnaby Rudge and his raven, little Paul Dombey, terrible Fagin. Mother took the books away because the print was so fine, but the next day she had them again. Then she tried the red books, taller, just as fat, that stood next. "Adam Bede"—she couldn't understand just what happened in that.

Finally Roger was well again. They had both peeled like snakes.

The house was fumigated. That was exciting. The books had to go into the oven, like cakes, and came out with their covers bulging. Paper pasted over the cracks of windows and doors. A smell, potent and distressing, filling eyes and throat with sharp tears. First upstairs, then downstairs. Papa came home, and one day Mamie came, the hack rattling up to the door, Mamie carrying James in her arms, the driver following with the baby carriage. Mamma seized James, crying, "Oh, my baby! my baby!" and James wrinkled up his pink face and screamed. Mamie took him, saying severely, "You frightened him, Kitty!" Then mamma cried,

"He's forgotten me, my baby!" and while Mamie hushed
the baby gently, mamma looked at her, her eyes hot and
tear-shining, and Jean moved away, troubled. She looked
as if she didn't like Mamie!

XV

Jean was not to go back to school that year. She had
missed too much, and she was ridiculously young, her mother
said—only eleven. Roger could go, because he was in a
lower grade. So she stayed at home. She read all the red-
covered books, but she didn't like the people so well as David
and Dora, or Paul Dombey, or even Fagin. She found a
terrible book. Purple, with thorns across the cover, and
the title, "Thorns and Briars." She found it one rainy
day, while mamma was lying down and James was asleep.
Sitting on the floor of the library, she read. Stupid at first.
Battles. The Civil War. It looked funny, because so many
of the pages had sentences too short to reach across the
page. Then two men found an old negro woman. Jean
grew stiff with strange, seductive horror as she read. They
threw the woman over a fallen tree and whipped her. Jean
felt the cruel whips tearing her own soft flesh. She couldn't
put the book away. The men whispered, and the woman
cried, "Oh, massas, not that! Beat me some more!" But
they did something; and the woman, when they had gone,
crawled into a swamp. Old Jupe, her husband, found
her floating there. An ecstasy of horror racked Jean as
she turned page after page. Her mother said, behind her,
"What have you got?" and the book was gone.

Jean never saw it again, but she had read it once. Sometimes before she slept, when she wound her dreams together,
one would come, perverse, horrifying, but thrilling with a
terrible delight, a dream of that old colored woman, beaten
with wands of willow. She told that dream to Anne Bishop,
one night, but Anne thought it silly. Anne was engrossed
in a mysterious something which had happened to her.
Jean withdrew from knowledge too complete.

In the afternoon mamma dressed James in his white coat and bonnet and told Jean she could take him for a walk. Jean liked best to wheel his carriage around to Mrs. Dunkert's. There she left him on the porch with Mrs. Dunkert sewing, while she climbed the stairs to Sam Dunkert's room. Sam had gone away to college, but he had left all his books. "From Cabin Boy to Captain"; "Bootblack to Merchant"— alluring titles, all of them. Jean read them, one after the other. Boys could do anything! They could turn into anything. No matter how poor and wicked they might start, they finished in riches and happiness. There were no books about girls like that. Just the Dotty Dimple books in the Sunday School library, or the stupid books about a curious girl named Elsie Dinsmore, who had but one exciting moment, when she refused to play for her father on Sunday and fell off the piano stool.

One day Jean asked her father a question which troubled her.

"What did the girl in 'Adam Bede' do that was so wicked? I've read that part three times. She just went into the woods."

Her father looked at her, his eyebrows puckered. They were in his office. Just then someone knocked.

"She let the villain kiss her, Jean. What are you reading George Eliot for? Come in." And in came a strange man before Jean could ask another question. She knew at least that it was wicked past words to be kissed. In the woods. By a man.

The house next door had been empty until that spring. A man and woman moved in. Young married folks, mamma said. Jean could look at the house from her window. One night after she had gone to bed, a light splashed on her ceiling. She ran to the window. The woman was in the kitchen, setting dishes on the table, her hair soft yellow under the light. She turned her face toward the door, and then the man came in, tall, his face white between his dashing black mustache and stiff black hair. Jean watched, enchanted. It was like a story in a book. He sat down at the table. They talked, for their lips moved. Then the woman sat on the corner of the table and laid her hand on his shoulder. He looked at her and laughed. He ate something, and suddenly while Jean watched, he pulled the woman into his lap and kissed her. Jean drew back from the window, shivering. When she looked again, the light had gone out. She crept into bed, wondering, wondering. They were married. They didn't quarrel. Perhaps because there weren't any children. Was it wicked, that kiss? She felt a delicious shiver through her body.

Occasionally Anne Bishop took Jean with her to see a little boy who lived in the next block. He was older than James, and he had beautiful things for toys, things Jean had never seen. Once his mother came in, fragrant, elegant, silken-clad, before she went away for her afternoon drive. His father was quite old, Anne said. One Saturday when Jean went to see Anne, she found her black eyes full of excited glints. When the two girls were in Anne's room, Anne explained. Mrs. Thomas, the little boy's mother, had killed herself, last night. Chloroform and a pistol both! In the bathroom.

"Her husband was too old," said Anne, wisely. "She married him for money, not for love."

Jean remembered quickly the song that Elsie, the hired girl, was always singing:

"She's only a bird in a gilded cage,
  A beautiful sight to see.
You might think she was happy and free from care——"

She taught the words to Anne and they made a signal whistle of the first line.

That was Jean's small self. Eager, wistful, oversensitive to the atmosphere about her, desiring the beauty that lies in peace more than any other quality in life; aware of pain as a thing possessed of morbid fascination, tenacious of everything her senses could grasp; her shell of childhood tight to bursting now, opened only to admit strange particles of life, not comprehended; not yet thrust apart for any out-going of herself.

PART II
FILAMENTS

PART II

FILAMENTS

I

FATHER had lost his position. Jean, pretending to know nothing about it, listened fearfully to bits of conversation. Darwin came in, somehow. Her mother said, "Even if you must believe in Darwin, you needn't say so to a trustee! You have to be careful."

"He asked me pointblank! Do you want me to lie? Darwin's old history to everyone outside this damned college."

"You believe in bread and butter for your children, don't you?"

"Brown wants my job for that nephew of his. You know it. He's been down on me straight along."

"All the more reason for being careful then. You don't care about Darwin! You're just stubborn. That's all. Stubborn."

"Brown's a decrepit old bigotist! He said, 'Would you tell your students, these young souls we entrust to you, that the doctrines of Darwin have more truth than the Book of Genesis?' What can I say?"

"A lot less than you did say! Losing your temper over a book. Is your family to starve?"

Jean waited on the steps until her father came home that night.

"Who is Mr. Darwin, papa?"

"You, too?" Her father pulled at his mustache.

"Well, I wondered." Her eyes, intent on his, insisted, "I don't think you were stubborn; it is you I wish to know about, not this Darwin." But she added, "I heard of him."

43

Her father sat down on the porch railing.

"He's an Englishman who has worked out a theory of life, Jean. Evolution. Life growing through change. First tiny cells. Then slowly animals. Monkeys. Finally men. Development through ages of living. Sometime I'll give you a book about it."

"What is bad about that?"

"Who said it was wrong?" Her father slipped to his feet, his fist shooting out in a gesture of defiance. "It's the most hopeful theory of life the world has known! Think, Jean, life growing! Going on, step by step—we're only a stage! What may come after us?"

Jean glowed. Her father had forgotten her; light ran through him. That was the way he talked from his platform, his hands sweeping the air.

"Then Adam and Eve and six days are just a story?" she asked.

"They are a myth——"

The door opened. Jean turned, guiltily, and the fire died in her father's eyes.

"Supper is ready," said mother, her upper lip thin like a hard parenthesis. "When you finish your lecture."

An afternoon later, Jean was in the library with James, playing a new game. She braced James against a chair and retreated slowly, halfway across the room. Then she held out her arms, and said, "Ready, go!" In a soft, clumsy rush, the baby ventured toward her, arms and feet wobbling in haste to reach her knees before a fall. Jean caught him, buried her nose in the little hollow at the base of his neck, the baby made soft gurgles of delight, and Jean laughed. Then they started from another chair. As Jean lifted her face from his silky head, she heard voices in the hall.

"It's settled." That was father, short and dry.

"They've——"

"Brown's nephew gets the job. With a raise! My services are valued, but perhaps in some larger center——"

Mamma was crying, short, difficult sobs.

"What are we going to do? What——"

"Brown's a stinking hypocrite! If I get a chance, I'll tell him——"

"No! You've got to have their recommendations."

"He's hated me since he heard my name. The students—they were on my side. They made a petition, Kitty."

"That doesn't pay our bills, does it? If you had been careful——"

"It's settled. Careful! I've spent the year walking on eggs!"

James wriggled out of Jean's arms and descended to his sure method of locomotion, on hands and knees. Jean let him go. She shut her eyes against the tears. Her father had lost his job. Now they would starve. Her mother said so. The baby—would he starve, too?

Her mother cried out, "My baby!" and Jean heard James's "Mum-mum," as she swept him into her arms.

"What are we to do? Innocent children! You have to think of something besides yourself and your ideas!" How her voice crackled!

"You'll frighten him. Come, don't take on so. There are other places. I've written that agency, last week."

Jean couldn't tell them that she knew. Her grief ran over into unnoted ministrations. She helped the girl set the table, filling the glasses to the brim. She arranged the little bathroom table with soap, powder, and special towels that mother needed for the baby's bath. She met Roger at the door when he came in from playing ball, and warned him in a whisper that he must be quiet and wash his face and hands without a word. Then she followed him upstairs and watched him splutter into soapsuds. "Here's your towel." She gave his neck a friendly rub as she handed it to him. She drew him into her room.

"You got to be awful good," she said mysteriously.

"Why?" asked Roger.

Should she tell him? He was so little to starve, and he was thin, already. But she had to tell someone!

"Papa's lost his job, and there won't be any money for

anything! Mamma cried, and——" She stopped as her father called,

"Supper!"

Roger, oppressed into silence, tiptoed downstairs, Jean behind him.

Silence, while papa served the creamed potatoes. Suddenly mamma threw her napkin in a heap and shoved away her chair.

"I can't eat! It chokes me!" She went hurriedly upstairs.

"Nothing chokes me," said Roger, valiantly, and his father absently piled more potatoes on his plate.

In the days that followed, Jean poured out her anxiety in services. The hired girl went away, and Jean washed dishes as if she prayed. She watched to see how much the family ate. They weren't starving yet, at least. Roger said,

"When I'm big, I'll be a nengineer, and I'll take care of everybody."

"You aren't big now," was Jean's miserable rejoinder. She pried open her iron bank and counted the money. Mostly pennies. Three nickels, a dime, and one quarter. One day she emptied them all into her father's top desk drawer. He might find it before they starved.

Father went away. The days stretched out endlessly between the postman's knocks each morning. One day mother said, "Jean, we are going away."

Jean's heart grew heavy, like a wooden block, and sank down until it hurt her insides. Now they would begin to starve!

"Your father has a new position. He writes he will be home to-morrow."

To-morrow would be father's birthday, too. Jean helped mother make the cake, beating the eggs until they flew like suds. She watched the trial cake, in the tiny cover, until it was brown. Then she and Roger divided that and devoured it, still warm, while mother poured the creamy batter into the big pan. When the cake had been frosted, Jean pushed the red candles into place.

Her father had come! He hugged mother and tried to make her dance with him, while James crowed and chuckled, and Jean laughed.

"It's only for a year, mamma," he said. "Smithers has leave of absence. It's a grand chance! Smithers might die or find another job. Let's celebrate!"

They led him out to the dining room, where the cake sat proudly on the white cloth.

II

Mother was dressing for a party. Jean, fingers awkward in her excitement, hunted for the hooks concealed in the lace at the shoulder, and fastened them. Then she stood off, with quick breaths of delight, admiring her mother in her blue dress. She fingered the little spangled fan and the lace-edged handkerchief, she sniffed at the white gloves with their faint odor of sachet and dusty kid. Father's suit was laid across the bed; mother had fitted the studs deftly into the gleaming shirt front. Father hadn't come home yet.

"He ought to be here." Mother dabbed powder on her nose and wiped it carefully off.

Jean looked hopefully up the street. Not in sight. Mother gathered up her fan and gloves, and holding her skirts away from her shining patent leather shoes, went slowly downstairs.

"You and Roger must be quiet and not wake up Jamesie," she said. "You can eat supper now if you want to."

"We'd rather wait till you go," said Jean, running again to the window. Roger was knocking croquet balls about the lawn, but her father was not in sight. Mother sat down in the wicker rocker, tapping one shiny black toe.

"Where *is* he? It is almost time to start!"

"Will there be lots of people there, mamma?" Jean circled her mother, stooping to touch very gently the coiled dark hair. She longed to say, "You look lovely!" but the words lay in her throat, unuttered.

"I suppose so. Don't fidget, Jean. Isn't he coming yet?"

"I think so——" Jean peered down the street; someone was coming—the figure passed the house. "Perhaps he had to stay and work."

"He said he'd be home early."

"I'll go over to the office——" Jean was at the door, when her mother called her.

"No. He won't be there."

Silence. Her mother drew her watch from the ruffled silk at her bosom, looked at it, snapped the lid shut. She rose, and walked into the parlor. Jean watched her part the lace curtains and stare down the street.

"Roger could run over in a minute," she ventured.

"Well——"

With the half permission, Jean bolted out to the yard.

"Roger, run and see if papa's in the office. He ought to be home. It's time to go to the party! Run!"

Roger dropped the mallet and ran.

Mother walked back and forth, from library to parlor. Jean sat on the steps, waiting for Roger's thin legs to dart around the corner again.

Presently he puffed into sight.

"Door's locked," he panted. "Janitor says—he says——"

"What?" Jean clasped her hands. "Oh, what?"

"He went away—long time ago."

"Wasn't he there?" Mother was at the door. "I thought so. He's down town. Playing billiards. He knew I wanted to go."

She disappeared into the house.

"We've got to find him, Roger." The children looked at each other darkly. "Mrs. Dunkert's got a telephone. You go ask her to call up the lodge and ask if he's there. Tell him to come quick!"

Roger was off.

Mother's face had lost its pleasant flush; her lips had thinned into a parenthesis. Jean stood in front of her, wretchedly searching for words.

"I think he'll be here in a minute," she said. But her

mother turned and went into the parlor again, her skirts fluttering ominously.

If he only would come! Perhaps something dreadful had happened to him. He had been hurt. Jean went out to the steps again. Her desire showed her a hundred times the figure of her father swinging around the corner. A hundred times fear cleared her eyes and she saw that no one came. There was Roger! She ran to meet him.

"He's coming," said Roger. "He'd forgotten it was to-night."

Jean rushed into the house. Her mother was no longer in the parlor. Suddenly she heard the sound she had, unknowing, listened for. Crying. She fled up the stairs. Her mother stood in the middle of the room, her lovely blue dress a heap about her feet, her fan and gloves on the floor.

"Mamma, he's coming! Roger found him. Put your dress on, quick! He'll be here——"

"Let him come! Does he think he can lug me in, hours late——" She stepped over the dress, dragging it after her.

With a little cry of despair, Jean gathered up the fragrant, rustling silk.

"Please put it on," she begged, following her mother's flight about the room.

"Leave me alone! He knew how much this meant to me! He stayed away on purpose! I'll show him if he can treat me like this——" She was wringing her hands in a dread gesture.

Jean spread the dress on the bed beside the limp black clothes that father had not come to wear, and tiptoed out of the room. She found Roger at the foot of the stairs, his eyes wide.

"Gee, she's mad, ain't she!"

Jean sat down on the lowest step and began to cry. She had looked so beautiful! Now it was spoiled. Roger put his arm around her shoulders.

"Don't you cry, Jeanie," he said stoutly, "we didn't do it!"

"Oh, Roger! He might have come in time!" Jean choked.

Her sobs rose from an injury deeper than she knew. "It was all so nice——"

Roger sniffed at her shoulder and she threw up her head, blinking violently.

"I—I'm not crying, Roger. See!" She smiled tremulously.

Just then a loud step on the porch, and father, rushing into the house.

"Where's mamma? Did she go?"

"She's pretty mad," said Roger, accusingly. Jean looked at her father. An hour ago she had longed to see him, had feared unmentionable things. Now, for the first time, she shrank away from him.

"Oh, Lord! It isn't too late. I forgot. Thought it was to-morrow."

He took the stairs two step at a time. The children listened.

"You decided you'd come, did you?" A door closed, and only the indistinguishable sound of their awful voices floated down.

They went out on the porch. Dusk had come along the street, making shadows under the trees. Soon father banged the door and pelted past them. He wore his best suit. Still that crying above them.

"Let's eat our supper," said Roger. "I'm hungry."

"It's all on the table. I don't want any." Jean gasped, echo of her frustrated sobs. She had planned that she and Roger would have a party.

"Aw, come on, Jean. It's lonesome."

Scarcely had they sat down, when the sound of a carriage stopping at their door hurried them into the hall. A hack! Father stepping out, stopping to speak to someone inside, dashing past them upstairs.

"Kitty!" They heard him at the door. Mother had locked it, then. "They want you to come! They have special seats for us, a farewell dinner. Miss Matthews has come with me. We've got a hack——"

The door flung open.

"Tell your Miss Matthews that I was ready. That I waited. And you deliberately refused to come! Tell her that! Go with her. That's what you wanted."

"Hush, Kitty! She'll hear you!"

"Hear me! If you don't leave me alone——" The door closed, the voices rumbled. Father stamped downstairs and out of the house. The hack door slapped shut. The horses pranced away into the dark.

Jean's chin quivered. The poignant tragedy of a lovely thing gone to ruin under her very eyes ached within her, almost past endurance.

"Well, I should think she'd go anyway," said Roger. "Prob'ly she'd get her dinner even now."

"It isn't dinner." Jean choked. "It's——" She stopped, lest she cry again. Her father was to blame. If he had come! He shouldn't have forgotten. Soberly they returned to their supper.

But days later, when mother would come down to breakfast again, and even talk with father about the plans for moving, Jean could not forget the hours she had waited, while pleasure decayed within her sight. The roses which father brought home with him that night stood vividly for a symbol. Mother had thrown them into the garbage pail.

III

Jean took James to stay with Mamie while the family moved. Father and mother went to the depot, and father climbed into the train with them.

"Now you just sit still here, until the conductor tells you to get off," he said, after he had found them a seat, and James was bobbing his nose again the window pane in delight. "I've spoken to him. It's not much over an hour. James will be all right."

"I can take care of him." Jean was reassuring. "Oh, the train's starting! You'll be left——" Father ran down the aisle, and a moment later Jean saw him on the platform, waving to them.

Jean thrilled at her responsibility. Maybe people would
think Jamesie was her baby! The woman across the aisle
smiled at them.

Mamie met them, her puckered, anxious frown vanishing
as she hugged them both. Then they had to see that James's
go-cart was put off the train. They climbed into the rattly
station bus.

Jean loved the approval which met James.

"What a pretty baby!"

"He's my brother," was her unvarying reply.

After a week, Mamie went back with them, to the new
home.

Father met them.

"Well, you've grown so I wouldn't know you!" That
was always his greeting to Mamie. "Climb in!"

"Is it your horse, papa?" Jean sparkled when she saw
the small black mare.

"In a way." Father picked up the lines. "She goes with
the place. We're four miles from town," he explained to
Mamie. "We've rented Smithers's house. He's the man
whose place I'm taking. Furnished. Stored our lugs.
Rented the horse, too. Gid-ap, Peggy!"

They drove a long way, Jean thought, through country
level and green, and finally they turned between stone
pillars on to a graveled drive.

"Campus begins here," said father. "Those are faculty
houses. •That's the President's."

Past houses, past dark green fir trees, stopping finally
before a red brick house.

"At last!" Mother ran out to meet them. "It takes so
long to drive from town!"

Jean wandered through the house, with Roger at her side,
pointing out marvels. Nothing familiar. A bathroom with
red tiles. Strange furniture. High ceilings. "Here's your
room," said Roger. A big yellow bed and dresser, instead
of her own small white bed and white bureau which father
had painted. Her bookcase stood near the door, with the
old books showing her their familiar titles.

"It's fine here," said Roger. "I've been riding most every day. An' swimming in the river with papa! An' there's some boys lives near here. It's grand!"

Jean felt a clutching inside her chest, as if she were lost. Perhaps she would like it, after she knew the furniture better, and forgot how the old house had looked.

Father's new office was very grand. Two rooms. In the first, a desk where a stylish young woman sat. The secretary. On the door in gold letters, "Dean." The inner room, where father stayed, had heavy chairs with leather cushions, and a great roll-top desk. Outside the window rose an old arbor vitæ; Jean liked the pungent odor which floated in under the morning sun.

"Does 'dean' mean you boss the college, papa?"

"Not quite. Instead of teaching, I have to manage the students. Tell them what to study. Keep 'em in line."

The stylish young woman came in with the mail, smoothing down the front of her stiff white waist. Jean felt her impressiveness.

Mother said, "Why on earth do you need that snip in your office?" Father just shrugged.

Jean couldn't settle into a home feeling. Like visiting. An undercurrent of tension in the life around her gave her a tingle of suspense. She heard Mamie, the morning before she went home, talking quickly as if she wanted to say something before she was stopped.

"You must be careful here. So close to the rest of the teachers. Your tantrums never do any good. Try to control yourself. James'll need some help. He wants to make a success——"

Mother just looked at her. Jean, in the hall, saw her face, and felt a shiver along her backbone. How did Mamie dare talk that way? But mother only looked at Mamie, with that queer, shut-in look, and then went slowly upstairs without one word. Mamie had to go up to her room to say good-by to her.

One night Jean heard her mother and father.

"Everyone is watching you to see what you do." A pleading tremor in her voice.

"I can't do more than my best, can I?"

"I don't trust that snip in your office."

"She's got to stay. She was Smithers's clerk."

"If you only behave yourself——"

"How the devil would I act? If I say good morning to a woman, you suspect me of starting something!"

"You know what I mean. And that Miss Murray—dean of women! She says with her smirk, 'Mr. Winthrop has never done anything but teach before, has he?' She is sly."

"She's all right. Friendly enough. Likes to show me how much she knows, that's all."

"A woman can fool you every time!"

Jean strained her ears, anxiously, but the voices dropped to indistinctness.

Everyone had to be careful, evidently! The next time Miss Murray came in, Jean peered at her. Plump, with wavy white hair and pink cheeks, she looked like a kindly grandmother. But when mother said, "I don't trust that woman! I can feel something," Jean, who had heard her add, often, "You know how often I'm right about people! If you would only listen!" felt that there must be signs she was not wise enough to read.

IV

School started. Jean had to walk out to the gate of the campus and wait for the chunky red street-car. Father went with her the first day, and she was entered in the classes the scarlet fever had interrupted. Cæsar again, with his tiresome marches; Silar Marner; the first weeks of repetition gave her so little to do that she sat, much of the time, watching the girls and boys about her. Many more of them here. They divided into sets, with a few people, like Jean, on the outside.

Jean's hair had grown long enough to be parted and tied

with two bows, one behind each ear. The other girls wore
only one bow, large and stiff. Jean tried to tie her hair
back in one bow, but the ribbon slipped off. She explained
to the girl next her that she had been so sick the nurse had
cut her hair; then she was more comfortable about her
deviation from one ribbon.

Four of the girls lived at the edge of town toward the
college, and sometimes they waited for the car with Jean.
One of them had dark eyes and hair, a little like Anne
Bishop, except that her hair curled, and her face had red
spots on it instead of the pale smoothness of Anne's cheeks.

"Why don't you come to our church on Sunday?" she
asked. "We have a club."

After that Jean went to Sunday School with them, and
belonged to their set in school. Their class in Sunday School
sat in an alcove of the balcony; during the opening exercises
they moved their chairs out to the railing and sang very
loud, never looking across at the boys' class opposite.

The club met on Saturday afternoon. They sewed and
had refreshments. Sometimes the mother of the girl at
whose house they met would sew with them. But once no
one was in the house except the club. That afternoon the
girls told stories. First they said, "Jean, haven't you
got a fellow?" Jean hesitated. "Well, not here," she
said.

Then the oldest girl, Daisy Thoms, who looked a little
like Anne, told stories. In a low voice. Peeking toward the
door now and then. Jean, listening in wonder, tried to understand them. She pretended that she did, and when the girls
laughed, she laughed too. Furtive stories, with a perverted
Rabelaisian flavor. If she didn't laugh, the girls would
think she was a baby.

There was another set of girls whom Jean watched,
enviously. They wore astonishingly pretty dresses, and
they had an air of complete exclusion of everyone outside
their set. They talked of "frat" parties and giggled.
"Awful snobs!" Daisy Thoms declared them. They paid
no attention to Jean, except when one of them, a slender,

fair girl who sat near Jean, asked how to work the problems in geometry, or how to translate a sentence in Cæsar.

Jean did not feel like herself. Sometimes her body was heavy, languid, difficult to move. Sometimes her head dragged on her neck. One day, as she stood at the board working out a geometry problem, the sounds about her receded endlessly. A whirring, like distant wings, and Jean opened her eyes to stare up into the startled face of Professor Bent.

"Stand back!" he was saying. "Give her air!" A circle of staring eyes around her. Her head throbbed. She tried to sit up.

"Wait a minute, Jean. Drink this." He held her with one arm and the water trickled over her chin.

She went home in a hack, with Daisy Thoms. Daisy watched her avidly for the first mile.

"You don't think you'll faint again?"

"I guess not. My head aches."

"You hit it on the platform when you fell."

"Did I fall right down?"

"I should say you did! Whack!"

Jean was at home for several days, resting on the living room couch. Mother hovered about her, tender, solicitous. It was nice to be sick, especially when you didn't really feel sick. There seemed to be a queer kind of pity in mother's attention. Jean wondered at that.

She felt almost distinguished when she returned to school. Professor Bent came into the assembly room to ask how she felt, and the girls stared at her.

College opened. Over night the campus changed from a stretch of sleepy, evergreen trees in front of sedate faculty houses and old red buildings with empty windows to a place full of exciting voices, girls' voices raised in greetings, boys' voices thundering across the lawns. The students came in groups, like flocks of chattering bright birds. Jean watched them pass the house, the girls with arms interlaced, their voices gay, light. What did they talk about? She longed to be grown-up, to walk with them, arm in arm. But what could she say, if she were a part of that enchanting, endless running on of voices? Perhaps, when she grew up, and went to college, then she would know.

Father rushed into the house late for dinner, and rushed out again, the spoke-like wrinkles at the corners of his eyes never smoothed out.

Mother said, "You can't keep this up! Use some judgment——" and he snapped out, "Who'll do it if I don't? Things have to be seen to. Plenty of folks are ready to take advantage of my being a new man."

Jean felt that his thoughts went on, running, even when he sat down in the evening with his paper.

The first excitement diminished; Jean grew accustomed to the sight of girls in bright dresses, to the sound of voices. Perhaps the first chorus subsided a little, too. But father seemed to keep his harassed wrinkles and he never seemed to have time to walk slowly.

The house with its strange furniture, the waves of sound about it, the irritable rush in which her father lived, a white, shut-in look on her mother's face—all these pulled at Jean, invisible, tormenting threads.

New tensions within Jean herself. Once at the table father laughed at something she said, and unexpectedly she burst into wild tears and flung herself out of the room. Roger wasn't as nice as he used to be. She found her little desk open one day, the writing paper thrown around, the pencils out of their box. In a fury she flew out, searching for him. Her ribbons dropped off, her hair tumbled like a mænad's. She shook him, crying, "You've got to leave my things alone! You bad boy!" Roger wailed out his surprise, and mother came, to pull Jean away and send her in disgrace to her room. Tears flooded away her rage and left her as amazed as poor Roger.

She heard her mother telling father about it, and at his, "What ails Jean? She's never acted like that!" she crept forlornly away. They all hated her. Nobody liked her—until more tears came.

Sometimes for days Jean was her old self, untormented by

unbidden rages or griefs. Then, as if a demon entered, she lost herself. Mother said, "I'm ashamed of you, Jean. You act worse than the baby!" Jean said nothing. In secret she groveled.

V

Christmas was coming. Jean found her old joy in planning gifts that she could make, in going into the woods to help select the tree, in popping and stringing corn to trim it. She and Roger whispered together, amity restored. Jamesie was old enough this year so that the tree was to be especially his, and Jean and Roger could help decorate it. Christmas morning Roger's shrill cry woke them, "Merry Christmas! Happy New Year!" He was scrambling around in his pajamas, although it was as dark as the middle of the night. But father and mother called "Merry Christmas!" sleepily, and then their light was on.

"You get dressed and wait at the head of the stairs till I come back," said papa, hurrying into his clothes. Roger pulled his pants on right over his pajamas, but mother caught him and made him dress. James didn't have to be dressed.

"James first. Roger take his hand. Then Jean. Then mamma. Then me." Father met them at the head of the stairs. "Now! Ready, march!" He played a tune into his hands, and they filed downstairs.

The first glimpse of the tree always made Jean ache. It looked strangely different, even when she had wound the tinsel through the branches herself. She could see it as they had found it, dark, snow-laden, pointed. Now its branches were full of pointed golden lights from the candles; the popcorn looked like snow. Myriads of packages had appeared at the base. The golden flames seemed to sing a fine, unheard song, as they trembled against the dark branches.

A long time later they had breakfast. James stood his fat woolly lamb on the shelf of his high chair, and shrieked in protest when Roger seized it and thrust it head downward into his bowl of oatmeal. "Lamb ought to eat," insisted Roger, but James cried, and Roger subsided ruefully into his chair, the lamb safe on the shelf. Jean sank into her chair with a queer feeling in her stomach. Christmas had come; they had seen the tree; they had untied all the red ribbon and unwrapped all the tissue paper. It was over—the beautiful thing for which they had worked and waited. A year now, a whole long year, before another. It took so long to wait for a day, and when it came, it rushed past you like wind!

But when she had eaten breakfast, she forgot that forlorn sensation. Roger wanted her to coast with him. James was bundled into a fat white lump, and they drew him around the yard, first Jean and then Roger holding him on the sled. Then Jean, her blood singing with the sharp air, went in to help stuff the turkey.

"They're going to have music at church this morning," said mother. "Special music."

"Want to go?" Father had just assured Jean that never had he so enjoyed a shave as that he had just had, with Jean's present of shaving papers tied under a hand-painted cover.

"Of course I'd like to go." Mother pounded loudly into the large brown chopping bowl.

"Come on, then."

"I suppose you'll stuff the turkey if I go?"

"Can't Delia do it?"

"She's never roasted a fowl, she says."

"Let her boil it, then. Come on."

Mother gave a bang with her knife.

"You'd like boiled turkey, I'm sure!"

"Couldn't I do it, if you want to go?" Jean looked uneasily from her father to her mother.

"Oh, go away, both of you!"

"If you want to——"

"That's as reasonable as you ever are. You say 'Come on,' and then you're satisfied, no matter what I have to do."

Father left the kitchen hastily. Jean watched the danger

flags spring into her mother's cheeks. But Delia said, "Ain't that like a man, though?" and mother, after a decided "It certainly is!" seemed to forget the incident.

Dinner, with Roger sighing because no amount of unbuttoning would permit him to eat more. Jean helped Delia with the dishes, becuse she wanted to get off early. Mother went upstairs to rest, Roger sat down on the floor near the tree to examine his new magic lantern. "To-night I'll give a show," he said, holding the slides up to his eye and squinting. "It's too light now."

"Umm," said Jean from the chair where she sat humped over "The Arabian Nights for Children," one of Roger's presents.

"Animals!" declared Roger. "I see a tiger——"

A sweet, clear jingle of bells at the door. Father, with Peggy hitched to a sleigh.

"Tell mamma to wrap up and come for a ride," he called. "We can all pile in."

As mother came downstairs, a man and woman stopped to speak to father, and he jumped out, threw a blanket over Peggy, fastened the strap to her bridle, and came into the house, the people following him.

"Here's Professor Thorpe and his wife," he said. "My wife, Mrs. Thorpe, Professor Thorpe. My daughter Jean, and Roger. No, come right in. We can drive later."

They were shaking hands, Mrs. Thorpe with many flutters of the plumes on her big black hat.

"We've meant to run in all the fall, Mrs. Winthrop. We won't detain you, though. On Christmas, too."

"We can drive any time." Father led them into the parlor.

Mrs. Thorpe was like a bird, thought Jean; so little and quick, with red hair curling against her velvet hat and a piece of fur around her throat, soft and velvety like a bird's breast. Her husband was tall and bald, with a smile which he put on and forgot. Roger went out to tramp in the snow, dejectedly, and Jean, taking off her coat, sat down again with her book.

The voices floated between the sentences.

"Lovely children! Your husband has told me how domestic you are!"

"Oh, you've met before?"

"I just ran into his office. I knew dear Mr. and Mrs. Smithers so well, I really forgot there would be a strange man in that office!"

"Hope you'll forget it often," said father.

Jean looked up through the draped portières. Mrs. Thorpe sat where she could see her and father. The others were behind the curtains. The feathers on Mrs. Thorpe's hat danced and trembled, and father was looking at her, his fingers jiggling his watch chain.

"It's too bad you didn't forget a strange woman was in Mrs. Smithers's house," said mother. Jean puzzled over the tone; the words sounded silly, but the tone——

"You find it comfortable here, Mrs. Winthrop?" That was Professor Thorpe. Slow, thick.

"Yes. Although not having our own things—we thought it would be easier just to take the house."

"Smithers is having an interesting year."

Jean tried to read again. Queer, when grown-ups talked they said things, and underneath they meant other things. Sometimes the underneath things pushed so close to the surface Jean could almost hear them.

"No, we didn't hear the music," mother said.

"I begged Mrs. W. to go, but turkey meant more to her than Christmas carols!"

"Really! Dear me, I always go anywhere I am asked."

"Yes, a turkey would never keep Mrs. Thorpe at home, not if I had to eat it raw."

Jean looked anxiously at the dancing feathers, at her father's restless fingers.

"A mother learns she can't go when she wishes," said mother, gravely.

"We have no little darlings——" Mrs. Thorpe drooped, a violent palsy afflicting the longest plume.

"Do you find the country here pleasant?" Professor Thorpe cleared his throat.

"What I've seen of it." Mother was short.

"Nice place to drive."

"Perhaps you'd like a run!" Father jumped to his feet. "Let's take them for a sleigh ride, mamma, shall we?"

"Oh, how sweet!" Mrs. Thorpe smiled, her head on one side. "I adore sleighbells!"

"You've just come," said mother.

"We can come again—any time!"

"Get your things, Mrs. W. It'll be a tight squeeze—four of us—but I guess we can manage."

Mrs. Thorpe laughed, although Jean saw nothing very funny.

"I don't believe there'll be room for us all—" said mother.

"Well, Mrs. Thorpe and I are going, aren't we? If you folks want to come"——Father was at the door, Mrs. Thorpe hesitating gracefully, poised on one toe.

"Do you think that—er—that we can be accommodated?" Professor Thorpe had risen.

"I don't know, I'm sure." Mother's voice sounded as if it came through snow, but she went swiftly to the hall rack and took down her coat. Jean wished her mother had a fur to wear about her throat.

"I'll take you and Roger when we come back," said father, hurrying out to strip the checked blanket from Peggy. Jean watched them climb in, a chill which had nothing to do with the wintry air settling over her. Something was wrong. Very wrong. Mother didn't like Mrs. Thorpe. Although she was pretty.

Roger came in through the kitchen.

"Stingy old pigs!" he muttered. "Going off instead of us!"

"There's Jamesie, awake. You go get him, Roger, and we'll build houses for him." Jean heard the faint metallic jangle of vanishing bells.

They built houses for the baby's rag doll, and a barn for the lamb. Roger rolled over in glee when James tried to eat the lamb's shoe-button eyes. Jean told them stories. Roger, curled against her knee, listened with Jamesie to the old "Three Little Pigs, Brownie, Blackie, and Whitie." The early winter twilight floated down through the branches of the Christmas tree.

"We could have our show now, Jean. It's most dark."

"Maybe we ought to wait."

"Aw, I can work that lantern. You watch!"

Jean pinned one of James's blankets on the curtain, and the show began. The smell of hot metal and smoky oil, the round yellow spot on the blanket with colors suddenly thrusting across it. Back of that, in Jean's inner self, a dread, a waiting. James talked his mysterious soft language whether Roger showed them tigers standing on their heads or giraffes right side up.

Faintly sleighbells sounded again, louder, jangling to a stop outside. Roger rushed to the door. "Can we go now?"

Mother brushed past him into the house.

"Can we go now, mummie?"

"Of course not. It's dark. It's too cold." She went upstairs without another word. Father had driven away. Jean and Roger heard the sound of the bells come sharply back as he turned the corner toward the barn.

"Maybe to-morrow we can go, Roger." They went back to their magic lantern. But James was tired and whimpered in his cushions.

Jean climbed the stairs. Mother sat by the window of her room, her cloak and hat still on.

"Did you get cold?" Jean tried to throw her words out casually.

Her mother did not move; her profile showed like a paper face against the window.

"Do you want me to give baby his supper? He's getting cross."

"Yes."

Her mother did not move. Jean waited, but except for the monosyllable, not a word.

"Is she mad?" whispered Roger as she came downstairs. "Yes, she is!"

"Needn't bite *my* head off!"

"I got to give James his supper."

"Nice way to act on Christmas," Roger mumbled. "Want my supper, too."

"I'll take baby upstairs and then we'll get our supper."

James sat on the bottom step and wouldn't budge.

"Put your arms around Jean's neck, then." Jean bent over him, felt his hands clutch back of her neck. He was heavy! Slowly she climbed the stairs, her arms tight about the softly dragging body.

"Here's baby, mamma," she said from the doorway. "Shall I undress him?"

"Give him to me!" Her mother enclosed him in a clasp so sudden that James shrieked and pounded her shoulder, thinking she had started a new game. "Don't, Jamesie!" Her voice came from some deep, shut-in recess.

Jean turned on the light.

"I'll see to him." Mother swung her chair away from the light, her back to the door, and Jean, her feet loud in a flurry of rage, clumped downstairs. She had done nothing! The glimpse through the curtains of the Christmas tree, its dismantled branches a curious green in the light from the sitting room, a long string of popcorn dangling from one point, drained off her anger in a sharp gasp.

"Oh!" she cried, and one hand flew to her throat in a gesture of her mother's. "Oh, it was so beautiful! And it's spoiled." She wanted to fling herself down and sob out the twisting ache. But Roger called her, his voice anxious.

"Jean! Papa's here. An' he says we can eat cold turkey. C'mon!"

Jean knew there was something feigned in her father's loud "Here's where we put the end to turkey forever! What'll you have, Jean? His front leg?"

"Gimme his hind wing!" Roger jumped around the table. "Ole hind wing! That's what I want."

"What does Jean want? Here's where we drive Turkey

out of Europe!" Her father looked at her challengingly,
and swiftly Jean answered his look.

"I'll have Constantinople!" she cried, and Roger laughed
until he choked and had to be patted between his shoulders.

In a moment Jean discovered that pretending to be jolly
actually changed your inside feeling. Father chewed the
wishbone, pretending he was a dog, and Roger growled like
another dog, trying to get it.

Then Jean and Roger held the wishbone ends, solemn a
minute while they made their wishes. Jean's wish was,
"Make mamma feel better!" But the bone pulled apart,
and suddenly the head snapped off, leaving neither of them
with a wish coming true.

"Where's that other wishbone?" Jean and Roger laughed
at father peering into the hollow of the back.

Jean heard it first. A faint sound, the pushing of a slipper
on a rug. She stopped abruptly, not daring to turn her head.
Father looked up.

"Come on, mamma," he exclaimed, "and find me the other
wishbone. Christmas turkeys always have at least two,
don't they?"

"We didn't get our wishes at all," said Roger, beaming
from a smeared little face. "The head flew off!"

"I should think," began mother, and Roger swallowed
his smile with a gulp, "that you'd be too ashamed to come
back to your innocent children!"

"Now, mamma, play you feel good!" Father brandished
a bone toward her. "It's Christmas, isn't it?"

"And you let that woman come into my house on Christmas, to insult me!"

"Come, Roger." Jean seized his hand, and slid past her
mother into the dark library.

"You—you——" The voices buzzed from the kitchen,
father's protests losing their high, strained merriment,
mother's voice riddled by heavy breathing.

"Let's go to bed," said Jean. "You take your lantern
up with you." She helped Roger pick up the scattered
slides. He went ahead of her up the stairs. When he had

gone into his room, Jean crouched at the head of the stairs.
What were they saying?

"I don't know what you're sore at now!"

"No, you don't! You think I'm a fool! Shut up where
I don't know what you do! You don't know what Miss
Murray said to me, do you? 'You haven't met Mrs. Thorpe,
have you, Mrs. Winthrop?'" Jean shivered at the thin,
mocking imitation of Miss Murray's speech. "'No, I
thought you hadn't.' They moved down town because that
woman carried on so with the men! And you—what does
she come to your office for? 'I hope you'll forget often!'
Squeezing up to her in the sleigh! Oh, I wish I was dead!
You could have your strumpets——"

"Hush, Kitty! The children——"

"Hush? What do you think of the children? You think
I don't know!"

Jean wondered feverishly what strumpets were. She would
look up that word to-morrow. Mother's voice had broken
into sobs; she was pacing back and forth, father's voice
chasing her. She stopped sobbing, grew articulate again.

"You want to ruin us. You don't care. They're watching
you. Miss Murray was warning me. The children! They
didn't know why you felt so lively, did they? Oh, no!
They don't know their father drinks, do they? They think
I'm to blame for trouble. I've shielded you!" Her sobbing
began again.

"I'll tell you one thing!" Jean sat straightly against the
railing. This was a bad one! Her father was angry, too.
"I haven't looked at the woman. I will, though. I'll give
you something to make a row about if you want it. A
glass of beer is getting drunk, is it? I'll show you! If
you want something to row about, I'll give it to you!"

A terrific slam of the kitchen door, silence, and then the
low, continuous sobbing. Jean crept down the stairs into
the kitchen. Her mother sat at the table, her head down
almost in the platter of turkey remains.

"Mamma, please don't." Jean touched her shoulder.
"Please—come up to bed——"

"Leave me alone!"

Jean was crying.

"Go on to bed! There's nothing for you to cry about."

"Please come, mamma!"

Jean's sobs were real enough, but she had a distant wonder whether if she cried harder, her mother would come. She was moaning, long, sobbing moans. Jean stood, irresolute. Then a torrent of grief swept over her, and she ran until she was in her own room, shaken by her own tears. Roger came in.

"What you crying for, Jean?" He pushed awkwardly against her where she had flung herself on the bed.

"Go 'way!" cried Jean. Then she heard it, like an echo of her mother, and she sat up, tears rolling down her cheeks. "I'm not crying now!" She hugged Roger violently.

"If they want to get mad, let 'em," said Roger. "I guess Christmas is a strain on 'em. You don't need to cry, too."

"No, I won't." Jean mustered a laugh. "You'll get cold in your pajamas, Roger."

"C'mon and see how I fixed my lantern," he coaxed her.

Jean followed him into the little back room. The lantern sat shiny and black on top of the box, the slides laid in a row on the table.

"All ready for another show. I sorted 'em out. That was a pretty good show, wasn't it?"

"Yes, it was. You hop into bed and I'll put up your window."

"Gee, it's too cold!"

"Just a crack." Jean turned out the light and raised the window. She looked out at the firs, black against the snow. "Good night, Roger." She hesitated. She wanted to kiss him good night. But that would be silly.

"G'night," he murmured, sleepy already.

When Jean had undressed, her door closed against sounds from the kitchen, she lay for a while staring into the darkness of her room. What had happened? Rows didn't just come. Something made them. That woman—she would look up strumpet. That might explain things. Had father come back? She lifted her head. No. Her throat ached. Things could be so beautiful, and then in a whiff, smash! She ought not to sleep, with her mother in the kitchen. She couldn't go downstairs again. Would her father come back —drunk? Probably the cool air would calm him down. Old Murray was to blame. Saying things to mother out of her fat cheeks. Oh, she wished—she wished—— She drowsed off. Some noise dragged her bolt upright. What! Had father come? Nothing but darkness, silence, with that distant, dreadful sound. A dream, perhaps. Then she slept.

Life smoothed out quickly that time, perhaps because Delia came back in the morning, perhaps because they lived so near the other faculty houses. But under the surface, Jean felt brittleness, and for days she walked with care, alert for signs of breaking. She thought that once or twice, in the night, she heard voices, low, struggling, but those were easy to forget.

VI

Spring came. The bright broad leaves of skunk cabbage unfurled in the ditches along the car line. The evergreens on the campus pushed out tips of pale, tender green. Jean felt tired. Restless. The baby was a nuisance. Roger plagued her. She wandered moodily from room to room; even books were stupid. What *did* she want? She locked the door of her room and cried. She heard her father say, "What ails Jean, anyway?" and mother, "I don't know. Nothing interests her. She mopes all the time."

"She comes by it honestly," said father, teasingly.

"She may have her father's temper!"

"I meant on the other side."

"Of course! All her bad traits come from her mother. Her father is perfect!"

He meant she was like mother, going off to cry! She stood up, stormily. She wouldn't be like that! Some of the college girls went past, singing. They made her feel unhappy, too.

Father decided that she needed to get outdoors.

"Peggy's as safe as a hearse," he said. "Jean can drive her."

She drove with father several times, and then he said, "Ask someone to go riding with you. You can manage her."

Jean thought. Mother was nervous about her driving. She didn't want to ask one of the girls. Suddenly she remembered Mrs. Pratt. She had heard Miss Murray talking about her one day.

"Nothing but a waitress in a hotel when he married her, my dear! She's very pushing. Expects to be taken right in because her husband's on the faculty. Her blue eyes caught him all right."

"Was she a waitress?" Mother sounded interested. "She has nice manners. But I thought there was something—— She may be all right, of course."

Their tones stirred rebellion in Jean. She had seen Mrs. Pratt on the campus; her house was a tiny cottage on a side street off the main faculty row. Her blue eyes looked hungry.

Jean thrilled with importance as she drove up to Mrs. Pratt's house, holding the reins tightly, as if Peggy were really a difficult horse to manage. Mrs. Pratt climbed in beside Jean.

"Your father thinks the horse is safe?" she asked.

"Oh, I can drive her!" Mrs. Pratt looked like a kitten, thought Jean, with her fluffy yellow hair, her small pink mouth, and her round blue eyes.

Jean clucked at Peggy and off they went, through the campus at Mrs. Pratt's suggestion. Miss Murray bustled past them, nodding, staring at Mrs. Pratt.

Mrs. Pratt sucked in her lower pink lip.

"She's sort of plumpish, isn't she?" said Jean, comfortingly. So Mrs. Pratt didn't like the dean of women, either!

"I should say so!"

They drove along the river road, under the maples with their young leaves distinct and perfect against the spring sky. The river in spring flood held trees within its course, their trunks mysterious and black as they stood up from the ripple of the current.

Mrs. Pratt asked questions. About school. About her brothers. About father.

"Your mother hasn't called. Of course she just came this year, and yet it's my first year, too."

"She's pretty busy with the baby and all."

"Perhaps it's really my place to call. I'd like to! Your mother looks so sweet. She's young, isn't she? It's hard to know just what to do in a new place."

Mrs. Pratt spoke in staccato entirely, with unexpected emphasis. The breeze blew tendrils of yellow about her ears. Jean decided she was beautiful.

"Oh, violets!" Jean yanked at the lines. "You hold Peggy, while I pick some." She was down on her knees in the bit of meadow which touched the road, breaking the delicate, thin stems. "Aren't they lovely?" She stood by the wheel, looking up shyly. "Would you like them?"

"Awfully sweet." Mrs. Pratt took them. "They don't smell a bit, do they?"

"They are the very first I've seen." Jean slapped the reins on Peggy's haunches. She was happy. The inexplicable, vague restlessness which had tormented her had drifted away. She did not know why. Nothing had happened— except the violets.

When they stopped before Mrs. Pratt's house, the woman said, "This has been such a nice ride. It's the first nice time I've had," she added under her breath.

"Would you go again sometime?" Jean leaned toward her, shy seriousness on her face.

"I'd like to ever so much!"

Jean's dream that night before she fell asleep had Mrs. Pratt as chief actor. She said to Jean, "You are my only real friend," and Jean said, "You are mine, too."

They drove again, Saturday after Saturday. Mother said, "Why not ask some of the girls instead of that woman? What do you find in her?" Jean said only, "I think she's nice."

"What do you talk about?"

"I don't remember—things we see——"

"Don't tell her things you ought not to. She may be prying——"

One afternoon, Jean, home from school early, ventured around to Mrs. Pratt's door. No one answered her ring, and she had started down the steps when the door opened.

"Come in, Jean. I didn't know it was you."

Mrs. Pratt's eyes were glittering with tears, and her small mouth trembled.

"Oh, what is the matter?" cried Jean.

"Nothing—I——" and the woman was crying, not as mother cried, but gently, like a little girl. "They're so mean to me—I can't bear it—I don't mean to cry." She dabbed her eyes with a wad of handkerchief. "What did I ever do to them? Just because I worked——"

"Has somebody been mean?" Jean stood close to Mrs. Pratt, her hands clasped. "Oh, I'd like to tell them what I think!"

"You're a sweet girl." Mrs. Pratt seized her hand, held it to a damp cheek. "You wouldn't understand. It's just that they won't pay any attention to me. I spent just hours hemming curtains for the parlor—and not a soul——" She sat down and drew Jean near her, an arm about her waist. "I don't know what I'd do without you. Will says"—her tears flowed again—"that I should go out and see folks! How can I? Men don't know——"

Jean stood rigid in the woman's embrace. A fury of pity ran through her. How could people be so mean? She was so pretty and sweet! Mrs. Pratt shook away her tears.

"If I should tell you some of the things they've done! Christians, they call themselves! Christian cats! Claws! They've talked to your mother, I know."

"Don't think about them," begged Jean, with a guilty recollection of her mother and Miss Murray, talking. "They're just old things!"

Presently Mrs. Pratt, her eyes dry, little points of fire still sharp in them, took Jean out to show her the pillow she was embroidering. Shaded roses. Mr. Pratt came in. Jean felt his relief at finding her there.

"Maybe she cries when he comes home," Jean thought, as she rose awkwardly, saying that she must go. She always wished that she could just say presto and vanish; making proper farewells was difficult. Mr. Pratt, thin and little, with a high forehead and scanty light hair, stood between her and the door, rubbing his palms together.

"Yes," he repeated. "Nice of you to run in. The wife gets sort of homesick, er, that is, lonesome, you know. I have to go off and teach physics. Can't stay home. Can't earn a living that way. Now can I, Lottie, eh?" His eyes hung on his wife, like a humble dog, thankful for a pat.

"Men always run away, don't they, Jean?" Mrs. Pratt came to the door. "Don't say anything, Jean dear, about— you know." She kissed Jean's cheek quickly. "Come again, won't you?"

The next Saturday mother wanted to drive into town, and Jean could not have the horse. The following week was rainy. Jean cherished the afternoon she had gone to Mrs. Pratt's as too sacred to repeat. She must wait until she could take Mrs. Pratt for a drive. She walked past the house in the twilight, hopefully, but the shades hung behind the ruffled curtains, and no one looked out.

VII

Father was sick. The house had a stillness like a cellar in all the rooms. Jean tiptoed in to listen and then tiptoed out again to keep James happy and quiet. She stayed home from school, since mother was too busy to watch James. When she was out in the sunlight with the baby, she could almost forget the feeling of the house. But when she stood in the empty sitting room, the stillness was like a wild beast, crouched to leap upon her. Mother came downstairs with swift, noiseless feet, and Jean followed her into the kitchen.

"Is he dreadfully sick?" The hot water gurgled into the bag mother was filling.

"We don't know. Take good care of James. That helps mother most."

Her eyes were withdrawn, concentrated; her voice had a quality of the stillness in it, under its tenderness. Jean watched her in curious awe.

Saturday the doctor came three times. The last time his horse pawed a great hole in the gravel, so long did he stand there. Within an hour, the doctor drove back, a second doctor with his black case climbing out after him.

Jean waited, James clinging to her hand, through long heavy minutes until the men came down into the hall. Mother was with them, crying softly.

"Well, Mrs. Winthrop, the worry is over. It isn't appendicitis. With your excellent care——"

"The fever has dropped since morning. No operation, fortunately."

"You are sure? It won't come back?"

"No danger now, so far as mortal eye can see." The new doctor came out, stopping to tweak James's cheek as he passed.

Jean still listened, holding her breath.

"He's in bad shape, though, Mrs. Winthrop. He wouldn't think of trying some other work? He came in a month or so ago, and I told him he was burning out. All nerves. He's too young a man."

"I don't know." Mother had her company tone, suddenly. "It's been a hard year."

"Take it as easy as you can. He'll need good care for a while. I'll run in early to-morrow."

Jean stood on the steps in the path of the doctor.

"Will he get well?" she demanded.

"Well? Well!" The doctor's face was round and pink. "Well! I should say so. Ain't I taking care of him? What a question!"

Jean stared resentfully after his carriage. He thought she was nothing but a little girl! Suddenly happiness broke over her, flashing, tumultuous, and she seized James by both hands.

"Come on, Jamesie! Let's dance!" She whirled around him.

He was better. When Jean, a few days later, tiptoed in to see him, a lump in her throat melted into hot tears at the sight of his face, gaunt and shadowy against the pillow.

"Scare you, Jean?" His voice wobbled. "Like my beard?" He lifted his hand, and Jean laid her cheek on his in a swift, shy caress. He was stubbly! Mother came in, and Jean tiptoed away, swallowing hard.

Later she could sit by the bed and read to him, dry articles in the paper she didn't think about at all. Mother came with a tray.

"Pays to be sick, eh?" Father grinned. "That's the way to get treated fine. Nothing but kind words and orange juice."

Mother set the tray on a chair. "I know where you are and just what you're up to!" But she smiled as she spoke.

Jean went back to school. Father was up, and could even go to his office for an hour. There were new shadows under his cheekbones, even after he had shaved off his sick-beard.

There grew a new trouble at home, formless, vague, with faint rumbles like distant thunder. Father acted as if he scarcely saw any of them. Mother had her white, shut-in look. Jean waited, fearful.

"I told you that Murray woman was double-faced." That was mother, one night. "I warned you to be careful of her."

"But to say such things! To take advantage of me—when I was flat on my back!"

"You needn't have made an issue of that girl."

"I couldn't let her expel a girl for a silly thing like that—disgracing her for life!"

"It gave her the chance to complain. That you interfered with her discipline. That you wouldn't discipline girls—if they were pretty!"

Bit by bit Jean pieced out the trouble. Father had lost his position again. Smithers wasn't coming back, and he had expected to stay. But they had thrown him out. That was his terrible phrase—*thrown him out*. Miss Murray had done it. She had friends—trustees. She never liked father. Father was going to try something else. He was sick of the whole damned academic mess!

"Perhaps it will be better." Mother had the same tender concentration of father's illness. "Something where an enemy can't destroy all your good work. It's a risk——"

Jean couldn't pour out the sympathy which ached within her. They hadn't told her anything. She had just puzzled it out. Mrs. Pratt would understand. It had been a long time since that afternoon. Mrs. Pratt hated people, too. Jean wanted to ask for Peggy. But if they were thrown out, perhaps she shouldn't have Peggy.

On Saturday, however, father and mother drove away together. Jean knew she was supposed to stay with James. But he was taking his nap, and Delia said she'd listen for him.

Jean went through the yard, across lots. The lilacs behind the sheds had, over night, opened their tight purple spikes. Jean picked an armful, and went hastily on, the fragrance swimming about her.

Mrs. Pratt opened the door, the ruffles of her blue dress swinging.

"I thought you'd like these, maybe." Jean thrust the lilacs forward. Above the lavender blossoms she saw Mrs. Pratt's eyes, blue, but hard, hard like unopened lilac buds. Was she angry because Jean had stayed so long away? "My father's been sick—and I couldn't come."

"I heard he'd been sick." Mrs. Pratt made no motion toward the flowers. Her mouth was tight.

Jean drew back a little.

"They have the horse to-day, so I can't take you riding——" Jean trembled. She wanted to run away from those eyes, staring so strangely at her. Something within her curled up, away from the warm out-rush which had carried her to the door. And then the woman opened her tight little pink mouth and said a dreadful thing.

"You needn't bother! Your mother's acted too stuck up to call on me, but I don't wonder! My husband keeps his jobs, anyhow, and behaves himself." Then she shut the door.

Jean crossed the road to the path. She felt sick. The sweetish lilacs—she dropped them to the grass.

Late that afternoon her father called her. She went reluctantly to the door. Mother stood by the carriage, father still held the reins.

"Don't you want Peggy? Take Mrs. Pratt for a drive?"

"I'd rather kill her!" cried Jean, and then fled, aghast at her outcry, to her room.

"What is it, Jean?" Mother followed her, bent over her where she huddled against her pillow.

Jean quivered.

"Have you been over to Mrs. Pratt's?"

A single angry sob.

"Tell mother, Jean." Mother sat down on the bed. "What did she do?"

Jean sat up abruptly.

"Nothing!" Her eyes fled from her mother's gaze.

"She wasn't nice?"

"I never want to see her again, ever!"

"What did she say?"

Jean shook her head, her lips pressed together.

Mother was silent a moment, then she sighed.

"I suppose she said something about father. Did she? She's a scheming thing. She thought if she was nice to you, she'd get in where she wanted to. Now she thinks she wasted her time. Don't feel so bad, Jean. What was it she said?"

Jean threw her arms about her mother's neck in a passion of loyalty. In her heart lay a dead thing, hurting her. She could feel it under her hand, right in her chest. But stronger than the hurt was her anger. That woman had said things about her folks! Mother patted her hair gently.

Jean felt like a tiny girl, held close to her mother's soft breast.

"I'm sorry, Jean. Sometimes people are like that. You mustn't feel bad. She was too old for a friend, anyway. I didn't like your going off with her."

Jean drew away. She was grown up, again, too old for the soothing comfort of arms.

Days later she saw Mrs. Pratt walking toward the corner. She felt a leap within her, an animal, craving flight. But she walked stiffly past, her eyes on the dusty ruts of the road, pretending she had seen no one.

You couldn't tell whether people felt the way they acted or not. Pretending they liked you. It must be hard work, Jean thought. She would be sure to forget, and act the way she felt. She remembered the little boy's mother who had killed herself in the bathroom. The bird in the gilded cage. She couldn't stand it. Maybe she had tried to pretend for a while. Mother never pretended. Jean could see just which people she liked and which she didn't like, from the way her mouth turned into a line and her eyes shut part of herself away.

People knew what happened to your folks. They talked about it. Jean walked softly as she came up to two of the faculty ladies. Did she hear them say, "The Winthrops"? But they nodded pleasantly at her, and she went on, the conviction wretched within her that they were saying things about father. Perhaps they knew about the quarrels, too. She hurried, to shut herself behind the door of their house.

VIII

School was over. They were going to move down town. Mother and father had found a house the Saturday they drove away with Peggy. Father was going into business, a vaguely promising phrase. Perhaps they would be rich, now.

The house seemed very public, with a tiny yard between it and the street in front, and other houses crowding against

it on either side. Jean missed the green slopes and pointed
firs of the campus. Moving itself was uneventful. The
house was settled with their own furniture, taken out of
storage, and then the trunks were packed and moved down
from the college. Wandering through the rooms, Jean
tasted flat disappointment. She had thought she would love
the old things, but somehow during the year they had grown
strange, too, and when she came to her own room, she saw
that the paint was dingy on her dresser, and the iron of the
bed showed through. Father was away all day. Jean
dreaded the moment after he had taken his hat and started
for the door.

"Will you bring home some meat for dinner?" mother
would say.

"What do you want?"

"I don't know. You can see, in the market. I haven't a
cent for the milk. The man asked for it yesterday."

"How much have you got to have?" Father's gesture
toward his pocket looked as if he meant to hold his money
from jumping out.

"You know what the milk costs as well as I do. Ice, too."

"Good Lord, where does the money go? I'm not made
of it!"

"I'm not asking for any for myself."

Jean shut the kitchen door and poured the water into the
dishpan. Poor father! And yet, mother had to pay the
milkman.

There was nothing to do. Roger found a boy down the
street to play with. James cried because Roger wouldn't
take him, but Roger said he couldn't have a baby tagging
him every step! Jean hated the hours, with dust floating
into the rooms from passing wagons. Sometimes she sewed.
Mother helped her cut a shirtwaist out of chambray—ox-
blood, she called it—and Jean sewed it, tucks and seams and
boxplait down the front. A brief pleasure in running the
machine as fast as her feet could make it go, another in the
fastening together of strange shapes of cloth and seeing a
waist grow. The tedious process of finishing it up, as mother

called it, ended in a buttonhole on the wrong side, and tears
from Jean.

"You have to have some patience, Jean!" Her mother
took the waist out of her hands. "You can't finish it up in
a second, the first waist you ever made."

"I hate sewing." Jean dashed away her tears, ashamed,
and yet driven on. "I hate everything!"

"Go and read or something. I'll fix your waist."

"I've read everything."

"Go and see one of the girls, then. You need some air.
You're worse than James."

Jean sat on the front steps, her face doleful, her eyes still
wet. What *could* you do? Endless, hot, dusty days. She
thought of Mrs. Pratt, of the beautiful content of those
afternoon drives. Feet of clay. She had read that phrase,
and liked it. That was Mrs. Pratt. Feet of clay. Some
day—an indrawn tenseness swallowed the dolorousness—
some day Mrs. Pratt would come to her. "Jean, dear, I
have wronged you. I have not been happy since that day.
I cared for you more than I knew. Will you forgive me?"
Jean extended a graceful hand; she was very dignified.
"Don't think of it, Mrs. Pratt. I forgave you long ago.
But my feeling for you is dead." Mrs. Pratt was on her
knees before Jean. Would she kneel? Jean frowned. Of
course! "Can we be friends again?"

A wail at her feet startled her out of her dream. James,
on his knees in the grass, one hand gyrating.

"What'd you do, Jamesie?" Jean tumbled beside him.
"What is it?"

"Pwetty bug," James sobbed. "Hurt baby!"

Jean pried open his dirty little fist.

"See, Jee——" He stopped crying to point at a fuzzy
bumblebee, crawling into a clover blossom. "Pwicked baby!"

"Oh, he stung you! Poor baby!" Jean carried him into
the house, and by the time his swollen thumb was anointed
and bandaged, and Jean had beguiled him out of his woe
with stories, supper was ready, and another day gone.

Mamie wanted Jean to come to see her. Alone. Mother

packed the telescope, not so bulging this time, with only Jean's clothes.

"I don't like it," said father. "The children belong at home. When you grow up, Jean, home is gone. You never have it after you are young. Stay here. You don't want to go, do you?"

Jean nodded. She wanted to say that she wouldn't care if home did disappear, but instead she said, "I wouldn't be gone long. I haven't seen Mamie for a long time."

So she went. In her new ox-blood chambray shirtwaist.

Mamie's house looked smaller than she had remembered, and the yard had shrunken. After supper Mamie sat down in her rocking chair and began to talk. Jean sat soberly opposite her, sedately conscious of advancing years. Almost as she talked with mother. About the neighbors, about the drouth. Finally she said, "Is your father doing well, do you think?"

"Yes." Jean wondered. Mamie spoke with some sharpness.

"Does he like his new business?"

"I guess so."

"Seems dangerous, changing out of one thing into another, with a family."

"The doctor said he ought to," cried Jean.

"I know it. Does your mother like it?"

"I guess so."

"How is she?" Mamie pursed up her lips, and Jean knew what she meant. But Jean couldn't talk about that, even with Mamie, who knew.

"She's pretty well," she said.

"Your father's awful trying sometimes." Mamie sighed. "I suppose men are. But your mother oughtn't to take on so."

Jean flushed to her ears. She rose, stiffly.

"I guess I'll go to bed," she said. "I'm kind of tired, after the trip."

She was to sleep alone, in Mamie's front room. Mamie tucked her in.

"You're a big girl," she said, sitting down on the bed. "About as big as your old aunt." Then she added in a half whisper, "Haven't you ever come round?"

Jean twisted over to the other edge of the bed, shame leaping through her.

"I should think you were old enough."

"Yes." Jean shot out the miserable word.

"That's good," was her aunt's amazing rejoinder. Then she kissed Jean and went away.

After the first day, restlessness seized upon Jean again. She went with her aunt to call on people who had known her mother.

"So this is Kitty's girl! Hasn't she grown! She hasn't a look of her mother about her, has she?"

"She takes after her father's side," Mamie would explain.

On the way home, they stopped in the bakery, warm, full of the heavy odor of cakes.

"Pick out what you want, Jean."

She picked doughnuts and sugar cookies. They never had those at home.

Grandmother stayed in her own room all the time now. Jean was no longer afraid of her. She scarcely thought of her. On Saturday Grandfather went over town to the barber shop. The rest of the time he sat in the shade near his woodshed, whittling small bits of white wood.

Jean liked to go over town. One block of stores, along the base of the triangular park. On the corner stood the white hotel, next it the saloon, then the drugstore, two grocery stores, and two general stores. The hardware store, postoffice, and bakery were down the next side street. Always there were men and boys, chairs hitched back against the buildings, and a few women standing at the doors of the stores, talking. Jean walked along briskly, her head up; they must all know she was from a city. Perhaps they knew who she was; perhaps they said, "Can that be Miss Stephen's niece?"

Mamie didn't like to walk past the lounging men. "Nothing to do but sit there and stare!" she fussed.

Jean had been to the postoffice for the morning mail. She had gone over a second time, for a loaf of bread. She wrote a letter to mother, with a special note for Jamesie, and pulling on her straw hat, called to Mamie that she was going to the postoffice.

"You don't want to go over town again!" Mamie hurried in from the kitchen, wiping her hands on her checked apron.

"I want to mail my letter." Jean stepped out of the door.

"Wait till this afternoon, Jeanie. You've been over twice."

"I want to mail it now. It's only a little walk."

"You can't go now!" Mamie held the door ajar. "I don't want folks seeing you running the streets all the time. It isn't nice."

"Why, what harm is in going to the office?" Jean's voice rose.

"You come in the house. There's plenty of girls in this town walk up and down the main street, showing off. I won't have my niece doing it."

Jean stood in the little porch, the cloying fragrance of honeysuckle dropping about her.

"That's silly!" she cried. "There's nothing else to do in this old town, anyway!"

"We'll go this afternoon, Jean. Come in."

Jean banged the door after her and rushed past Mamie into the little bedroom. She flung herself face down on the bed and cried. Mamie treated her like a baby! She hated this town. She wanted to go home! If Mamie came in and found her crying, she would be sorry she had been so foolish! She had expected to have a beautiful time—Mamie was mean and silly.

Mamie didn't come in. Presently Jean's sobs stopped and she rolled over. The crisp white curtains at the window, looped back in exact folds, filled her with remorse. Mamie had washed and ironed the curtains because of Jean. She hadn't meant to cry. She sat up. She could see herself in the mirror of the dresser, eyelids red, mouth dangling! Suppose Mamie did have funny ideas. All old maids did, mother often said. After all—she stood up, looking out of

the window. She hadn't cared about going over town.
That wasn't it. Just doing what she had started. Was
that it?

Why, she had acted like mother. Shutting the door, and
crying. Jean felt an uncomfortable warmth tingling up to
the roots of her hair.

"Jean!" Mamie called from the kitchen.

Jean blew her nose and went out.

"Will you spread the frosting on this cake?" Mamie's
hair blew in little curls about her heat-flushed face. "Dinner's most ready. Grandpa brought in some fresh peas."
Jean felt her anxious, entreating glance.

She spread the frosting, dipping the silver knife in a glass
of water, standing off to observe her work.

"That's fine!" Mamie's tone had a pleased under-note.
"Now would you rather have preserved strawberries or
peaches?"

"Let me go pick them out." Jean went down the low,
uneven wooden steps into the cellar. She loved the
feeling of the cool twilight in which the preserve shelves
hung.

Mother wrote that Grandfather Winthrop was dead, and
father had gone to his home. Jean had better come back
soon. Saturday Mamie went to the depot with her. When
the train puffed in, Jean threw her arms about Mamie's neck,
clinging to her as if she were a little girl again. That was
the way she had wanted to feel, all the time she had visited
her. Why hadn't she? Dear Mamie! Tears in Mamie's
eyes as she kissed her, and handed her telescope up the steps
to her. Jean found a seat on the depot side of the train
and smiled at Mamie until the train dragged her out of sight
of the figure on the platform.

IX

Jean was glad no one met her. She liked the important
feeling of climbing into a hack alone and giving the address
to the driver. She leaned near the glass of the door; per-

haps someone would see her and know that she had come
back from a visit. Mother and Roger and James were all
on the porch when the hack drove up. Jean paid the driver
solemnly with the last quarter in her purse, and rushed up
the steps. They were glad to see her again! She was glad
to be home.

Father had not come back.

"He wanted me to go," said mother, "but I couldn't take
the children to a funeral, and there wasn't anybody to leave
them with."

"I can take care of them," said Jean, "if you want to go."

"It's too late now. And anyway, I couldn't leave you.
We can't afford the carfare."

Jean wondered how bad father felt. She hadn't seen
Grandpa Winthrop for so many years that he was little but
a shadowy mixture of beard and peppermints. She supposed
she should feel bad, since he was dead, but somehow she
didn't really. Mother's voice was hushed a little when she
spoke of the funeral, but Jean suspected that she didn't really
mind. Not very much.

Then father came back. Jean wanted to tell him she was
sorry, but he seemed so busy that she couldn't find any
time when they were alone.

"I've got to go back next week to see to things," he told
mother.

"I should think one of your brothers would do that."

"Father asked me to."

"You ought not to be away just now, when you're starting——"

"Some things won't wait."

Mother was silent. Later Jean heard her ask, "Did your
father leave much?"

"Enough to keep mother comfortable. That's about all.
A lot owing him that probably can't ever be collected."

"I thought he had a good deal of property."

"He'd given the houses to the boys. The home's got to
be sold, to give mother an income. She's going back with
Dorothy."

"So you are to do the work and the rest get the money! You might think of your own family once in a while!"

"I've got to see to affairs. That's all there is to it! I won't argue about it, I tell you."

"You mean you won't listen to a word I say."

Jean closed her door. That sounded like a danger signal, and she couldn't bear to listen.

She lay staring at the dark square of the window, while the voices spread about her, a murky flood, receding, sweeping up over her. Her door opened, and Roger stood in the faint light, a thin, woe-begone figure. The voices poured in, loud.

"I'll tend to my own business!"

"Tend to it by leaving it! How much money did I have last week while you were gone? Do you think they'll let you stay in that office?"

"Jean!" Roger's whisper shot through the noise. "You 'sleep?"

"No, I'm not," said Jean. "Go to bed and don't listen, Roger."

"It's James. He's crying. Scared."

Jean swung herself out of bed and followed Roger, bare feet sticking to the hall matting. James was sitting up in his iron bed, under the window in Roger's room, sobbing with little heart-rending catches of his breath.

"Shut the door, Roger." Jean picked up James, her arms tight around the soft body, warm through her nightgown, and sat down on the plaything box.

"What's the matter, Jamesie? Here's Jean." She rocked gently back and forth. Roger stood near her, twisting one bare foot around the other ankle. "See Roger, baby! He thinks he's a stork! There!"

James stopped sobbing and peered through the dim light, his breathing still full of catches.

Roger pulled his foot farther up his leg, wavered, fell over against Jean.

"He isn't a very good stork, is he!" Jean wiped James's

cheeks with a fold of her nightgown, and James choked over a shaky giggle. "That's it. Now Jean'll tell you a story."

Roger crawled into bed, and Jean lifted her voice to drown out the voices clamoring at the door. Presently James slept again, one hand curled in the hollow at the base of Jean's neck. He sighed in his sleep. Jean balanced cautiously, rose, and let him down on his bed, pulling her arms slowly away.

"He's all right," whispered Roger.

"Now you go to sleep, too," said Jean.

She opened the door a crack and slipped out, closing it quickly. The voices had stopped; just the sound of sobbing from the front room. Father must have gone away. Jean pressed against the door, then turned back. Nothing she could do.

Day after day. Summer would never end. During August there was not even Sunday School. Father went away and discomfort brooded over the house. Mother said, "Why don't you go and see some of the girls or ask them to come here?"

"I don't want to see them," said Jean.

But she went upstairs and dressed in the blue dimity mother had just made for her. She would go out to see Daisy Thoms.

Daisy came to the door in answer to Jean's knock. Her eyes were red-rimmed, and her black hair disorderly about her face.

"Oh, you!" she said. "Ma, it's Jean Winthrop."

"Sit on the porch," came Mrs. Thoms's reply from the dark hall. Daisy brought out two rockers and the girls sat down.

Jean told about her visit to Mamie, but Daisy kept glancing at the house instead of listening. Finally she leaned forward and lowered her voice, "I'm going to tell *you*. You won't repeat it, will you? My sister Bessie's home. She came this morning. With her baby."

"Is she?" Jean looked into the hall. Why couldn't she

repeat that? Something seemed to creep out through the rusty screen, sluggish, ominous.

"She's left her husband." Daisy sat up straight, tears in her eyes again. "The baby's only a month old, too. She's never going back. He was a brute!"

"Oh!" Jean's eyes, still on the door, darkened.

"Ma's awful upset. She wants her to go back. Bessie won't. We've cried all day."

"What did he do?" Jean lowered her voice to hushed inquiry.

"Awful things. Chased women. I don't know. Gee, men are fierce, aren't they? She says what she's stood from him!"

Jean wriggled, fingering the ruffle that edged her sleeve. She ought to go home. Daisy wouldn't want company.

"But what are you going to do? You have to marry them or be an old maid, now don't you? Say, listen, Jean. *Would* you get married?"

"Daisy!" Mrs. Thoms's voice rasped out to them. "You've got to get the baby's bottle. Bessie's sick."

"That's what I'll get out of it, you see!" Daisy rocked darkly, not offering to rise.

"I'll have to go." Jean jumped up. "Come see me if you can, Daisy."

"You come again. The baby's real cute. Some other day you could see her."

Jean sped down the street, no longer careful not to stir up dust with her new shoes. A weight settled deep in her throat. She had seen Bessie once, before Christmas. She had a vision of her, little, with untidy curly hair, coming home with a tiny baby, and the house full of crying women. Oh, she hated it! Were men brutes? That was what mother said, sometimes. Her father wasn't! Roger and James—why, they were just folks, like herself! She wished she hadn't gone to see Daisy Thoms.

Jean shut herself into her room with books. She read again the fat gray Dickenses, with their warped covers, the red George Eliots. She was sorry for Tito. He couldn't

seem to help the wrong things he did. She puzzled again
over Adam Bede; she felt as if she almost understood it
this time—no, it slipped away just as she thought she had it.
She tried Guizot's "'French History," bright blue with gold
edges, eight volumes. Father had said, "You read too much
fiction, Jean. You are old enough for something solid,"
and he had tried to make her read an hour every day in the
blue volumes. She never could get past volume one. Fine
print, battles, crowds of people, kings—she had to read
slowly instead of gulping, and she thought it very dull. One
day she explored the top shelf of the big bookcase, where
the little books stood. Hegel. Kant. Curious titles. "The
Critique of Pure Reason." She sat at her father's desk,
frowning over the sentences. They looked easy, but she read
them over and over, and they didn't say anything. Mother
came in.

"What are you reading? For goodness' sake, what
possessed you to try that?" Mother put the book back in its
place and looked at Jean with queer animosity flashing in
her eyes. "Leave your father's books alone."

"I'd like to know what is in them." Jean sulked.

"A lot of good they've done him! If he had as much
sense as he has learning——"

"I'm going to read them by and by," insisted Jean.

"I hope you'll get some sense first. With all your getting, get understanding."

Jean felt herself linked wth her father in an obscure
accusation. Mother went back to the kitchen, and Jean
stared at the shelves. Another title leaped at her. "Thinking, Feeling, and Doing." She opened that book. Pages
of diagrams. A bird and a cage. You moved the book
slowly, and the bird walked into the cage!

She carried that book upstairs before she was discovered,
and spent the afternoon reading the directions under the
plates, thrilling over her experiments. Stairways that turned
into cornices as she looked at them, spots that disappeared
at a certain distance. Funny, that your eyes could fool you
that way. She would ask father why, when he came home.

She found a paper-covered book, "A Story of an African Farm." She had supposed Africa was a wilderness from which negroes came. The somber cruelty of the veldts gave her a new dream, of exploring that strange country. She reread, with painful, sweet shame at the core of her being, the chapter where the little boy was beaten. The next day the book was gone. Mother must have found it. Well, she had read it!

Her father was home again. Between him and mother hung sharp opposition, tightening life until Jean struggled to shut herself into an ignoring shell.

X

Finally September came with school again. Mother said, "Thank goodness you'll be kept busy now!"

The first days were deliciously exciting. Eddies of boys and girls in the halls. Swift rivers of them from one room into another. Discussions of electives, a term satisfying in the importance it conferred. A seat in the Junior Assembly room. When the principal looked at Jean's program, he pulled his black mustache.

"Ah, Jean Winthrop. You're taking full work this year."

"Yes, sir."

"Let's see, your father was acting dean at the college last year, wasn't he? This year——"

"He's gone into business." Jean spoke loudly. She wanted to affirm the dignity of his move with all the fiery words she could summon, but fear held her silent. So the principal knew, too! Oh, what did they say about her father?

"Yes, so I heard." He scrawled his initials at the bottom of her sheet. "I hope you will make a record as good as last year, Miss Winthrop."

"Miss Winthrop!" Jean repeated the phrase under her breath.

The new history teacher was pretty. Jean sat in the middle of the row of recitation seats and gazed at her. Small, with brown hair coiled round and round her head until it seemed heavy for the slender throat; the most beautiful eyes Jean had ever seen, large, gray, with astonishingly yellow glints. She wore immaculate white waists, with black ribbon crossed under a turnover and tied in a jaunty bow. And her hands! Jean hid hers at the edges of her skirt, they seemed so huge!

Her name, too, was lovely. Miss Dorothy Adair.

Jean found in the book of home songs from which she played, one about Robin Adair. "What's this dull town to me——" She played it over and over, after she had studied her history lesson in the evening, until mother said, "Play something else, Jean, or go to bed."

The history of the Egyptian dynasties, the rise of the Roman empire, were glamorous links in the chain of hours, one each day, when Jean sat in front of Miss Adair, holding her hands clenched in her lap to repress her eagerness, until Miss Adair might say,

"I am sure Miss Winthrop can answer that question."

The family was to attend a new church, one near the house. Jean dreaded the first Sunday, with new people. When she had been assigned to her class she glanced across the room, and her heart jumped to her throat. There sat Miss Adair, in blue silk, surrounded by her class of boys. Perhaps she went to church, too! The next Sunday Jean went with mother, sitting erect in the pew, her eyes bright with hope. She studied the hats ahead of her, the profiles across the aisle. She saw her! Down toward the front, a great pink rose on one side of her velvet hat.

She thought out questions about the old Romans, so that she might stop after class near the desk, and watch Miss Adair's pearl-like fingers ruffling the pages of her record book; even, sometimes, look up into her eyes in quest of those flashing bits of yellow. She longed to say things to her, light, careless things, such as she sometimes heard the seniors toss her. But her face grew warm, and her tongue was stubborn.

One day she made a turnover, hemstitching it, and tried to wind a blue ribbon about her throat as Miss Adair wore

hers. The bow was limp—the ribbon was too old for stiffness—but Jean went proudly to school. When the bell rang
for history, she lingered at the door, afraid to enter. Suppose Miss Adair noticed and didn't like it! Miss Adair
smiled at her. Had she seen the ribbon?

Father and mother were going to join the church. They
had their papers transferred. Father was indifferent, but
mother said, "It's the best way to meet people." Miss Adair
was joining, too! The minister announced their names one
morning, in church.

"Could I join the church?" Jean stood by her father, who
was reading.

"Do you want to?" He laid his book aside.

"Yes."

"Why?"

"I don't know." Jean twisted on one foot. She didn't
know. "To believe in God."

"If you want to, you can." Her father's eyes crinkled.
"The minister has a communion class, I think."

The class met on Saturday. One woman, three older girls,
and one young man. The minister, his eyes sharp and black
under his white hair, prayed with them. About entering
God. Jean felt a quiet ecstasy mount within her, as if she
had dropped into a warm, sustaining flood. She wanted to
enter God.

"You are sure, Jean Winthrop, that you are ready to give
yourself to the service of the Lord?"

Jean nodded, tears brimming. This was what she had
wished, surely.

The Sunday came. In the front pews sat the people who
were joining. On one side of the aisle were those with
letters—mother, father, Miss Adair, several men, another
woman; on the other side, the members of the class. The
minister lifted his head, his hair floating back like an aureole,
and prayed. Jean closed her eyes, the quiet ecstasy climbing through her. Her face was serious and white. Entering the service of the Lord. Abandoning yourself to Jesus.
Beautiful phrases! You could no longer be wicked, you

would be good, washed in the Blood of the Lamb. That was
queer—washed in blood! The prayer was over. Jean looked
at her father and mother. A doubt squirmed into her ecstatic
mood. They had abandoned themselves to Jesus a long time
ago, and they seemed—well, like ordinary folks. Miss Adair
stepped forward, her gray eyes solemnly lifted. The doubt
slunk away. When the minister read "Jean Stevens Winthrop," the syllables seemed to consecrate her through in-
finity. She sobbed as he touched her bent head. Miss Adair
had seen her enter the church. She walked back to the pew
behind her mother, her head lifted, her eyes brilliant.

That afternoon she started to read the Bible through. The
phrases resounded. "Let there be light: And there was
light." Later chapters dragged. Curious things in the Bible.
Could you find God that way? And old man on a throne,
with a long beard.

One day as Jean started home from school, someone
shouted her name. Daisy Thoms was hurrying to catch up
with her.

"Say, I hardly ever see you nowadays." She tucked
her hand under Jean's arm. "Don't you go to Sunday
School?"

"Oh, yes. I've joined the church. But down town."
Jean tried to pull away from Daisy's hand without hurting
her feelings.

"Did you? You're a funny kid. I'm going along your
way. Down to meet my sister."

"Is she here yet?"

"You bet she is. Say, her husband came after her, and
there was some fuss! She wouldn't go back. Not one foot.
He's trying to get the baby. And listen, she's gone back to
work. Bookkeeper at the factory."

Jean had freed her arm under pretext of straightening
her hat. She didn't like the way she saw Daisy's gums when
she laughed. Moist, red things!

"Does she like working?"

"She says it's a cinch after being married. She says not
having to ask anybody for money if she wants a pair of rub-

bers is worth the price of admission. Say, men have it easy, don't they?"

At the next corner Daisy left her, hurrying off with elbows swinging, and a loud, "Well, so long! Come and see us."

Jean walked slowly. Money. When you got married, you asked your husband for it. Still, it didn't seem nice for a married woman to work. One of the girls had told her that Daisy's father and mother were divorced. Awful word, scarcely to be spoken aloud. Perhaps that was why Bessie came home. Ran in the family. Girls worked, in stores and factories. Or teaching. She was going to be a teacher. Some married women worked. But it wasn't very nice for their husbands. Folks said, "He doesn't earn enough." Still, if mother had more money——

XI

Jean had a new friend—Esme Maurey. She was a year ahead of Jean in school, and Jean had never seen her until one day Esme waited for her at the door, and went down the street with her.

"You are Jean Winthrop, aren't you?" she said, while Jean marveled at the ease with which she spoke. If Jean had wished to approach a strange girl, she never could have done it! "I'm Esme Maurey." How long her eyelids were, under fine arched brows, and how her hair shone in the sun, fine separate fair hairs catching the light in splinters around her face.

"I'll walk home with you. You're the girl who's got a case on Miss Adair, aren't you?"

Jean's secret was a startled rabbit within her, seeking covert. She stared at this bold girl.

"I know you are. That's why I want to know you. I love her, too."

She swung along at Jean's side, light, astonishing, saying what she felt, what she thought, what she wanted, with an effrontery which fascinated Jean. The two girls stood in front of Jean's house.

"My sister is a senior at her college this year. She is lovely," said Esme, her short upper lip caught between her teeth in a sigh. "I haven't any friend just now."

"I haven't, either," said Jean.

They looked at each other, a fire back of Esme's blue gaze. Jean flowed out toward her; she wanted to touch her, to be sure of her, to be possessed by her. But she was silent.

"Do you like poetry?"

"Some," said Jean. Esme's leaps of thought were part of her astonishing quality.

"You come over after school to-morrow and I'll read you some. I love it."

The next day Jean's thoughts of Miss Adair were mixed with those of Esme Maurey. Esme had gone to see Miss Adair! She walked home with her, some days. Her house was near the place where Miss Adair roomed. Miss Adair had held Esme's hand, because Esme had said, "I was so ashamed of my finger nails! Hers were manicured and beautiful!" Esme dazzled, like fire; she *darted* at you!

Jean waited for her after school. They walked slowly, the leaves drifting from the maples about them. Esme told how she felt when she saw Miss Adair, and Jean listened, shy, flushed. Finally Jean told about her song, Robin Adair.

"We'll have that for a signal! The first bars——" Esme whistled them. "That's the call. And the next—'Ro-o-bin—'s no-ot here!', that's the answer. Then we won't have to ring doorbells."

They whistled it softly until they came to Esme's house. No one else was home. They went up to Esme's room.

"This is my sister Laura." Esme handled the silver-framed photograph gently. "Isn't she sweet?"

"Yes, she is." Jean studied the face. Perhaps having a sister grown up, like Miss Adair, gave Esme her fire, that thing that leaped out, that caught even Miss Adair.

They sat on the floor near the bookcase, while Esme pulled out book after book.

"Laura gave me most of these. She used to read poems with me. I haven't had anyone to read them with, since she went away. Most of the girls would just laugh!"

Jean had never bothered with poetry. It mixed stories up, when it told any, and the halting, clumsy reading in school had never captured her ear. Esme opened a soft green leather book.

"Tennyson," she breathed. "Do you know his poems?" Jean shook her head.

And so Esme read.

> Tears, idle tears,
> I know not what they mean——

"It's the way you feel, deep inside," she said, softly. "Sometimes I almost cry, just reading that."

"Read me more," begged Jean.

Suddenly she saw that the room was so dark that Esme could not see the words plainly.

"Oh, I must go home." She scrambled to her feet.

"Probably your folks have a copy," said Esme. "If they haven't, I'll let you take this."

"Good-by," said Jean. She was full of delicious vague music, words melted into sound, sorrowing love, beauty. "Come and see me, soon, Esme."

"We've got to be friends," exclaimed Esme, clasping the book to her breast, "since we love the same one!"

"Oh, yes!" sighed Jean.

"You ought not to stay so late," said mother, "the first time you go to see a girl. Was her mother home?"

"No, she was at a church meeting, I think." That sounded safe. Jean hastened to set the supper table. "Mamma, have we a copy of poems by Tennyson?"

"I guess so. Put two spoons on, Jean."

Jean hurried through supper, hurried to wipe the dishes, and then stood in front of the bookshelves, searching. No green volume, with gold letters across the back. Then she saw it, brown instead of green. She tucked it between her school books.

"Are you studying Tennyson now?" asked mother.

"We're going to, I think," was Jean's reply. How tell of her beautiful hours, of her great discovery?

She found the songs Esme had read her. They looked different, in their irregular black lines, until Jean tried reading them just under her breath. Then the magic came back to them. She found a long poem, "In Memoriam." Arthur Hallam must have been a friend of Mr. Tennyson. She didn't understand all of the verses, but she liked the way the rhyme clipped shut at the end of each stanza.

> Strong Son of God, immortal Love
> Whom we, that have not seen thy face,
> By faith, and faith alone embrace,
> Believing where we cannot prove;——

She felt the unhappiness, the struggle, without understanding.

> "The stars," she whispers, "blindly run;
> A web is woven across the sky;"

Immense and stirring, that figure!

> An infant, crying in the night——

That was like James, only she would have preferred the word *baby* to *infant*.

There were days of rain, with leaves sodden in the gutters, and the maples a black network against gray clouds. Esme waited at the corner for Jean, and they walked under one umbrella, Jean flushed, with little breathless gusts of confidence, Esme a swift dancing figure, sometimes radiant, sometimes prostrate in dejection.

"I saved my allowance for two weeks," she said one morning. "To-night I shall buy roses for Her."

That night Jean waited until mother had taken James up to bed.

"Father." She had changed from papa and mamma because Esme never used those childish names. Mother objected, because it made her feel old, but Jean insisted, her color heightened whenever she used the words. "Father!" He looked up from his paper. "Could I have an allowance? So much a week?"

"What for?"

"For—well, for anything. You know. The other girls have them."

"Maybe their fathers have more money. I give you what you need, don't I?"

"It's different, having an allowance." Jean trembled; she wanted it so much! "Some of them have as much as fifty cents a week."

"What for? I buy your books and clothes. What else do you want?"

"It's just having it."

"Candy and gum! No, I won't. You can ask me, and if I have the money, and it's something you need, I'll give it to you. You've just bought all your books. You don't need anything more, do you?"

He settled back with his paper.

"Sometimes I might want something I didn't want to tell about." Jean was hot with humiliation, but she couldn't stop.

"Then you oughtn't to have it, that's all. Don't begin to bother me for money, like your mother!"

Jean felt a cold fist shut tight within her breast. With her books, a blur dancing before her eyes, she climbed the stairs to her room. Door shut, she sat down by the window. She wouldn't cry! She squirmed in enraged helplessness. It wasn't because he was poor! He just wanted to make her ask for things. She leaned her forehead against the cool glass. Suddenly she lifted her head. A whistle! Clear and low, the first bars, "What's this dull town to me——"

She pushed the window wide and knelt to whistle the response. She saw Esme in the dark street, vaguely beckoning. She ran downstairs and closed the front door softly behind her.

"Jean!" Esme seized her arm, her voice rippling in delight. "I took them! She was home, and oh! Jean, she kissed me! Pink rosebuds. She said they were lovely! She kissed me!"

They were at the corner, and Esme's face was a pale star under the flaring arc lamp. Jean gazed at her, caught into the delight of Esme's beautiful evening.

"Now I must run. It's late. But I had to tell you——" Esme threw her arm over Jean's shoulders and brushed Jean's lips with a sweet, flying kiss. "Good night, dear!"

Jean tiptoed back to her room, glamour shimmering about her. Esme had come to share her lovely moment. Esme was wonderful. Before Jean slept, her eyes flew wide with the recollection of her father's refusal. "I've got to have some money," she said aloud. "Some they don't know about!"

The next morning the world seemed to have shared their joy. The rain had gone. The sun hung low and golden, a mellow lantern swung in hazy skies. Color had come back to the trees, golds and browns of oak leaves and pointed beech, papery, slow drifting in the windless air.

"Indian Summer," said mother. "I'm glad the rain has stopped. This family tracks in more mud!"

Jean thrilled to it. Like poetry. Her feet moved to some unheard rhythm.

Esme was not at the corner. Jean saw her in the hall, heavy eyelids, somber mouth.

"I couldn't sleep," she said, swiftly. "Something's haunting me. I don't think I can tell you."

The class bell rang, and reluctantly Jean left her. Instead of studying, she wrote to Esme. The sweet, golden day pressed around her, and the embarrassment which held her silent, melted. She could write—anything she felt. She was an acolyte, swinging freshly lighted incense for her first worship. The bell ended the period, startling her from her devotions. She thrust the note into her volume of Ovid, and went to class to sit in a soft dream while the story of Baucis and Philemon was dragged forth from the Latin.

That afternoon Esme walked home with her. Jean wondered whether she dared give her the letter. But Esme's silence, her dark mood, rose like a wall between them.

Mrs. Winthrop was not home. Roger, playing with James in the yard, said she had gone to the Ladies' Aid meeting.

"You take James now." He glared at the baby. "I been stuck here ever since I got home."

"You play with him, Roger," Jean begged him, "and I'll— I'll give you my pencil with the glass end."

"Don't want your old pencil." Roger dug his toes into the pile of sand.

"It's most new! I'll give you that and I tell you, I'll sew up your school bag. It's most done. Come on, Esme." They hurried into the house before Roger could protest further.

"What is it, Esme? You were so happy last night——" The door shut them safely into Jean's room.

"It's terrible." Esme sat on the bed, her arms clutching her knees. "I remembered it last night."

"Tell me!"

"I think I ought to tell Her. She liked me. She thinks I am nice. You remember—'I could not love thee, dear, so much—Loved I not honor more!' It's like that. She ought to know."

"What, Esme?"

"About me. What I used to do. Dreadful." Esme threw herself sideways on the bed, her head down on her arm.

"I don't think you ever did anything bad!" cried Jean. She longed to touch Esme in evidence of her faith, but she could only hover near her.

"Oh, you don't!" Esme jerked herself upright, her face scarlet. "I did the worst thing you can think of! I wasn't a nice little girl. I didn't know—I did, too! But I didn't feel the same——"

"Oh!" Jean sat down. The vague shadow of the "unpardonable sin" in the Bible touched her puzzled thoughts. She had never understood what that was. Did Esme mean something like that?

"Ought I to tell her, Jean? She ought to know how bad I've been. It isn't right——"

"That was a long time ago," said Jean. Esme thought she knew; she couldn't ask—that would sound stupid. "You aren't like that now."

"I did it, though." Esme's flush vanished and her eyelids trembled. "I feel as though I had to tell her. Does it make you hate me?"

"No." Jean waited an instant. "No, I feel just the same, Esme dearest. No matter what!"

"Then I will tell her! I'm going right there!" Esme was on her feet, her despair drowned in new excitement. "Good-by, Jean!"

She ran down the stairs, and Jean, behind her, heard her mother, "You seem in a hurry!"

"I am!" Esme was gone.

Mrs. Winthrop stood at the bottom of the stairs.

"What have you been doing up there?" she asked, and Jean's nerves curled at her tone.

"Just talking," she said.

"What about?"

Jean was silent.

"Jean, I don't want that girl ever to come here again. You aren't to go to her house."

"Mamma!" Jean's cry broke off at the sight of a sheet of paper her mother held.

"This nonsense would have been enough." Mrs. Winthrop struck the sheet with her fingers. "Morbid, absurd!"

"Give me that!" Jean tried to seize the note, but her mother held it. "You—you read that?"

"I pick up one of your school books, and this falls out! That girl is ruining you. I have heard—that doesn't make any difference. You understand, Jean, you are to have nothing more to say to her or do with her. I always thought you were a sensible girl. But this!" Her mother held the note off, as if she didn't like its smell.

Jean crept upstairs. She was ashamed, ashamed to a deep core, as if she had been thrust naked into the street.

That letter which she had not even shown to Esme! What had her mother heard? Not—fear crumpled her. Not what Esme had said! Oh, 'not that! Mother had not liked Esme. Never. A bold face, she had said.

"Jean, I want you to set the table."

She did not move. Her door opened.

"Jean, did you hear me? It's supper time."

Jean stood up. Her knees were stiff. She must shut inside of her every sign of feeling.

Roger stared at her, round-eyed. Had he heard, too? Finally she could take her books up to her room. She crept into Jamesie's bed, and laid her cheek softly against his hand, clenched on the cover.

What could she do! Not see Esme? She would tell her not to come here. She *would* see her.

"Jean!" Esme whirled up to her in the coat room, pulled her along into a corner. "Jean! She doesn't care! She understands."

Jean had forgotten Esme's crisis in her own rebellious misery.

"When I said there was something I ought to tell her, she just said 'When did you do it?' and I said years ago, and she said not to tell her. That everybody had things in their past to be ashamed of! That she understood!"

Against the dingy walls, with their scrawled names and couplets, Esme's joy leaped like a live thing. She wore a new waist, scarlet wool with tiny gold buttons, and the color seemed to shine up on her lips and cheeks.

Jean caught her hand.

"I'm awful glad, Esme," she said. "I have something to tell you—something—" she was afraid to throw it at Esme.

The bell clattered over their heads; a girl cried to them, "Come on, you moonies!"

"Tell me to-night." Esme gave Jean's fingers a quick pressure. "After school."

"Well," thought Jean, "I've got to go home with her this once, to tell her."

Mrs. Maurey looked up from her sewing as the girls went

through the hall. She was older than Jean's mother, with gray hair, and eyelids long like Esme's, with curious folds above the eyes.

"How do you do, Jean?" she said, and Jean winced at her politeness. If her own mother would only speak that way to Esme! "What are you girls going to do, Esme?"

"Oh, study Latin," said Esme carelessly, as she went up to her room. "We might, you know," she said to Jean, with a little elf-like grin. "Mother doesn't understand anything! If I said we wanted to talk, she's probably come right up with us."

"They act as if they thought it wouldn't be safe for us to talk," said Jean, sagely.

"Now what have you got to tell me?" Esme threw herself on the bed, her chin propped on the palms of her hands. "Oh, I feel so good, Jean! 'Sif I'd just had a bath!'"

"My mother says I can't see you any more." Jean was tragic, but under her wretchedness ran a thin sense of drama. Frustrated love!

"Why?" Esme stared, her nostrils widening.

"I don't know."

"Is that all she said?"

"She found a—a letter I wrote you. I never gave it to you. She said awful things about that."

"She doesn't know anything about me!" Esme pushed herself upright, her eyes angry. "My land, I guess I'm as good as you are!"

"She gets ideas about people. You can't change her."

"She forbids our friendship?"

Jean nodded, tears in her eyes.

"Jean!" Esme pulled Jean down beside her, an arm close about her shoulders. "Why, you are my nearest friend! I tell you everything! Don't cry, Jean."

Jean shook her head.

"I won't spot your new waist," she sniffled, and they both laughed.

"Mothers don't like me, I've noticed," said Esme, suddenly. "I don't know why." Her thought strained at her face, making it hard. "But nobody can dictate your friends, now can they?"

"No!" cried Jean. "I shall love you till I die, Esme." She trembled with defiance. "I'm coming to see you anyway! You can't come to our house. I'll meet you places——"

They were silent, hand in hand, while the fall twilight deepened sweet around them.

"Esme!" They started apart at Mrs. Maurey's call. "Jean's father wants her. Is she still there?"

Esme kissed Jean. Jean tasted tears on her lips; was Esme crying, too?

"Never mind!" cried Esme, fiercely. "They can't separate us!"

Outside on the walk stood father and Roger. They stared at Jean without a word, and she went hastily past them. She heard them behind her, and her feet stumbled as if the guilt in which she walked were tangible.

At the door of their own house her father spoke.

"Go to your own room. Your mother is sick, but she had to send for you."

Jean sat by her window, staring into the dark street until spots circled before her eyes. She wouldn't go to bed. Sorrow like this should keep her from sleep. She wished she could die. If she lay dead, her eyes shut, perhaps her mother would say, "I was wrong. I never should have forbidden——" But no, mother would never think that she was wrong. The door opened, and Jean shrank away from the figure on the threshold. Her mother. Roger behind her, thrusting his head curiously into the dark room.

Mother closed the door after her and snapped on the light. How bright her eyes were!

"I can't trust you any more. Deceitful and disobedient." She paused, but Jean could not move. "How do you think I feel, having a daughter like that?"

"I had to tell her what you——"

"You did not! You disobeyed me deliberately. I can't trust you. I may have to take you out of school."

Jean gave a sharp little cry. Mother's voice had its awful tone, her eyes were blue stones.

"That, or send your little brother for you each day. How do I know whether you will mind me or not?"

Jean had a picture of Roger, his face solemn and accusing, waiting for her at the school door.

"I won't go there again."

"How can I trust you?"

"I promise." Jean was sobbing now; her heart was a swift wheel dashing through her body. Her mother would do what she threatened! "I'll promise! I won't go there again."

"Well." Her mother gazed at her. "I don't know whether I can trust you or not. I'll see." She went out, leaving the door ajar.

XII

Esme was scornful of the promise.

"When folks make you promise things, you don't have to keep them!" she said. "That's no promise, dragged out of you. Cross your fingers if you have to make one!"

"She'd take me out of school," protested Jean. They were in the dim corner of the coat room again.

"Oh, well! Do what you want to!" Esme dashed off, catching at the arm of Grace Torrance, a plump, curly-headed senior whom Jean disliked because she seemed always to be laughing at her. Jean stood, twisting her fingers together, a great hollowness settling in her stomach, as if she had eaten nothing for days. If Esme deserted her!

She walked to the corner with Esme, glancing furtively ahead, lest she see Roger waiting under some tree. Esme said, "You're as good company as a funeral!"

At night Jean sat up in bed, rubbing her eyelids awake. She wouldn't sleep! She would grow gaunt and haggard from sleeplessness, until her mother would see how she suffered. Her mother still watched her with blue stone eyes. Let her!

On Sunday she refused to go to church. Her mother said, "I should think you might be too ashamed, acting this way just after you joined the church, too!" Jean crept away, her face scarlet. She wondered miserably where that peaceful, ecstatic feeling had gone. You could enter God and not stay there! She read the poems Esme had shown her. "Tears, idle tears"—she was crying again.

"May I go to see Miss Adair, my history teacher?" Jean did not look at her mother.

"Where does she live?" and when Jean had explained, "How do I know that is where you'll go?"

"I've kept my promise."

"You must be home by half-past eight."

Jean fled through the quiet streets, her heart sounding louder than her footsteps. What would Miss Adair say? She had never dared go to see her. She pushed the doorbell before her courage vanished.

Mrs. Smith, tall, somber, in her widow's dress and cap, opened the door.

"Is Miss Adair home?" Jean shrank from the austere gaze.

"I think so. Dorothy?" she called, and then from above, the soft voice answering, "Yes?"

'Here's a girl to see you." Jean felt her disapproval.

"Who is it? Oh, Jean Winthrop! Come up."

Jean climbed the stairs, wishing that she might dodge that gaunt figure at the door and run away.

"Come right in, Jean." Miss Adair led the way into her room, a square bedroom, with dark red furniture and ruffled curtains.

"Were you busy?" Jean stammered, an agony of shyness upon her.

"Just writing some letters. Sit down here. Take off your hat, won't you?"

Jean sat down, trying to pull her feet under the chair. Miss Adair, in her blue silk, sat near her.

"I'm glad you came in. Esme's been talking so much about you."

"Has she—did she——"

"Yes, Jean. She told me all about it."

Jean's shyness was swept away in a sudden outrunning of her need for comfort.

"I can't bear it," she said, stormily. "I——" She stopped, to check the rising tears.

Miss Adair drew her chair close and took Jean's hand. At the warm touch, the sullen ice melted, and Jean lifted dumb, adoring eyes.

"You mustn't feel so bad, Jean. If you and Esme are friends, being separated a while won't make any difference." Miss Adair went on, spinning silken phrases, touching Jean's cold little fingers softly, while Jean listened, half believing, hoping, thrilling with her adoration and her secret, unhappy sense of drama.

The little white clock on the dresser began to strike. Nine! Jean jumped up, horrified.

"I didn't know it was so late!" She hurried into her coat.

"That's not very late. You must come again." Miss Adair stood close to her, smiling, the yellow glints shining in her eyes. "You and Esme are the two most interesting girls in school."

Jean gazed at her, silent. She wanted to say things—all sorts of strange, lovely things, the kind Esme would say— but she was silent. Then Miss Adair kissed her gently.

"Good night, Jean," she said. "Now don't be unhappy any more."

"Oh, no!" breathed Jean, like a prayer, and slipped out of the house on wings.

The street was dark, except for the yellow spots of corner lights. Perhaps if she took the side street and ran across the empty lot she could reach home more quickly. Out of breath, still wing-borne, she opened the door.

Her mother stood in the hall, her hat and coat on. She looked at Jean without a word, and abruptly the wings crumpled.

"Where have you been?"

"At Miss Adair's."

"Tell me the truth!"

"I am." In a flash had gone Jean's fierce sweetness of resolve to be good, to be obedient, in the hope that some day things would come out right.

"I've been down the street where she lives, and just come home. This minute. You weren't there."

"I was too! I came across lots. I didn't know it was so late."

"You've been at that girl's again!"

"I said I hadn't! Didn't I?" Jean tried to pass her mother, but sharp fingers closed on her arm.

"What did you come another way for, then?"

"I thought it was shorter. Let go!" Jean wrenched her arm free and ran into the sitting room. Her father looked up from his book.

"What are you up to now?" he said, and his voice was as cold as mother's.

"What's the use of telling the truth anyway, or trying to be good?" cried Jean, shaking with rebellion. She hated them! She had come home, determined to give them the daughter they wanted, and now!

"Well," said mother behind her, "you can see what happens if you are deceitful sometimes."

Jean doubled her hands against her thumping heart and stared at the corner of the room. She wouldn't cry! That silly picture was crooked!

"Go on to bed and don't look abused. After this you can stay at home nights."

Jean stood in front of her bureau. She wished she could die. They all hated her. No use trying to be good.

Esme—she crushed down the flame of panic at the thought of Esme. She would lose Esme, too! Esme didn't like it, her promising.

She opened the medicine cabinet of the bathroom, to take down the tooth powder, and stood, her hand poised, empty. A large brown bottle. A skull and crossbones under the label. Muriatic tablets. Poison. The sly, gliding picture

of herself dead, pitied, loved again, insinuated herself. She
lifted the bottle. Almost empty. A few white pellets in the
bottom. She shook one into her hand. She had only to
swallow that, and all her trouble was over. The door knob
turned.

"I'm in here!" she called. Then, as if someone else lifted
her hand, she dropped the tablet on her tongue, gulped it.
Strange metallic taste, making a great shiver run over her.
She drank some water, but the taste clung, the shiver repeated itself.

No need to brush her teeth. She opened the door, clinging to the handle. Roger was in the hall. He looked at
her accusingly. He must have heard mother talking to her
again.

"Roger! Kiss me good-by," she whispered, bending
down to him. He pulled away, saying with conscious virtue,
"You'd better behave yourself!"

She shut her door. Roger, too! No one cared. In the
dark she lay rigid, waiting, waiting. How would it feel to
die? She wished—too late now. That queer shiver again!
Like licking corroded brass. Was she dying now? Would
they let Esme see her? The darkness settled around her,
heavy, cold.

She was dragged up out of a black pit. Her head ached.
She was sick! Nasty sick! She stumbled out of bed, felt
along the wall to the door, almost fell into the bathroom.

Later, with the chastened feeling of after-nausea, she
lay again in her room. She hadn't died. No one had heard
her. It must be almost morning, from the pale, swimming
light at her window. They didn't know that she might have
died. If they found out, they would be sorry. A long sigh
carried her back into sleep again.

In the morning she felt heavy, sick. This was the morning they were to find her dead, and regret their cruel treatment. Jean sat on the edge of her bed, dramatizing the
scene. Roger would be sent up to call her when she failed
to appear at breakfast. Mother would run up the stairs.
A queer thought dropped a sudden curtain over the scene.

If she had died, she wouldn't have been there to see them feeling sorry! Where would she have been? She peered with melancholy eyes at her reflection. How queer her eyelids looked, all white! Her face was thinner, too.

She couldn't eat.

"Do you feel sick?" Mother was wary.

"I'm not hungry."

"If you'll begin to act like a nice girl again, you'll feel all right."

XIII

Jean sat in history class, her eyes blue wells of pathos never for an instant diverted from Miss Adair. Once Miss Adair smiled at her, a quick flash, and Jean's heart climbed straight into her throat. She remembered last night, then!

She did not see Esme until after school, when she waited in the coat room until the seniors marched in.

"Hello, Jean!" Esme brushed past her to the hook where her coat hung.

"Let me hold it." Jean seized it, and pulled it up to Esme's shoulders.

Esme turned, and Jean saw that she was on the crest of some rippling excitement.

"I'm not going your way to-night," she said, under her breath. "What do you think, Jean! I've got a bid to the Delta's! Isn't that wonderful?"

"You mean the sorority?" Jean drew back.

"Of course I do. I never expected it—because I moved here only last year. I'm going home with some of them— my sorority sisters."

"Who belongs?" asked Jean dully. She knew. The set she had watched, enviously. Snobs. They spoke to her only when they wanted help with Cicero or a geometry problem. Esme would be one of them now.

"Oh, you know. Most of the best girls. See you to-morrow, Jean."

Jean walked home with lagging feet. The beautiful

Indian summer had gone; a cold drizzle touched her face, rustled through the brown oak leaves. The drizzle penetrated her thoughts, became the chill fear within her. Esme, her Esme! She would walk home with those other girls, now, talking about parties—or boys—laughing about their secret jokes. Esme wasn't like them. But she could be. They would never ask Jean to join them. She knew that. She couldn't be like them. Perhaps because her father had lost his job. Was that it? Or because she had her lessons. She had lost Esme. This new tragedy had no drama for Jean. It lay deeper than any phantasy relief. If she could only see Esme, she could keep her. Esme had loved her. Jean felt inarticulately the impatience, the pride, the changing hues of Esme's intensities.

That night she wrote to Esme. If she would wait, in a few years Jean could be her friend, openly. No one could love her so much. The other girls—Jean stopped. Rage shook tears into her eyes. She hated them! When she had finished the letter, she hesitated. Her mother might look in her books, after she was asleep. She would put it in her jacket pocket. Safe there. She tiptoed downstairs and tucked it deep into the pocket.

She ate her breakfast in silence. For the first time in her life she had no feelers out for the surrounding atmosphere. She had strapped her books together and stood in the hall, putting on her coat, when her mother came to the door. Instinctively Jean's hand plunged into the pocket. The note was gone! She lifted terrified eyes to her mother's stern face.

She had it! Jean opened the door. She wanted to escape before the thunder broke about her.

"Jean!"

She stopped.

"Do you expect us to feed you, to clothe you, to keep you in school, while you deliberately defy and deceive us?"

Jean shrank against the edge of the door.

"I take down a coat to sew on a button, and find—" she made a grimace of distaste.

"You shouldn't have read it! It isn't yours!" cried Jean.

"Don't be impudent as well as bad! Don't you see how chance brings everything wrong you do right to me? What am I to do with you? You break your promises——"

"I don't! I never said I wouldn't write—I had to——" Jean quivered.

"Don't talk to me! You promised to be done with this girl. She shows what she is in her influence on you, leading you on in disobedience——"

"They've taken her into the best sorority! She's better than we are! Her folks——"

"Jean, be still! Haven't I trouble enough, and your father, too, without this? This is your last chance. If I catch you again, you can't go to school." She paused. "Don't stand there and think insolent things! I see them in your face!"

Jean turned her head away, putting one hand over the tremble of her lips. She could think what she pleased! They couldn't stop that!

"I won't ask another promise. But I am watching. To see whether you deserve to stay in school. Go on, now."

Jean went, blindly, outraged. No one had the right to read your letters! The sense of her importance made her breath come short and difficult. Esme—she would write her again, in school! She didn't care what they did to her!

Miss Adair had a bunch of violets, darkly purple and fragrant, pinned at her belt. Esme had given them to her. Jean knew.

At noon she asked her father for money. Two new Greek books. A grammar, an Anabasis.

"See that you earn it by behaving yourself," he said, as he handed her a bill. "That's all I've got. Bring me the change."

On her way home from school Jean bought the books. She held the two silver dollars tight in her hand as she left the store. She hadn't seen Esme all day. Had she begun to avoid her, already?

She crossed the street toward the corner drugstore, and

then loitered before the window, held irresistibly. Half
of the window held flowers, green jars of them, carnations,
roses. The dollars pressed ridges into her hand. She flung
herself through the door, and feverishly, her voice shrill,
demanded the price of the flowers. She thought the clerk's
shiny black eyes had suspicion in them.

Half running, she came to the door of Miss Adair's
house. Mrs. Smith looked down at her, along her sharp
nose. She, too, was suspicious. No, Miss Adair was
not at home. Yes—this grudgingly—she would give her
the package. Carnations, crimson, pungent. The smell
was still in Jean's nostrils when she entered her own
home.

She gave the money to her father. A dollar and a half.
The books were a dollar and seventy-five cents each, she
said. Neat, black volumes with red edges. She hurried
upstairs. Easy to lie.

"It's an outrage!" Father's voice floated after her. "They
think they can charge anything! Why, no textbook should
cost that much!"

Jean stood at the head of the stairs, fear whirling through
her.

"Something ought to be done, I should think." That was
mother.

"Indecent!" How loud her father talked.

"Can't you do something?"

"I know what I'll do. I'll write a public letter. To the
paper. Public opinion should be stirred!"

Jean's knees melted and she sat down. The voices roared,
unheard, over her head. Presently she went downstairs,
slowly, her face paper white. She couldn't let him write to
the paper. That would make people laugh at him.

"The books were only a dollar and a half," she said. "I
spent the rest."

Her mother sucked in her breath loudly.

"Spent it!" Father's anger against the bookseller swung
over to her. "Spent it! When the books cost three dollars! You spent it! What for?"

Jean refused to tell. Finally she crept upstairs, numb, despairing, and went to bed. She was wicked. She stole. She lied. No depths of sin were too black for her. She should be dead. She couldn't go to school to-morrow. A little, licking flame of defiance—Miss Adair had the carnations! Red, spicy. But she would not like them, if she knew.

Everything was wrong, and Jean was the vortex of the wrongness. She felt the life of the house revolve about her, as a rope might twist around a stick, tighter, tighter, until she wanted to scream. James alone was not part of the tension. Jean spent herself on him in a passion of attention, yielding to his whims, playing with him, cuddling him until he squirmed to get down from her arms, and her mother said, "Leave him alone, Jean!" Jean heard in her tone the implication that James might suffer from the contagion of her sins.

It would have to last forever, thought Jean. If she died, they might forgive her, but living——

She went back to school on Monday, listless, solemn. She could at least show Esme and Miss Adair that she knew how to love faithfully. Esme, the new sorority pin flashing on her scarlet waist, nodded at Jean and passed her, arm in arm with one of the girls. But Jean met Miss Adair going through the hall with quick little steps.

"Oh, Jean! The flowers were sweet." She paused an instant. "I didn't get home till Sunday, but Mrs. Smith put them in water. They were scarcely faded. So sweet of you to bring them." She hurried on. She hadn't seen them till Sunday!

When Jean reached home that afternoon, she found she was no longer the vortex of family strain. Her mother and father were upstairs, and their voices swept down upon her. She hung her coat on the rack, indifferent. Maybe they would forget about her, now. Strange phrases, bucket shops, stocks, markets; what were they fighting about!

Father's voice, furious, "I don't know how you got your

nose into this! I tell you I thought I had a sure thing. God
knows we need money."

"Nose? You leave your papers lying around——"

"Lying in my pockets for you to snoop after, you mean."

"Taking the little you make—after the way I've slaved
this year to help you—throwing it away in a wicked gamble
——"

"It's my money! I'll use it as I please."

"It doesn't belong to your wife and children, I suppose!"

Father crashed down the stairs and out of the front door.
Jean went into the library. Did he feel like her, when he
was caught that way? But he could go off—and do what
he wanted to.

That was the beginning of the winter. Jean's ego turned
in upon itself in a warped passion of suffering. She watched
Esme and Miss Adair with wistful, pleading eyes. She had
a secret, formless, wordless thought, that at least her grief
must interest them. She heard several girls talking one day.
They knew about Esme and her. Esme had told them, "Oh,
Jean's no fun any more. She just goes around feeling bad
all the time!" Her twisted self found pleasure in the comment. She haunted the places where she might see Esme.
Library, coat room, certain corners. When she saw her, a
hectic tightening of her muscles, a flushing of her face, were
her only responses, as she pretended to be busy with a book,
or to be joking frantically with her companion.

Her mother insisted upon her taking a tonic, bitter, unpalatable.

The doctor had said, "She's growing fast, that's why she's
thin and languid. This will brace her up."

She knew with a dull certainty that her father's business
was failing. Because he went away to see to Grandpa Winthrop's estate, mother said. When she heard the ominous
mumble of their voices, she pressed her hands against her
ears. She wouldn't let them make her cry, not any more!
Only if Jamesie woke, would she pull herself from under the
covers to comfort him.

The weeks swung past. Mamie couldn't come to visit

them, as Grandma Stevens was not well. Jean asked timidly one day if she might go to see Miss Adair.

"I thought that nonsense was over!" said mother sharply. "No."

Jean had no rebellion left. She wove Miss Adair and Esme into a ritual of misery. Sometimes she dreamed herself a victim of the Inquisition—they had reached that in history—imagining the instruments of torture until her body had the curdling, half sickening thrill of twisted ecstasy of pain.

One day early in March Grace Torrance, the curly-haired senior who always laughed at Jean, waited for her in the library.

"You know, Jean, I think it's a shame," she said abruptly. "I told Esme I was going to tell you, too."

"What?" Jean shivered a little.

"You think Esme likes you, don't you? And just your mother won't let you go with her."

Jean waited. Grace had plump white hands, moving always in soft curves, as if she knew they were pretty.

"They talk about you, awful. They say—well, Esme says you are just morbid and weak, to mope so long. And Miss Adair does, too! They talk together."

Grace looked at Jean. Her brown eyes were solemn, but Jean wondered quickly whether she was glad. She had been jealous of Esme—— Then she realized what Grace had said. Weak. Morbid. This was the reward of her faithful love!

"Do they say that?" She sought for some blustery phrase to throw out as a shield. "I don't know as I care what they say! I don't know as they know anything about me, really."

"I just thought——" Grace pursed her full lips, puzzled. "I thought if you really did care, you know, you ought to be told what they said."

"Thanks, ever so much." Jean pushed her mouth into a smile. "You see, no one knows about my life. But thank you, Grace." She hurried out of the library, and, head down against the sharp March wind, went home.

XIV

Her mother called as she opened the door.

"Jean? Is that you? Come here. I've been waiting for you."

Her mother's eyes were red and swollen, and she cried again as she spoke.

"My mother is very sick. I've got to go to-night. Do you think you can be good and take care of Roger and James? If—if she dies—your father will have to come. But I've got to go."

Jean helped pack the little bag her mother was taking, listened to last instructions about the boys, and when the hack drove up, threw her arms about mother's neck in a sudden rush of pitying love. Poor mother! Of course Jean could see to things. Perhaps grandma would be better. Father was in the hack, to go to the station with mother.

Father came back soon, and they all got supper together. Jean lost her feeling of lassitude; it was fun to watch father's solemn air as he broke the eggs into the mixing bowl and pulled up his sleeves to stir them. Jean sat in mother's place. Like playing house, only nicer. In the evening father rode Jamesie pickaback up to bed, and then helped Jean with a difficult geometry problem. When, at last, it was time for bed, Jean stopped by his chair and kissed him shyly. She wanted to say something, about the strange, clear feeling that had supplanted the dark past. But she only said, "Perhaps grandma won't die. We can manage, can't we, till mother comes back?"

"Yes." Father patted her shoulder. "You're grown up enough to take responsibility now, aren't you?" And Jean thought that she heard, like the bass notes in a chord, his recognition that she had, some way, been purged of her difficult, twisted emotions.

She undressed peacefully. Dear father! He was so funny and nice when he felt good. Smart, too. Not many girls had fathers who could work original problems. It would be nice if no one ever had to feel cross. She remembered for an instant the thing Grace had told her, but hastily she thrust it away. Weak! It was strong to suffer so much. She was sure of that. She wouldn't think of it, to-night. She curled up in bed, in the drowsy crescent of her childhood. How easy it was to-night to forget the doubts that harassed her; doubts of father, lest he really was to blame somewhat for the rumpuses. She had won back to her old pride in him, to that tender, ineffable over-flowing of herself around the thought of her father. It was as if she had wound back all the filaments her growing self had spun and thrown out in quest of new mooring. Too long the gossamer threads had been broken, thrust rudely away. She coiled them again within her heart. The old allegiance was better. Sleepily she dreamed that when her mother should return, she would show her the old Jean, the child, content to love within the walls of her home.

That mood hung about her when she went downstairs in the morning, after helping Jamesie with his bath and leaving him for Roger to button into his overalls.

The kitchen was full of acrid smoke. Father rushed about, opening doors, seizing cloths to rub off the stove, scraping a bubbling black mess into the fire.

"Oh!" cried Jean. "What did you do?"

"Get the mop! Wipe up the floor!" he shouted, and Jean ran for the mop. It was only oatmeal; it had boiled over, and when father rushed to rescue it, he had knocked the kettle over, too. Then he had used mother's best checked dishtowels to wipe up the slithering stuff. Jean dabbed soberly at the floor.

"The oatmeal should be cooked at night!" declared father, hotly. "There's no system in this house whatever!"

"I'll fix some more," said Jean.

"I can't wait all day for breakfast! Get me some eggs."

Jean wanted to laugh, he looked so funny and exasperated, but she wisely kept her face demure. Just like a man. That was what mother would say. The coffee boiled over, too. That was less messy. At last father had gone, the boys had eaten their breakfast, Jean had bundled James into his red reefer and stocking cap and sent him outdoors with a warning to Roger not to let him get cold.

She stood in the middle of the kitchen. Piles of dishes. Father certainly was more reckless with dishes than mother. Smeary floor. Black wafery curls on the stove. Ruined cloths. She would clear up the mess and then she might bake a cake. And sweep. Mother always swept on Saturday. The beds, too; they must have fresh sheets.

It was late when the kitchen was finally in order, and Jean sat down for a moment by the shining brown oilcloth of the table. She would bake first. A cake with fig filling, because father liked that. Frosting. She measured and mixed with slow delight. This was more fun than cleaning up. Making something. At length she dropped a spoonful of the creamy batter into a baking-powder can cover, and set it in the oven to try. She hurried into the dining room with a creaky carpet sweeper while that baked. It came out perfect, and she poured the batter into the round tins and slipped them into the oven. She needed more wood. Roger ought to fill the box. She opened the front door just in time to hear a frightened shriek.

Roger was pulling James up from the ground, and Jean saw, with a terrified shrinking, that blood ran down the little, distorted face.

"Oh, baby!" She was at his side.

"He climbed on the rail. I told him not to!" gasped Roger.

Jean tugged him into the hall.

"Get me some water, quick! There, Jamesie, let sister see! Don't cry so! Why, that isn't much——" She wiped his forehead gently; a long scratch over his nose was bleeding, and a bump was rising over one eye. "There, sonny, be a big man!" Roger came at such speed with the water that he sloshed it all over Jean's dress. "See, Jamesie, Jean's all wet! That doesn't hurt much, does it?" James stopped his shrieks to say, with puckered, piteous mouth, "Does hurt! Hurt Jamesie!"

"Well, not so much. Roger, get some vaseline. Upstairs."

Finally, vaseline besmeared, little wet points of hair sticking to his forehead, his lips still tremulous, James let Jean take off his coat, and laid his head against her shoulder with a sigh.

"Now I know something nice! Roger, you get the little cake on the kitchen table."

Roger came quickly back with it.

"We'll make three pieces——" Jean broke it, her arm still about the child. "There!"

"Is he hurt much?" whispered Roger before he tasted his piece.

"Just a scratch. Scared him mostly, didn't it?"

"No. Wasn't scared." James nibbled his cake, happy again.

"I guess the oatmeal's still scorching," said Roger.

"Oh, my land!" Jean set James down and ran for the kitchen.

Her beautiful cake! Burned. She set the pans on the table, and caught her breath in a half sob. Roger and James stood beside her, their faces disconsolate.

"I'd eat it anyhow," said Roger stoutly, "don't you care, Jean!"

"If you'd taken care of James——" Jean stopped, abruptly. If the cake was burned, it was. No use scolding Roger. She tried to scrape off the blackened surface, but not much was left.

And while she worked, father hurried in the front door.

"Isn't dinner ready?" He looked about the kitchen. "I said I'd be here at twelve."

"I didn't know it was so late!" wailed Jean. "The cake burned and James fell off the railing——"

"Never mind. I'll cook this steak. There's bread, isn't there? Get me some onions. Fry 'em——"

Another hour and father had gone again. The kitchen was a wreck of its neat self. Father told Roger to wipe the dishes, but first James had to be put to bed for his nap, and Roger was mournful. He had promised a boy to come over at two. He would be late. They were going to make a wagon in the boy's father's workshed. Jean told him to run along and stop fussing.

The afternoon was a paradox; short as the morning, still its hours were interminable. When Jean had cleared the kitchen again, James woke. He followed her querulously about. His head ached from the bump. Jean made the beds, four of them. She swept the sitting room and dusted. When she finally sat down in the clean, quiet house, her legs ached, and her back ached, and she wanted to say cross things to James when he begged her for a story. Supper came next, she thought, and more dishes!

Suddenly she sat erect, her face intent. Every day was like that! Over and over. Maybe that was why mother sounded cross sometimes. Father, Jean, Roger, all went away. Mother stayed. Dishes. Cooking. Dishes. Sweeping. Dishes. Over and over. It didn't do any good to do things once. You turned around, and there they were again! You couldn't go away, like a man. Jean remembered wistfully her delight of the early morning. She had thought it would be fun to manage things. You didn't manage them. They managed you. Her burnt cake—— "I'd rather be a man," she said, rebelliously. "Doing stupid things—mother doesn't like it. Household drudge, she says."

Father came home early.

"Your grandmother is dead," he said. "Your mother wired me. I'll have to go in the morning. I don't know what to do about you kids."

"I can take care of them all right," said Jean.

"Well, you'll have to try. Just a few days. The funeral's Tuesday. We'll come home that night. Two nights you'd be alone. If you stay out of school, you can catch up."

"Of course." Jean thrilled gravely under this new responsibility.

They had a good time, the three. Jean had a sense of guilt that she should enjoy the days so much when Grandma Stevens had died. She wondered how bad her mother felt. But James was so pleased to have Jean at home and devoted to him that he pattered about with soft radiance on his face and wasn't cross once. Roger came hurrying home from school to help keep house. They had easy things to eat, and Jean took the routine of dishes, dusting, cooking, as an unconscious ballast to her responsible pride.

Then it was over. Mother and father came back. Mother cried as she kissed them, and sat down with James on her lap, rocking back and forth, crying softly.

"You better go right to bed, Kitty," said father. "You've had a hard siege."

Mother sobbed, "Yes, but I want my children first."

Father carried James upstairs. Then he came back and led mother up, his arm about her waist. Jean watched them, solemn eyed. Grief did that!

"I could stay home from school to-day," offered Jean the next morning.

"No, you've missed enough," said mother. She had come downstairs heavy eyed, her mouth compressed, but her voice was gentle, almost caressing. "You've been a great help, Jean. Things look nice and clean. But you mustn't stay out of school any longer. I can get along. I'll feel better working."

Jean went back to school.

"You been sick?" Daisy Thoms called to her.

"No. My grandma died, and I kept house." Jean saw Esme at the end of the hall, and turned away without a quiver.

"All alone?" Daisy admired her.

Jean wondered a little at her release. She didn't know what had happened, but she accepted with a contented passivity the draining away of the hectic hours of the winter.

That night Jean dreamed her mother was dead. She saw the shiny hearse with plumes on the horses' heads, and her father riding in a slow hack, Jean beside him. They both cried, and father said, "Now you will have to take her place, Jean."

Jean's waking, her face wet with tears, seemed an indistinguishable part of the dream. Was her mother dead? She slipped out of bed, shivering in the gust of wind that tore through her room as she opened the door. Where was mother? Then she stopped, the dream drifting away. She could hear father's voice, behind their closed door.

"You'll just make yourself sick. No reason in your taking on so. Your mother was old, and she's better off dying quickly without pain, than if——"

"Oh, leave me alone! You don't care how I suffer. If only I had made her happier. I meant to." Mother broke into sobbing.

"She was as happy as she could be. You couldn't leave your family to stay with her, could you?"

"She knew I wasn't happy. That grieved her. I never told her a thing. But she knew."

"I don't know what she had to worry about, unless——"

"You think she couldn't see! She knew! She knew you were breaking my heart!"

"Damn it! Everyone has trouble."

"Oh, leave me alone! You haven't any heart."

"I know you feel bad. My father died, you know——"

"She was the best mother. Devoting herself to us. I never did anything for her. Now she's dead and gone."

"She left her own mother, didn't she? What are you——"

"She had to! That was why she grieved so, lonely, missing her. I meant to help her, and I could have done so much, if you had been what you ought to, and——"

"Blame it on me! You'd have been a model daughter, only you married me! That ought to satisfy you."

"Ah—h!" Mother's cry rose like a wavering line of smoke.

Jean pushed open the door and ran to the bed. Father stood beside it, mother lay with eyes closed, pounding her hands on the counterpane.

"Mother!" Jean took the icy, rigid hands. "Mamma! Don't cry. Don't feel so bad." She drew herself close. "Here's Jean."

Her mother opened her eyes for a wild moment, and threw her arms about Jean, dragging her flat against her body.

"Jean," she sobbed. "Always love your mother! If you don't—some time will come—you'll repent it—too late——"

"Here!" Father put his hand on Jean's shoulder. "Here, Kitty! Drink this. Get up, Jean."

"Too late!" gasped mother.

"You shouldn't talk to the child like that. Of course she loves you. Kiss your mother, Jean, and go to bed."

Jean withdrew from the tight arms and slid to the door, her eyes still on her mother's face. Father sat down beside her, one arm under her shoulders.

"Drink this!" He lifted her and she drank. "Go on, Jean! She'll be all right."

Jean drew her knees up to her chin. She was frozen. Her teeth chattered. The bed was like ice water. Suppose her mother had died! Then it would be too late! She must be very good. People might die any time. Then, alien thought —father didn't act that way—didn't he love his father? Would she, Jean, act like mother? She edged away from the thought. Thoughts like that would make her sorry, if ever——

For days she was docile and obedient with a queer, frenzied ardor. If she sat still and read, she fidgeted; her legs had the jumps. When she found something, dusting, straightening her bureau drawers, which would bring an approving smile from her mother, she flew at the work feverishly. She invented a society: "W.W.B.G." she printed in red ink on squares of ribbon. James wore his with pride, but when she explained to Roger that the letters meant, "We will be good," he sniffed.

"That's silly," he protested. "Mebbe we will. I don't know how I'll be to-morrow, do I?"

XV

On Sunday Jean went back to Sunday School. She kept her eyes righteously away from the corner where Miss Adair sat, but somehow she knew that Miss Adair wore a new hat, a blue one with a green feather. When the superintendent announced that the church was to raise funds for its debt by means of an entertainment, and asked for volunteers, Jean waved her hand vigorously. That was the beginning of an exciting three weeks. Every day after school the people met in the church to rehearse.

"A Dream of Fair Women, with occasional dances and singing." So the programs ran. Jean was part of an occasional dance. Mrs. Lebec, a small woman with fluffy red hair and countless sparkling rings, trained the dancers.

"She's very stagey," Jean told her mother. "She isn't exactly an actress, but she goes around training folks."

Eight girls in Jean's dance. Spanish. They were to carry tambourines and wear roses over their ears. They stood behind the pillars which supported a gallery of the Sunday School room, and, when the music started, they slid around one pillar, reversed, returned, kicked to the left, to the right, and slid back around another pillar.

> I met my love on the Alamo—(slide)
> When the moon (reverse!) was on the rise.
> He-er beauty quite outshone (kick!) the night,
> So-o radiant (slide) were her eyes.

Jean slid and reversed and kicked with a nervous resolution to win the approval of Mrs. Lebec's sharp green eyes.

"Lift up your feet, girls! They ain't lead, are they? Or glued down? Now kick! Kick! Don't you know a kick?"

The ladies of the committee sat in a row on the platform, whispering as they watched. The last evening as Jean pulled on her coat, Mrs. Bates, the committee chairman, took her arm and drew her into the corner behind the piano.

"Jean," she said gravely, "there is something I want to tell you."

Jean waited expectantly. She had hurled herself into the Alamo with abandon that day.

"Most of the girls kick real genteel," went on Mrs. Bates, her plump pink cheeks shaking gently, "but I think you ought to know you kick too high. It doesn't do any hurt at rehearsal, but your mother wouldn't like you to kick that way in public."

Jean's cheeks flamed.

"Mrs. Lebec said to!" she answered, unsteadily. She was tired and warm from the dragging rehearsal. "She told me I did fine!"

"She's a sort of an actress, you know, Jean dear. You remember when you are on the stage, won't you? It's for the church, you know."

Jean fumed her way home. "Old fatty! What does she know? I'll kick higher than that! You have to!" She hummed the tune. Slide, reverse, kick! Always around the pillars.

Mother had the costume finished. Black paper cambric skirt and jacket, called by Mrs. Lebec a bolúro. Red rose from the ten-cent store. "Father didn't have the money for the slippers to-day, but he said he'd have it to-morrow."

"You have to have slippers!" Jean looked down at her shabby high shoes.

"He said he'd have it to-morrow."

Jean's dream before she slept that night was of herself a famous actress, bowing graciously to rows and rows of faces. She *would* kick high! She would show them that she had the real spirit of a Spanish dancer. Someone would say, "Did you notice Jean Winthrop? Next the end? I never realized she could dance so well."

School dragged that Friday. Xenophon's progress, to the strains of the "Alamo," which echoed louder than his marching orders, was dull enough. Even Miss Adair, who was to appear as one of the Fair Women—Jean didn't know whether she was Cleopatra or Helen of Troy—had dancing glints in her eyes and forgot to assign the Monday lesson. Jean was sure everyone must be talking of the entertainment, even the unfortunate girls who attended other churches.

"Did you get the slippers?" Jean ran into the library.

"Your father will bring them. My head ached too much to go over town."

He might forget them. He did forget things. Jean

trembled with anxiety. She hurried upstairs to dress, straining to hear his step on the porch. A white waist of mother's, with elegant leg o'mutton sleeves and lace at the neck. The full skirt. Her legs looked long, sticking down under it! The bolero. The rose. Jean tipped the glass to see the effect. She could see only half at a time, the upper half or the lower, as she swung the mirror back and forth. *Did* she look Spanish! She should have black eyes. She peered at her face, high forehead, serious mouth, fine dark hair combed back and tied. Why, she couldn't wear a ribbon and a rose! She borrowed hairpins from mother's dresser and rolled her braid into a pug. The rose wobbled above her ear. Jean turned away from her reflection, sighing. She wished she were beautiful. But she would kick so professionally that no one would notice her face. Father had come. She sped down the stairs.

"My slippers! Did you get them!" She pulled the brown paper from the parcel and gazed at the shoes. High heels, straps, they looked very long. She sat on the lowest step and unbuttoned her boots. They were too long. She took a cautious step. "They're too big!" Her lips trembled. "They'll come off when I kick!"

"Let's see." Father pinched the toes. "Stuff 'em with paper. I got them long so you could use them next year. Use them longer, see?"

"I told you what size," said mother, sharply.

"They didn't have it. This was all I could get. Wear your shoes if you don't like it. I can't afford them, anyway."

"The store would be shut now," mourned Jean.

"I think I can fix them." Mother stuffed them, tied a piece of black ribbon around Jean's instep and said, "There! They'll do."

Jean kicked gingerly. They didn't fly off. They wobbled when she walked, but perhaps that was because of the heels.

She met the seven other Señoritas at the church, and together they hurried to the adventuresome stage entrance of the town Opera House. The special numbers had been re-

hearsed there, but Mrs. Bates thought the influence on the
young girls was better if they practiced only in the church
parlors. So Jean's first glimpse of behind the scenes came
when they climbed the dusty stairs and found themselves
among high shadowy pasteboard walls at alarming angles
overhead, with people rushing back and forth like chickens.
Jean's heart leaped. Between a scabrous tree and a piece
of house wall, she could see the stage, with a throne in the
center and lumpy branches behind. The background looked
like the southern jungle of Uncle Tom's Cabin, but the
throne with its flowing draperies—were those the portières
from Mrs. Bates's house?—was impressive. Across the
stage trailed a white-gowned woman, long yellow hair spill-
ing over her bare shoulders and arms.

"How am I ever going to climb that, I'd like to know!"

"You can get up before the curtain rises any way you
want to!" That was Mrs. Lebec, more glittering than ever.

Confusion. Dust in your nostrils until you had to laugh
because the committee all sneezed at once. Shouting. The
sound, dim and mysterious, of violins being tuned. That
was the Sunday School orchestra, beyond the great gray
curtain. All the Spanish girls corralled in a stuffy corner,
where they could just peer out around a jagged bit of scenery
at the stage.

"Now don't you open your heads!" warned Mrs. Lebec.
"The music's starting!"

Faint rhythms. The yellow-haired woman clambered up
the throne, someone smoothed the green portières under her
feet, she draped her arms negligently along the throne, Mrs.
Lebec pulled her hair forward over her gown.

"Now!"

Outside the clapping of hands. The curtain rose, creak-
ingly; Jean could see, across the stage, the old man who
turned the crank. Then the elocution teacher, resplendent
in black satin, stepped forward near the glaring footlights,
and read in a loud, slow voice, "A Dream of Fair Women."
This was Helen of Troy!

The curtain fell. Helen scrambled down, Cleopatra took

her place. Miss Adair, with a green papier-mâché snake!

Their number came next! Jean felt her body freeze into rigidity.

Mrs. Bates's daughter Cordelia, who sang in the choir, in a black lace shawl, stood in the middle of the stage.

"Ready, girls!" Mrs. Lebec stood behind them. "Shake your tambourines! When she begins the chorus——"

Up went the curtain. The orchestra boomed out, "I met my love on the Alamo." Cordelia Bates sang as loudly as she could, but the orchestra made more noise. Now!

Jean saw in front of her, like white stones under water, faces, faces, receding. Where were the pillars? Slide, reverse—no pillar! The girls were kicking! Her feet were stuck to the floor. She lifted one—the slipper wobbled!

It was over. Clapping. Had she kicked at all? Mrs. Bates bustled up.

"Cordelia's voice was fine, wasn't it? Jean, you kicked just right. Isn't it a lovely audience?"

Jean, in the corner, biting her lips against tears. What had happened to her? She hated the dusty, smelly place. She wanted to go home. She couldn't watch the next numbers. Finally she could hunt for her coat and escape. Father was waiting for her outside the door.

"Well," he said, "fine show you put on. Didn't know there were such pretty girls in our church."

Jean walked beside him, her feet unsteady, her spirit drowning in a black pit of despair.

"Think you'll take up stage life?" Father whistled the first bars of the Alamo chorus.

"No, I don't." She hesitated. "Did you notice anything about my dancing?"

"Oh, you all looked nice."

At home, shut in her own room, Jean wrenched the rose out of her hair, pulling at a strand caught on the wire stem. It flew down under the bureau. She pushed away the shameful recollection of her feeling of wooden panic. Her dream was gone. She didn't want to think of it, ever, ever!

Life was empty again. She couldn't regain her content-
ment at home. She was sick of dusting, of setting tables,
of taking care of James. She wanted—what did she want?

Monday she discovered a new power, one never suspected.
She walked home from school in a group of girls, some of
them from the Spanish chorus.

"How'd you like Miss Adair as Cleopatra?" asked one of
them. "She didn't care how low her dress was, did she?"

"Had to have a place for the snake to bite," retorted
Jean.

The girls laughed. "Say, that's pretty good, Jean!"

"Cleopatra had a little snake," chanted Jean, a confused
impulse rising within her, "and it was awful green. And
everywhere that Pattie went, the snake was—was often
seen!"

The laughter brought color into Jean's cheeks; it healed,
obscurely, a hidden wound. Miss Adair had betrayed her
with Esme. The entertainment had betrayed her.

"And Helen of Troy made eyes at a boy." She stopped,
breathless with her own laughter. "She must have borrowed a nightie to wear, and she forgot to comb her hair."

"Jean! Aren't you the limit!" That was Daisy Thoms,
seizing her arm and hugging it. "Tell us some more!"

"Well, didn't she look 'sif she was going to sleep, while
Miss Briggs elocuted about her?"

Jean went home, glowing. She could amuse them! They
liked her when she said things. Something expanded, floated
around her as she walked. Just saying things—that was
easy. She could think of lots of things to say.

She did. And it worked. Anything that came into her
head! Not many days later, as she stood on the corner with
Lora Tate, a thin round-shouldered girl in her own class,
Lora said, "I've got an awful trade-last for you, Jean!"

"What is it?" Jean was eager.

"It's a trade-*last!*"

"Well, I can think of lots for you."

"Yes, you can!"

"Yes, I can, too! Just the other day someone——"

"You have to say who."

"Daisy Thoms. She said she thought you were the sweetest girl in school. So there!"

"Mine is better than that. It was Grace Torrance, too. She said——" Lora waited, tantalizingly. "She said she always knew you were smart, but now she thought you were the funniest girl in school, or anywhere. She never heard funnier things than you said. What do you think of that?"

"Oh——" Jean tossed her head. "I can't help thinking funny things. They just sputter out."

Lora laughed at that, too, and Jean carried home the glittering secret bauble of her triumph. Sometimes she felt almost ashamed. As if she took a beautiful thing, or a cherished thing, and rubbed dust over it. When she said Miss Holmes, the Greek teacher, looked like a sprouted potato. Miss Holmes liked her. But she had to be funny!

XVI

Spring came late that year. Snow flurries in April and days of cold rain. The last Saturday of April came with a spurt of rain. But toward noon Jean went out on the porch with rugs to shake. She flapped them over the railing until her arms ached and then she leaned against the post to rest. The rain had stopped. The sky had lost its cold impenetrable look. Still gray, but with a luminous quality; masses of clouds, through which you guessed at light. Jean watched them. On earth there was no wind, but overhead the cloud shapes were full of motion, steady westward motion. At times the masses rolled apart for a translucent instant; then they piled upon each other, always westward. Jean listened. She could almost hear the rushing of that high, swift wind, far above the world. How quiet it was around her! She drew a long breath. Almost as if the earth had ceased to turn. Waiting. Suddenly she tingled with soft joy. She knew! Spring! She smelled it. Winter was done. She wanted, unaccountably, to cry. But mother called to her.

"Bring in the rugs, Jean."

The next morning a pale spring sun shone through the black wet trunks of the trees, and Jean saw from her window that the tips of the branches were swollen. Spring! The soft, expectant delight lingered all day with her. In the evening mother and Roger went to church, and Jean told stories to James, not knowing why she chose the old Norse tale of Freja and Loki. When James slept, she went softly down to the porch, and wrapped in her coat, sat on the step, her head against the pillow. Stars overhead, a narrow lane above the houses; the street lamp at the corner shone between her and the sky.

Father was coming. Jean saw him at the corner, walking in a brusque, swift stride. Funny, she thought, how he always seemed to hurry.

"Hello!"

"You're out here?" Father stopped, one foot lifted to the first step. "Where's your mother?"

"She took Roger and went to church."

"Warm enough out here?"

"It's spring." Jean threw the phrase at him in a half challenge.

"Spring?" He sat down just below her. "You smelled it, too, did you?" He took off his hat and fumbled inside his coat for a match. The light, shielded in the palm of his hand, glared briefly on his face—prominent cheekbones, strong, square chin, eyelids in folds over blue eyes. He was frowning, and his mouth twitched about his cigar.

"Are you tired?" asked Jean. Her expectant mood flowed out to include him. It was nice to sit there——

"I guess not."

"You look sort of excited." Jean wondered at her saying that; somehow he seemed like—well, like a person. Not just her father.

"I've been talking—was your mother feeling pretty good?"

"Um—yes. Kind of sad. She was talking about Grandma."

Her father made a gesture with the hand that held the cigar, a bright arc of impatience.

"Why does she feel so bad?" asked Jean. "She didn't see her so very often."

"I don't know. Some folks take death that way." He was silent so long Jean forgot her question. "It's this way, Jean. We all go along, planning things for to-morrow. To-morrow we'll be different, we'll reform. We'll hold our tongues. We won't get mad. We—oh, everything! Then someone dies. To-morrow is gone. That's the trouble. To-morrow is gone. It was her mother——"

"But she believes in Heaven." Jean frowned. "And God. And so Grandma must be better off——"

"Logic, Jean! Logic don't matter much to feelings. When you feel bad over death, you feel bad for yourself. Be good to-day, Jean. Or bad. But be what you mean to be to-morrow. Don't put it off!"

Jean hunched up her knees, clasping her arms about them. The quiet darkness, the faint, pungent breath of spring, the few stars, her father there beside her, talking—she thrilled slowly to the moment; it enclosed them like a soft cloud.

"Being good is funny," she said. "You think you'll be good——" Strange things bubbled within her, things un-thought as yet. "You mean to be good, and then you aren't, and you have to think it all out again."

"Philosophers have observed that, Jean." Her father leaned back, stretching his legs down the steps. "If man were required only to meet some one great moment, to do some one great deed, life would be easy. It is the constant repetition of petty things—drops of water on the rock— that makes failures of us."

Jean felt her love for her father brimming her heart, drop by drop. She wanted to touch his forehead, indistinct and pale, to pour out her heart about him. He was unhappy; she felt his presence as a demand for comfort. But she sat in silence, longing toward him.

"What are you sitting out here for? You'll catch cold. It isn't summer yet!" Mother and Roger stood in front of them, dark shadows.

"We were discussing philosophy, mamma," said father, rising. "That warmed us."

"Huh!" Mother brushed past them into the house.

Jean scrambled up. She was stiff! She wanted to hurry up to her room, before the golden moment had been blown away.

"Was the sermon good?" Father stood in the hall, watching mother draw the pins from her hat. He had a nervous animation in his eyes and voice. "Roger, I hope you profited by it."

"Roger doesn't need it as much as his father, I guess!"

"He's still young enough to be impressed. Kitty, I saw Donnelly to-day."

Mother turned, alarmed.

"He's made me a fine offer."

"Not that traveling salesman position?"

"A hundred a month to begin with, and ten per cent commission besides."

"And you on the road a month at a time! You can't do it."

"Go along to bed, children," said father. His voice rasped, and the vein on his forehead stood out. Jean fled up the stairs, Roger padding after her.

For a long time she heard the voices downstairs. Mother wasn't crying. She was talking, in a steady, solemn tone. Father came in sharp, bitter, loud. Finally she heard them come upstairs, past her door.

"You're not the kind of man who can stand that life," mother was saying. "You know it! You can't keep safe even when you are home. What would you do——"

"Good Lord! What do you think I'd do?"

"I don't know. Anything! I won't risk it. I'd rather we starved. Get a job digging ditches!"

Jean slept. Later she woke, to hear the voices still chording. Mother was crying now.

"If only you'd go back into teaching. That's your profession. Nothing will be right until you do."

Jean pulled the covers over her head and slept again.

In the days that followed father was sulky, quick-tempered. Mother went about with a quiet air of triumph. Jean never heard again a word about traveling salesmen. She caught references to letters, to names of teachers at the college, to applications, to agencies. And one day, as she sat in the library, she heard father rush into the house and out to the kitchen.

Silence. Then mother,

"You didn't get it?"

"No. They—see, they considered me—favorably, they say—but they appointed Chase. I'll never try again! Never!"

"One attempt isn't final. There are plenty of chances——"

"I won't humiliate myself so! I tell you, I won't! I did this because you wanted me to. Now you can see it's no use. I won't grovel in their muck! Filthy little schoolmen!"

School ended. Jean went with her class to the commencement exercises. Esme had one of the senior orations. Jean listened to her as if she were a stranger. How could she think of all those long sentences, about life and struggle and poetry? Her eyes shone out of a white face, and her voice trembled a little as she began, but steadied before she was through. People clapped and clapped. Jean twisted her cold fingers in her lap. Esme—she wanted to cry. Esme would go away now, east to college. Jean would never see her again.

The first weeks of vacation were confused, tiring weeks. They had to move, to a house at the edge of town toward the college. Mother called it an old hole, but father defended it.

"It's the best we can do at our price," he insisted. "They'll fix it up. Room for a garden, too."

"No conveniences, but you don't care about that! More work for me doesn't matter!"

"They'll put in electricity right now. A bathroom in the fall."

"Well, you can't pay this rent. But it's a frightful hole!"

Jean liked the high-ceilinged rooms. But moving was work! Nothing fitted. Curtains had to be hemmed up, the carpets were too small and had to be eked out with brown filler. The chairs looked shabby. Jean had not noticed, until she helped place the parlor set, how the velvet of the upholstery had lost its nap along the edges.

"If we have to move again, the rags and sticks will fall apart on the way!" said mother, bitterly. "Not a new thing for years!"

"What is there to get new things with, I'd like to know?" Father came in from the kitchen, smears of soot on his face, his hands black. He had been helping the men set up the stove. "Who wants new things? These are plenty good enough."

"Plenty good enough for me, I suppose." Mother sat down. Her hands lay, palms upward, on her knees, and her body had the same empty curve of dejection from head to knee. Jean looked wistfully at her father; her glance said, "She's tired, and she'd like pretty new things, don't you see?"

"Good enough for us, eh, Jean? Come and clean up the kitchen for me."

Jean felt, obscurely, that her father found some virtue in shabbiness, even in the lack of bathroom and lights. As if those things said, "See how hard I am struggling!"

Jean liked the yard and the fields behind the house. Almost country. The city had grown a lean tentacle along the car line, and slowly the side streets crept after. Not yet had the new frame houses reached the block where this old house stood. Behind it lay a meadow, still green in the early summer, and in the distance a small patch of woods broke the even horizon line.

"Remember Bishop, back at Cygnet College?" father said one day at dinner. "He was in this morning. Traveling for a store fixture firm. Looks like an old man. His daughter —say, they had two, didn't they?"

"Jean used to play with one of them," said mother. "Anne, I think her name was."

Jean, who had gone to the kitchen for fresh water, stood

in the doorway, rubbing her palm on the cold steam of the glass pitcher.

"Yes, Anne. That's the one. She ran away with the boy who brought groceries."

"Um-m——" Mother made a sound of disapproving sympathy. "Her poor mother!"

"Bishop said she took that pretty well, when Anne was so young. But she died this spring. Childbirth. Mrs. Bishop's had a breakdown."

"Sh-h!" said mother, with a quick glance at Jean. "Did you hear that, Jean? You remember Anne?"

Jean did remember her: soft, dark, whispering to her in the night!

"She's dead. She broke her mother's heart and died."

A flare of resentment mounted to Jean's tongue. The instinctive resentment of youth against reproving age.

"I guess she wasn't so happy herself!" she cried, "to die having a baby!"

"Jean! She ran away with a grocery boy. That wasn't nice."

"Maybe he was a nice grocery boy." Jean sat down at the table, her cheeks flushed. Anne was dead, and it was unfair to say she had broken her mother's heart. Anne, with her dark eyes—Jean had not thought of her for a long time.

"Don't be foolish, Jean, when you don't understand."

Jean was silent. When, after dinner, she heard her mother say, "Did Mr. Bishop tell you any more?" she closed the kitchen door and rattled the dishes in the pan. She wouldn't hear them!

That afternoon Jean went alone across the meadow to the wood. Part of the meadow was swampy; she stepped from one grass hummock to the next, liking the way the ground yielded to her foot-pressure and followed with a spring as she lifted her foot again. In the wood she came to a little brook, a trickle between boulders smudged over with thin moss like green mould. Violets there in the spring; she saw the green clusters of heart-shaped leaves. Standing close against the rough trunk of an old oak and looking up through the branches, she could think she was deep in a forest, although if she looked away in any direction, she could see sunlight on the meadow.

Anne was dead. Jean could almost feel her, sleeping beside her. She pressed her cheek against the wrinkled bark. Anne's dying was a different thing from the death of old people. Anne was no older than she! A subtle antagonism crept through Jean. She knew how mothers would say in their warning tone, "See how she broke her mother's heart!" What could they know of Anne herself? Jean knew. Anne had wanted to find out what life meant. *Life*—strange, outstretching word. *Reality*—as vague, as elusive, as tentacled. When you know more about life. Older people said that, their eyelids drooping wisely. When you understand reality. Who had said that? What did they mean? Jean pressed her forehead against the tree; she felt the ridges of bark push on the bone under the thin skin. Anne had dared to rush out on her quest. She saw the old people of the world, hands linked in an endless wall, standing to hold her away—not her, but everyone who was not already old—keeping them shut in—from what?

An ant crawled down her chin, tickling. Jean brushed it away, and looked out at the meadow. Long shadows crept out of the woods and lay across it, blue shards. Suddenly she laughed aloud, then stopped, half ashamed. How funny that would sound, laughing alone in the woods! But the source of that laughter bubbled within her. Inarticulate, intangible, formless, it bubbled and laughed. This it was: strength, secret, indomitable. Youth, seeing in a flash that all the old people clung together, hands linked, tongues dropping the same warning tones, because they were helpless! They turned their faces away from their helplessness, pretending to be strong. Anne had broken through their wall! Nothing stopped you. Death? Anne had broken through the wall before she had died. None of this lay in Jean's consciousness as thought. It pushed up from depths as a living spring; it moved in her as antagonism, a secret rebellion upon which her strength might feed until she too broke through the wall.

The summer days grew interminable. Housework. Dull, stupid, meaningless repetition. Father had a new position. An office with another man. "Jessup and Winthrop, some combination, eh?" But mother refused to smile about it.

"I don't like that man. He has a bad face."

"Can I pick a partner for his beauty?"

"What kind of broker is he, anyhow? His family doesn't look as though he made much—that poor little wife——"

"Insurance, stocks, bonds, mortgages. See the head on his stationery?"

"No good will come of it."

Jean went to the library day after day, and carried home books. F. Marion Crawford. She read them in gulps, skipping the parts that smacked of history. Historical novels, "Janice Meredith," "When Knighthood Was in Flower," "If I Were King." She liked to read at night, when the house was still. Lying in bed, her pillows propped against the footrail, a handkerchief wrapped around the globe to keep the light from shining under the door, the irregular drumming and whirring of moths against the window screen. One night the acrid smell of charred cotton floated across the romantic presence of the book. She looked up, saw the handkerchief spurt flames through the smoke, and terrified, jumped to drag it down. It scorched her palms, but she crushed it, and flung it out of the window, leaning to watch it smoulder below, a sulky star. After that she pushed a rug against the door.

She found "Les Miserables" on the bookcase at home, four green volumes. She carried them all to her room. Fantine fascinated her, selling her hair, her teeth! Jean shivered. She read and read, turning the pages frantically to escape the long battle of Waterloo. Javert, with his terrible struggle. The sewer. When finally she closed the last volume, she could scarcely raise her head, she was so stiffly rigid, and she discovered that the electric globe stood out with pale filaments in the mist-gray of dawn.

She went down to breakfast, after a few hours of heavy sleep, her eyes bister-circled, her head tired.

"Have you been reading at night?" demanded her mother. "You have time enough through the day, I should think."

That night she fell asleep early. She woke, startled. Her mother, crying! She crept to the head of the stairs. At the foot, staring out of the window, her face a white mask in the light from the corner lamp, sat her mother. Watching for father to come.

"Mother, come to bed," she begged softly. But her mother did not answer.

After that if she woke in the night, she went out to look down the well of stairs, with the band of light across the foot. Sometimes she found her mother there. Then she hurried back to close her door and burrowed into her pillow, trying to sleep before her father came and a storm broke. Sometimes the lowest step was empty. Then she could lie in peace, weaving secret dreams.

One night the voices dragged her ruthlessly out of sleep. She heard them pounding up under the floor, like a great tide. Roger came to her door.

"Can't you stop them, Jean?" he asked. "James and I can't sleep."

Jean started down the stairs, Roger behind her. But as they went, mother came through the hall, crying out, "I'll kill myself! I won't live! You can gamble and keep your strumpets and drink! I'll kill myself!" Jean heard her on the porch, saw her flying down the street, hatless, wild, past the pool of light at the corner, into the night.

"Get some clothes on, quick!" She pulled Roger up the stairs. "We'll have to stop her!" Blindly she found her shoes and stockings. "I'll just put on a coat—" she was off again. Her father was at the door. "Where is she?" cried Jean. "Where has she gone?"

"She won't do anything," he said grimly. "Go after her if you want to."

Roger came after her, his shoestrings making a trickling sound as he ran.

"Go down toward the river," said Jean. "I'll go around this block."

Panic, excitement, despair, drama—all in the night wind on her face as she ran. For hours, it seemed, she ran, past dark, shadowy houses, along empty streets. At last her heart thumped in her side until it ached, and she stopped. Where was she? Almost to the river herself. Then she saw them, her mother and Roger, coming swiftly toward her.

"Go back to bed!" said mother sharply. "You have no business out this time of night!" Jean lagged behind them. Roger, clinging to mother's hand, puffed a little as he walked. But he led mother into the house and up to her room. Jean peered into the library. Heavy breathing. Her father, asleep on the couch, his clothes rumpled, his mouth open. Anger stirred in her, that he could go to sleep! She hated the sound of his breathing.

She tiptoed into Roger's room.

"Where was she?" she whispered. Roger was climbing into bed.

"Down on the bridge," he said, disgustedly. "Looking at the water. I said, 'Come home, mamma, I'm sleepy,' and she came."

Jean shivered.

"You were a good boy, to go get her."

"Wisht they'd have their fights in the daytime!" Roger turned toward the wall.

Jean knew, suddenly, that his petulance was the reverse of his recent suffering.

"Never mind, Roger." She bent over him fleetingly. "We'll stick together." She patted his cheek, and quickly, shyly, he made a grab at her hand.

"You bet!" he muttered. "G'night!"

XVII

Jean wandered between the stacks in the library. The books looked dingy, their brightness smeared away by sweaty fingers. The still, hot afternoon air hung full of the odor

of binder's paste and cloth covers decaying in the heat. She
had read all the good books. She was tired of books, anyhow. Flat people, falling in love over and over. The librarian looked up with her patient, round eyes, as Jean passed
the desk.

"Don't you want a book, Jean?" her restrained whisper
followed the girl.

"Read 'em all!" said Jean. She heard the librarian's
whisper. "Guess you have!" and was pleased for an instant.
But when she came to the street, with the limp leaves overhead, and the sidewalk warm through the worn soles of her
shoes, she pushed her sailor away from her face with a
vicious little gesture. She hated it! The street, summer,
everything! She heard her name called with a tantalizing
split into two syllables. Around the corner trotted a little
mare, with a road cart, red wheels spinning, and Esme in
white, a boy at her side. Esme was going with Sam Burt.
They shot away, dust swirling up and settling slowly around
Jean. Life was never stupid for Esme. Jean pretended to
herself that she could see Esme now with not a flicker of
emotion. But deep below the surface touched by thought,
like the slow rise of bubbles at the bottom of a kettle before
the water boils, was always that quick constriction, and a
thumping of her heart as if her veins closed against the flow
of blood.

If she had kept Esme—if her mother hadn't—it would have
been different. She hated those words—— If! Would have
been!

She walked on, dumb anger muffling her thoughts. She
stared down at her hat, dangling from its elastic. The
yellow daisies around the crown were faded to dirty white.
They had been pretty in the spring.

This was the street where Lora Tate lived. She might go
to see her. Lora wasn't exciting, but her admiration for
Jean had an anodyne quality.

Lora's mother came to the door. She was like Lora, only
thinner, more rounded of shoulder, more pathetic.

"Oh, Jean!" she said. "*How* do you do!"

"How do *you* do?" How silly that sounded! "Is Lora home?"

"Oh, didn't you know? Lora's working this summer. At the ten-cent store. She wanted to earn some money, and I let her work."

"She is?" Jean gazed vaguely down the street. "Could I see her in the store, do you think?"

"Well, I go in sometimes. If she isn't busy, then you could see her."

Jean hurried under the limp maples down to the main street. She stood a moment in front of the flaring red store, looking at the windows, pyramided with shapes and colors. Everything!

The long narrow store, with counters down each side, and a row of tables in the middle of the aisle, seemed cool at first, so dark and chasm-like it stretched after the glare of the street. Jean walked among the women who filled the meager aisle, looking for Lora. A girl behind each counter, monstrous pompadours, the back of each head flat, the front a strange face. She saw Lora, almost at the end of the store, her face pallid, her shoulders stooping, her hands wrapping a bundle of tin dishes. Jean waited until the fat, red-faced customer waddled off with her bundle.

"Hello, Lora!"

Lora turned, her pallor rippling into a smile.

"Jean! Why, I *am* glad to see you."

"How long have you been here?"

"Oh, three weeks, I think. It's warm to-day, isn't it? There isn't much air in here, hot days." Lora leaned against her counter.

"How much do you get?"

"Three dollars a week. It counts up quite fast, too. I'm saving it for clothes, this fall."

"Could I get a job?" Jean felt her anger and restlessness fuse into swift resolve. That was what she wanted!

"Oh, Jean! That would be nice! Ask him—Mr. Florent, he's manager. Let's see——" Lora stood on tiptoe, peering along the aisles. "He's not in the office—" she pointed to the bright yellow railing which enclosed a platform in the rear corner. "There he is! That dark man, see him? Go ask him!"

Jean watched him come down the aisle, his black eyes roving over the counters, over the pompadoured girls, among the shoppers. Her hands clenched at her side, and her tongue felt dry. Did she dare?

She followed him to the steps of the office.

"Do you—" she cleared her throat— "that is, would you like another girl?" She strained eagerly toward him, her voice intense. "I'd like to work here."

"What?" Mr. Florent turned and looked at her. His eyes, his hair, were like black velvet, thought Jean; and his skin was white as silk. He smiled at her, showing teeth like peeled nuts, pointed, strong. "You want a job, eh? How old are you?"

"Fifteen."

"Ever worked?"

"Not yet." Like some kind of animal, thought Jean. Not a mole.

"In school?"

"I graduate next year."

"Oh, you do."

Jean waited in an anguish of doubt. She was humiliated by her fear lest he reject her.

"Your name?"

Jean told him.

"Miss Wattles!"

Surprisingly there appeared over the yellow railing a head as yellow, but more frizzled, small blue eyes, full red lips, and finally a pink waist, low at the throat.

"Pay off the girl at the glass counter. I told her I'd let her go as soon as I found another. Miss Winthrop here will take her place. Put your hat in the coat room downstairs," he added, and stepped through the swinging door of the office.

"It's just at the foot of the stairs," whispered Lora.

When Jean came up from the musty dimness of the basement, the girl at the glass counter had gone, and Mr. Florent stood in the aisle.

"Everything on this side is ten cents," he said. "Keep the counter looking decent. Put the money in the till before you wrap packages. No, wait till morning before you clean up. Store's too busy now."

Vases, plain, colored; pitchers, sugar bowls, fruit dishes. An infinite array. Jean fumbled deliciously with the paper and string when she had sold the first vase. Lora smiled at her across the glitter of pieplates and tin spoons.

She went home in winged fear. What would they say?

"You're late," said mother. "Supper's all ready. Where've you been?"

"I've got a job," said Jean, cheeks scarlet. "Three dollars a week. At the ten-cent store."

"Jean!"

"Lora Tate's working there, and the manager's real nice, and I like it, and you can save the money for me, and then——"

"What's that?" Father had just come in.

"It's all right, isn't it? We need money, and I can earn three dollars——"

"There's plenty of work for you here, helping me," said mother. "Without your getting into such a place——"

"I'm sick of staying home!" Jean quivered with rebellious anxiety. "You don't get paid at home! I want to earn some money."

"Let her try it," said father. "She's old enough. Lord knows even three dollars a week will help out."

"I can buy my clothes," said Jean, eagerly. "Lora's going to."

She was too tired to read at night, now. Standing behind a counter from eight until twelve, from one until six, and then until ten on Saturday, made her willing to crawl into bed as soon as she finished supper. Mother put up a luncheon for her, and she ate it in the back room of the offices father shared with Mr. Jessup. A strange place, that office. Up two flights of stairs, then a few steps down. No windows.

Skylights, gray with dust, the sunlight filtering through on old leather-covered chairs and desks littered with papers. Sometimes father was there, or Mr. Jessup, with his bristling little black beard and shoe-button eyes. Sometimes the office was empty. Jean would spread her sandwiches on a newspaper, pull up an armchair, and eat slowly. Her arms stuck to the leather, coming away with a sucking noise. Then she washed her hands in the queer-smelling little hole at the end of the hall and went back to the glass counter.

Every morning she wiped the glasses with a cloth and brushed off the green felt of the counter. Then she arranged them. She liked that, trying different places for the various shapes. People straggled in through the morning, usually women. In the afternoon people walked through the aisles in a steady, trickling procession. A little boy came with ten cents tied in his handkerchief to buy a present for his mother. Jean glowed as she helped him decide. She felt subtly the approach of customers; some of them liked to order her around; some of them smiled at her; some of them were cross and slow to decide. And always she watched for the passing of Mr. Florent, manager, with his velvet eyes and soft, purring voice.

She liked to step gingerly down the steep stairs into the basement. The air seemed to reach out gray, wet fingers to her face, flushed a little in embarrassment because she had to ask Mr. Florent to leave her counter. The fetid toilet, so dark that she could only guess at the noisome legends scrawled on the walls, made her shrink. But the rows and rows of bins, from floor to ceiling, filled with packages, with wrapped china, with bulking tinware, pleased her. It seemed a secret place, to which she alone had access. One day she drifted into the dusk, between the pressing bins, silently, hastily. Excelsior under foot; at the end of the tunnel a pale star. A sweetish smell. She peered upwards at the labels. Chocolates! The boxes misshapen, sunken, dark smears down their sides. She felt under a cover, and drew her fingers back, sickened by the formless softness.

"What's the matter with the candy downstairs?" she asked Lora, later that day.

"Oh!" Lora frowned. "It's awful, his leaving it. This spring, don't you know, that time the river flooded all the basements? Well, it got in here, they say. And spoiled lots of the goods. He just left it all on the shelves. A girl ate some of it——" Jean shuddered. "It made her sick. I think he ought to clean it up. But he's funny that way. Awful stern up here on the floor. He don't seem to care about the stock."

Sometimes mother came into the store, with James. Jean was always secretly delighted if she had a customer, and they had to watch while she sold and wrapped a dish.

"What can I do for you, Madam?" Jean giggled. Mother laughed and said, "Nothing to-day."

"You should say, 'I'm just looking!'" said Jean. "Do you like these plates?" She ran out to the china counter. That morning the stock boy had brought up new plates, small, thin, buff china, with pale flowers, lavender and blue.

"They're real pretty," said mother.

That night Jean carried home six.

"They are to be taken off my salary," she said, proudly.

Saturday night grew feverish. The store became a contracted chasm, with stagnant air hanging thick above the counters, over the bent heads of purchasers. The gas lights hummed and sang overhead, throwing glittering refractions over the glass and tin-ware. The piano behind the music counter rattled under the hard, flying fingers of the music girl. Seven o'clock boomed on the town hall clock. Eight. Ages later, nine. Finally, to a dull beating back of Jean's eyes and a dull pressure low between her thighs, ten o'clock.

Father waited for her in the office. They went home together on the street car. Jean slept until noon on Sunday, waking heavily, a little dazed.

"What is your father doing when you go into the office?" asked mother often.

Jean looked at her, innocent-eyed.

"Why, writing letters. Or talking to a man."

"He gambles up there. Poker." Mother was sharp. "Haven't you seen him?"

Jean shook her head. Poker meant those white and red and blue discs. Silence was safer. She wondered whether mother wanted to know about the woman she saw there at times, a slinking, drab little woman with drab eyes and a multiplicity of watch chains and pins on her dress. "Jessup's typewriter," father had said, when Jean asked him. She didn't tell mother about her, although she hated to find the woman's drab eyes touching her; like a snail, she thought.

Lora stopped work, because her mother was sick. The new girl at the tin counter chewed gum when Mr. Florent wasn't looking and giggled whenever a man stopped near her table. One day she said to Jean,

"Say, old Florent's awful hard hit by that bookkeeper, ain't he?"

Jean looked up at the office, startled. She could see the frowsy top of Miss Wattles's pompadour.

"Ain't you seen his wife coming in to spy on them?"

"Is that his wife, that pretty woman who comes in?"

"I wouldn't say pretty. Too meeching. She comes in all right."

Jean had seen her. She stood sometimes by Jean's counter, watching Jean. She had smiled at her, and Jean had been sorry for her, without knowing why. Something in the soft line of heavy brown hair over her ears, the gentle droop of her neck, the lifting of her dark-lashed eyelids. Like an animal that is hurt, Jean thought.

"She's in the family way, too."

"Oh, no!" cried Jean.

"Gee, where's your eyes, kid? Say, did yuh see that farmer's wife in here yesterday? Big as her farm! I should think they'd be ashamed, running out in public like that."

Jean walked to the other end of the counter, troubled. She had not seen the farm woman. Why should she be ashamed? And yet—that girl smirking about her! She began to watch for Mrs. Florent, to notice the sleek, dark top of Mr. Florent's head next Miss Wattles's canary pompadour.

Late in the afternoon Mrs. Florent came in, to wait for her husband. Jean heard him say to her, "Go on home, Thea. You oughtn't to tire yourself, waiting around here."

Mrs. Florent moved her head slowly on her slender, drooping throat.

"I'll wait for you," she said. Jean thought Mr. Florent's velvet eyes hardened.

The next Sunday she heard her father and mother talking in the dining room as she pulled herself slowly up from sleep. Low, secret voices. When she had dressed and gone down to breakfast, her father was gone. Her mother had a queer, excited look, a contraction about her nostrils and mouth.

"Jean, have you heard anything about that manager and his bookkeeper?" she began.

Jean looked up warily. Mr. Florent seemed to link himself with father!

"No," she said, and poured the milk over her oatmeal. "Why?" Vividly the pale, drooping face of Mrs. Florent shone before her.

"His wife shot herself last night." Mother's voice was shocked and bitter. "She was going to have a baby, too. She left a note about that—that shameless——"

Jean pushed her chair away from the table, pity darting through her, a sharp knife in her bowels.

"You must have seen him, the brute, in the store!"

Jean shook her head stubbornly.

"Men!" Her mother's voice rose. "Oh, they're all alike! They say she was crazy, sick, but who made her that way?"

"She was so pretty." Jean stood in the middle of the living room, her hands pressed against her breast. "That other girl—why, she's horrid! He couldn't have liked her better."

"What is she like?" Mother followed her, her nostrils avid.

"I don't know." Jean went to the door, staring out at the patches of sun on the grass. Dead, with those bands of heavy brown hair around a white face. It hurt her!

"Well," said mother, sharply, "you can't go back there to work again. I only pray they won't drag you in. They've arrested him!"

"Me?" Jean turned blankly.

"As a witness. Because you worked there. If anyone, *anyone,* asks you, don't you know a thing!"

"I don't." Jean felt those two faces pressing on her, Mr. Florent, black velvet, white silk, his wife with piteous eyes.

The next week Jean slept and slept, as if she never could be rested. She hunted for the daily papers, but they disappeared. She went down to see Lora, and the two girls shut themselves into the room Lora shared with her mother.

"They arrested that Wattles girl, too," said Lora. "Haven't you read about it? She swears she is innocent, and they had doctors examine her and everything and they say they can't tell."

"How could a doctor tell anyway?" Jean was scornful.

"Oh——" Lora hesitated. "Well, someday you'll know. But they can't always tell."

"They couldn't tell," said Jean somberly. She didn't know what Lora meant, but that pale face of Mrs. Florent hung in her thoughts. "Maybe she just saw him look at her—if she loved him so much."

"The verdict was that she was temporarily insane, due to her condition. The poor thing was going to have a baby, Jean!"

"Yes."

"Love is awful, isn't it?" Lora shook her head. "I don't think it pays."

"Perhaps he really didn't do anything," protested Jean. "Maybe she imagined it." Again Mr. Florent stood beside her father, a figure demanding her sympathy, her understanding. "Sometimes people, women, imagine things. She had such a pretty name—Thea Florent."

XVIII

Mother with James went to visit Mamie. Mamie could no longer visit them, as she could not leave Grandpa.

"He has failed fast since Mother died," she wrote.

"When are you coming back?" asked father, as they waited for the train.

"I don't know," said mother. She looked at him, and Jean shrank back. Something secret, fierce, compelling in that exchange of glances. "Maybe not at all, once I get away!"

"Oh, yes you will! You couldn't leave us alone."

"Maybe you'll find out!"

Jean knelt by James, her arms closely around him. Dear Jamesie! He wriggled in her grasp, his eyes deep blue stars.

"Train coming!" he cried. "Goo'by, ever'body!"

Father, Jean, and Roger ran along the platform, as the train moved slowly out. James had his nose buttoned against the window, behind him mother waved her hand. They were gone. Suppose something happened to them—the train ran off the track—she never saw James again!

"I'll be home this noon," said father, swinging on to the step of a moving street car.

"Now we can do what we want to, can't we, Jean!" Roger grinned at her, shoving his cap back from his forehead. "Gee, we'll have fun!"

Jean liked the empty house. She thought, "I won't touch it! We can clean up just before mother comes home." She read. Sometimes she sewed. She went down town, walking quickly past the ten-cent store. They had a new manager, Lora said. What was Mr. Florent doing now? She climbed the stairs to father's office. The small woman sat in one corner.

"Well?" said father.

"We need some groceries," declared Jean, hostilely.

"Give me the list. I'll get them."

Jean went away, humiliated. She had wished to buy them.

She found Roger on the floor in the library. He looked up, his thin face tense.

"What are you doing?" Jean looked over his shoulder.

Roger closed the book in haste. A large black book from the lowest shelf.

"Just a physiology," he said, sticking it back behind the curtain. He went off, whistling defiantly. Jean drew the book out. Human anatomy. Pages of plates. Colored, black and white. Forbidden, secret things. A baby, not born! Jean felt faint, sick. She pushed the book away from her. Roger was only a little boy. He ought not to see such things. He was standing behind her, accusingly.

"You mustn't look at that book." Jean thrust it into its place.

For an instant the two looked at each other, a terrifying, naked instant, with veils rent away, and thirst, hunger to know, a driving inquiry crashing together from their eyes. He was a boy. She was a girl. Jean felt that like hot iron pressed into her flesh. Her brother!

"Don't look at it, Roger!" she begged, suddenly. He was so little! He ought not to know—she was frightened.

"I didn't like it much," said Roger, indifferently.

Presently she heard him in the woodshed, pounding, whistling. He was building a rabbit house, he said. For a rabbit that he *might* get.

They went to bed early, lacking anything else to do. Father came home late, and slept downstairs on the couch. One morning Roger came to Jean's door.

"Jean!" he sounded alarmed.

She opened her door.

"Father isn't here! He never came home at all."

They stared at each other, dismayed. Just then they heard him, banging kettles in the kitchen.

"I guess he did, after all," said Jean. But she was afraid to ask him.

A strange feeling grew about the house. Something tense, forbidding. A faint, distant ripple of dissolution. Jean shut herself away from it, pretended she did not feel it.

Saturday father brought home a turkey. Enormous, naked, yellow, with claw feet and limp head, filmy eyed.

"I can't cook that!" cried Jean.

"We'll take it to the bake shop and have them roast it."
Father was irritated at her reception of the bird. But he
carried it off.

Sunday morning Jean tiptoed through the empty house,
unable to escape that faint note of dissolution. Like a creeping tide. As if she heard the plaster of the walls rotting.
Roger had gone swimming with some of the big boys down
the street. Father wasn't home.

Finally she put on her hat and went forlornly down town,
resenting the air which hung so still and close about her.
She climbed the musty stairs to the office. Her father sat
in one of the leather chairs, asleep, his head on one side.
Jean stared at him, at his hair thin about his temples, at his
grayish, unshaven face, at his open mouth, at his clothes,
wrinkled, spotted, and suddenly a wail escaped her lips. He
started awake.

"Are you sick?" Jean twisted her hands together. "Are
you sick?"

"Sick?" Her father laughed, sitting forward, rubbing
one hand over his chin. The sunlight dripped upon him
through the coated skylight. "Trying to josh me, eh?" He
stretched himself.

Again Jean heard that note of decay. She shivered back
toward the door.

"What d'you want?"

"We ought to get the turkey," she said in a half whisper.
She walked beside him to the bakery, her cheeks flaming.
She was ashamed! He looked—oh, he ought not to look like
that! She had no articulate thought as to the reason back
of his appearance. She had only a violent protest, a burning
shame. And in that violence and heat one strand of her
being curled up, twisted, and was consumed. The part of
her which had flowed out toward her father fled back deep
into her self.

The next week Jean had a strange impulse. She wondered
how starving felt. If you had nothing to eat for days and
days—— Her wonder started from a story of shipwreck,
gruesome, tragic. She would try it. Not easy, since she

had to cook for her father and Roger. But she could do it.

They did not notice that she left her plate untouched. People didn't notice much. The creamed potatoes for supper the end of the first day drew her with their aroma, but she moved her fork about in them and did not taste. Her legs were like lead as she dragged them up to bed. The next day was easier. She had a light feeling, as if she floated about. She wondered whether drinking water ought to be banned, too. She might drink just a little.

The colors out of doors grew unbearably vivid, blue, green, yellow, the scarlet of poppies in a garden down the street. Sounds, the plop, plop, of horses' feet far down the dusty road; the cries of children playing in the sun; she could even hear the soft flutter of the dust as it settled. She looked at her hands. White. Thin. The blue veins made an H on her left hand, an M on the right. That was funny. How long could you starve? Lassitude, like the weight of deep green water, pressing upon her. She didn't sit down for supper that night. Father said,

"Don't you feel well, Jean? You look sort of peaked."

Jean looked at him. His nose was a strong beak; she could see tiny red roots in the corners of his eyes.

"I'm not hungry," she said. "It's hot." Then she went floating, floating, out to sit on the steps.

"You'd better go to bed." Her father touched her shoulder. She felt as if she were a filmy veil floating from his fingertips as he led her into the house.

The night was strange. She did not know when she slept or when she woke. She saw herself floating about the room, beckoning to her to follow. Hunting, searching, for what? Something darkly obscure, but compelling her. She must find it. That self, that floating self was lost! She must find that. Across a great swamp, brown, green where she touched the brown scum, where monsters floated, monsters with wrinkled, warted hides and scum drawn over their lidless eyes. Hands clung to her, holding her, pulling her down into the green slime. Weights at her ankles. She must go on. Out of reach of those clinging fingers, in quest of that floating, beautiful self.

She woke, crying. The tears rolled down her cheeks. Morning. Her hand rose, wavering, to brush away the tears. She stared around her room. Familiar, and yet strange. Suddenly she pushed herself out of bed. She wanted her breakfast. What a silly fool she had been! What would folks say if they ever knew? She dressed with slow difficulty and slipped downstairs. You shouldn't eat much at first. She drank a cup of milk, slowly. She had been foolish. But under that admission, deeper, lay a curious pleased pride.

Mother was coming home that afternoon. Father swept until the dust flew in clouds, Roger shook the rugs, Jean dusted. The house was spotless again.

"Did you miss me?" mother said, walking through the house, adjusting the crooked window shades.

"Yes." Jean looked through the rooms. They had lost that faint, unmistakable murmur of dissolution. Strange days! Yes, she was glad mother had come back.

"Here, Jean." Mother called her into the dining room. She had a folded piece of cloth on her knees, one hand stroking it. "Mamie sent you this. She bought it for—for my mother. But she had never used it. We thought it might make a suit for you."

"It's lovely." Jean touched it. Fine blue serge.

"She never wore it." Tears in mother's eyes.

"Could you make it?" Jean asked, hastily.

"No, I can't make a jacket." Mother wiped away her tears. "But there's your money that you earned. You could have it made."

The dressmaker lived not far below them. A dumpy little woman like a pin-cushion, thought Jean, with her mouth and bosom full of pins. She patted and twisted Jean, and sat back on her plump legs to squint up at her work.

Jean made herself pique collar and cuffs, starching them until they were like white boards. Sunday morning she came downstairs, her face radiant. She had revolved before her mirror, almost disbelieving that stylish reflection. She

peered between the coats into the hall glass. Father came
up behind her.

"Don't I look nice?" Jean spread her hands in a little
gesture of revelation.

"Where'd you get those duds?" Father stared, his eyes
heavy, hard. "Where'd you get money to buy those?"
he flung at mother, who had come in from the kitchen. "I
can't have you going out like that! Church! Pshaw! All
the men I owe will look at you and then come hunting me
down for debts. You oughtn't to dress like that, when my
affairs are in such a state."

Jean's pride fed her spurt of anger.

"I paid for having it made myself!" she cried, and then
was silent as mother broke in,

"She can tell people that my dead mother furnished the
cloth," she said, in a white whisper. "I'll pin a sign on her
shoulders, 'Her father did not buy these clothes!' Must
she go ragged because you can't dress her?"

"You see what you've started, don't you?" Father's face
twitched into redness. "Go upstairs and take them off!
You've got to dress like my daughter! People needn't give
you clothes!"

"Go on to church, Jean!" cried mother. "If your father
wants to advertise his shame, he can do it himself! Go on!"

Jean's fingers plucked at the little cloth buttons of her
jacket. She had a wild impulse to tear it off, to hurl it at
her father, to burst out at him almost as her mother might.
Suddenly she turned, and with her head stiffly erect, went
down the steps to the street in sedate, sure strides. As she
walked, the flapping of the pleated skirt about her shoe tops
comforted her. They could settle their own squabble! She
would wear her new suit.

Her father was gone when she came home after church.
Nothing more was said about the suit. A week later, just
before school opened, Jean went to the office.

"I've got to have some shoes for school," she said, thrusting out her scuffed, grayish toes. "Can I get them to-day?
School begins Monday."

Her father looked at her, a queer tightening of the lids over his eyes.

"So you can't furnish your whole wardrobe yourself, yet?" he said.

Jean drew her feet back. She knew what he meant. He was still angry. She was silent, rejecting the furious little answers which pushed up for utterance. If she made him mad, he wouldn't give her the money.

"Well," she said, cajolingly, "I didn't earn much. Just twelve dollars altogether. No, eleven dollars and forty cents. I bought those plates."

"Still need your dad's pocketbook?" pressed her father.

"The soles are worn through, and there's a hole on my ankle bone, and they've been tapped twice." Jean turned her toes upwards to show him, meekly.

As she descended the stairs, the money in her hand, she kicked her heels viciously against the treads. If you wanted money, you couldn't say what you thought! Trucking! You had to have money yourself—— Mother was waiting at the foot of the stairs, and Jean put aside her anger.

"Did he give it to you?"

"Of course!" she said blithely. "Which store do we go to?"

XIX

School opened. Esme had gone to college. Miss Adair had left to be married. Jean was a senior. Roger had entered high school, a little freshman in knee pants. Sometimes Jean saw him in the hall, looking absurdly small.

Class meetings. Jean sat in the rear of the room and made wild flurries of jests to the girls around her. The officers were chosen. Jean imagined herself rising to her feet, making a speech, as some of the boys and girls had done. Her hands froze in her lap at the phantasy. Now they were to choose the performers for the end of the year, Class Day, Commencement. Lora Tate sprang to her feet.

"I nominate Jean Winthrop for Class Prophet! She's the smartest girl in our class!"

Jean shrank back in her seat, a tumult of fear and dizzy hope driving the blood into her face. She couldn't do it! Get up on a platform! Swiftly her mind leapt at bits of prophecy—it would be fun. Someone nominated another girl, Rebecca Northwood, a tall, fair girl with wonderful curling yellow hair. Jean knew. Rebecca would be chosen. Because she was so pretty. The announcement of the tellers had no surprise for her.

"She hasn't any brains at all!" fumed Lora as the girls left the building. "They just elected her because she'd look nice standing on the platform! I think you'd look all right, dressed up."

"I didn't want it," said Jean, earnestly. "I couldn't think of things to say. I don't know half those folks!"

But that night she lay awake, restlessly wondering. She was smarter than Rebecca Northwood. Rebecca was always saying, "I don't think I know!" But she smiled under her filmy yellow hair, and the boys hung around her after school. Jean doubled her arm under her cheek.

"I could do it!" she thought. "But I wouldn't look nice on a platform." She pressed her lips together. She didn't care. She visualized one by one the seniors who had been chosen. They were different, somehow. She lined herself up, not as a visual image; she never thought of herself as she looked in a mirror. Her consciousness of herself was an intense composite, like a knot of tense wires. What did they have that she lacked? Not brains. People noticed them. They stood out. Dimly, without quite bringing her idea to the surface of her mind, she felt: "They are like bottles with the stoppers out. I'm like a jug, sealed up. I can't get out. I could do things, but I can't get out!" For the first time she felt strongly herself apart from others, different. The knot of self strained under new tensions. She wanted to burst out, to startle them into awareness, to lose her awkward, fearful constraints.

Jean spent Christmas with Mamie. The house looked smaller; the yard, with mounds of snow over the bushes, narrow chasms along the paths, seemed shrunken. Mamie

looked smaller, too, and grayer. Jean took the coal scuttle
away from her and lifted it to the top of the sitting room
stove, letting the coals rattle in.

"You ought to have somebody help you," she said, ma-
turely.

"You'd better stay here." Mamie laughed at her. "You're
so big now you could boss me around."

After supper they sat and talked.

"Your mother says your father isn't doing very well."
Mamie pursed up her mouth with her little "tch—tch—"
sound.

"He's working hard." Jean was cold.

"I don't think your mother seems well. She never was
strong, and having so many children, and all——" Mamie
"tch"-ed loudly.

"Well, what did she have us for?"

"I told her she was to blame if your father wasn't doing
well. I made her awful mad, but I just spoke my mind
right out."

Jean stared at the crimson glow behind the isinglass doors.
She wanted to talk. To say some of the things she thought.
But the dumb loyalty of her childhood held her silent.
Mamie went on,

"I never said a word while you were little, but you are
growing up now. She's hard to get on with, your mother.
Just like Grandma. Why, there never was a man so patient
as your father, when they were married."

Jean's eyes filled with tears. Her father, when she was
little!

"Many's the time I've seen him, when he had to study,
walking the floor with you or Roger on one arm, because
you were teething or something, and a big book in his other
hand. Back and forth. Back and forth. Never a word of
complaint!" Mamie hitched her chair toward the stove.
"Mind, I'm not defending him if he's taken to doing wrong
things. But you have to look at both sides if you can."

Jean couldn't speak. Grief lay heavy in her throat.

"Your mother, now, she never liked housework. But

if you marry, you have it to do. You ought to be cheerful
about what you have to do, I say."

"I'm not going to get married!" said Jean. "I don't
want to do housework and ask a man for money and everything! I——"

"Sh, Jean! Marriage is a woman's destiny. You don't
know what you'll do when *he* comes along."

"You aren't married!"

"No. Sometimes I think I'm better off, too!" Mamie's
eyes snapped. "But it's lonesome. And your mother'll
have you children to look out for her, no matter what happens. Who'll I have?"

"I'll look out for you!" Jean felt her future, strange,
heavy with promise. "You needn't worry! If I get married, it won't be till I'm old—oh, twenty five at least!—and
then he'll have to have a fortune—ten thousand dollars—in
a safe place where he can't lose it!"

"You're a great girl!" Mamie smiled at her. "What are
you going to do while you wait for your rich husband?"

"Teach school. Latin, I guess. But I have to go to
college to teach that. Maybe I can't go."

"When you were a baby," said Mamie, with the quick
little air of a bird dragging a worm from an unexpected
hole, "they took out an insurance policy. To come due in
twenty years. For your college. I don't know what they've
done with it. But I remember just as plain. I was there
that winter, and they talked about where they'd send you
to college."

Jean tingled. A fear, never caught in daylight before,
came bobbing to the surface like a dead fish in a flood of
warm hope.

"Oh, then I can go! Probably they kept it for a surprise! Or maybe they even forgot it!"

Mamie pursed her lips.

"You can't forget it. You have to pay on it every year."
The fear flicked its tail; was it dead?

"Much?" asked Jean.

"I don't know exactly."

For a long time that night Jean lay awake, listening to the soft rattle of shifting coals in the checked stove. She watched a tender, vivid picture, her father and mother when she was a baby—she did not imagine them younger, as they were then, but vaguely as she knew them now—planning for her when she grew old enough to go to college. New dreams, now. Jean at college. Jean, with a wonderful position. Earning lots of money. She would give it to them, and then things would smooth out again. It was beautiful of them, when she was only a baby, to think so far ahead for her.

At home again, the dream still clung. She wanted to ask about it, but when she tried to speak, something held her silent, partly fear, perhaps, but partly a soft shyness, as if she hesitated to intrude on a dream that belonged to them.

One day in chapel exercises the state commissioner of education spoke; he was round and little, with a voice rolling out great phrases over the heads of the students.

"Consider your futures, young men and women! What are you planning to do with your lives?"

After school the girls discussed these futures. Lora meant to take stenography and go into an office. So did Daisy Thoms. Several of the girls were going to the university in the fall. "What you going to do, Jean?"

"I don't quite know." Jean felt her dream glow within her, brighter than truth. "I may go to the university, and I may go east to college."

"Have you applied anywhere?" That was Jessie Smith, a practical, downright girl with a homely, freckled face. "You have to put in an application for the eastern colleges. Esme Maurey did, oh, long before Christmas."

"My father is going to at once," said Jean, guiltily.

"I'd like to go to college," said Lora, "but I'm not really smart. There's money in offices, anyhow. You meet fellows there, too."

Jean moved slowly through the routine of supper and dishes. She had to ask about that insurance now. She had committed herself.

She told her mother about the speech.

"That must be Whitelaw." Her mother sighed. "He came to dinner with us once, when you were little. You wouldn't remember."

"Am I going to college?" Jean flung the question breathlessly.

"Don't ask me! You ought to go. Ask your father. If he can't pay his grocers' bills——"

"Isn't there—didn't you have an insurance for me?" There! It was out!

Mother turned, her eyes darkening into tragedy.

"Where'd you hear about that?" she asked.

"Mamie told me." Jean felt her dream wither, root and branch.

"Pity your aunt couldn't keep still." Mother's mouth hardened.

"Wasn't it true?"

"Yes, it was. But it's gone. Your father had to borrow on it when we moved from Cygnet. He never paid it back. We had to have it to pay doctors' bills. It's gone, like everything else."

Jean's dream was heavy within her, crumpled, dead. Then she saw her mother's eyes, and she felt for a poignant instant that behind them lay another dream, dead, heavy. The pity of it ached more bitterly than the weight of her own perished dream.

"Never mind," she said, hastily. "I'll go, anyway!"

"I begged your father not to touch it," began mother, but Jean fled up to her room.

As she stood by her window, she could see, where the light ran from the library out across the field, tall weeds pricking up black from the thin snow. Again she heard that faint rippling sound of dissolution. What hurt so, until she pressed her hands against her throat? Not disappointment. She knew now, that under her hope had lurked, fed by Mamie's phrase, "You have to pay each year," the knowledge that she now had. Pity! That was it. They had dreamed beautiful dreams, too, her father and her mother.

It was Jean's first clear glimpse of the pitiable human tragedy that lies in the discrepancy between intention and accomplishment.

But she was too young to hold it long. It terrified her. She fought away from it. It was a quicksand; if she lingered, it might suck her down, negating her own life. She would forget it, thrust it deep out of memory. A subtle instinct of preservation worked in her, and presently she sat down with her books, thinking, "It was mine, when they planned it for me! They were pigs to use it!" As she opened her Odyssey and gazed at the page, the rhythm of the sonorous hexameters rising in her, she thought, "They'll see! I'll go, anyway! I won't be stopped!"

"You must have spring fever," said mother. "You're as thin as a rail and you look all washed out. I'm going to get a tonic for you."

Jean swallowed the bitter medicine indifferently. She wasn't sick. But she felt tired all the time. School was dull. Things out of books! She was tired of sitting on wooden benches while a teacher went round the class with questions, ending all too often with, "Miss Winthrop, you can answer that!" She was tired of home. When she came in from school, she stood in the hall, listening, feelers out for the degree of tension. Sometimes things were calm. Sometimes father was there, arguing.

The seniors gave a reception for the freshmen. Roger wanted to go, and Jean apathetically dressed in her last summer's white dress and went with several of the girls. She stood in a corner of the hall, conscious of her old dress, of her buttoned shoes. She couldn't dance. Silly things, she thought, watching the sliding, revolving couples. The freshmen were playing games in the next room. She saw Roger darting past the door, his face scarlet, in slipping flight after a girl, the dropped handkerchief in his hand. Children! Daisy Thoms rushed up to her.

"Come on and dance, Jean! Who needs a fellow!"

"Can't." Jean turned away from her. Daisy was so loud! Then she saw a boy edging toward her. David Sterrill.

She had seen him in some of her classes. He stood beside her, his heavy eyebrows meeting over his thick spectacles.

"Want to dance?" he blurted out.

"No, I don't care to." Jean was frigid. She wanted to talk, to hold him there beside her, to escape the sense of elephantine conspicuousness which overwhelmed her. But she couldn't find a thing to say!

"Let's get some ice cream, then." He looked at her imploringly, his hands dangling out from the sleeves of his new blue suit.

"I don't want any." Jean couldn't walk across the room with him! Everyone would see her.

"I tell you, I'll bring you some over here. You wait!"

He went off, hitching his shoulders awkwardly as he slipped on the polished floor. The music stopped. Perhaps he wouldn't come back.

But he did, his face twisted in earnestness above the two plates with spoons thrust into the pink mounds. Jean ate slowly, feeling his hasty glances from behind the thick spectacles.

"Say, do you like this sort of thing?" he waved his spoon.

Jean looked at him. Why, he hated it, too! Suddenly her stiffness melted.

"Silly, I think."

"Um, I do too!"

"Sounds like a room full of monkeys!"

"Monkeys, that's it!"

"I just came because my brother, he's a freshman, wanted to come, and he wanted me to come."

"Dunno why I came."

David carried her empty plate away. Jean stood in the corner, an armor of contempt shielding her. David was at her elbow again.

"I tell you, let's go home. You live out my way. I'll go home with you. It's nice outdoors."

"I'll have to tell Roger."

"I'll tell him. The little kids are in there. You go get your things and I'll meet you at the door."

The sky had the clear transparent darkness of spring. The air touched Jean's cheeks gently, after the close hall.

"Want to take a car?" They had reached the Avenue.

"Let's walk."

In silence they went past the darkened store windows, across the bridge.

"I've got a canoe," said David. "Like to go, some day?"

"Yes, I'd like to." Jean looked back at the smooth, black water. "I'd like to."

"I know your father," said David, later. "I've been to his office. Reporting. I'm on the paper."

"Oh, are you?" Jean felt a twisted thread pull at her, part fear—what did he know about her father?—part interest; reporting!

"Um. I'm going to have a steady job there this summer."

They stood a moment at the door of Jean's house. Jean had a new importance. A boy had seen her home! To be sure, David was rather queer. She had heard the girls laugh at him. But he was smart. He reported for the paper.

"Some day I'll let you know, and we'll go up the river."

"All right," said Jean. "Good night."

At breakfast Roger grinned.

"Jean had a fellow," he announced. "He took her home. I saw him."

"Who was it?" Father looked up quickly.

"Oh, one of the boys. David Sterrill. He said he knew you."

"That boy, eh?" Father looked at her queerly. Jean felt that he was pondering something.

"I'm going canoeing with him some day," she said.

"You be careful about the river!" Father's voice had an undercurrent of hostility. "You don't know whether he can manage a canoe or not."

Jean was silent. She was going, just the sam—ee!!

She didn't see David again in the weeks before Commencement. Perhaps he hadn't liked her. As if she cared!

She didn't care about anything. Not even her new dresses for the graduation exercises.

"What's the use of trying to do anything for you, anyway?" Mother had just come from the dressmaker's with her. Jean's head ached from standing and standing while lace and ruffles were pinned in place.

"I don't want you to do anything!" she cried. "Keep your old clothes! I don't want them!" She ran up to her room, to sit silent, unthinking, brooding inarticulately.

School was over. She would never go through the dusky hall, up to the assembly room again. A vague melancholy hung about the thought. She didn't care, exactly, but the finality had a tinge of sorrow.

One night there was a dreadful quarrel. Jean pressed her hands against her ears, but the devastating words roared between her fingers. Finally she crept down the rear stairs, out to the long grass behind the house. She lay there, face down, sobbing, when Roger came to kneel beside her.

"Don't, Jean, please," he begged. "What's the good of your crying, too?"

Jean lifted her face. She could see him indistinctly, his thin, square face held in determined rigidity.

"Let 'em fight," he said. "What difference 's it make to us?"

"None!" cried Jean fiercely. She sat up, pressing the coarse stems down beneath her palms. "I'll never cry again! Never! No matter what they do."

Roger sat down beside her. They could see the lighted windows of the living room, and occasionally a figure flurried past the long rectangle. They could hear nothing. Shoulders just touching, they sat together, while Jean's breath grew regular, until her tumult had died and her heart beat slowly again.

"They get worse all the time," said Roger. "No good letting them make us feel bad."

"It does make you feel——"

"Don't me!" Roger waggled his head. "I'm sick of it.

Sick an' tired. Some day I'm going away. That's what I'm going to do."

"So am I. I tell you, Roger, when I get a job teaching school, you can get another job, and we'll have a house together."

"You can keep house for me," interrupted Roger. "And I'll earn the money."

"I'd rather teach or something. I tell you, we'll have a hired girl. Oh, Roger, wouldn't it be nice! No fights—we wouldn't ever fight, would we?"

They went softly toward the house. No sounds. When they tiptoed through the kitchen, they found father bending over the couch, trying to pour water between mother's clenched lips.

"Go telephone the doctor!" he said hurriedly. "She's made herself sick! Get some hot water, Jean!"

"Where'll I go?" Roger hesitated.

"Next door. The folks are up yet."

Jean lighted the oil stove, panic in her fingertips at the sound of her mother's low moaning.

"My heart! It's stopping! My hands are dead!"

Endless, hectic, frightening minutes before the doctor drove up. Terrifying hovering outside the circle of father and doctor, with the nucleus of that moaning figure.

"An attack of angina pectoris. She's coming around. Keep her in bed a while. Did she have a shock of some sort?"

A new fear, now, that a quarrel might end thus. Her heart was weak! Jean kept house. She carried fresh water, or a tray with toast and egg, up to her mother's quiet, darkened room.

Her father, haggard, unshaven, skulked through the house.

"You'd better be careful—" Jean spoke abruptly—"not to make her mad!"

Her father stared at her, the whites of his eyes flushing; then he swung on his heel and rushed away from the house.

Mother came downstairs again. Summer drifted along,

dusty, warm, empty. For a time father came home for supper and stayed there in the evening.

One night Jean woke to hear her mother's rapid, irregular walk, back and forth, from parlor to kitchen.

"Mother!" She seized the fluttering hands. "Mother, come up to bed. You mustn't! You'll just make yourself sick again."

"Leave me alone! Where is your father? Do you know what he does? You think I'm to blame—getting mad— making a scene! Well, listen to me! Your father you think so fine—he drinks! That's what he does! I never told you that! Now you know! Leave me alone!"

Jean stood aside, impotent before the tearing fury in her mother's voice and hands. Did she think that was news! Did she think they never heard what was said in the wild nights?

She woke Roger.

"You'll probably have to get the doctor again," she said. "She's wound up. If father doesn't come soon——"

The same thing. But this time Jean held her panic in cold reserve. She heated water, she mixed mustard plasters, she brought glasses of water for the frowning doctor, and through it all, like a shrill cricket, she heard an inner comment, "She could help it! I won't feel bad! I won't!"

One day David came to the door.

"Would you go canoeing this afternoon?" he asked, his thick eyebrows meeting. "Take our supper?"

Jean met him at the boat-shed at three. He had taken off his coat and rolled the sleeves of his striped shirt up from thin forearms, amazingly hairy. Jean looked away, embarrassed. But the thrill of the slim canoe slipping from the rack across the platform into the water, the sense of comfort in arranging pillows in the center for her, the slight wavering motion as David swung the canoe out into the current, filled her with delight. David wasn't very big, she thought. All black and white, like a drawing, with faint dark shadows on his lip and chin. He sat before her, his arms moving in a slow cadence, and Jean relaxed, content.

Shanties along the river edge, with ragged washings fluttering among the trees. Then fields, sloping, full of sunlight, to the gray shore.

"In spring the river's awful high," said David. "Up over
that gray line."

Around a long curve, and they were slipping between
woods, tall dark trees with wind in their branches, ghostly,
mottled cottonwoods with crooked dead branches hanging
out over the water.

"I brought a book along. You like to read?" Jean
nodded. "A fellow in the office gave it to me. Thought you
might read it——"

"Horseman Against the Sky," read Jean. "I never heard
of that."

"A new writer, I think. Ambrose Bierce. I read some
of his stories. Weird. That's why I liked them."

Jean looked at David. She didn't suppose boys liked
books. But David was different. He wrote, himself. She
began to read, awkwardly at first, conscious of an audience,
eager to read well. Then she forgot David in the strange
disturbing sentences. She finished and looked up from the
page. Above her a gaunt, sandy cliff rose straight from the
water, a high bank eaten by the river. For an instant she
saw, against that sharp blue of summer sky, the figure of the
horseman!

"I'd like to write like that," said David, solemnly.

They ate supper on the shore, with a fire, and David cooking "wienies" on a stick, his dark face flushed.

Then they floated with the current, between banks sweet
with dusky twilight, the water about them mysterious with
faint light, until at last they reached the low boat-shed. Jean
sighed as she stepped out on the platform.

"It's been beautiful, David," she said, as they climbed the
hill to the street.

"Would you come again?"

Often through the next month David came for her. Jean
tried once or twice to paddle, but she discovered that David
liked best to have her stretch out on cushions facing him,

and read. She thought, "Well, some day I'll have a canoe, and then I can paddle!" Sometimes she found him watching her as she looked up from a book; she shrank a little, disturbed by a flicker of pleading under his dark eyebrows. She felt his darkness as a distant menace. But for the most part she read, or watched the shore, centered strongly in herself, dreaming vague dreams, aware of David only as a means to the wonder of twilight on water, or to the discovery of books she had never read.

One day, as she flew about the kitchen, putting up a hasty luncheon to take, her mother came to the door.

"You go off with that boy too much, I think, Jean. You—what do you do up the river so much?"

"Oh, read—eat! Where's that salad dressing?"

"Right there in the cupboard. Jean, you aren't getting fond of him, are you?"

Jean whirled, spoon in air. Something hidden in her mother's face probed at her, sought secret places.

"He isn't strong. Your father says he's sickly. I don't want you mixing up—— You're too young, anyhow!"

Jean laughed. "What a funny idea! Why, David—— Gee whiz!" she cried, and laughed again at her mother's grimace of distaste for such language. "David? Why, he's like a girl. Only he likes books and things, like me. David!"

"Well, he may be getting fond of you."

"We have fun, and there's nothing else to do. You don't want me just sticking around here all the time, do you?" Jean stirred her potato salad vigorously. "He's going away next month, anyway. To Detroit. He's got a fine job on a paper there."

"I'm glad of it!"

That afternoon Jean peered furtively at David. Was he fond of her? He wasn't silly. What foolish ideas mothers got! Then David brought out the book, a new one. "The Open Road."

"It's made to take outdoors," he explained. "There's one poem there—do you like poems?" He opened the book and handed it across to Jean.

Jean read it. She was a little afraid to read poetry. Reading it seemed to betray something of your inmost heart. So she read cautiously.

> There's a schooner in the harbor
> With her topsails tipped with fire,
> And my heart has gone aboard her
> For the islands of desire."

"It's lovely, David!" Her eyes filled with light. "It's——"

"There are more," he said, gruffly.

Jean kept the book. David wrote in it, "For Jean S. Winthrop, from her friend, David Sterrill."

The next week David went away.

"Would you write to me, sometimes?" he asked, the night he came to say good-by. "I don't know anybody in Detroit."

"If you write to me. Tell me all about your new job. And the city." Jean stood on the top step, her hands loosely clasped. She felt forlorn.

"Some day I'll come back to see you," David said, his voice queerly husky. "If I find some good books, I'll let you know."

He held out his hand. Jean laid hers in it, felt a hot, quick grasp, and then David swung off, his shoulders hitching with his awkward, gangling stride. David! She would miss him. The lovely hours of the summer had been those on the water. Perhaps she would never see him again. Perhaps he would become a famous writer! Her mother stood in the hall. Had she been watching? Jean shrugged, with a little spurt of anger. A lot she'd see!

That was Jean Winthrop, at seventeen. The shell of her small self had expanded, had opened for shimmering filaments, which had recoiled within the shell again. She had knowledge beyond her comprehension, knowledge curiously separate from the emotional currents of her days. She had torn away the unquestioning devotion of her small self, and the pain of that sundering had served to thicken the shell which enclosed her. Strongly egoistic, carrying always the sense of herself as opposed to others, she still kept a wistfulness, a desire for the beauty of peace. She was like a sea anemone, with the delicate flowering tentacles drawn inward. She was like one who runs, breathlessly, his heart held cuplike in clutching hands, while he seeks feverishly along a strange road for a place to pour out the brimming, unknown contents of that heart. But, however shy or cautious or overconscious she might be of self-betrayal, one thing she possessed. She had no fear of what she might become. She meant to "do things," vaguely, still resolves unformed, indefinite, but hard like a rod of iron through her flesh.

PART III
WITH THE WIND

PART III

I

In the fall Jean entered the college outside the town. Her mother had suggested the State Normal, but Jean was stubborn in her refusal to consider that. She was vague in her reasons; perhaps the strongest was that she didn't like the two girls from her class who were going there. College was like school. Jean took the car each morning, went to classes, ate her luncheon in the basement room with the other town girls, went to classes, and rode home again. Sometimes she went up to one of the double rooms in the dormitory shared by the out-of-town girls. She envied them. Away from home, with trunks full of new clothes, a whole winter's supply, they seemed to live a separate, vivid existence, quite unlike her own.

The rushing season of the four literary societies caught Jean into an emotional vortex. The girls didn't talk about the rushing; that was against the rules of the game. But strongly, through all the life of the fall term, ran the currents of rivalry, of desire, of excited hope. If one of the seniors spoke to you, invited you to tea in her room, you were being rushed! She might ask you to a meeting of her society. Some of the freshmen were rushed by all four societies. And some of them——Jean thought disdainfully that they were like little, hungry dogs, running around with tongues out and tails wagging, in quest of some senior to toss a friendly bone. Jean was as hungry, but she couldn't wag!

If father had stayed here, as dean, they would all want

175

me, she thought. *But they know about things. Things,* to Jean, meant that faint, inevitable, increasing sound of dissolution. To escape the constant pricking of shame, she built up her defenses of clowning. She discovered that mimicry delighted her audiences, particularly when it held a kernel of biting truth. She learned to retell a simple incident—Grace Torrance forgetting to pay her fare, the algebra instructor requesting "less chatter and more matter, young ladies!"—with exaggerated emphasis. She knew that when she came into the basement room where the town girls studied, gossiped, ate their luncheons, there was a slight flurry of amused expectancy. And out of her need for material grew, slowly, a greater awareness of people around her. She had to watch them, to listen to them, to ponder upon their motives, if she was to re-create them as a joke.

In the algebra class Jean sat next to a drowsy, swarthy senior, a girl so dark that some of the freshmen whispered, "Colored blood, I'll bet!" Jean thought her beautiful, with her heavy, curly hair, her great brown eyes, her pouting full lips. She belonged to the oldest society, the Homerian, that which all Esme's sorority sisters, if they came out to this college, entered by right of custom. Jean wanted to belong to that society. She came to recognize its members by their dash, their accompanying hordes of boys, their dress. She wasn't like them. She admitted it with bitterness. Esme would have joined that. Several times Jean was invited to the society next in age, the Agora, by a staid senior, in long plain skirts swirling sedately around her shoes, a tiny diamond on her left hand proclaiming that she was engaged —to a Methodist minister in her home town. Jean felt the tone of Agora, more subdued, more serious, less sparkling. But she liked the meetings in the long narrow room, where the girls danced after the short program.

Then one day Emilia Wright turned her sleepy eyes on Jean.

"You're awful smart, aren't you?" she said. "I've taken this course three times, and if I fail this time, I can't graduate! I wish I had some of your brains!"

After that she copied Jean's problems, hastily, in the few minutes before the instructor appeared. After class, she walked down the stairs, her arm through Jean's, her soft, small hand just touching Jean's wrist. At the corner of the building she withdrew her hand and stood, waiting, while a tall bulky senior, Clark Clarkson, her lover, came toward her under the drooping firs. They went off together, and Jean thrilled at the passionate rush of the two figures toward each other as they disappeared. Emilia asked Jean to a meeting of her society. Jean, in her white graduation dress, waited in the town girls' room. Other seniors came in laughing, and carried off their freshmen. The Agora senior came through, looked at Jean with grave reproach, and vanished. Had Emilia forgotten her? Emptiness within her. Spots of desperate red on her cheeks. She heard the rhythm of pianos down the hall. The girls were dancing! In rushed Emilia, her hair a cloud about her face.

"Jean! Clark kept me so long! You've been waiting——"

Jean sat in confused awkwardness in the corner of the room, watching the other girls. She couldn't dance. Emilia floated past, turning to nod. How beautiful she was!

The next week came the mid-term quiz in algebra. Jean, working easily over the problems, heard her name whispered. Emilia, staring at her with sorrowful dark eyes. "Help me!" her lips formed the words.

Back and forth in front of the room paced the instructor. The Walrus. Jean had given him that name, and it stuck to his shiny small bald head and melancholy sandy moustache. Emilia's eyes were tragic. Jean folded the bits of yellow paper on which she had worked the problems and awkwardly, her face pale, slipped them across the aisle into the sly, greedy hand stretched out for them. Had the Walrus seen her? He wouldn't think of watching her; he was openly proud of her work. His protuberant pale eyes grazed her, and Jean flushed. She had cheated. Cheated!

"Well, Emilia's got it easy," said one of the freshmen, at the end of the hour. "The Walrus almost caught you, Jean! He'd been surprised if his model pupil got caught cheating."

"Oh, he'd have talked it over with the Carpenter," said Jean, but there was an unpalatable flavor under her tongue. Even Emilia's soft, "You saved my life, you sweet thing!" as she hurried away with Clark did not ease her dry throat.

The following Monday Emilia was not in class. Jean wondered. This was the tense week when the bids for the societies came out. On Wednesday she asked one of the older town girls.

"Emilia Wright!" The girl looked at her mockingly, Jean thought. Did everyone know she had tossed her honor into Emilia's hand? "Hadn't you heard? She's gone home. Going to marry that man she's crazy about, at Christmas."

All day Jean pushed away thoughts of Emilia. She wouldn't think of her! The freshmen talked in flurried corners, stopping guiltily if an upper class girl approached. Societies. Which one——

That night Jean sat by her window, her eyelids heavy, warm. Emilia had never cared about her. Not the smallest shade of caring. She had only pretended, in that soft, darkly sweet voice, because she wanted to use Jean's brains. Jean hugged her knees, her forehead down against the window sill. What smelled of lilacs, through the faint smoke odor of late fall? Suddenly Jean sat erect, her body shrinking, contracting, as if it attempted withdrawal into some secret corner of herself. Mrs. Pratt! Years ago. At the college. She had forgotten her. They had done the same thing, Mrs. Pratt and Emilia. People were like that. That old ache, with the sickish fragrance of lilacs.

"I'm a fool!" said Jean aloud. "A fool!" She remembered things her mother said to her father. "Anyone can get anything out of you if they use a little soft soap! You're soft."

That was it. She was soft. She wanted to be hard. Like steel. Using other people. She paused, her breath quickening. Had her feeling for Emilia been clear? Emilia, the Homerians. If Emilia had belonged to no society——Jean didn't know. Perhaps, after all, she had been working

Emilia. Somehow that thought slipped in beside the heavy
shame of her cheating. Would she like being hard, using
people?

The town room, the next morning, whirled with excitement. The freshmen went about with an air of ostentatious
obliviousness to the tiny pins which their sponsors had
fastened to their waists. Jean watched, furtively, while
waters of despair, blacker than any she had ever known,
closed over her head. No one had wanted her. One other
freshman wore no pin—stupid, fat Pearl Jones. Jean knew
she followed her, trying to corner her, to talk with her. As
Jean came into the room for her lunch-box, the girl rushed
at her.

"Say, aren't they the limit, stuck up?" she cried, her cheeks
moving up to her little eyes, venom in her voice.

Jean glanced behind her. Had anyone heard? Terrible,
to spit out your feeling like that! She looked at the little,
red-rimmed eyes. Poor Pearl! Who would ever want
her?

"Never mind, Pearl," she said, quickly. "It doesn't make
much difference."

But she seized her lunch-box and slipped away from the
building, out to a clump of firs. Their dragging branches
shut off the chill November wind; she could see the low,
gray sky through points of dark green. As she tried to eat,
someone called her. Jessie Smith. Jean shrank against the
rough trunk, but Jessie had seen her.

"Jean!" She sprawled beside her, her freckled nose
wrinkled earnestly. "I've been looking for you." Color
rose under her freckles. "They wanted me to ask you.
Well, you see, it's this way." Jean saw her Agora pin,
under her stubby fingers. "Your Agora senior, Mary Bird,
thought you were going Homerian. Emilia sort of rushed
you. She thought you didn't care about Agora. But she
wants to know—before you get your bid——"

Jean looked away. She could see yellow spheres circling
against the gray sky, as she strained her eyes and held her
lips firm. Shame! What could she say! Reject it? Mary

Bird was punishing her. Righteous, stern Mary Bird. Humbling her, because she had liked Emilia better!

"Don't be silly, Jean," Jessie's homely face was disturbed.

"If they wanted me—" Jean's voice was low—"why didn't they ask me?"

"They are! They do! They think you're the smartest girl in the freshman class. I guess you are, too. Come on, Jean." Jessie pushed her head through the scratchy branches. "Mary Bird's waiting, down in the Agora room."

And so Jean, cheeks burning, walked into the Agora room, and let Mary Bird pin the small emblem on her shirtwaist. The bitterness of her outcast morning lingered as a background for days, making her silent and awkward during the initiation ceremonies and the first weeks of the society meetings. She avoided the Homerian freshmen, but when she found Pearl Jones staring at her pin with red, hostile eyes, she felt ashamed of her jump of pride.

Then the freshmen had to take charge of a program.

"Write a funny story, Jean!"

A panicky excitement filled the week. Jean's thoughts rushed about her story. She had vague dreams of something beautiful—the pungent odor of fall among the great firs of the campus, the clear gold sky of a November sunset. But the girls wouldn't like that. Something funny. She wrote a burlesque, an imaginary dialogue of the faculty, with the Walrus, a gray Hippopotamus—that was the dean —a Giraffe—the thin young sister of the dean, who taught English—and so on through the menagerie, discussing the Agora girls. Jean was a mouse with a skinny tail in one corner. The dean had been friendly to her—not the same dean of women who had hated father. Jean felt sorry for her sister because the girls disliked her. She was part of their stock gossip, with her affairs with senior boys. Recklessly Jean shoved aside her sense of fine loyalty to them; you couldn't be funny and sympathetic at the same time.

When she came into the Agora meeting, she found the

Dean there, on the front row. What could she do! She
wanted to run. Then—if she said things, she ought to dare
say them before people! She would stay, would read everything she had written.

Her feet stuck to the floor when the president called her
name. Her voice boomed out fast, loud. Then, as the first
ripples of laughter broke the silence of her audience, she
forgot her terror. When finally the mouse crept out into
the empty office, hunting for a few crumbs which the faculty had left, and found a bit of Mary Bird, who had been
too tough to be entirely destroyed, Jean folded her sheets of
paper, looked down at the dean with a queer little smile,
and went to her seat.

All the dean said was, "You are a naughty little mouse,
Miss Winthrop! We'll have to be careful what crumbs
we leave for you!"

The girls were uproarious in their delight. "Let's have
Jean on the program every night," someone suggested, and
the clapping that followed washed into Jean's heart her first
conscious triumph.

II

At the end of the first semester, Agora gave a party, the
annual Agora Dance. Jean had been learning to dance.
Enough to go to the party, the girls insisted.

"But I don't know anyone to ask!"

"We'll find you a man. Plenty of them want to go to that
party!"

Jean shook her head, faint anticipatory terror rising. But
the girls were insistent.

Jean, on the committee for decorations, forgot her dread.
The party was to be given in the old Armory, a great bare
room.

"What can you do with a barn?" The committee stood
in the middle of the floor, staring around at the spaces, the
dusty windows. "Wax the floor and call it done!"

"We can do lots!" Jean squinted along the walls. "Lanterns over the globes, in our colors, black and gold. Alcoves, fir trees——" She grew ardent, incoherent, as a vision of transformation shimmered before her.

For days they worked on the lanterns, cardboard, with tissue paper designs. They piled up evergreen boughs; they draped yards of bunting. The Armory was lost in a strange disguise. "It's the best ever!"

Then one late afternoon, when the winter twilight had already settled over the gleaming snow, Jean waited at the side door of the dormitory with Rachel Cousins, a sophomore. She was to meet the *man*, who had consented to be taken by her to the party.

"What'll I say to him?" she wailed. "I don't know him!"

"Just ask him to go. There they are!"

Rachel introduced them. He was a friend of her man.

"Meet Miss Winthrop, Mr. White."

Jean stammered a "Glad to meet you," and found herself walking beside him, after the chattering couple. Short, stocky. His face looked red; perhaps that was just the twilight. Jean tried to chatter; she talked very fast, although she couldn't recall later a thing she had said. Finally the walk was ended.

"Lessee, you'll be out here?"

"Yes. I'm going to stay with Rachel that night. You come with Mr.—Mr. Rachel's man."

He laughed.

"That's good! I'll tell him that. Mr. Rachel's man!"

"Do you like him?" asked Rachel.

"I don't know. I talked so fast I'm hoarse. He said he'd go, anyway."

Jean resolved to make a conquest. She pushed out of mind the haunting recollection of a red face above stocky shoulders, and dreamed of floating to real music, an orchestra, with a man for a partner, a vague, shadowy man.

Rachel curled Jean's hair. It looked rather queer, but Rachel said it hid her high forehead.

"You look so—so smart!" Rachel complained. "That's why you don't have fellows. They don't like smart girls."

Jean looked wistfully at Rachel's pink silk dress, with the tiny ribbon rosebuds around the low V neck. She wore her white dress. She had asked for a new party dress, but mother said white was always pretty. She wished she had cut out the collar. Still, the bones showed at the base of her throat. Rachel's neck was beautiful, soft, round, without a bone!

"Try cocoa butter. Rub it on twice a day," suggested Rachel.

Then they went down to the parlor. Jean wore her winter coat, sighing again as she saw Rachel's blue cape.

There they were, Rachel's man, looking very tall and elegant in a dark blue suit, and her man—well, suppose he did have sandy hair and a reddish face! He looked—healthy!

Jean started toward the Armory, chattering wildly. Would she have enough to talk about the whole evening?

"Here are your programs." Jessie Smith stood in the cloak room, distributing them. Jean looked at hers. She had helped design them, and their jaunty black and gold lay in her hand like a rebuke to her rising panic.

"What do I do with them?" she asked Rachel, who stood preening before the little mirror.

"Fill them out, of course! One's yours, one's White's. Get dances for him. Here, I'll trade the second." Rachel scribbled her initials with the tiny gold pencil.

Jean stood at the entrance to the Armory. Across the floor came the whine of violins being tuned. The lanterns, the dusky alcoves, the gleam of the waxed floor bolstered her heart for a moment. Then she saw Mr. White, peering about under sandy lashes, and click! the band shut about her heart. What could she say to him? She had already said everything, everything!

Fill up your program, dance after dance. Jean went slowly toward him. The girls were drifting about, strange and beautiful creatures, in party dresses that floated and trailed about them.

"Do you like the decorations?" She stopped beside Mr. White.

"Real nice." He looked redder than ever.

"We cut out designs for the lanterns until I thought I was a pair of scissors." Jean's chatter began again. "Thought I'd come to the party and find myself with a light inside, turned into a lantern!"

"You did?" Mr. White stared blankly at her. "You did?"

Jean's chatter died abruptly. He couldn't see a joke!

"I have to get some partners for you." She tried again. That sounded ungracious. "Fill up the program. Who'd you like to dance with?"

His glance wandered about the hall.

"Oh, anybody," he said. "Lots of pretty girls here."

"Just wait, and I'll be back." Jean started valiantly on her task. She didn't know any of the men. She couldn't ask them. What did you do! She brushed past Rebecca Northwood, swaying in blue silk ruffles like a fresh sweet pea. "Would you trade a dance, Rebecca?" she begged.

"My program's all full, Jean. Haven't you made yours yet? Gracious! Who's your man? Don't know him." Rebecca floated away.

The music started for the first dance. Clumsily, her face scarlet, Jean edged her way back to the door. Mr. White had his arm around her, one hand warm and heavy between her shoulder blades, and they were off. Panic in her heart, fear in her feet. Could she dance! Was it a waltz or a two-step? She tried to remember which way to move her feet. Drops of perspiration between Mr. White's pale eyebrows. Did you have to talk as you danced! They collided with Rachel Cousins, and her man put out a warning hand.

Jean's nightmare began. The evening lost all reality. It grew horrible and vague, a viscous flood through which she wallowed, the terrible net of inexpertness enmeshing her. She was a stranger in a strange land, unversed in customs or language.

The second dance, with Rachel's man, was little better. He made kindly remarks about the decorations, but when

Jean tried to talk, her feet entangled themselves with his. His silence, when the orchestra began the encore, marked her as a failure there, too. Rachel whispered hastily as she came up with Mr. White, "Cheer up, Jean! This isn't a funeral! He's not so bad."

Jean tried again, that third dance. As if sinking, she came to the surface for a third frantic effort, scrambling and splashing. Mr. White's hand pressed moistly between her shoulders. Was it a waltz? She was trying—he slipped, recovered himself, and they stood, breathing heavily, in the middle of the floor.

"Have to get out of here," he muttered, and Jean sank for the last time. Sank into the thick flood of shame, of humiliation, of despair. Boiling oil had been easier to bear!

Midnight. The orchestra played "Home, Sweet Home," and the lights were lowered. The sentimental melancholy of the last waltz filled the hall like fragrance. Jean, huddled in her coat, her throat fuzzy past all power of speaking, walked toward the dormitory with Mr. White, silent and red, beside her. A choked, hasty, "Good-by!" and she fled past the lingering couples, through the hall to Rachel's room.

Rachel came in, humming "Home, Sweet Home," turned on the lights, and glanced at Jean, who sat white faced and rigid at the foot of the cot.

"Tired?" she asked, carelessly. "Wasn't it a grand party? That orchestra can play!" She tugged at the shoulder of her dress. "Unhook me, that's an angel child."

Jean, with fingers cold and dead, fumbled for the hooks. Rachel hadn't noticed! Perhaps no one had seen. Into her stark despair came an amazing thought. You could feel like that—as she had felt—as she felt now—and another person, a person near enough so that you touched her, did not know it! You could lie, drowned in the engulfing seas of humiliation, and no one would know, no one outside yourself.

"Did you like your man?" Rachel lifted her rustling pink

silk over her head and shook it out with little caressing movements of her soft white arms.

"No."

"Sort of stupid, I thought. I told Everett I didn't think much of his friend. He says he's a nice, honest fellow, though. Country boy. He couldn't dance. Walked on my feet as if I was one of his old cow paths."

Jean couldn't talk about him. She undressed quickly and lay in the dark on the narrow cot while bits of the evening, harassing, terrifying, drifted past her, like sea monsters along the vasty deeps where she had drowned.

"Anyway," said Rachel abruptly from her cot, "he ought to ask you to the spring party of his frat."

"No!" Jean gasped. "He won't!"

"He'll have to, after you took him."

"I won't go."

"How are you going to meet any man you do like, if you don't take what chance you get? That's the only way. All last year I went with a fellow I couldn't bear, and then in the spring I met Everett."

Jean did not answer. He wouldn't ask her! She knew. She was safe there. She would never go to a party again, as long as she lived.

"You ought to go to a men's party," murmured Rachel, sleepily. "Then they have to do the work. Lot's easier."

Jean wondered miserably whether she had a fever. Her cheeks burned, and her throat had a dry ache in spite of glass after glass of water. Would she be sick? Could she never sleep? That moist hand still pressed against her back. It had smudged her white dress. She tried to count sheep, jumping a wall. The third turned its head and stared at her with pale eyes between sandy lashes. Four, five, six, over they went, to the tune of "Home, Sweet Home."

In the morning she woke with a dry, hot feeling back of her eyes, as if she had not slept at all.

"Did you have a good time?" asked her mother, as she closed the front door and dropped the pasteboard box which held her white dress.

"Oh, pretty good." Jean turned away from her mother's eyes, to hide the resentment which leaped up. Why hadn't they taught her to dance? Other girls knew! Or how to act at parties, like the rest of the girls.

"You look half dead," said mother. "I suppose you talked all night, didn't you?"

"No, we went to sleep." Jean was halfway up the stairs.

"Your father didn't like your going with a boy we hadn't ever seen. Is he going to come to call?"

Jean pretended she had not heard.

She never spoke of that party again. For a time she feared that Rachel might bring it up. Rachel's silence gave Jean a new discomfort. Mr. White was a friend of Rachel's Everett. He had probably said things! But Jean never asked. The attrition of the days wore off the sharp pricking edges of her feverish recollections. One thing stayed; she was determined to dance well. Instead of sitting at the back of the society room, waiting for someone to notice her and ask her to dance, she grew bold in her ventures. Gradually she lost her consciousness of feet, and came to love the rhythmic motion. When Roger spoke of dancing, it was Jean's fiery insistence that gained him permission to use part of his weekly wage from the paper route in lessons at the assembly down town.

One thing in the college work held interest for her. Zoology had changed miraculously from the dissection of clammy corpses reeking of formaldehyde—frogs, cats, rabbits—to microscopic work on lower forms of life. Evolution! She remembered Darwin and her father, years ago. She loved it. She had learned to conceal her interest; it would mark her as a greasy grind! But the glowing hours of the spring were those in the laboratory, her eye screwed to the cold top of the microscope until the brass grew warm and pulled at her flesh, her hand poised over the drawing sheet, while she exulted in the etching-like sketches of the strange life she was finding. She speculated. The Bible was a story. Darwin was truth. The world wasn't made in a week. It was growing. Amœbas up to monkeys—monkeys, then people. No one made the world. It was making itself. Growth. Change. Constant, continuous, unfinished! That was the fascinating thought. Nothing done yet. In the making.

Then the year was over, with the final weeks of commencement parties, alumni reunions, commencement itself. Jean was again on a committee for the Agora party. When the girls asked whom she was taking, she grinned at them, as if she had an entertaining secret. The night of the party she wandered restlessly about the house, in aimless search for something to blunt the edge of her feeling—a mixture of disappointment and relief. She was a failure, as the girls counted things. She had been invited to not one of all the parties. She had no one to invite to her own society party. At least she was safely at home, with no dreadful repetition of another night that dwelt at the periphery of her consciousness, a haunting shadow.

III

Summer started with dusty premonition of disaster. Jean felt the swirls of hot air from the road grit on her temper. James had caught the whooping cough from a neighboring boy and had hacked himself thin and irritable. Jean spent hours with him, sitting on the floor, constructing marvelous scenes with the wooden clowns and animals of his Humpty Dumpty circus. Roger was driving a delivery wagon for a grocer. Sometimes Jean saw him in front of the grocery, a solemn, small boy perched under the huge cotton umbrella on the high seat in front of piles of baskets.

There was a new theme for disputation. Jean unraveled it slowly. Mr. Burgess, a restaurant keeper in town, wanted father to take charge of some land and sell it for him. Something was wrong about his wife.

"What's she got to do with it?" father shouted. "Money's money, isn't it? What difference 's it make what she was? He'll pay well for the work."

"I won't touch their dirty money. Made gambling and

selling booze, blood money of wives and children. You've let that—that woman work you! She's about your kind."

Father stamped out of the house.

One afternoon mother and Jean went down town. It was an adventure, starting off together. Mother's cheeks were pink, and her hair curled under the brim of her shabby little black hat. It was time she had a new one! The bow of ribbon hung rusty and limp over its wires. Jean helped her mother up the step of the car with a gesture of warm gallantry. Her mother was pretty when she felt well. If only she could have pretty clothes—a new waist as well as a hat. They sat together, talking in low tones, quite as if they were polite acquaintances.

"We'll buy you a hat like that one!" Jean pointed to an expanse of rose-bedecked green straw ahead of them. Then Jean and her mother giggled deliciously.

"Just my style," said mother. Then she added, seriously, "I hope I can find a nice fine straw, a small shape——"

"We'll look at Miss Purdy's store."

"We might go round and look first at several places." Mother's eyes were blue and soft. "I haven't had a new hat for three summers."

Mother waited at the foot of the stairs while Jean went up to the office to ask for the money father had said he would give them. Shoes for James, a hat for mother. Jean climbed reluctantly.

At the door she hesitated. People. A tall man with a shock of white hair over black eyes. A plump woman with chalky pink cheeks and a checked silk dress.

"Come in, Jean!" Father had his hasty, jovial air. "My daughter, Mrs. Burgess, Mr. Burgess. She's so big I hesitate to own her. Where's your mother, Jean?"

"She's waiting. She had an errand."

"Wants money, I bet." Father laughed, and Mr. Burgess joined him.

"Trust the women folks! That's their number."

"Tell her to come up," father blustered. "Want her to meet these folks."

"We had a good many things to do." Jean poised near the door, tiny flames of humiliation licking at her. She hated the jokes men made about money and women! Sometimes father wouldn't give her the money; he insisted that mother come up to the office. Jean was bruised, a buffer between contesting wills.

"Won't take but a minute to run up. Tell her I'm afraid you'll spend it all if she doesn't come."

Jean gazed at her father, warning and entreaty in her eyes, but he jerked away, scattering papers over his desk. Mrs. Burgess had scarcely looked at Jean; she watched the men, dimples in her plump cheeks, not soft dimples but hard, small dents.

Impotently Jean descended the stairs.

"Wouldn't he give it to you?" said mother, her mouth hardening.

"He wants you to come up." Jean frowned helplessly. Should she say that the Burgesses were there?

"What for? Who's up there?"

"I don't know them. Burgess——"

A sharp, explosive sound from her mother, a hand thrust out to grasp the handrail. Behind them the door of the clothing store swung open and the sleek head of Mr. Abrams, the proprietor, protruded a moment.

"How 'do," said Jean hastily, with a glance at mother. Mr. Abrams withdrew.

Her mother gasped. In the shadowy recess her face hung, fungus-white. Suddenly she darted to the street, Jean after her.

"Where are you going?" Jean could scarcely keep at her side without running. Her mother shook her head. "Wait for a car," begged Jean. But her mother went on, along the glaring sidewalk, her head down, her shoulders contracted.

Jean followed. They had meant to have such a nice time. Ice cream at the new candy store after the shopping. Spoiled.

"Mother, there's a car!"

"I don't want a car. We can't afford to ride. Let him ride around with that harlot. She's got an automobile. We can walk."

When they reached the house, mother rushed up to her room, and the bang of her door smote Jean as the final blow to the destruction of the day. James had seen them from the yard where he was playing, and came puffing into the library.

"Where's my shoes?"

Jean's lips trembled.

"We'll get them some other day, Jamesie," she consoled him. "We couldn't to-day."

"Wouldn't he give you the money?" asked James wisely.

"No. But never mind. What are you doing? Come outdoors and tell sister."

"Don't you care!" James tugged at her hand as they went out through the kitchen. "When I'm a big man then I'll give you lots and lots of dollars."

Jean hugged him.

"You're a darling kid brother!" she cried. "What do you want to do?"

"We been making a tightrope to walk. Only Hughie fell off and it bloodied his nose and his mother she said not to make it any more." James looked solemn, his blue eyes very round. "Folks does walk 'em only they have to learn first to walk 'em."

Jean laughed.

"Circus folks can walk them, but I guess it's pretty hard. Let's do something else. Let's go for a walk and see if there's any water in the brook."

They went down across the meadow, James clinging to Jean with his hard, warm little hand. Wisps of thought in Jean's head. Nice of me to take James for a walk. Might have sulked myself. Afternoon spoiled. Nice of me not to sulk. Don't cry any more. They can't make me feel so bad. James is sweet! Jean could see herself as a young girl taking her small brother into the woods when she might have yielded to bitter feelings. She had an indistinct vision

of herself dramatized. She laughed. Wasn't she silly?
She *liked* going with James.

"See me jump this gulf!" James balanced on a hummock, his thin body bent into an exaggerated horseshoe,
swung his arms violently, and landed a foot away on another
hummock.

"Can you jump this tree, do you think?" Jean pointed to
a milkweed stalk. She looked gravely at James. She loved
the way he listened to her nonsense, his blue eyes caught profoundly into hers, while he pushed beneath her mask of
seriousness.

"Prob'ly not." He poised again, pretended to breathe heavily. Then he jumped so elaborately that he landed in a
heap on the milkweed.

"Goodness!" Jean laughed, and he giggled, the fugitive
dimples about which Jean teased him coming in his cheeks.

He liked Jean's jokes. Sometimes she told him long,
grave stories of impossible happenings, piling up details
about the looks of the people or the place. Roger would
listen impatiently and break in with, "But that couldn't
happen, Jean! That isn't so!" James would listen, his face
as serious as Roger's, with a searching difference, a searching for the clue Jean would give him. Then they both
laughed and laughed.

When they came back to the house, father was just hurrying up the street.

"Where did you go?" Hostility bristled in his voice.

"Home."

"Why didn't you have your mother come up?"

"She wouldn't."

"I suppose you told her who was there?"

"She asked." Jean was sharply defensive.

"You needn't have said till she came up! She insulted
those people. I've got to make a good impression on them.
You weren't even civil yourself. You expect me to feed
you, don't you? They've got the power to make us
rich."

"You knew mother wouldn't come up! We'd planned

such a nice afternoon and you spoiled it!" cried Jean. "You know she doesn't like them."

"I suppose she's in a tantrum?"

Jean shrugged.

"One of her notions! That woman's perfectly respectable now. Has been for years. Respectable as anybody—as your mother!"

"What did she do?" Jean's curiosity dulled her anger. Her father was excited enough to be caught off guard.

"Some story your mother got hold of. She thinks Mrs. Burgess was a bad woman. Kept a house—you know. I tell you it isn't so! And if she did, her husband's rich and he wants me to sell that land. If you raked up everybody's past, where would we be? Good Lord!"

"She's upstairs. You better be careful."

"She can stay there. I'm not coming home to be rowed." He wheeled and was off down the street so fast the dust spurted from his feet.

Jean saw Roger coming, his face dirt-smeared, his thin, growing body slack and weary.

"Come on, Jamesie." She seized James's hand and ran toward the house, forcing a note of gayety into her voice. "We'll get supper for Roger and eat it out under the trees."

"Picnic?" cried James, in swift transition from his gloom. "Goodie!"

The summer twilight was cool and green under the great elm. Jean drew funny faces on the hard-boiled eggs, and James laughed so at his that he had to roll over and over on the grass. Roger told about a fat woman who had scolded him because the yeast was not in her order, and all the time it was there, under the bars of soap. Finally the boys went to bed, and Jean sat reading when her mother came noiselessly down the stairs.

"Didn't he come home?" she asked.

"Yes." Jean looked up. "He had to go back to the office."

"Important business!" Her mother sneered. "Jean—" she had a white intentness. "If that woman is ever in the

office, I don't want you to go inside the door. You oughtn't
to be in the same room. She's wicked."

"Why?" asked Jean cautiously. "She's married, isn't
she?" She had meditated upon her father's hasty comments but they eluded her.

"That doesn't change her! She—— Jean, I don't know
how to tell you. She kept a house of ill-fame. Young
girls—— That Burgess met her there! In her shame! If he
had no more shame than to marry her, does that change her?
She is defiled. I wouldn't breathe the air she breathes. Did
you speak to her?"

"No."

"I'd starve before I touched a penny of theirs! And if
your father won't listen to me, I'll go to them and tell them!
I'll tell the authorities. I won't be dragged into their mire!"

"I should think a person might be bad and then reform."
Jean was troubled. If her father could make lots of
money——

"Never! Not out of that life!"

Her mother's white rage silenced Jean. But she thought
about it for a long time before she slept. That was her
mother. Uncompromising. A straight, clear, unbending
sense of right and wrong. Father was different. He didn't
care. Was he wrong? Because he—well, because he was
less *good* than mother? Couldn't people ever change? Were
you always what you did, once? Things were like that in
books. People were one thing or the other. Jean didn't
feel that way. She wasn't sure—wasn't sure what was good
and what was bad, always. If it was all black and white,
rigid, unquestioned, then she must be bad. She had bad
thoughts. Well when mother was cross, she said, "You're
just like your father!" Maybe she was.

Jean never met the Burgesses again. She saw them one
day; their shining black automobile was a thing people
stopped to stare after. Father's deal with them had fallen
through, and she guessed vaguely that he blamed mother.
She wouldn't help him with it. But she never heard any
further discussion.

Perhaps it was the Burgesses that set mother packing her trunks with suppressed fury. Jean didn't know. She came in from the library one afternoon to find mother in the storeroom, piling things into the little trunks with their high, arched lids.

"What's the matter?" Jean peered at the disorder. Clothes, bundles of letters, everything.

"I'm going home." Mother crushed a winter coat into the trunk. "You can stay here if you want to. I'm going."

She would say nothing more, but Jean knew the storm signs, distended nostrils, wide, hard eyes, thin lips. James clung to Jean on the station platform as the evening train swung its headlight around the curve, and then they were gone.

Soberly Jean and Roger walked back to the quiet, empty house.

"Do you think she's gone for good?" asked Roger.

"I guess not. They always get over being mad."

As they came up to the porch, father rose, a stocky shadow, with a cigar glowing redly on his chin.

"Where's your mother?" he demanded.

"Gone to Mamie's." Jean was non-committal.

Her father sucked in his breath.

"Where'd she get the money?"

"I don't know."

"What did she say?"

"Nothing."

"She took James?"

"Yes."

Silence for a moment, the house bulking dark, ominous behind them.

"Well, she'll get over it. She'll be back soon enough." Father went into the house, and the sitting-room light leaping into the windows scattered the dark fear.

The next day Jean went about the house, putting it in order. In the storeroom, behind one of the locked trunks— why had her mother packed them, if she hadn't taken them? —Jean found a small package of letters. The string about them had slipped loose, and as she picked them up, they scattered. In grayish ink, the inscriptions were all, "Mr. J. Winthrop, Arcola, Ill." The date of the round postmark was too faint to read. The writing was her mother's fine, regular hand.

Jean sat down on the floor. They weren't her letters. Wicked to open them. But they were old letters. The pale ink, the yellowed edges. Her mother to her father, years ago. Not curiosity, but something deeper, tumultuous, driving the blood from her face into her heart so that it could scarcely beat, an inarticulate need to understand. Her fingers were stiff so that she dragged out the folded sheet clumsily.

The brief note opened in her hand. Like a long wailing note from violins, the phrases rose from the gray ink.

"My Beloved: One short week and we shall never again be separated. Katherine Stevens will be gone and I shall be your wife, your Helpmate. My darling, I pray that I may be worthy your great love. I dream of nothing but you."

Jean folded the sheet and slipped it into the envelope. She could not finish the note. Her finger-tips resting on the letters, she stared ahead, where motes gyrated slowly in the shaft of light from the tiny southern window. In her forehead a dull pounding. Her mother had been a girl then, scarcely older than Jean. Never had Jean thought of her as a girl, in love. What had they done? Beauty—— For a long time Jean sat motionless, a mourner in a ruined temple, where loathsome creatures crawled with slimy tracks over broken altars.

She thrust the letters out of sight behind the trunk. The phrases lingered, without words, merely the poignant vibration of a violin string.

As she went slowly downstairs, she gazed around at the rooms, strange now in their familiarity. The worn place by the register where the darns showed in the carpet. The chipped gilt frame on the dull oil painting of trees and a river. Dust on the rounds of the chairs. The faint sound of dissolution had ceased. She knew now. The tide of destruction was at the flood.

That afternoon an obscure restlessness drove her to the desk. She sat gravely with paper and pencil before her. What was it she wanted to say? A poem. The house where love once dwelt. She scribbled phrases on the paper. Ashes of roses. The rose of love has turned to gray. But she stared at them in disgust. The rhymes made her say things she hadn't thought of. The words sounded—well, like songs or poems she had heard. Not what she meant. She crumpled the sheet and, cupping her chin in the palm of her hand, made queer designs along the margin. A story! That was it. She wrote feverishly, page after page. A story of a girl who waited for her lover. She found a package of letters, her father's and mother's. They were divorced. When she came down the stairs—Althea, Jean named her, and she gave her gold hair and eyes like spring violets—she told her lover she would never marry. He departed, and Althea sank fainting on the stairs. Better keep love beautiful rather than destroy it!

Jean relaxed, looking at the sheets of paper on the desk. A strange excitement tingled through her; the aching pity of the morning had gone. What had she done? Her body felt light, weight-less, as if she had poured it out.

It was a wonderful story! She would send it away, to a magazine. She folded the sheets until she could push them into an envelope. That magazine on the desk—it had a section called "Storiettes." She would send hers to them!

After she had dropped the fat envelope in the postbox on the corner, panic seized her. If they published it, her mother would see it! She would know Jean had read the letters! Jean poked a stick under the clattering lid, but she couldn't touch the bottom. Should she wait for the postman and demand the letter? He wouldn't give it to her. Perhaps her mother wouldn't ever see the magazine.

For days Jean rushed into the hall at the postman's whistle. She found nothing but a letter from mother, or a bill for electricity. Never a letter from the magazine saying,

"Dear Miss Winthrop, we have received **your wonderful** story——" What else would they say?

IV

One afternoon, several weeks after mother's departure, the bell rang. Jean dropped her book and hurried to the door. David Sterrill stood there, red mounting under the steel blue line of his clean-shaven chin and lip as he saw her.

"David!" Jean held out her hand. "Why, you!"

"Hello," said David. "I had a vacation, and so I came."

"Come in." Jean retreated into the sitting room.

"Want to go up the river?" David seemed excited; he gulped at his words.

"I'd love to! Wait till I dress up." Jean ran to her room. She wished she had sewed instead of reading. Then the blue dress would have been ready to put on. She buttoned herself hastily into a fresh white blouse and rubbed the toes of her oxfords with an old stocking. Then she ran down again. David was walking around, staring at the pictures, the books.

"I haven't anything to take——"

"I had a lunch put up. Your father said you were home."

He had seen father! Did he, she wondered, know——

All the way to the boathouse David talked. He had never talked so much, Jean thought. About his job. About the stories he had covered. About the men in his office. About how lonely a city was. His eyebrows had grown heavier over the bridge of his nose; they gave him a perpetual frown above the thick lens of his glasses. He had a new suit, gray, oh, very stylish!

Jean settled into the cushions with a sigh of delight.

"I haven't been up river for ages!" She dabbled her fingers in the water, watched it ripple from the silent blade of the paddle, looked at the familiar shores slipping by them —the same ragged washings fluttering behind the shanties, the same stretch of meadow.

"Did you bring a book to-day?" she asked.

"No. I thought we'd talk." Red mounting again into David's dark pallor.

Something was gone. The old lazy comfort—perhaps the pillows weren't so soft. Tightness in the air.

A flurry of wind across the river where it widened at a bend plashed little waves against the canoe. The blue was gone. More wind, puckering the surface as it ran across the water.

"Gee, look at those clouds!" David pointed with the paddle, silvery drops gleaming on the polished wood. "Rain!"

He looked so unhappy that Jean laughed at him.

"Maybe it won't really rain," she said.

"We couldn't get back to shelter in time." David paddled violently. The trees swayed toward the water. "We'll have to land. You haven't even got a coat, have you?"

"I don't care if I get soaked!"

A flash of lightning, then a long rumble of thunder, which the river caught and held along its surface. The first drops, splashing up from rippled water.

David pointed the canoe shorewards. He helped Jean out, and dragged the canoe up the shelving bank.

"We can sit under this," he panted.

"Here!" Jean seized the gunwale and pulled. The canoe came up sulkily. Pillows on the ground, the canoe arching over at their backs, they sat in silence watching the rain rush across the river in a gray sheet. David tried to wrap his coat around Jean, but she pushed it away.

"I'm not cold. I think this is glorious!" Her face glowed, and she laughed when a clap of thunder startled her.

The rain ran over the edge of the canoe down their necks. It drove in on their feet. David opened the lunch box and found the sandwiches in a puddle.

"They taste just as good!" Jean grinned at him as she bit into hers.

"I wanted to have a good afternoon!" David mourned.

The daylight had been sucked into the storm. As they huddled in the half darkness, Jean felt again, more defi-

nitely, that strange tension. What was the matter with
David? What did he want? She turned toward him as a
sudden prolonged flash sent a green-white glare over his
face. His sleek black hair, shining wet, the black curling
hair along his arms, his eyes, mysterious behind gleaming
spectacles, his mouth twisted somberly—— Suddenly Jean
was afraid! He wanted something of her! She moved
away, a quick, wild motion, and the canoe rocked almost over
on them. She pushed her fear out of her thoughts, but it
lingered, heightening the storm excitement. She talked—
about anything—college, people David knew, books, anything.

Finally the rain stopped and the wind dropped abruptly.
The dark, wet world seemed amazingly quiet. Around them
was the steady dripping of drenched leaves, below them the
plash of the wind-driven river; but those were quiet sounds
after the storm. The strong odor of soaked forest mould
and the cool fragrance of wet leaves hung about them.

"We'd better start back." Jean stood up, stiff from her
long cramping. "Guess I must be getting old."

"You won't catch cold?" David rose near her, solicitous.

"Old, I said. Not cold!" Jean clasped a damp pillow
under one elbow and pulled at the canoe. Together they
slid it into the water. As David knelt to hold it for her, he
seized her hand, and Jean thought she heard a whispered,
"Please, Jean!" But she stepped hastily in, and settled herself.

"This pillow's oozing wet!" she cried. "Are yours dry?"

"Put my coat around you. I don't need it paddling."

"But it's your grand new suit, David! I'll wrinkle it."

"Pshaw! You take it!" David tossed it into her lap, and
Jean wriggled into the sleeves. It wasn't too big, much.
David wasn't much larger than she was. A paper crackled
in a pocket. She wondered what it was. A faint aroma of
pipe crinkled her nose.

"Do you smoke lots in your office?" she asked, as David
pushed out into the stream.

"Oh, some."

The collar scratched her neck. Woolly.

She could see David only as a dark shape in the stern. The river was a strange place at night. They had never stayed so late. It stretched between strange banks, where enormous trees never seen by day hung twisted branches. In silence they ran down with the current, pushing through the damp, cool fragrance of the woods. When David rubbed the bow along the dock Jean stared, amazed.

"Is that you, Jean?" The lighted doorway showed her father, hurrying down the platform, Roger after him. "Well, of all the crazy nonsense! What were you thinking of, going off in such a storm?"

"It wasn't a storm when we went." Jean climbed out of the canoe.

"I thought we'd better wait, Mr. Winthrop." Poor David, how wretched he sounded! "We turned up the canoe and kept pretty dry."

"In another minute I'd have sent a boat out in search of you!"

Jean smiled secretly. He was cross because he had worried!

"I'm all right, really, father." She tucked her hand into his arm an instant. "David gave me his coat and we ate soaked sandwiches and there's nothing to worry about."

"Well, don't do it again for the Lord's sake!"

"We've been down here hours," said Roger reproachfully. "Should-a thought you'd known better."

"We didn't, did we, David?" Jean laughed. "But we're all right."

"Come along, Roger. I've got to get back to the office. I've wasted enough time."

The boathouse keeper came out with a lantern, and David followed Jean to the street.

"I'm awfully sorry," he began miserably.

"Now there's nothing to be sorry about! He had to fuss because he was scared, but I loved it."

"Let's take a car. You'll get cold."

"We're sights!"

"You look all right. You always do." Jean retreated from the quaver in his voice.

"I don't mind." And, in fact, she rather enjoyed the short trip, with the conductor saying to David, "Got caught with your girl, eh?" and the passengers turning to look at her in David's coat.

As they hurried up the steps of the dark house, Jean said, "Aren't you hungry, David? Come on in, and I'll rustle up some food."

But David stopped in the hall and caught her wrist. His fingers were cold and hard.

"Jean!" he said, and the fear which had crouched all the evening just behind Jean's thoughts, leaped out, huge, dominant. "Jean!"

Jean dragged away from him, into the sitting room, and felt for the button; the light showed her David white, his lips quivering, his eyebrows ponderous.

"Jean!" He had her hand again, the fingers folded into his palm. "Please, Jean!" He was drawing her toward him.

"Oh, don't!" Jean had one hand against his lips before they reached her face. "Please!" A kind of sickening terror such as she had never felt rushed over her.

"Jean!" David's lips against her hand were hot, eager, "Jean!"

"Oh, no!" Jean begged frantically. "No!"

Suddenly David let her go. He stood back against the wall, his face so white that the dark lip and chin were smears on it.

"You don't like me!"

"Yes—but not that!"

"You don't." Rage, like the sudden wind on the river, rippled over his face. Its darkness threatened her. "You don't! You let me think you did! You don't know, all this time, the way I—I didn't do things—things the rest of the fellows did—because of you! I've been good, Jean. Keeping myself for you!"

Jean's teeth chattered when she tried to answer him.

"And all the time you didn't care! Maybe you've even got 'omebody else." He turned away, his hand over his eyes, and Jean's fear was melted into pity. His unhappiness threatened her far less——

"David." He did not move. "David, I do like you."

"Well, then!" His teeth shone out, strong, square. "Why don't you let me kiss you? I want to marry you. I've got money enough now. I've just been waiting, and——" He choked.

"No." Jean hesitated. "I don't know why—but never, never!"

He stared at her for an endless moment. His lips drew back from his teeth in a snarl, his face was a mask, black eyebrows, white teeth. He rushed out of the room, down the steps. Jean listened. She looked at her hand, steady—and saw the sleeve of his coat.

"David!" She saw him stop under the corner light. He would think she wanted—that! "Here's your coat!" She dragged it off and left it on the step. As she ran up to her room, she thought she heard him in the hall again, and panic filled her throat. But he did not come in.

She sat in the dark, her hands twisting. Why had she been so frightened? She wanted to put her head down on the pillow and cry. She wouldn't! David—— The dancing lights in his eyes. That dreadful shrinking within her—curds in her veins.

The thin mull blouse she had worn lay across a chair in the morning sunlight. She stared at it, her throat tightening. One sleeve was crumpled into a bright red stain from the pillow she had leaned against, in the rain. She scrubbed at the smear in vain. Then, sickening a little with an echo of her fear, she thrust the waist into the stove. She couldn't bear it! The mark seemed, in an incomprehensible way, to stand as a symbol for the evening, stirring her panic to fresh life. The acrid odor of burning cotton filled her with pleasure. Now she could forget.

For days Jean started at sudden noises. If the bell rang, she peeked from the parlor window before she went to the door. But David never came back. Presently she did forget her strange horror.

Father said nothing about the canoe trip. Jean suspected that he was rather ashamed of his temper, especially after Roger told her how he and father had walked back and forth on the bridge watching the storm, and how finally father had routed out the boathouse keeper and had sworn at him for renting a boat to young folks in such weather. Jean said,

"He was silly to make such a fuss," but secretly she was pleased.

Her father did ask about David one day.

"What did you do to that boy, Jean? He said he was going to be here a fortnight, and then he sneaked off without coming back to the office at all."

"I didn't do anything," Jean's eyes were remote, but she felt that recurrent flutter of panic.

V

Jean thought of clerking again. When she spoke of it, her father was loud in his rejection.

"If your mother goes off, someone's got to run the house. Roger and I are working. Your place is here."

Jean was apathetic. She had more time to read. She didn't care what happened to the house. When she washed dishes, she propped her books against the window sill over the sink. Easy to learn poems that way. Arnold's "The Forsaken Merman." She loved the swinging movement of that, like waves, and the pictures—clear green caverns, cool and deep. And "Dover Beach." The cool melancholy touched her. Ah, Love, let us be true to one another. Lovely words!

One morning as she leaned against the sink, dishes forgotten in cooling water, while she read a new poem—"My Last Duchess," this time—father came in with the breeze of a new idea rushing him along.

"Jean!" She turned. "There are some folks out here, Mr. and Mrs. Cochran, from the south. Mississippi. Here on business. If they can find a place to stay, I can pull off a big deal with Cochran. Got a nice little girl. Come meet 'em. Thought we might put them up here."

Jean, dismayed, followed his rush to the porch.

"My daughter, Jean." Father waved his hand. "Bigger than your girl, eh, Mrs. Cochran?"

"Well, well!" The man looked at her; florid, with bright blue eyes and sweeping mustaches, his suit a blue almost purple in its brightness, his heavy watch chain a cable across a rotund vest. His wife, small and dark, her slight figure moving restlessly in her chair. The little girl, long dark curls and petulant small mouth, ruffled silk dress.

"You-ah fathah thought we might have a room heah." The southern drawl sounded queer to Jean. "I cain't stand hotels, and Theodore wants to stay for business. Don't pull mothah's hand, pet."

"Just come right in and give the place the once over." Father led the way, knocking against a chair, his joking tones floating back to Jean.

She saw the house afresh through strange eyes. Dusty. Old. Shabby. What a mess it was in! She hadn't taken care of it. Father shouldn't have brought them!

They were on the porch again, and father bustled out to Jean, standing in the kitchen.

"They'll come. Now you just go get that woman who washes for your mother. Have her come and clean up. Ask her to help get dinner. We can see to breakfast. Twelve dollars a week they'll pay!"

"Father! Mother won't——"

"She's not here, is she? You can have half the money to buy something for her. Hurry along!"

The two weeks were curious. Jean watched the Cochrans intently. She had never seen outsiders at such close range. Mrs. Cochran hung about her huge husband, touching his arm, asking him questions with a fluttering lift in her voice, calling him pet names until Jean felt her cheeks grow warm. The little girl, Dora, was fretful; she didn't like any of James's toys and she didn't like Jean's stories. But Jean paid little attention to her. She was fascinated by the relation between the man and woman.

One night she sat on the porch after they had gone up to the front room. Their voices floated lazily out. Jean heard "De-ah," over and over. When her father came silently up the steps, Jean was crying, her head down on her arm.

"What's the matter?" He bent over her.

"Nothing." Jean choked. Then, violently, "They're so fond of each other—they say such nice things—— Oh, why aren't you and mother that way?"

Her father sat down heavily beside her, sighing.

"We are fond of each other, Jean." He paused. "We don't act the same way——"

Jean sniffed. Her sobs had stopped.

"There never was any other woman for me but your mother—never will be."

"But everything's so—so wrong!"

"Well, she has to say things. That's her way." He slumped in his chair. "She thought I was perfect. That was the trouble. When she found I wasn't, she couldn't stand it. So she tries to yank me up. I don't yank much. I ain't perfect. But I'm not as bad as she thinks I am and maybe she doesn't think so herself. She gets mad—— Don't you feel bad, Jean. It'll all come out in the wash."

"But things could be nice—— If you did what she wanted, and she didn't talk so——"

"What she wants! Damned if I know what she wants sometimes. I don't mean to start things. Not that I'm perfect. I'm not. Why, the first year we were married, I used to start off in the morning to college, and I had to go back a dozen times because she was crying so. Why? She was lonesome. She didn't like to stay home all alone. What could I do? Had to earn a living." Jean felt him brooding darkly over years past. "The first time she knew I smoked —you'd have thought I'd murdered someone. Jean, she made me cry! Like a baby! But later, I got hardened. Your mother's a good woman. She's a good deal better than we are. But she—she's not easy."

They sat in silence for some time. Jean went over, one by one, the things he had said. She heard a subtle undertone of apology, that repeated, "I'm not perfect." She was sorry she had cried.

"Maybe she'll feel better when she comes back." She rose. "Good night, father." She bent and kissed him, her arms tight about his neck for a straining moment. Then she ran up to her room. Oh, the pity of it, the pity of it! It ached in her breast like a great wound.

The next day Mr. Cochran came home with his floridness redder than usual, and his slurring accents more uncertain. When he had stumbled upstairs, Jean heard the familiar rumble of a family storm. When her father came in, she told him, a droll twinkle in her eye, as if she said, "After all, they do it, too!"

"She thinks he drinks too much," said father. "I guess he does. He isn't panning out very well. I'll be glad when they go."

Jean would be glad, too. When they came in for breakfast the next morning, she peered at the woman. Circles around her dark eyes, a tinge of red on the lower lids. Still calling Mr. Cochran "De-ah" in every sentence. Jean was sorry for her. She had a little jump of illumination. The woman called him pet names because she was afraid! Afraid of what he did when he was away from her. Afraid of what he might do to her! She glanced at the man. Sulky, his high color yellowed vaguely.

When they had gone, Jean demanded her twelve dollars. Father gave it reluctantly.

"I didn't get a thing out of him but words. Who's going to pay for the food they ate? I paid that Dutch woman you had helping you."

"You said I could have it." Jean was stubborn. "I earned it! I'm going to see Mamie and mother and Jamesie for a week, and I'm going to buy things for them."

Jean did not write that she was coming. The hack rattled up to the doorway of the little house. Mamie came running to the door.

"Why, Jean!" Her arms were warm about the girl. "How nice! Why didn't you tell me you were coming?"

"Wanted to surprise you!" Jean's hug swung her aunt clear off the floor. "Where's mother? And James?"

"James is over town. Your mother's in her room." Mamie turned her head slyly toward the rear door. "She stays there most of the time. She isn't well, Jean. I can't do a thing with her. She's—well——"

Steps in the next room, and mother was there, a thin, haggard whiteness on her face.

"Jean!"

Later Jean unpacked her valise, and drew out proudly the things she had bought. Silk gloves for mother and Mamie, a necktie for James, lots of things.

"Where'd you get the money?"

When Jean told her, mother cried.

"You let strangers come in my house, use my things——"

"They didn't hurt anything," protested Jean. She had known her mother wouldn't like it. Her gifts, vain placations, lay on the floor. "They've gone now."

That night Jean slept beside her mother, restlessly. She didn't like the consciousness of someone so near her. It haunted her dreams. She woke to find mother slipping quietly about the room, dressing.

"Did your father say anything about my coming back?" Her cheeks had bright pink flecks.

"He said to give you this." Jean reached under the bed to drag out her valise. "If you'd come home." She handed a sealed envelope to her mother.

Money! She saw the dull green of folded bills before mother had thrust it hastily away.

"I can't stand it here. Mamie doesn't want me. She acts as if I had no right here, in my father's house." Jean drew the sheet up to her chin, shivering at the bitterness in her mother's voice. "She's got so many old maidish ways, living alone. I think I'll go to-day. You can stay a while if you want to."

VI

Jean did not go back to college in the fall. Her mother was not well, there was little money, and after a few days of vague phantasy, in which Jean saw herself dramatized as heroic and self-sacrificing daughter, she offered to stay at home and keep house. The matter-of-fact way in which her offer was received disappointed her. But she stayed, concealing her feeling of righteousness.

By spring she looked over the winter as a wayfarer, caught in a stagnant marsh, might gaze back at the almost imperceptible signs of his trail. She had planned to study, French, painting, history. The French class: Alicia Jones, daughter of a hardware merchant, just back from a year in Paris, started a class while she worked up her vocal culture trade. An offer for a concert tour ended that; Jean could say, "Je ne parle pas français," and she had a few curious details of French life which Miss Jones had imparted in whispers.

Painting: hours in a cluttered, dusty attic, with Miss Margaret Pennington flying up the stairs to peer over her shoulder at the drawing board, to throw strange phrases at her before she hurried away in answer to the faint, querulous call of her crippled mother.

"You see too much, Miss Winthrop! Forget it, all but its essence! See that purple shadow that holds the leaves together."

She was gone, leaving Jean to stare at the spotty water color of the cyclamen, at the plant before her. What was its essence? She had been putting in leaf after leaf.

She thought Miss Pennington queer, at first. Faded, drab hair, skin with a pale gray bloom, eyes that narrowed in their gaze, as if to see only essences. Miss Pennington had meant to be a great artist. She had studied abroad. She had exhibited. She had taken Academy prizes. Her mother had been thrown from a carriage. "My brothers were married and busy, of course," said Miss Pennington, "so I came home to take care of her." Her father, an old man with apostolic beard and eyes, spent his days in the study, writing a history of the Pennington family.

Miss Pennington would come in, umber shadows about her eyes, a slight tremor on her lips. She would drag an old art magazine from the clutter along the walls, and hunt for some sketch. Then, her absorption laying petals of brilliant color in the hollows of her cheeks, she would talk of composition, pure color, line. Slowly Jean's feeling of awkwardness, her sense that Miss Pennington was *queer*, slipped away into a new recognition, one almost awe-touched. She was in the presence of a strange passion, a devotion not to a person, nor to a thing, but to creation itself, to beauty. Under that drab and worn body ran live currents, stronger than the prosaic ways her body followed. She gave Jean books to read, the notebooks of a dead artist, and Jean read, while the strings of her spirit grew taut. Here, too, the strange passion for creation. The struggle to project into paint and canvas something unique, something infinitely personal.

"I don't see what you do down there," said mother. "Your father pays a dollar for every lesson, and you haven't painted a picture yet."

Hesitantly, Jean took her mother with her one winter afternoon. She felt hostility in the shabby attic chamber. Her mother thought Miss Pennington *very* queer.

"You're just wasting time and money," she said, as they went home. "I don't want you going there any more."

"I'll paint you a picture soon," said Jean, pleadingly.

She asked her father why her mother didn't like Miss Pennington. She had stopped at the office for the dollar.

"Well—" father looked uneasy. "She's afraid—sometimes older women like that sort of take a fancy for young girls, strong, healthy girls like you."

Jean flushed. She heard, behind his words, dim accusation of something which threatened to smear the quiet, tense growth of this new beauty.

"You'd better plan to stop," said father.

Jean went hastily down to the old Pennington house. She

wouldn't stop! She couldn't. But Miss Pennington came to the door, subdued, ghostlike.

"My father's quite ill," she said. "I'm afraid I can't help you to-day."

Jean looked at her forlornly.

"I found that little verse I couldn't recall, and copied it for your scrap-book." She went to her desk and came back with a sheet of paper. "I'll let you know, if he's better."

Jean stopped at the corner to read the poem. The fine, slanting lines seemed like Miss Pennington.

> I have a little brook in the depths of my heart,
> What does it matter if the day be dark or drear?
> Colored like a tourmaline, winged like a lark,
> Voiced like a nightingale, and sings all the year.
>
> Small bright herbs on the banks of the stream,
> Moon-pale primroses and tapestries of fern.
> This is the reality and life is just a dream——
> Iridescent bubble that the moon tides turn.

Jean pasted the sheet into her old notebook. That was Miss Pennington. Something within her, more real than life itself.

She never went to the attic room again. Old Mr. Pennington died, and the shock, so the papers said, affected Mrs. Pennington seriously. Jean went down to the house, but the somber, drawn shades filled her with inarticulate fear, and she hurried away. Guilt, as if she had failed in a task, hung about her feet. A few days later she wrote to Miss Pennington, a stiff little note, and then she read in the evening paper that "Miss Pennington has taken her mother to the Brookfield Sanitarium. She will live in Brookfield in order to be near her mother."

But never again could Jean copy painstakingly a pen drawing of lovers, by Gibson. She was ashamed of the large sketch which she had framed and hung in the library with such silly pride. Perhaps she couldn't paint. At least she possessed, incoherently and vaguely, a new desire. Her own sketch of weeds, black above a stretch of snow, tiny mounds of snow caught in their dead leaves—that was hers!

The rest of the winter—— She had meant to be patient, sweet tempered. But queer things had happened to her disposition. The days when mother stayed in bed—— Jean felt them as a dreary chord, the notes resolving themselves into a darkened room, a white face on the pillow, dark hair straggling about it, slops to empty, trays to carry up, meals to prepare. Other days—— Jean found slight things mother said spurting flame, as if she were sandpaper! She didn't mean to be cross. But she smothered, caught in a stagnant marsh, standing unable to move. What did she want? Sweeping, dishes, food—over and over and over. The garbage pail, with its recurrent need of a scrubbing stood as a malodorous symbol. Her allegiance swung back to her father. He went away and she wasn't shut into a dull routine with him. Her mother felt that, in spite of Jean's attempt at disguise. One noon father forgot to bring in the groceries they had ordered.

"He expects to find food without buying it! Thinks we can make that of nothing, too!" Mother bent wearily to spear the baked potatoes. Snap! Jean's intention broke.

"After all," she cried hotly, "he is my father! I wish you wouldn't jaw at him all the time!"

Mother turned, her cheeks scarlet from the heat of the stove, her eyes terrible. She said nothing, but Jean slipped out of the kitchen aghast and defiant. It was true, wasn't it? She shouldn't have said it, but it was true!

That her mother remembered it she knew, a few days later, when out of some slight argument came a swift storm.

"Did you stay at home this year just to throw it up at me! Is that what you go sulking about! You needn't think you are so indispensable to me, you——"

Jean retreated to her room. It was her fault. She had been saucy, as her mother said. Where was that sweet vision of herself as noble, self-sacrificing daughter? Swiftly she linked herself with her father. What difference did it make what you did, or why? If she could get away! Anywhere!

During the early winter Jean had gone occasionally to the meetings of her society at the college, her sense of heroics sustaining her in the face of the girls' chatter of parties, exams, crushes. But as the winter drained the virtue from her heroics, leaving her dingy and subdued, she no longer cared to go.

On Sunday afternoon she went occasionally to call on Miss McNealy, the teacher who had followed Miss Adair in high school. On her way to the house Jean would think, "Suppose I told her everything! What would she think? Could she help me?" Then the hour in Miss McNealy's pleasant sitting room would drift past in talk of the weather, the sermon that morning, books. Jean, looking at the friendly, serene face, was unable to draw the talk from the elevated, impersonal level down to the unabashed intimacies she longed to pour out. "She would be shocked, and think I was wicked to say such things. Or she'd think I was exaggerating. I'm a child to her." So she sat self-consciously, hunting for answers to gentle inquiries as to what she thought of this or that, while within her rose a cry—egoistic and a little histrionic, perhaps, but nevertheless fundamental—"I am lonely, I don't know what to do! Help me!" She wondered at the animation with which an idea filled Miss McNealy. The decorum, the serenity, the assurance of Miss McNealy's thoughts stood before Jean in a curious mixture of barrier and ideal. The unattached tendrils of her affection pushed out around the woman. Perhaps some day they could be friends. Equal. "She can't really care what I think"——Jean was humble and grateful. "It's good of her to let me come."

VII

Spring grew into a cool rainy summer, with Jean scarcely aware of changing seasons. Then, after a violent flare-up, mother had packed her trunks again, taken James, and gone to Mamie's.

"Do you suppose she'll come back?" asked Roger that night, as he and Jean sat at supper. Father had not come home.

"She'll cool off at Mamie's." Jean was scornful.

"Say Jean——" Roger bent industriously over his plate, the tips of his ears reddening. "Say, I got some new clothes. Long pants. I'll have 'em Saturday. I'd of had them this week but I had to give some money to mother for her fare."

"Long pants!" Jean looked at Roger. He had grown tall, as tall as she.

"I'll be a senior next fall." He defended himself earnestly. "Would you go out to the Park some night next week? To dance? I can dance pretty well now. But I'd be scared to ask a girl to a party. I kind of thought if we went together, you could show me, you know."

"Of course!" Jean glowed softly. "We'll pretend I'm your girl."

"Can't go Saturday, on account of the store keeping open. But there's an awful tough bunch there Saturday. We don't have to mix with any of them, of course."

Roger, in his new blue serge, with long trousers, and a neat blue tie, very serious in his intention to learn just how to conduct a lady to a dance, was subtly different from the younger brother in knee pants.

"We'll pretend we aren't related at all," said Jean, "and then we'll have a much better time!"

The pavilion in the small park along the river was crowded. No one whom they knew. It was fun to stand at one side while Roger bought tickets for the dances, to wait for an opening between couples, to slip out on the floor. After the second evening Roger lost his sober concentration upon his feet, they lost their horror of a collision, and began to joke about the other couples.

"If there was some system as to how a fellow ought to act, now——" Roger unfolded the immaculate square of his handkerchief and wiped his forehead, glistening from the exertion of introducing Jean to a boy from the store, and being in turn introduced to the boy's girl. "Now I don't know *how* to act!"

"You did that all right, Roger." Jean's eyes threaded the crowd in search of the boy and girl. "No one would have known you weren't born introducing!"

"He wanted to trade a dance," said Roger, still miserable. "But I didn't want to dance with that Jane!"

"Nor me with him! He had pimples!" declared Jean succinctly.

"Should you say, 'Meet Mr. Smith, Miss Winthrop,' or 'Meet Miss Winthrop, Mr. Smith'? Or should you put the Jane in first, or what? I've got to know, if I'm going to parties." Roger's chin and solemn eyes had a fierce determination.

"Ladies first." Jean pondered. She was uncertain herself. "I think it sounds nicer to say, 'May I introduce you to—' don't you? Then you say, 'Pleased to meet you,' or something like that."

"Let's dance," sighed Roger. "I can do that pretty well now."

"You know," said Jean, one night late in the summer, as they sat in their favorite seat on the open car, just back of the motorman, and felt the cool breeze from the river— "you know, we have good times, Roger, when we don't act as if we belonged to a family."

"Let's act that way right along!" Roger pulled off his cap, and his high forehead gleamed above his spectacles. "Families are bunk! Thinking you have to nag at everybody, fuss over what they do!"

"We're sort of nice, now, aren't we?" Jean slipped her hand under his arm. "We don't fuss."

"I'd as soon go to a dance with you as any girl!"

"Well, I'd rather go with you than any boy I know."

Shy after such unwonted courtesies, they rode home in friendly silence. But they said good night solemnly, feeling that a compact had been made. Jean stretched out in bed in the comfortable relaxation that dancing gave her body, thought over their conversation, and the evening before it. The trouble with families was that they thought they had to butt in. With friends, you never said quite all you thought. You kept some things to yourself. Even if you were angry, or disapproving, you didn't always say so. If families could act that way! Maybe she could. With Roger. With James. With father—most of the time. With mother—she sighed. She felt strongly, without analysis, that her mother wouldn't permit such handling. She would insist upon coming in. What was it? Jean had the feeling without an adequate word. A feeling of an intense personal attitude. Perhaps mothers had to feel that way.

She and Roger would be friends. Roger was nice. Thoughtful. Quiet. He didn't lose his temper. He hadn't once suggested that Jean ought to have a fellow of her own, like the other girls at the Park.

A letter from Mamie. Mother must have some money. She was sick, and she wouldn't have a doctor because she had no money.

"Tell her to come home. Doctors enough here," blustered father when Jean showed him the letter. She had hidden the last sheet, where Mamie had written, "Your father ought to be ashamed, letting her come home penniless."

"But if she's sick, she can't come back, can she?" urged Jean.

"She makes herself sick."

Roger pushed his chair back from the table, his face white.

"If you won't send it to her," he said, his voice husky, "I'll borrow it and tell 'em what I want it for!"

Jean jumped to her feet as her father's face reddened and the vein bulged on his forehead.

"Father'll send it, Roger." Her voice begged for peace. Roger looked at her, his eyebrows threatening.

"When I ask you to tell me how to run my affairs!" roared father.

"Now see here!" Jean spoke hurriedly. "What's the use of getting mad? You'll be late to work, Roger." She laid her hand on the boy's arm and propelled him toward the door, feeling the tense quiver of his muscles. "Don't say anything, Roger!" she whispered. "I'll get him to send some. You keep your shirt on!" She squeezed his arm, heard his low, determined, "I meant it, just the same!"

"Impertinent young whippersnapper!" Her father stood by the table, but Jean noticed, even in her distress, that he made no move to follow Roger.

"He was worried," said Jean. "After all, mother's our affair, too. You'd better help her out."

"When she deserts me for weeks at a time?"

"If she's sick, she's better off thei e."

"You're all siding with her against me!"

"I'm not siding." Jean pressed her lips together. She mustn't flare up! There was a queer twitching in her father's cheek.

"Send her that!" He threw a crumpled wad of bills on the table. "Tell her it's the last cent I'll give her unless she comes back where she belongs!"

When he had gone, Jean counted the bills. Eighteen dollars. She left the breakfast table in disorder, and hurried to the postoffice, distressed that she had to break one of the bills to pay for the money order. At least she had sent the money.

She told Roger that evening. She wanted to add, "You must be careful how you talk," but she swallowed the words. That would sound too much like fussing. Roger stared at her, as if he felt and resented her warning.

"He'd better look out!" he exclaimed. "He ought to support his wife! He has money enough for what he wants. Look at those game cocks he's bought!"

Jean nodded. The new chickens in the poultry yard worried her. When mother saw them!

School opened the day after Labor Day, and Roger went off light-heartedly in his new long pants. He came into the kitchen that Tuesday night to stand silently near Jean, who was paring apples for sauce.

"How'd school go?" Jean asked. Then she noticed Roger's face, tired hollows in his cheeks.

"Don't know. Say, is *he* home yet?"

"No. What's the matter, Roger?"

"He says I can't go back to school. He was waiting on the corner this morning. Says he can't support us all in idleness. If I spent all my money on clothes and dances this summer, then I can go on working. That's what's the matter." He sat down by the table, his shoulders dejected.

"Roger!" Jean was aghast. "Not go—why, it's your senior year!"

"What can I do?"

"Is that all he said?"

"Oh, he got off a lot more about how he wasn't making anything and we ate it all up and everything."

Jean dug her knife into the apple.

"You can't stop!" Was Roger going to cry? His eyes were bright, and his straight lips quivered. "Maybe I could persuade him——"

Roger shook his head.

"No use. He's set. Old Thomas will pay me more, now the other fellows are gone. I thought some of running away, but I couldn't make enough outside of school to pay my board.

"I'll get a job," cried Jean. "Then you can go back."

"He says you'd better get to work, too. He says he's earned as much as any man ought to have to. He's got it all added up. Twenty thousand or something. I don't know."

"If mother were here, she wouldn't stand for it."

"And he says education's no use anyway. Maybe it isn't. I can get quite a lot after a while, prob'ly."

"Oh, Roger! Only hicks and low-down folks take their children out of school! You've got to go on. To college, too!"

"Sh-h! He's coming!"

After a silent supper, Jean, feeling that she twisted her slim courage like a rope between her hands, went out to the porch where her father sat smoking.

"He's such a good boy, faithful, hard working," she finished her breathless plea.

"He's an impertinent upstart, that's what he is!" answered her father. "He told me I ought to be earning more! He can taste his own medicine."

"Mother will——"

"She can say what she pleases. She's not here. I'm running things."

Roger was waiting at the top of the stairs. Jean shook her head in dumb misery.

"I told you so," said Roger.

"I'm going to write to mother."

"Better not. Just stir up an awful row." Roger went off to bed.

The next morning as Jean watched him hurry down the street in his shabby work clothes, instead of his blue serge, and thought how he had pressed his suit so carefully on Monday evening, she bit her lip furiously to keep the tears from falling. She would write mother. A row would be over, some day. Surely Roger was worth it!

At noon she sat at the desk, screwing her forehead in an effort to tell the story in phrases which might have some conciliatory effect. Suddenly she heard the clear, light vibration of James's voice.

"Jamesie!" She ran to the door, and bent to hug him in frantic joy. "Why, Jamesie!" Mother stood behind him, suitcase dragging at her arm. "Mother!" Shame, despair, relief, all went into her straining embrace. "Oh, I'm glad you've come back!"

"I felt a little better," said mother, as she dropped into a chair and unpinned her hat. She pushed her fingers through the fine hair flattened on her temples. "The doctor thought I ought not to come yet, but school begins this week."

"Oh, yes!" Jean hovered near her, one arm around James's shoulders. "You've grown, Jimmy!" she sang out. "You're most as big as sister!"

James went off to explore the house and yard, in quest of change during his absence.

"Is Roger in school?"

"No." Jean looked at her mother. How could she put it best, so that mother would *do* something. "I was just writing to you."

"Your father kept him out!" Mother laid one hand over her heart. "I felt it here. I knew something was wrong. That's why I came. I wasn't fit to travel. I knew something was wrong, something needed me."

"He—he said he couldn't afford——"

Mother nodded. Her eyes had a strange, withdrawn gaze, almost, thought Jean, as if she communed with a secret voice which had warned her homewards. She rose and pinned her hat on again.

"Where're you going?" Jean was frightened at the tense remoteness of her face.

"Down town. To see him."

Jean never knew what was said. Roger came flying home and up the stairs. Jean, hurrying after him, found him throwing his old clothes off, dragging his best trousers on, swift repressed joy in his face, in his movements.

"Golly!" he cried. "Guess I haven't missed much! First day doesn't count!"

"You're going back?"

"You got it! Watch my smoke!" He rushed down the stairs.

"Had your dinner?" Jean shrieked after him.

"Haven't got time!"

"Roger, you come eat something!" She fled after him, pulled him into the kitchen. "Here's bread and butter and milk——"

Mother came home presently; she sat down in the library, and stared at the books in the cases, still with her remote, white face. She refused Jean's suggestion of dinner.

"College opens next week," she said abruptly. "You're going back this year." Then, tensely, "I guess you children need me some, after all!"

What had she said? How had she done this? Jean wondered, but she did not dare ask. There was never any reference, that winter, to mother's mysterious and potent interview.

Father went with Jean to the college, to arrange her work. Jean watched, with a furtive hostility, his animation in the discussion of courses and program. How could he, after what he had said about schools? Suddenly her hostility was washed away in a rise of pity. He wasn't pretending! This was a spurt of an old enthusiasm. Suspicion, alert and piercing: he had kept Roger out of school because of mother! To make her come back.

She pushed away her thoughts to listen to the discussion. The dean suggested a regular course this year. The course for women, leading to a certificate in domestic science and art. Jean grew rigid with protest.

"The supply of such teachers is small as yet," said the dean in her brisk, professional manner. "The salaries paid are much higher than those usually given women."

"But I don't want to teach cooking and sewing!" Jean cried.

"Peculiarly fitted to women," went on the dean with suave ignoring of Jean's protest. "Salaries almost as high as those paid to men!"

"I'd rather starve!" Jean sat forward, intent, determined. "I want to teach Latin or English or anything with thinking in it!"

"My daughter is not very domestic," said father, with a jocular air. "She will never be a domestic artist."

The dean smiled, and lifted a deprecating hand to the sleek, austere braids about her forehead.

"Of course, I suggest the practical aim."

"Can't I take just what I like? History and economics and——"

"The president is discouraging specials." Jean was on the point of declaring that she wouldn't come, then, when the dean added, "But Miss Winthrop's record is so uniformly good that perhaps, if she does not choose too light a program——"

So it was settled. When the girls gossiped about the

positions last year's seniors held, with salaries up over the
thousand mark, Jean grinned and said, "Ought to be worth
more, keeping your nose in a bread pan for a year!"

VIII

She liked that fall term. She liked the scarcely concealed
deference the freshmen gave her as an upper classman, and
a society member. She rushed a freshman from town, Cordelia Peavy, a slender brown-eyed girl whose family had just
moved to town. Cordelia flirted with everyone, boy or girl,
lifting her eyelids suddenly over her large, wistful eyes, turning her small head gracefully on her slim throat. Jean liked
to make her laugh, to see her small shining teeth, like kernels
of young corn.

"Why don't you have beaus, Jean? You're as pretty as
lots of girls who get them!" asked Cordelia one afternoon, as
they waited for the streetcar.

"I can't roll my limpid eyes at them the way you do!"

"Your eyes aren't bad," said Cordelia seriously. She
had been initiated into Agora the week before, and her
deference toward Jean had shifted into an attitude of spon-
soring. "I'm going to get you a man for the fall party.
There's a boy here I knew in Owosso. He can dance, oh,
grand! He's on the football team, and he's sort of fun.
Luther Wallace. You wait!"

"I couldn't, Cordelia! I wouldn't know what to say to
him!"

"Never say anything much to a man." The girls climbed
into the car and sat down together. "Let him say it! Ask
him what he's been doing, you know, anything. Then you
listen. That's what they like. I expect you know so much
you scare them off."

Jean stood at the window of the town girls' room; her
chin came just to the high sill, her eyes were on the level
of the ground outside the building. The November twilight
threw mysterious shadows under the dark pine boughs and
into the hollows of the campus. She could see, between the

branches of the great white pine above her, the broken shimmer of light in one of the faculty houses beyond. The wet pine needles reflected the light in brittle stars.

"Jean!" She turned her head. "I was afraid you had gone!" Cordelia's pointed face hung dimly at the door. "Luther's out here, and Shelley. They belong to the same frat! Isn't that sweet? We can go to their fall party together. Come along. Luther's crazy to meet you. I told him your real man had gone away, David, you know. And so—but come on! They're waiting."

"Cordelia! I said I didn't want to meet him." Jean crossed slowly to the door.

"Piffle! You do too!" Cordelia seized her hand with small chill fingers and ran down the corridor to the side door.

In the shadow at the rim of light spilled from the overhead lamp lurked two figures. They stepped forward. Shelley—— Jean had met him. Cordelia's present follower. She didn't like him. He was too dark and saturnine, with bristling eyebrows and bushy hair over a square forehead. She said hello nonchalantly and then looked at the other boy, Luther Wallace. He shook hands gravely. Tall, broad, fair, his nose hooked slightly—baseball hit it, he explained later—mouth like a small boy's, with protruding upper lip.

"Well," giggled Cordelia, "now let's go down by the bridge and get acquainted. Luther, you behave yourself!"

"'Slong's you aren't too close!" Luther slipped his hand under Jean's elbow. "Cordelia's a caution, isn't she?" He had to bend his head to look at Jean.

"Isn't she just?" They walked around the building, down the graveled path to the small bridge across the brook. Cordelia's light voice through the dusk spurred Jean. She would act like Cordelia, if boys liked that!

"Don't call me Mister! Makes me sound like a grandpa!" Luther had his face close to hers.

"All right." Jean edged away from him, leaning against the rail. "This your first year?"

"Do I look that green! You weren't here last year, though, were you?"

"No. I was home."

"I knew I'd remember if I'd seen you."

"You haven't seen me yet! It's too dark——"

"Here, what are you doing?" Cordelia and Shelley loitered up to them, shadowy blurs in the night.

"Never you mind!" Luther laughed. "Give us time!"

"You interrupted just as I was going to propose——" Jean stopped at Cordelia's giggle. That was a good joke— their kind! "—Propose that Luther go to our party."

"You bet!" sung out Luther. "Let's try a step here!" And whistling softly he pulled Jean into his arm, and danced along the rough planks. Cordelia and Shelley whirled slowly behind them. The soft whistle, the slow rhythm, the pale gleam of the threaded water below—Jean loved it! She would make him like her. She didn't care how silly she acted. This was *life!*

The boys walked to the car station, and Jean settled into her seat after a last glimpse of Luther sweeping his cap in a broad circle of farewell.

"Do you like him?" Cordelia wriggled down against Jean's shoulder. "You got on fine!"

"He's just a kid, isn't he?"

"He's a grand dancer," declared Cordelia, on the defen- sive. "And I think he's good-looking."

"I can manage him," said Jean. Her cheeks were warm; her blood ran swiftly, singing. In the snatched dance she had felt challenge.

"I ought to tell you"—Cordelia glanced sidewise at her, her small nose wrinkled amusingly—"he's sort of soft, you know. But he's nice. I used to go with him a little. His mother keeps a store. He's her only child, sort of spoiled, you know."

Jean had a new dress for the party. Soft blue silk mull. Mother made it for her, working feverishly over the folds of the skirt, the line of embroidery at neck and sleeves.

"It's a darling." Jean stood in front of the dresser, the

mirror tipped back to reflect every inch. "I'd better curl my hair."

"If you weren't so skinny, it would be easier to make a party dress for you." Mother tugged at the belt. "But that isn't bad."

"Wish I had some party slippers." Jean still stared at her image.

"We'll rub whiting on those pumps. Don't scowl so, Jean."

Jean turned away, sighing. She thought, "No matter what I wear, I look—well, as if I liked to read and things——" She had seen a figure tall, a little angular, slim hipped; a face long, with high forehead and rather wide mouth, eyes far apart, wistful and blue. She could not see the swift mobility, the light floating of moods over lips and eyes, the quick change of color in her clear skin.

"Hold your shoulders back, too. You read so much you've got a regular bookworm's curve." Mother looked at her with restrained pride. "But you needn't be ashamed of your looks, Jean."

"Gee, you're some Jane!" exclaimed Roger, the night of the party.

"Do I really look all right?" Jean revolved before him.

"Wish I was your fellow to-night!"

Jean's eyes shone.

"You get a girl, Roger, and I'll get you a bid to the next party."

Luther had come. She heard his deep voice in the hall. She hurried down-stairs, panic just at her heels. Would she be scared again? Would she—but when she saw him, tall and straight, his suit pressed into knife lines, the aroma of powder and shaving soap faint from his clean, ruddy skin, she slipped into her winter coat and went off with him, gay as Cordelia herself.

She felt as if she had laid aside an old Jean, a dull, sober, humdrum creature, and taken on a new self, incredibly light, given to quick laughter, part of the music itself. Even the dances with strange men failed to break her mood.

"Don't trade too many dances," begged Luther. "I like to dance with you! You just fit."

When Luther said good night, on the steps of the dark porch, he held her hand closely. Jean's heart leaped within her. But he dropped her hand, said, "Then I'll come down Sunday, yes?" and dashed off, to catch the last car back to college.

Luther came on Sunday. Jean had dusted and straightened the parlor, had waited in a panic of excitement. Suppose he might not, after all, desire to come. They made fudge. James had a special saucer full as a bribe to stay out of the parlor. Then Luther wanted to sing. He had brought some songs. Jean tried the accompaniments gingerly. "Dreaming, dreaming, of you, Sweetheart, I am dreaming!" Luther's pleasant tenor voice filled the room. If he flatted occasionally, Jean was uncritical. He had a way of leaning toward her, his eyes significant above his pompously moving lips, when he sang, "Dre-eaming of you when the li-ights are low!" Another song. "Love me and the world is mine." The accompaniment to that was full of chords, whole handfuls of notes.

"You leave that and I'll try it over," said Jean. Then Luther spread the next on the piano rack.

The next day Cordelia told Jean with triumph that Shelley had said, "Luther's got an awful case! He thought that girl was one of these brainy skirts, but you'd never know it!" And Jean listened, her delight easing a subtle, curious prick of shame.

That was the beginning of a winter different from any Jean had known. Friday evenings she and Luther went to the Assembly in town, where they could dance every dance together if they liked. One Friday Shelley was out of town.

"I can't go to Assembly to-night," mourned Cordelia.

"Say"— Jean hesitated. "Would you like to have Roger take you? He's a good dancer." She was half sorry she had spoken when she saw Cordelia's dark eyes widen with delight.

"Sure! He's a sweet boy. Would he take me?"

Would Cordelia try to ensnare Roger? She flirted with anything! She even rolled her eyes at Mr. Winthrop! Well——

"I'll ask him to-night and he can telephone you. After supper."

"Aw, you're stringing me," replied Roger, when Jean proposed the plan. "She's got a steady."

"He's home this week. She—I think you'd have a good time. The boys like her."

"Sure." Roger abandoned his caution. "She's a good looker, and she doesn't look very old——"

"Don't let her jolly you too much," warned Jean. "She has a way——"

"I know her kind! Baby doll! I guess I can jolly her along, too. What's her number?"

Jean watched Roger and Cordelia during the first dance. She had never seen Roger with a girl before. He was good-looking. His shoulders had broadened, and he carried his head well up, a kind of stubborn, clean integrity about his face and manner. Cordelia was fluttering her eyelids at him as if he were a college boy. They came up to the chairs where Jean and Luther sat.

"May I have the next waltz, Miss Winthrop?"

Jean gave his arm a little hug as they stood, catching the beat of the music. "Glad you came?" she said.

"Sure!" Roger swung her off, expertly. "She's like a feather, dancing. She thinks I'm falling for her!" He grinned at Jean.

Luther had a new dance. The Barn Dance. When the melancholy little gray-headed pianist began to bang out a twostep, he led Jean out to try it. One, two, three, kick! One, two, three, kick! One, kick! Around they went. A rollicking, breathless dance. Roger and Cordelia had to learn it. Then, every twostep, off the four went. People watched them, enviously. It was thrilling!

The next morning Jean came sleepily down to breakfast just as Roger was hurrying off to work.

"Hello!"

"One, two, three, kick!" He whirled her around in the little hall. "Some dance!"

Jean yawned.

"Awful sleepy. Aren't you?"

"I got to hustle along. Say—" he stopped just outside the door. "Do you *like* that girl?"

"Didn't you?" Jean shivered in the cold morning air. "Oh, she's all right, I guess." Roger stared, as if he might have added more.

"She's good-hearted," said Jean abruptly. She knew what Roger was thinking, behind his gleaming spectacles! "I feel sorry for her, sometimes. She likes me."

"I just thought—— She's a funny kind for you to pick! So long!"

Jean stood in the hall. Cordelia's presence rose near her, not so much a visual image, as an impression, tone of voice, gestures, a dimly recognized effect of Cordelia as a person. Did she like her? What had she meant, saying she was sorry for her? Roger was critical of her. She had wanted him to know she understood Cordelia, wasn't fooled by her. She was sorry. Something flimsy, brittle, exerting every— every eyelash! Trying so hard to make her clothes look nice——

"Jean! Come eat your breakfast if you are up. I'd like to get this family fed sometime to-day!"

Saturdays Luther often met her after society, and walked across the campus to the car. Sundays he came to the house; fudge and songs.

"Who is that fellow that's hanging around here all the time?" demanded father one Sunday. "Are you going to college or have you lost your head?"

Jean flamed, but before she spoke, mother said, sharply,

"He's a decent boy, and I for one am glad Jean is acting more like normal girls instead of sitting around with her nose in a book every minute."

"Well, I'm footing the bills. You can't burn your candle at both ends. Out nights——"

"Just once or twice a week!" cried Jean. "My work's all right, too. Just ask anybody!"

IX

When, in May, she wanted a new dress for the Commencement party, father refused.

"You've had one party dress this year. That's more'n I can afford."

"Then I won't go!" Jean slammed the door of her room after her. She stood at the window, pressing her fists against her hot cheeks, when mother opened the door.

"I think that dress will do, Jean." She sat down on the bed. "He won't give me money for another."

"I've worn it everywhere all winter!"

"If you had long gloves and new slippers?"

"He wouldn't buy those. The other girls are having silk dresses."

"I've got a little money. I saved it from the groceries. White kid gloves——"

Jean lost her anger suddenly.

"Mother! Could I?"

Luther wanted a girl for a friend of his.

"Nice fellow. Sort of quiet, but a good sort. Know any girl like you?"

"No." Jean gave him a little sidewise grin, a trick she had borrowed from Cordelia. "Aren't any like me!"

"Sure, I know that! I didn't mean that, but any girl, nice, you know?"

"Well, there's Lora Tate." Jean had seen her the week before, and Lora had sighed at Jean's glowing tales of the winter. Lora was sick of office work. "She can dance, and she's real nice."

So Luther and Jean took Percy Johnson to call on Lora. Percy was solemn, stocky, literal minded, earnest. Luther shone beside him. But Lora, fluttering gently in her limp, ruffled dress, said she'd be pleased to go with Mr. Johnson.

Jean held out her arms in the long white kid gloves.

Amazingly elegant! They covered her nubbly elbows. They wrinkled sleekly over her arms. She scarcely minded her old dress; she had pressed it carefully, and the smudged place in the back where moist hands had rested didn't show in the mirror.

Cordelia had a new white dress. Princess style. She had made it herself. She had fastened her best corset about a pillow, bulging it above and below, and fitted the dress to that. It clung snugly to her slight, graceful waist. "Sags a little," said Cordelia. "But no man looks at that!"

It was Jean's first all-night party. She was tired, a little, at midnight, but strangely, with the next dance, she seemed lifted into a new region, where exhaustion never entered, where nothing dwelt but the drifting music, and Luther's eyes, blue, ardent, his warm breath on her cheek, the pressure of his arm about her waist. During an intermission they wandered out of the Armory, along the path. Suddenly ahead of them, just a glimmer in the dark trees, Jean saw Cordelia, a black sleeve around her shoulder, her face tipped back. Shelley! Even as Jean glimpsed them, Shelley's head shut out the blur of Cordelia's face. Jean turned quickly, queer hot pricklings of embarrassment running over her. Had Luther seen? He was silent as they returned to the lighted doorway.

It was strange to see the lights through the massed paper flowers grow pale, and the windows lose their opaque reflections, as the dark beyond them changed into gray. Dawn! Jean watched the faces floating past her. Flushed, some of the girls with hair straggling down, out of curl, some of them pale, shadows under their eyes. Suddenly the gray was luminous white. Night had gone. The orchestra began "Home, Sweet Home." The lights under the crumpled flowers were out. Jean, scarcely conscious of the movement of her body, felt Luther's arms lift her, carry her to the slow, languid waltz. Did she love him? He was so big and strong.

A special car waited for the town guests. Jean heard Lora's soft, "Wasn't it a grand party!" but she did not wish to talk. She leaned against Luther's shoulder, seeing through drooping eyelids the fields faintly green, as if color just stirred and woke.

"Sleepy?" Luther whispered above her. Jean shook her head.

They stood on the porch, the street quiet, the houses with drawn shades shutting them together in a queer hushed moment.

"Tired?" Luther whispered again. "My girl all tired?"

"No." Jean looked up at him. She was trying to see him—the real him behind his blue shining eyes. "No, I'm not tired." How strange it seemed, to dance through a night, and find morning again while they stood there, still together.

"Jean!" He had his arms about her, and his lips were on hers, warm, eager, in a long suffocating kiss. "There!" He looked at her, awkwardly. "I've wanted to kiss you all winter! I didn't know as you'd like it."

Jean's hands were against his breast. She felt the tense trembling of his body. Within her there floated something delicate, infrangible. She did not hear him, she did not see him. She swayed slightly, and he held her again, kissing her eyelids, her cheeks, her lips. Docile, submissive, expectant, that strange ecstatic lightness lifting her, holding her up to his lips.

"You're awful sweet!" His husky voice came close to her ear. "I've wanted to kiss you all winter. Didn't know—— Think what we've missed!"

Jean pushed away from him, her eyes dilated. What was he saying?

"All the fun we might have had!"

Why must he talk! If he would only—— Suddenly she saw him, his face flushed, his lips tremulous, parted. She didn't like him! She felt a wrench, as if part of the old Jean, hard, scornful, pried apart the new, soft quivering flesh, and entered home. She saw him, she wanted him to kiss her, but this wasn't love! It was——

"So long, Jean!" He held her firmly, while the inner,

scornful self jeered up at the ecstatic lightness. "Don't want to go bye-bye."

How silly he sounded! Dolorous! Jean slipped out of his arms and opened the door.

"Good-by," she said clearly, and did not watch him down the street.

Wearily she undressed. The tips of her beautiful gloves were dingy. The flush of dawn touched the familiar things about her with soft crimson tones. She shut her eyes, to feel that kiss again, soft, insidious, seeking out her veins with strange new languors. Was it wicked, liking that? Luther— "Bye-bye!" Scornfully she threw herself into bed. Silly! Cordelia and Shelley—under the pine tree. She didn't love him. She had shut off all her real self, playing with him, pretending. What did she want? A flimsy shell, patterned after Cordelia—he had liked that! Hard in her core rose a clamor, a great shout, for more than that. Was there, on earth, the lover she dreamed of? Perhaps kissing was love. Perhaps—and she slept.

High school Commencement at the Opera House. Mother's eyes were bright with tears as Roger marched across the platform for his diploma. James whispered,

"See, there's Roge!" and Jean shook her head at him.

As they waited for the streetcar, mother wiped her eyes. "Poor Roger, he's so patient and good," she sighed.

"He's not poor at all," declared Jean, indignantly.

"When I think about last fall——"

"There, don't think about that!" Jean peered at her father, who pretended not to hear. She hoped they could reach home without the kindling of a family blaze. "Here comes the car."

"Guess I'll run up to the office."

Jean caught her father's arm.

"You'd better come with us," she whispered hastily, as mother and James entered the car. "She's feeling bad——"

With a faint muttering which Jean did not catch, father stepped ahead of her into the car, and sat down behind mother. The night was saved!

Something white beside the doorknob. James pulled it away.

"Letter for somebody." He held it out and mother took it.

"Yours, Jean." She handed it over, questioningly.

Jean hurried into the house with it. Her name, scrawled in pencil. She knew, suddenly. That was Luther's writing. Uneven, like a school boy's.

"Just a note from Luther." She held it tightly in her fingers until she closed the door upon herself and it.

DEAR JEAN,

Sorry you aren't home. Got to leave town in the morning because my mother is sick. Wanted to see my girl again. You know why. Don't forget your Luther this summer and don't have any other beaus.

xxxxxxxxxx   LUTHER W.

Jean s eyes blurred. At the first words there had leaped in her an echo of that ecstatic lightness, the thrilling of her body to his kiss. But that row of X's! Oh, how could he? In a small passion of humiliation she tore the note to bits. Even Roger would have written a different note!

She undressed and sat down in her nightgown at the window. The soft June breeze touched her gently. She clasped her hands against her breast for an instant. Quickly she pulled them apart, dropped them on the sill. How foolish! Posing, as if someone watched her. Grit under her finger tips. Dust. What would David have said? David—she had not thought of him for ages. Queer, how a person came back whole, like a sound—no, like a distinct smell— and you felt him more clearly than you saw him when he was really with you. What was David doing? Why—a ripple of her old terror—why had she been so frightened of David? Suppose he had kissed her. Suppose——She leaned her head against the window frame, trying to imagine David's kiss. Would she have been frightened, then? She shrank hastily from the phantasy. David was too serious!

She could feel his dark, demanding presence. No, not David! What did she want? She thought of Lora, after the party, saying,

"Of course Mr. Johnson isn't very interesting——"

"Awful bore!" Jean had said promptly.

"But anyhow—if you can't get just what you want, you have to take what you get." Lora looked puzzled. "I'm most twenty-five, Jean. I hate office work. Sick to death of it."

She had stopped, but Jean had sensed, behind her gentle, pale face, a kind of buckling down to some rigid intention. Lora had made up her mind. Jean went no further; she couldn't hear it!

Perhaps you never found what you wanted. What did she want? She was lonesome. The quiet night sounds came up to her window—wind in the young leaves, faint squawks from the pear tree in the poultry run where the hens liked to roost, voices indistinct in the distance.

Luther and David. David and Luther. If she rolled them into one, would they do? She couldn't make them stay together. Love—that strange lifting within her, up and up. Then thoughts came in, spoiling it. Love should be something you couldn't spoil with thinking. Too big. Lifting you——

Perhaps you never found it. Perhaps they always said wrong things, and you always went hiding yourself. She wanted it, that ecstasy and lightness and vibration. But it should drown out everything else, even this hard, scornful core of self.

What had her father been like as a lover? Suddenly she felt him beside her; she had dwindled into a tiny girl, and he stood there, tall, handsome, his arm over her shoulders. Explaining something, something about the moon and the sun, and she was drawn into him, listening, adoring. Just an instant, and he had gone. She struggled to regain him. Only a picture of him on the street corner, hostile, muttering something.

She rose, shivering. She hoped she would never see

Luther again. She was never going back to that college.
Another year——

Summer. Long, dull days, all alike. Roger had a girl,
fair-haired, pretty. He told Jean with a subdued grin that
everyone thought he wanted to go with her sister, Elizabeth,
and all the time he had his eye on Molly. He had got rid of
her other fellows, he boasted.

"Too bad Luther isn't in town," he said one night. He
had hurried home from the department store where he
worked to rush into clean clothes. "We're going up river.
You could come——"

"Oh, I did that, too, in my youth." Jean was casual. She
wouldn't have Roger sorry for her!

James had grown into a chameleon. Some days he
couldn't stay in the house long enough to eat, so eager was
he to play with the boys. Ragged, dirty, cheerful, he bolted
his dinner and banged out again. Other days he slipped back
into a younger existence and stayed near Jean, giggling at
her jokes, begging her to take a walk with him. But Jean
saw that the little boy returned less and less often. He
played too hard, mother said, and came in irritable and
heated. Jean liked best the after-supper hours when she
could coax him into the armchair and read to him, until the
excited aftermath of his playing vanished, and he relaxed
against her.

There seemed less money than usual. One week Roger,
white with rage at mother's story of the way the grocer at
the corner had asked for his money, walked out of the house.
He came back with a receipted bill, which he flung down in
his mother's lap without a word.

"Did you spend your money for that?" Mother wrung
her hands. "When he's doing who knows what with
his!"

"I won't have corner Dutchmen saying things to you!
But you can tell *him* I'll take a room somewheres else if I
have to pay his bills!"

Jean ran after him, and they stopped at the edge of the
yard.

"Did it take all of your pay envelope?" she asked, despairingly.

"Just about." Roger thrust his hand into his pocket, his eyes avoiding hers. "I'm sick of this, when I pay board, too! Tell you one thing, Jean, I'm going to clear out some day pretty soon."

"Me too!" Jean nodded. They looked at each other without a word, and Jean felt staunch determination rising between them. "Only I'm sorry for James."

"Well, he's just a kid."

The next morning Jean dressed carefully in a clean white waist and a freshly pressed wool skirt. To her mother's inquiry she answered indirectly, "Oh, I don't know. I want to go down town."

She went in to see Lora. Alone in the office, dignified and impressive behind the large desk, with neat piles of typed letters, Lora shook her head at Jean's query.

"You don't know typwriting or stenography. You couldn't get a good job without those. I don't think you'd like it—office work."

"You don't, do you?"

"I hate it! Writing down letters, answering telephone calls, you'd hate it even more! You don't like to do just what someone else tells you all the time."

"I don't!" said Jean fervently, "how'd you know?"

"Tell by looking at you." Lora laughed. "You're too smart."

Jean felt a glow of affection for Lora. She liked her straight white teeth, she liked her hair, mousy-colored, long, even—it always stayed just as Lora combed it, in smooth waves about her small face. Her eyes were mousy-colored, too. She might be pretty, if she didn't look so tired. She was sweet!

"What are you going to do, Lora?" She leaned against the desk, poking at the manuscript piles, "if you don't like this?"

Lora glanced toward the door and spoke softly.

"Get married. That's the only thing for a woman."

"Who to?" cried Jean.

"I'm not sure yet." Lora looked up at Jean, her mouse-gray eyes inscrutable. "But I mean it!"

"Not that Percy!"

"He's not so bad, Jean." Lora leaned forward, earnestly. "He is kind and honest——"

Jean drew back. If Lora was serious, she couldn't talk about him.

"Well, me, I'm going to find a job somewhere. Maybe at the ten-cent store again."

"They've got an awful cheap set there this summer."

"It would be a job, anyway. But three dollars!" Jean jumped to her feet as Lora's boss came in. He scowled importantly at her, and with a small grin at Lora, Jean hurried out.

As she walked past the stores, she deliberated. The hardware store. No girls there. Meat market! Dry goods store. She hesitated. Then, across the street, she saw the double windows of the bookstore. She had gone there for school books. Probably in the summer they didn't have many customers. She'd try it anyway. A bookstore—glorious place to work.

Mr. Irvine stood in the aisle, in his shirt sleeves, his hands on his hips, his bald forehead gleaming as he stared about at his store. Jean drew her face down soberly. Mr. Irvine was the only man in town with an eastern accent. Jean and her mother had laughed at him often. He had gone to Boston one summer.

"Ah, good morning, good morning. What does the little lady want this morning?" He rubbed his palms together.

"Mr. Irvine——" Jean tried to smile at him beguilingly. He had a reputation for liking the ladies! "Don't you want a clerk, to sell books for you?"

"Eh? You are looking for a position? Let's see, it is Jean Winthrop, isn't it? Or Polly—or Sally?"

"Jean." Her eyes hurried past his face to the rows of paper-jacketed books, behind the counters. "I like books," she said. "I think I could sell them very well."

"You like books? A great talent, liking books. Do you know books? Do you discriminate in your affection for books?"

"Yes, of course." Jean had an access of courage. She lost the suffocating feeling of asking for a job and gained a queer sense of superiority. "But seeing books, lots of them, is nice. And so——"

"Ah, you have literary tastes? Now, here——" Mr. Irvine picked up a volume. "Have you read this? Chats with Howells. A remarkable man. A distinguished man. A writer. I remember when I was once in Boston, I met a man who had known Howells. Let me see, that must have been in the year of our Lord 1898. No, 1899. Well, let that be as it may. You wish a position. A remunerative, lucrative position. How much remuneration do you desire?"

"I worked once, several years ago, for three dollars. I think I am worth more now."

"Make it four! We will see whether you can entice the public with your own literary affections. The public—ah, sometimes I think——"

Just then a perspiring, undersized boy pelted through the store toward the dark rear. Mr. Irvine wheeled and pursued him.

"Roy, did you get those boxes?"

Jean, standing between the rows of books, laughed secretly. He was queer! She resented his pretentious manner. But he had given her a job.

She went across the street to the office to tell her father she would not be home for dinner.

"I'm going to work at Irvine's bookstore," she said. "But I haven't any money for food this noon."

"Here, I'll go get something and we'll eat up here. Cheaper than a restaurant."

"Mother will have dinner ready," Jean suggested.

Her father frowned.

"She doesn't know where you are?"

"No. I didn't know when I left home."

He flipped a quarter across the ink-stained green felt of

the desk. At the door he turned, his eyes puckered significantly. "You be careful in that store. You're older now—folks may try to get fresh——"

Jean stared at the door which swung shut behind him, her cheeks warm. Ridiculous! Folks didn't try to get fresh with her. She wasn't the kind. Nothing about her made anyone want to be fresh. She brushed away the lean, jeering spring of longing. Of course she didn't want to be that kind.

The rest of the summer Jean spent her days in the bookstore. Mother said wearily that she needed Jean's help more than Mr. Irvine did, and Jean retorted, callously, "I can't stand hanging around here!"

"What do you think of me, spending all my time here, and small thanks from anyone!"

Jean stifled innumerable rejoinders. She wanted to say, "Well, you wanted to get married, didn't you? This is your house, isn't it?" and other unpleasant things.

"You might try to save some of the money you earn," went on her mother, unaware of the smoky silence. "If you started a bank account, you could save. If your father had ever listened to me, he'd be better off to-day. I hope you'll start more wisely."

"You can put it all in the bank," Jean promised. She didn't care about the money.

She read book after book. Mr. Irvine seldom came in until noon. Neither did anyone else, except the agitated general utility boy. Jean dusted the counters, rearranged volumes, and then sat down in the corner near the window, her book concealed by the counter. Novels, love stories; she raced through them, gulping whole pages with a single swallow.

Then she discovered, on the other side of the store, under the counter level, a series of volumes, elegantly bound in red leather with crisp, transparent paper jackets. The Heptameron. The Decameron. Rabelais. Her reading became an anguish and a delight. She would have been faint with shame if someone had found her reading one of the books.

Sometimes a strange disturbance shook her, and she would slip the book into place until her hands lost their iciness and her heart ceased its violence. Wicked books! Fascinating books! Who read them? No one surely would dare buy such books, openly. Did Mr. Irvine keep them for himself? Still, here they stood, the most elegant books in the store. Someone had read them, for the pages were cut. Drifting crumbs of paper from the heavy deckled edges lay between the pages. She would resolve never to touch them again, but they drew her back to them. Some of the stories stirred faint recollections; they were like the stories whispered by the girls years ago in the sewing club. But those girls couldn't have read the books. At times she was ashamed of being ashamed. Something robust and vigorous stood out, reaching for her with cleansing power. But shame had tentacled roots of habit. She tried one day a thin volume, "What a Young Girl Should Know." It was mawkish and pale after Queen Margaret.

Dimly she struggled to comprehend all she read. It fitted into vague allusions, half guessed situations, hints, without ever making any clear entirely. And curiously, never did the stories connect themselves for an instant with her own longings, her own obscure and troubling stirrings of sex life. They were distressing, exciting, but always as things in books, things apart from the life around her.

In the afternoon, while Mr. Irvine stalked about his store, Jean rearranged shelves or sold pen points, paper, ink. If a customer by rare chance gravitated toward a book, Mr. Irvine flowed forward, pouring his verbosity over the sale. Jean was sure she could have sold books more skillfully than he; she felt sharp hostility at his approach, as if he usurped her right. She wondered why he had hired her, so few people drifted into the store.

Sometimes father came in, and inevitably he and Mr. Irvine launched themselves upon a sea of argument. About such things as absolutism, rationalism, Hegel, Kant. Father waved his arms, shouted a little. Mr. Irvine summoned longer and longer words. Then Roy jumped at Mr. Irvine with a bill of lading, or a customer appeared, and instantly the discussion melted.

One day in August a dapper little man with a small curled moustache and black eyes sought out Mr. Irvine at his desk. Jean saw deference in Mr. Irvine's greeting. Presently the two came toward her.

"You have come to exactly the proper place, Turner," Mr. Irvine was saying. "Here is a young lady, Miss Jean Winthrop, intelligent, industrious, with personality. May I present you to a possible candidate?" He thrust his fingers between the buttons of his vest. "Allow me to present to you Mr. Turner, the Honorable Mr. Turner, banker, citizen, head of the school committee. He is, I may say, fulfilling the latter function at present. He is——"

"How 'do, Miss Winthrop," interrupted the Honorable Mr. Turner. Jean felt his black eyes, shining and hard, ferreting at her. "Mr. Irvine has suggested that you might like to teach school. At Perry. This fall."

"Just so, just so," murmured Mr. Irvine, stalking an entering customer.

"You've been to college? Um. Haven't taught?"

"I substituted once or twice in high school." Jean stood very straight behind the counter. He needn't look at her as if she were a specimen! "I do want a position." She hadn't thought of it, but of course she did! Perry—little town—streetcar went through it.

"Think I know your father. James Winthrop? Used to be a professor, didn't he?"

"He's in business now." Jean resented his patronizing smile, as he flipped his watch chain.

"Can you give me references? Intermediate teacher's what we need. We've got our principal and primary."

Jean ran glibly over names. She would show him she was somebody!

"Um. Yes. Heard of some of them. I tell you, I'll see your school superintendent to-day. There's a board meeting Friday. At seven. You come over on the car. We like to see the teacher."

Father went over with her. The board met in Mr.
Turner's office, redolent of kerosene lamps. Two other
members, a farmer with a red beard, and the thin melancholy
village doctor.

"Miss Winthrop seems to have a unusual record as a
student," said Mr. Turner, pompously.

"She'd be a good teacher," interposed father. "Gets it
honestly, both sides of the family."

Jean wished he wouldn't talk! She didn't like his deprecatory eagerness. She wanted the position. But she wished
she could have come alone.

Jean and her father waited in a tiny outer room while
the board deliberated. Mr. Turner flung open the door with
an elaborate gesture.

"You are unanimously elected, Miss Winthrop. Your
contract—we have agreed, in spite of your inexperience, to
pay you forty dollars per month. Nine-month year. Beginning the Tuesday after Labor Day." He spread the sheet on
the table. "Sign here." Jean read the printed clauses.
Gross misconduct. What would be gross? She signed.

As she and father waited in the little shed for the hourly
car, father said, "Forty a month isn't bad. I got twenty
when I started." He glanced about the empty room. "Be
careful how you act. Two or three men out here—I
won't mention names—richest men—keep their families
here—and have women in town. You have to be careful——"

"They won't bother me!" said Jean. She was triumphant.
She had a real position!

"Now that Turner—you be careful how you talk to
him—" repeated her father. Jean knew suddenly that he had
felt Mr. Turner's patronizing manner. This was a way of
getting even!

The board requested that Miss Winthrop live in the village through the week. "We like to feel our teachers are
part of the civic life. Not merely present in the classroom. Living among us. Besides, that eight o'clock car's
likely to be late. Disorganizes your classroom."

Jean was to board and room with the janitor and his wife. Father disapproved. He suggested that Jean take the six o'clock car, but Jean, secretly delighted, announced quietly that she had to room in Perry. She would spend week-ends at home.

"Once you begin to live away from home, the family breaks up," insisted father. "You'll regret it later in life."

Jean glanced at his profile, close to her in the narrow seat, hooked nose, square chin, sharp lines through the cheeks, about the eyes. Did he really feel that way about the family, or was it—well, just an idea? She was silent.

XI

The afternoon of Labor Day Jean sat on the Interurban, her bag beside her. She wore a stiff white shirt waist, and in her bag was a second, with clean handkerchiefs, toothbrush, comb, and a necktie. She thought, "It's silly to feel so excited, just going off to teach in a little village school!" But her excitement lay deeper than thought could touch. She was off! This was only the beginning.

A boy at the Perry waiting room directed her to the janitor's house. "Right down Main Street. Last house on the left."

Main Street, crossing the car track at right angles, seemed to be all of Perry, a double line of houses with fields touching the edge of the yards. Could she ever be a part of the community life? Terrifying phrase. What did it mean? Did those windows hide people watching her, saying, "There goes the new teacher"?

Mrs. Collins came to the door of the white house. Gray hair, drab eyes, pale lips, thickened body in neat gray print dress. Jean flushed under her austere scrunity.

"I'm Jean Winthrop, the teacher. Mr. Turner said you would board me."

"Come right in. I wasn't expecting you till to-morrow. The last teacher never wasted any time in Perry. Here's the teacher, Jim."

The man in the armchair did not move except to hold out his hand. Big, grizzled, with bright blue eyes and sweeping mustache.

"Got your strap in that bag? All ready for the tough kids?"

"I'm ready for them." Jean laughed. She felt ready for anything!

"Tell the Missus to feed you well, so you'll have muscle enough to handle 'em."

"Mebbe Miss Winthrop can handle them without so much muscle." Mrs. Collins had an air of wariness, as if she waited to see how Jim and Miss Winthrop hit it off. "Here's your room, the parlor bedroom. It's warmer in winter."

A small room, immaculate; large wooden bed, washstand, dresser, chair, white ruffled curtains. Jean gazed about with inarticulate pride. Hers! She would pay for sleeping there.

"I'm sure I'll be very comfortable," she said.

"I hope so." Mrs. Collins jerked open a drawer. "You can keep your things in here. If you need more room, I could empty another." She stood at the door, her drab eyes gravely inspecting the girl. "I hope you'll be comfortable," she repeated.

Jean went over to the schoolhouse, a square box of a building in a field just off Main Street. Two rooms on the first floor, with a hall for wraps between. The first must be the primary room. Jean walked into the second room, and stood behind the flat desk, looking about. Rows of desks, black oiled floors, grayish blackboards, long windows, cracks in the gray plastered walls. Her knees quivered, and she sat down, her elbows on the desk. Her room! The year rose before her, a shining eminence she had attained. Her face glowed with pale intensity. She would be a wonderful teacher, the children should love her, she would do—oh, everything! What would they look like, those seats, filled with children? At a step in the hall she started guiltily away from her dreams.

"Miss Winthrop?" She rose to meet the tall, lanky man.

"I'm Miller, the principal. Glad to meet you, I'm sure."
He sat down on the recitation bench, his legs sprawling, his
sun-bleached curly hair pale above his tan, his queer, small
mouth showing rows of pointed, discolored rodent teeth as
he smiled at her. "Hope we'll get along fine. I always do,
with my teachers. Now, you haven't taught, have you?
Thought you might need some help with your program."
She had three grades, and each grade had seven classes.
By the time Mr. Miller had explained the system of including twenty-one classes in a day, the sunset lay golden on the
old seats and dark floor.

"Time for supper, I say." He poked himself erect.

Thought Jean: I wish he didn't have such nasty little
teeth! Can't ever like him much. Nice hair. But those
teeth! Country rube. Aloud she said,

"Thank you, Mr. Miller. I'm grateful." She looked at
the schedule. Fifteen minutes to a class. "I never could
have put all those things into one day!"

"That's easy." Mr. Miller pooh-poohed himself to the
door. "First year I taught I had eight grades!"

Jean walked slowly along Main Street. If he had only
been nicer, she thought, then we might have been friends.
He rushed upstairs as if he was afraid I might catch him!
Perhaps he was. Perhaps his teachers tried to catch him!
She didn't want him. What would the primary teacher be
like? She was new this year, too. From North Dakota.
They had to stick together, the three of them. They
made something, together. Jean turned her head, and saw
the peaked roof of the schoolhouse, with patches of fresh
yellow shingles. The exhilaration of the afternoon returned.
They were a *force*. They might accomplish wonderful
things in this small village. Together. Separately they
might not even like each other.

Jean reached the Collins's walk. She stopped a moment.
She could hear the faint running music of a little brook a
few rods farther, and off against the horizon of the rolling
fields a patch of soft maples huddled their subdued glory
under the fading sunset. To Jean the moment had a breath-

less quality of consecration. "I'm part of something," she thought, vaguely, "more than just me."

She was hungry. Mrs. Collins lost some of her austerity under Jean's praise of her pickles and creamed potatoes.

"The old woman's a good cook," said Jim heartily. "That's all she's good for, but she's good for that."

Mrs. Collins shut her thin lips and said nothing. Did she mind, wondered Jean?

Jim Collins walked to school with her, early the next morning.

"This Miller's got outlandish ideas," he grumbled. "Wants I should sweep every day! Once a week used to be good enough. Ain't worth what I get paid, I tell you. Goin' to tell the school board."

Jean couldn't listen to him. Her excitement mounted almost to a fever. What should she say to the children? Suppose she forgot what to do. As she hung her hat on its hook, she heard her name.

"I'm Rosa Porter." She whirled. "You're the other teacher?"

Rosa Porter was little, with a high pompadour of stringy, dull hair, and bright blue eyes in deep sockets. Her mouth was homely, but her smile had a swift genuineness that Jean liked. Her cheeks had spots of crimson in the hollows, and already chalk dust was powdered over her chin and dark waist. They stood side by side in the entry, looking at each other.

"This your first school?" Miss Porter chewed absently on a bit of chalk. Her large mouth looked a little chapped, as if she had eaten chalk for years. "Well"—she laughed— "it's not my first! But it seems a nice little town. If I can help you out any——"

Above them clanged the tower bell. Jim Collins stood in the hall, pulling the long rope. Startlingly loud and final!

In they came, boys and girls. Jean sat at her desk, her hands icy, her eyes smiling, imploring, searching. One of the big boys pretended to trip. Jean felt the children watching her. She smiled at him. He was being funny, like James!

She sat at her desk that afternoon, looking at the list of names, her head heavy and dull from the tense hours. In came Mr. Miller, Miss Porter tripping after him.

"One day gone!" They sat down on the long bench. "What's the news?" Mr. Miller's teeth leaped into view.

The tension melted. They made jokes about the children. They sighed over the dingy blackboards. Again they were subtly fused, a group, not individuals. Queer—Jean felt her identity running into that fusing. She counted, as part of the world, working.

She carried an armful of books to the house that night. "Huh! Teacher has to study!" cried Jim Collins, when he saw her.

"Got to know more than those kids," retorted Jean. After supper she sat down near the oil lamp. Mrs. Collins came in and pulled a chair near her.

"Could I look at the books?" she asked distantly. "I used to be a teacher. You wouldn't think it, but I did."

"I love it," Jean told her mother, at the end of the first week.

Mother sighed.

"I liked teaching," she said. "I was considered a good teacher, too."

Jean slept fitfully that night, the children trooping through her dreams. Eddie, sloping shoulders, small head, with dark fuzz like the down on a baby duck, pasty face and tongue that couldn't twist itself about words. Tola, tall, gawky, with swift, unintelligible speech, half Indian, Mrs. Collins had said. Samuel, the lawyer's son, heavy, sleepy, pimply-faced. "Retarded development," the lawyer had stopped her one day on the road, to explain. Little Lloyd Smith, squat, broad-shouldered, furtive-eyed. The family of Swedes, Frankie, Millie, and John, sturdy, sober towheads with pale lashes. Could she teach them? Could she wake up Samuel? Could she teach Eddie's tongue to say the long words?

Mrs. Collins liked to sit near her in the evening and watch

her go over the lessons. Bit by bit she told Jean her story. She had taught, had saved her money, half starving herself, Jean guessed, until she had gone to Chicago to the Cook County Normal. A shining half year there, and then her health had gone. Breakdown, she said drily. She had come home to a brother, who had not wanted her. Mr. Collins, then a comfortable farmer, needed a housekeeper. His wife had just died. Mrs. Collins said, "I had mind enough to do that, but my sickness had affected me. I couldn't teach. So I went to live with him. Then he thought we might as well get married. Cheaper for him to have a wife. What could I do?"

She was crying silently, tears slipping over the lines in her cheeks.

Jean looked away. She didn't know what to say! Mrs. Collins hurried out of the room. Later she came back with several books.

"These might help you. 'Method of Teaching Geography.' Parker was a wonderful man."

Another night she said abruptly,

"Jim was never educated. He thinks books are foolish. I've been a good wife to him——"

"Of course you have!"

"You don't know"—— She glanced at the door, her drab eyes haunted——"You don't know what I've had to endure! Terrible things! I couldn't tell a young girl like you."

Jean shrank violently from her. Mrs. Collins was staring up the narrow stairs to the chamber where they slept. She couldn't bear it if the woman told her more!

"Country men are like that, sometimes." Mrs. Collins knotted her worn fingers in her lap. "But I shouldn't talk this way. Only it tempts me—having someone here who studies, who likes books."

"You help me a lot," said Jean. "I don't know much about teaching."

"Do I?" Mrs. Collins looked up, her mouth trembling. Jean could feel the woman struggling against years of repression, struggling to speak out.

"Of course you do," she said, gently. "You're awfully good to me." Then she turned the pages of the reader hastily, to show Mrs. Collins that she needn't try to say anything more.

Some days the children were like an instrument she played perfectly. Some days they were like a wall, confronting her with solid, sullen impenetrability, Lloyd with his furtive eyes, Samuel with his heaviness, the outposts. She flung herself against them, bruising herself, her face white, rage trembling up to her lips. Once she flew out at Samuel, and the hush which dropped over the docile Rebecca and her cousin, the shocked, pale eyes of the little Larsons, ached within her the rest of the day. She wouldn't burst out in anger!

Jean had to rise at five on Monday in order to reach the down town corner in time for the car. By late November five seemed to be the middle of the night, and the empty, strained feeling of dragging herself out of bed stayed with her all day. Father woke her and went to the car with her. Jean thought, "He acts as if he was doing something great! He likes to make it seem important!" She decided to go back to Perry on Sunday night. Father disapproved, but Jean said, "I feel too tired all day Monday." She liked the hour on the Interurban in the winter night, with the headlight spraying its glow over the snow like the wake of a boat.

Friday afternoon had a pleasant excitement. End of the week. She closed school at three, told a story to the children, and dismissed them in time to run for the four o'clock car. Mr. Collins carried her bag to the station.

"Jim never would do that before," said his wife. "He likes you. You laugh at his jokes."

Home. Sometimes Jean felt that the walls of the house were pasteboard and a gust would topple them. Roger would say, "Awful row last night. But they smoothed out for the week-end!" They did seem to. As if she were different, when she was home only part of the time. James liked to hear about the boys in her room.

"I hope you lick 'em if they cut up. Don't you let 'em sass you!"

"You'll have to visit some day," promised Jean. "They're pretty good."

"I told my teacher my sister taught school," boasted James.

Saturday evening Jean went occasionally out to Agora meetings. She had lost her sharp self-consciousness in a pleasant sense of her own superior position, as one of the old girls, out in the world. The freshmen were children! But she liked the chatter and the dancing, and the slight expectancy that greeted her sallies.

She liked especially the dances with Dorothy Tiverton. She had watched Dorothy the previous year, one of four freshmen who had come from the same small town, a gay, bantering, self-sufficient group. Dorothy had scarcely noticed her, and Jean was incapable of aggression. Something in her walk, a swaying of her body from the hips which might have been awkward had she been less roundly modeled; something in her eyes, dark, under arched brows, with unexpected wistfulness even as the girl laughed; perhaps her mouth, with its beautiful curved under lip, and that upper lip—drawn into a straight line by the white wrinkle of a scar. Operation for hare-lip;, the girls had whispered. Wasn't performed quite right. Mustn't ever speak of it. Dorothy was frightfully sensitive. Jean never looked at the lip. It forced her eyes to cling to the dark eyes of Dorothy as they danced together. Perhaps the girl caught thus the affection which grew in Jean.

"She would have been lovely," mourned Jean. Dark hair, clear skin with texture like some heavy opaque flower—an Easter lily. Did she mind?

"You're a funny thing," said Dorothy one night, as they stood in the recess of a window after dancing. "You're as cold and impersonal as—as a toad! What do you think about, staring at us?"

"I'm not," protested Jean.

"Can't fool me. I've been dancing with you two years.

I don't know any more about you—— It's my opinion you've
got a wicked mind back of that calm face of yours!"

"Well, I've thought about you, lots."

"Listen to her!" Dorothy smiled. She had a trick of
ducking her head with a smile, as if to give her eyes a show
without the cruel grimace of her lips. "Come on upstairs,"
she added. "No one's there. I'm sick of this hubbub."

"That's the man I'm supposed to marry." She thrust a
photograph at Jean. "Like his looks?"

Jean settled herself in the wicker chair and looked at the
face. Thin, fair, something idealistic and eager even in the
huge glazed photograph.

"Lawyer," went on Dorothy. She perched on the arm of
the chair.

"He looks like a minister," said Jean.

Dorothy knocked the picture to the floor.

"He does! He is!" she exclaimed. "He's too good! He
lets me bully him. I want a man who'll not stand that!
Who'll—yes, who'd bully me!"

"What are you marrying him for?"

"Oh, known him all my life, got to marry some day,
mother's crazy about him. I tell John he ought to marry
mother!" She stared at Jean, her eyes somber. "Ever been
in love, funny little thing?"

"No."

"I was! Once. He kissed me. Devil! In the dark——"
She slid to the floor, hiding her face against Jean's knees,
sobbing.

Jean's fingers slipped fearfully from the soft hair down
to the smooth, firm throat.

"Don't cry, Dorothy!" She had the breathless shock of
coming too suddenly upon the secret spring of another's
whole life. Poor Dorothy! Could she say to her, "You
shouldn't care so much! You are beautiful anyway!" She
dared not speak of that.

"Who's crying?" Dorothy strained up against Jean's
breast, until Jean could feel in her soft bosom the tortured
beating of her heart.

Sounds in the corridor, the other girls, coming upstairs. Dorothy darted to her feet, her hands smoothing her hair, brushing at her eyes.

"Come home with me some time, Jean. Would you?" she begged, before the door burst open.

Christmas. The school had a Tree, the older boys dragging it in on sleds. Jean and Rosa Porter worked stringing cranberries and popcorn, in Mrs. Collins's kitchen. Jean recklessly bought a gift for each child in her room, pencils with colored stones at their tips, candy, little books—she found them at the ten-cent store, and gloried in the squandering of her precious wage. She dropped into the preparations with an abandon like that of the old days when, as a child, she had helped make Christmas. Mother and James came over to the Tree. Frankie Larson was so ecstatic that every white lock stood erect about his glowing face. He had never seen a Tree!

When it was over, and Jean left the empty schoolhouse to walk to the station, her feet lagged. Emptiness possessed her, as if the Tree, the gifts, the afternoon, had been herself, and now they were spent, leaving a void in place of the abandon of the past week.

"I'm silly—caring so much about such things," she thought, as she lay wakeful that night. "As if I were a child! But it *was* nice!"

Christmas was the following Monday. They had no tree at home that year. Jean thought James should have one, but there was little time, and she had no heart for it.

Her week of vacation dragged. Rumbles of a storm. Something about signatures on the deed. Roger explained that they'd been going on about that for some time.

"Mother won't sign. She thinks the property must be half hers if the law requires her name. It isn't really that, for father just took it for a deal. But you can't make her see——"

Father hung around the house late one morning, stamping up and down stairs, rushing out to the poultry yard, banging around.

Mother called to Jean from upstairs,

"You can tell him that he needn't wait around. I won't sign! That's all there is to it. If even the law protects me, I guess I have some rights." She sat on the bed, her shoulders huddled in an old shawl.

"You'd better come downstairs," said Jean. "It's cold up here."

"Not till he gets out. I don't want to spoil your vacation. He's bent on trouble." A door banged below them.

"What is it he wants?" asked Jean.

"He's got a little property. How he got it, I don't know He says he's got to sell it to clear the mortgage. What do I get out of it? We haven't had a cent here all winter. He's got to have my signature. I won't sign!" Her voice shrilled. "If it's partly mine, why should I? The money will go where everything else has. Some drab will get it! Or gambling." She stopped, one hand over her heart. "He can threaten me all he wants! You don't know how he acts, when you aren't around! Ugly! He's not himself. Sometimes I think he must be taking something besides just drink."

"Why don't you agree to sign if he'll give you part of it?" Jean stood by the door, the chill of the room, the terrible shrinking combining in discomfort.

"Because he wouldn't even if he said he would! You think I'm stubborn. Roger said I was! It's for you children. Trying to save something out of the wreck."

Steps on the stairs. Father was coming. Wracking tension at the pit of Jean's stomach. She wanted to run! The door flew open.

"Now I put it up to Jean, here." His face was red, heavy. "This is a business proposition. This isn't your property! It's mine! I got it to sell, to make money, for food and coal and clothes, everything! You're interfering with my business!"

"Business!" Mother spit the word at him.

"Why does mother's name have to go on that paper?" Jean's discomfort made her suddenly belligerent. "If she has nothing to do with?"

"Ask him that! He can't answer you!"

"Wait, mother!" Jean confronted her father squarely. "If the law demands her signature, it must give her some rights."

"The law's just for property owned by a man and wife. This is different."

"Different, is it?" Mother's sneer was vitriolic. "How much are you going to get?"

"None of your damned business!" roared father. "That paper's going to be signed this morning, or I'll put your name on it myself."

"I'll tell your party that you did!" Mother jumped to her feet.

"What's the use of yelling so?" Jean waved her arms at them. "You can't settle things that way——"

"Tell your daughter what you said last night! That you'd knock me down if I didn't sign! Tell her that!"

"I never laid a finger on you!"

"If you will give part of your sale to mother, she'll sign." Jean was coaxing now, eagerly. "If it's for food and coal anyway, why not give her half? If you have to have her name, the law must mean something!"

Father burst out of the room, stamping down the stairs. The front door rocked after him.

"If he forges my name, I will do something!" Mother began her quick, panting walk across the room, back and forth.

Jean fled down the stairs, seized her hat and cloak, and went out. She came back an hour later, her cheeks glowing from the cold and the contention of the hour, in her hand a deed and several bills. She sought her mother.

"Here's forty dollars," she cried. "He's going to get just eighty down. Now you'll sign, won't you?"

"He'll get it back from me." Mother's fingers closed over the bills. "When you're gone!"

"Put it where he can't! You sign here——" Jean held out the pen.

"It's not right." Her mother sobbed as she wrote her

name. "I try to save something, and you're all against me."

"Forty dollars is something, isn't it?"

The year swung on with its pendulum beat, Monday to Friday, Friday to Monday. Jean had an organ now, given by the ladies of the church. Rebecca Turner played a march for the children as they went home. Jean ground out songs, her voice lifted lustily over the organ sounds in the children's favorites. Poor Eddie listened, his blank face dreamily wistful. He couldn't even keep step in the marching. Tola giggled. But the other children liked it.

One night Jean went home slowly, burdened with several incredibly nasty notes she had found on the floor. She thought she recognized the writing. Lloyd's. What could she do!

Mrs. Collins read the notes, her thin lips puckered avidly. "Wash his mouth with soap! That's what I did, once. Teach him this is filth."

"Soap won't teach him. I ought to talk to him——"

"If you knew his mother, you wouldn't wonder! That shack off there—more than one man in this town has been seen sneaking out of it at night!"

"Poor Lloyd!" Jean could see him, squat, furtive, grinning. What was there she could say to him?

"Tola, now, she hasn't any chance, either. She's got two sisters. One of them's in the family way right this minute!"

"In this little town!" Jean's eyes were wide, frightened. What had she to combat such things?

"I guess this town isn't any worse than any other." Mrs. Collins was sitting very straight, a slight flush on her cheeks. "Why, when I was a little girl, we had a teacher once——" and she proceeded with a story which reached horrid tentacles around Jean, dragging her into an abyss of horror.

"What can I tell them? I ought to do something."

"You can't tell country children anything. They know too much already. Keep them interested in other things, if you can. I'd been wondering if you wouldn't find something——"

Jean couldn't escape the specter. When she looked at the faces of the children, she thought, "What are they thinking? What can grammar or geography do?"

That week-end at home the thing stayed near the surface of Jean's thoughts. She said nothing about it; she knew her mother's answer would be much like Mrs. Collins's. There should be some other answer!

On Sunday night, as she waited in the dingy, crowded Interurban station, she saw suddenly at the door, Luther, his eyes searching the room. She hadn't seen him since last June! She had heard that he wasn't in college. There, he saw her!

"Your folks said I might catch you here." Jean moved along to make room for him. "Thought I might ride over, have a chance to talk——"

The crowd surged toward the door at the whistle of the car. Luther had her suitcase. He found a seat. He was close beside her, the frost on his rough overcoat melting into runnels.

"How's my girl?" He was fumbling for her hand.

She saw his puzzled frown as she began a polite, frigid run of questions, comments. Everything was turmoil within her, Luther, that last dawn together, the week just gone.

They hurried up the dark village street, the wind stinging Jean's cheeks. Fortunately it was cold! Luther couldn't expect her to stand on the porch. Mrs. Collins rose, curious, and after the moment of stiff introductions, coerced her husband into the kitchen.

Luther fidgeted. Finally Jean said, "You'll have to go, if you want to get the car."

At the door he tried to catch her hands, to pull her toward him. Jean, the pupils of her eyes contracting, looked at him, and he dropped his hands limply.

"You don't like me any more, do you?" He was reproachful.

Jean shook her head. Then he had closed the door.

She thought about him that night. Perhaps he wasn't horrid—like men—or boys. But she didn't want him to touch her! Strange, how she kept the memory of that kiss as fresh as if it had been to-night! Was that a part of this terrible mess? It shouldn't be. The cold air, tingling in her nostrils, seemed to cleanse her. She snuggled under the blankets and slept.

Mr. Turner lived in a large gray house, half-way between the school and the Collins's. Jean looked at the windows as she passed. Caroline Turner was a senior in high school in town; no country school for her! She belonged to the sorority and next year would go east to a women's college. Jean had met her at the waiting room several times, and resentment at the girl's indifferent nod of recognition lingered after each meeting. Rebecca was sweet. To Caroline, Jean was nothing but the village teacher. Mrs. Turner was like Caroline.

One day in March Jean stopped at their door to ask about Rebecca, who was ill. Mrs. Turner opened the door.

"Oh, Miss Winthrop?" She lifted her dark brows with her voice.

"I stopped to ask about Rebecca." Jean shivered in the March twilight.

"Rebecca is quite well, thank you. Just a slight cold. I didn't wish to expose her to the draughty schoolroom until she was entirely strong again." Behind Mrs. Turner came a shout of laughter, a volley of chords on the piano. Caroline, with some of her friends from town——

As the door shut, Jean hurried away from the lighted windows, the wind over the bare frozen fields striking at her as if it sprang from her own bitterness.

"They needn't act as if I was mud!" she fumed. "Snobs! Because they are rich! Shutting the door as if I was a peddler!"

She stood for a moment on the porch, just out of the wind, before she went into the lighted sitting room and faced the Collins's.

"I don't know why that made me so mad," she thought, forlornly. She heard again the laughing voices, the chords of gay music, as if the answer lay in those sounds. The old humiliating feeling of inferiority—— They knew about her father, Caroline would tell them she hadn't been wanted in the sorority; she had no way of making them admit she was their equal. Jean felt that deeply, thorns festering under her skin. Oh, she would show them some day! And all the people like them!

That evening she said casually, "I wonder why the Turners live here. They spend so much time in town."

Mrs. Collins sniffed.

"Because Mr. Turner makes his money here. Mortgages, loans. He's got the upper hand of most of the farmers for miles around. I guess Missis would like to move, all right. She thinks she's so much better than the rest of us! They didn't amount to so much until her father died and left them property."

Mr. Collins looked up from his paper. He looked like a middle-aged faun, thought Jean, suddenly, with his bright eyes and tufts of gray hair in his ears, like horns!

"Handy for a man to have his family stuck out here," he said. "Leaves him to do what he likes without much chance of watching. Good and handy!"

"Well, Rebecca's a nice little girl. Smart, too," said Jean. She felt ashamed, as if her secret envies linked her with Mrs. Collins and other women in the village.

"They'll send her to town soon, I expect. They won't take any part in the church or the grange. Think they're so much better!"

On Friday Rosa Porter went to town with Jean. She rubbed off the chalk dust and dabbed powder thickly in its place. The bright spots of color which daubed her cheekbones faded as the car lurched through the country. She looked worn. Old.

"You going to stay here next year?" she asked Jean.

"I don't know. Are you?"

"I suppose so. It's a fairly decent place. Last year I had a much harder school."

"How long have you taught?"

"Years!" Miss Porter groaned. "More than I count up!"

Jean speculated. Years, and she thought Perry was a decent place!

"Well," she said crisply, "I think I'll try for another place. I can't bear the thought of Eddie grinning at me another year! And Tola and Lloyd!"

"You'll get other dummies wherever you go," was Miss Porter's retort. "Say, I'm glad it's Friday. If the week had eight days, I'd die."

"How'd you ever happen to come so far?" Jean stopped just short of adding, "to such a little school?"

"Agency. Went to a summer normal last year and joined a teachers' agency."

"How do you join one?" Jean built a swift vision of wonderful offers from an agency.

"They aren't much use. See, you got your job just by chance. That works as well as anything, I guess."

When Jean went to bed, she thought, "I must think about this. I must think hard." But Rosa Porter's face, grayed with chalk dust, above a dingy dark waist, wavered huge and dim above her thoughts until she fell asleep.

In the morning she went down to the kitchen in stiff white shirt waist and sateen petticoat, her serge skirt on her arm.

"Is there a hot iron?" She laid the ironing board, one end shoved into breakfast dishes, the other on a chair.

"What do you want to press for so early?" Mother, stirring a cake, complained.

"I'm going out to college, to see Professor Eldrich, about the school."

"What school?"

"That one between town and college. Where they're building, you know, where the fire was? He's on the board, and he liked me, in economics class."

"Can't you stay in Perry another year? You haven't lost——"

"Of course I can!" Jean banged her iron defiantly. She was all sharp edges against implied criticism. "But why should I stay?"

"If you don't stay two years, it looks as if they hadn't wanted you to."

"Not if I get a better school, does it?" Ssss, the iron steamed over the damp cloth.

"Why don't you try for a place right in town then?"

"You know I couldn't teach in town. Not without a state certificate. You can't get that till you've taught three years or gone to Normal."

"I wanted you to go to Normal."

"I didn't want to."

"You'd better eat your breakfast, then maybe you won't feel so contrary."

Jean started to cry out, "I don't feel contrary!" but suddenly she laughed. She did!

"There!" She stepped into her skirt. "Do I look neat and prim and like a school-ma'am?" She whirled about her mother. "Where's my coffee cup?"

"You act more like James," said mother, but Jean caught a warm pride in her tone, and hummed as she went into the dining room.

"What put that school into your head?" Mother came in to sit across the table.

"I don't know." Jean ate quickly. She didn't know. Somehow when she meant to think hard, she never did. Instead, things had a queer way of thinking themselves out; suddenly she had a new idea.

She came back at noon, subdued.

"Didn't you see him, Jean?" asked mother.

"Oh, yes. I saw him, and I had to see two other men. But some other girl has applied. I've got to send them references. Probably she'll get it. She applied weeks ago!"

"Don't feel so bad," said mother. "You can stay at Perry."

"I won't stay in that dump another year!"

"What dump?" James stood in the doorway, a football pinned under his muddy arm.

"James! Wipe your feet! Look at the mud on my clean floor!"

Jean led a Damoclean existence the next two weeks. She couldn't bear it if she failed to get that school! She wrote the County Commissioner, and in return had his letter. "To Whom It May Concern." Oh, he had said splendid things about her! Mr. Miller wrote her another To Whom, and even Mr. Turner.

She had it! A letter from Professor Eldrich, enclosing her contract. Fifty dollars a month! She would have to live at home, as the school was so close to town. But it was a better place. Her first clear thought, as she stared at the typewritten sheet, was, "I did it myself. I can get anything I want—if I can get steam enough to go after it!"

She told Mrs. Collins and exulted in her laments.

"Perry never had a better teacher. Couldn't you stay one more year?"

Mr. Turner came into the schoolroom one noon.

"Is it true you are leaving us?"

"Yes," said Jean, soberly.

"If we should offer you more? We are prepared to offer, say, forty-five?"

"I'm going to have fifty." Jean's inner thought was lusty and ribald. "Take that, old Smug! I'll show you yet."

Mr. Turner was sorry. The children liked her. They had hoped—— It was all sweet to Jean, a small triumph, but sweet.

XIII

Almost overnight it was spring. The road from school to the house sucked up Jean's feet in gulleys of mud. The swamp maples flamed in the hollows of the hills, and the children brought her tight, warm bunches of wind flowers and dogtooth violets. Restless days. Fine rain on the windows. Pages and pages in the textbooks to be covered before May ended.

One week-end Jean found an unfamiliar book on the desk, "Leaves of Grass," in a speckled pale green cover.

"Where'd this come from?" she asked mother, turning the pages curiously.

"That!" Her mother bit at her words. "Your father! I suppose he's been reading it with some of his lady friends, when they drop in on business!" She narrowed her eyes at the book. "Don't touch it!"

But Jean was already caught into it. Phrases leaped at her. The ragged lines, the broken bits of verse lured her with strange promise.

She asked her father cautiously if she might take it that week. She thrust it into her suitcase, under her clean handkerchiefs. She read it on the car, all the way from town to Perry.

Whitman. "O Captain! my Captain!" The children had learned that poem in February. But these others, disturbing, exciting, what were they about? What did he mean, sometimes? Safe in her room at Mrs. Collins's, she set the lamp on the washstand, propped her pillows against the foot of the bed, and read.

Afoot and light-hearted, I take to the open road.
Healthy, free, the world before me,
The long brown path before me leading me wherever I
    choose.

That was the way she wanted to feel! "I myself am good fortune!"

Camerado, I give you my hand—
Will you give me yourself? Will you come travel with
    me?

A challenge, like winds, thunder, fire!

I believe in the flesh and the appetites,
Seeing, hearing, feeling, are miracles, and each part and
    tag of me is a miracle.

Could she feel that way? About everything! People——
Jean wrinkled her nose. She liked people to be clean, not

smelly. Could you take them all, finding something, giving yourself? The vague, chaotic phrases rumbled past her.

She woke in the morning, to find the lamp smelling vilely of its burnt-out wick, the window closed, and herself stiff from the cramped position in which she had dropped asleep. But even as she stirred, sonorous phrases floated back to her. If she could take hold of life like that, proud, dominant, humble, reckless, without shame!

When she came into the house that afternoon, Mrs. Collins sat by the window, the copy of Whitman on her knee. Jean pressed her lips against an instinctive protest. Mrs. Collins always read the books she brought over.

But Mrs. Collins lifted furtive eyes.

"Do you think this is good poetry?" she asked.

"I don't know." Jean dropped her books and unpinned her hat.

"Wasn't this Whitman the man they put in prison for something awful?"

"I don't think so. Never heard of it." Jean stretched out in the old Morris chair. "He's supposed to be the greatest American poet. The Old Gray Poet. You know 'O Captain! my Captain!' don't you?"

"There was a man, English, a poet, put in prison," insisted Mrs. Collins.

"Well, Whitman wasn't English."

"Anyhow," said Mrs. Collins, and Jean felt that the opprobrium of prison still clung to Whitman, "I don't like what he writes about. Coarse!"

"He thinks everything in life is good," said Jean, slowly.

"It isn't! I know that if I'm not a poet. Some of it is bad and you don't make it good by calling names. There are some things in that book I'd be ashamed to be caught reading even to myself!" Mrs. Collins laid the book gingerly on the table and went out to her kitchen.

Jean stared at it. Would she be ashamed to be seen reading some of the lines? She wondered. She wanted not to be. She wanted to feel like the poems. But she hid the book in her suitcase. She thought about it through the days that followed, and at night she opened it, to read more, to reread poems half remembered. If she could feel like that, could she make the children—glad of their bodies, proud, not furtive, hiding, ashamed? The essence eluded her, vague, formless, buffeting, like a great wind.

The following Sunday she went to call on Miss McNealy. "Let's go for a walk," she begged. "It's lovely outdoors."

She answered Miss McNealy's kindly questions in a desultory fashion. The children behaved well. She thought she would like the new school much better. She glanced occasionally at the strong profile, while unuttered words pressed at her lips. They followed a side street out to the edge of town, unfamiliar to Jean. Bars, and a path across a meadow.

"Violets!" cried Jean, and knelt in delight among the tufts of spring grass, thrusting her fingers along the smooth delicate stems. Miss McNealy was smiling at her eagerness, she knew. The grass—what were the lines?

This grass is very dark to be from the white heads of old
    mothers,
Darker than the colorless beards of old men,
Dark to come from under the faint red roofs of
    mouths——

Jean rose, filling Miss McNealy's hands with her gathered violets.

"Miss McNealy," she cried, "do you like Whitman's poems? Do you——"

Miss McNealy lifted her gray eyes from the flowers and looked at Jean. Something disturbed, hesitating in the clear glance.

"I've been reading them." Jean stumbled over her thoughts. "I don't know——"

"What have you been reading?"

"All of them! 'Leaves of Grass.' My father had the book." Jean broke off the flood of her words. She had seen that look! It was like her mother's, like Mrs. Collins's!

"I don't think that everything he writes would be good for people." She could see Miss McNealy hunting for suitable words. "Some of the poems are lovely, of course. Much of it, however, does not seem real poetry to me. In form or in material."

Jean closed in upon herself. The outrush from the spring, the violets, the tumult of the week, shut tight within. Quietly she walked beside Miss McNealy back to her house. Talk about various things, the new leaves on the elms, the color of the sky, school. At the door Jean stood a moment, feeling in Miss McNealy's grave inspection a return to her question. She waved her hand in light farewell and hurried off.

The next week, when she tried to regain her thrill of power, of strength, shame entered. Perhaps nice people didn't feel that way! Was Miss McNealy never troubled about things?

When Jean came home the next week-end, mother unpacked her suitcase, to take out her laundry. She came downstairs, the volume of Whitman held off in one hand as if it had a vile odor.

"You haven't read this!"

Jean wished her cheeks wouldn't grow so warm.

"He's a famous poet," she said hastily. "I thought I ought to know——"

"Infamous!" Her mother threw the book on the desk. "Unspeakable and nasty! Why, Jean, they won't have the book in most libraries. I told your father—I can't bear to say it—but he reads it because he likes it! You can't write decent books about man's evil nature, calling it good! If you touch pitch——"

She went hurriedly out of the room, leaving Jean staring at the pale green speckled cover. Was it true? Her father— did he read it with women? Suddenly there swept over Jean a great consciousness of sin. All the insidious doctrines of shame, of guilt, of obscenity rose up and overwhelmed her. In a passion she rushed at the book, fled through the house, down into the cellar. She opened the furnace door. A light fire smouldered there, just enough to take the chill off the house. With a sob, Jean flung the book into the coals.

She watched the covers curl and twist and finally burst into flame. Then she closed the door and slowly climbed the stairs.

"I burned it up," she said to her mother. But, queerly, no response leaped in her at the pleasure in her mother's face. She was still shamed. As if she had failed.

Early in May the Perry church had a week of revival meetings. Mrs. Collins urged Jean to go with her.

"I can't go out evenings," said Jean. "I have too much to do."

"The ladies of the church got you that organ," said Mrs. Collins, insistently. "You never go to church here."

Thursday evening, Jean, thinking that perhaps this would turn out to be that mysterious taking part in the life of the town which had so eluded her, walked to the little frame church with Mrs. Collins. Jim refused picturesquely to go. "I'm no friend of the Lord's," he sneered. Mrs. Collins buttoned her lips, and Jean wondered whether she was praying for Jim's soul!

As they sat in the rear pew, Jean gazed about at the half-filled benches. Farmers and their wives. Mothers of some of her children. Some of the boys and girls. She saw Rosa Porter's flat back hair ahead of her. Then the services began.

"He can't even speak good English!" Jean watched the swaying, thin body, the large, bearded head. Scorn mounted in her with the superlatives of hell as he pictured its horrors. Finally he flung out his hands.

"I call on all those who have been saved to stand! Are there any unrepentant souls among us? Stand up for Jesus!"

Moored fast to her seat, Jean heard the scuffling of feet, the uprising of bodies. Mrs. Collins tugged at her sleeve. She shook her head fiercely. She wouldn't stand! It wasn't true, this harangue! Perhaps she had a glow of martyrdom as she heard the fiery words roll over her head.

"Souls still drowned in sin! In the black pit! Let us pray! Let us pray for them!"

Would she lose her job? She had marked herself an outcast.

In silence she walked beside Mrs. Collins's agitated skirts to the house.

"Aren't you a Christian?" The woman turned on her as she entered the sitting room.

"I don't believe a word he said," declared Jean, slowly. "I am sorry."

"I will pray for your soul, too!" Mrs. Collins's cheeks were scarlet, and her eyes had zealous glints. "You should have risen! Your pupils were there. They saw you!"

Jean went silently to her room. She wondered. Would it have been wiser to stand up and save a fuss and set an example?

"I won't!" she said aloud. "Not if I don't believe it!"

Mrs. Collins told her sorrowfully that several of the ladies had asked about it.

"I told them you belonged to another church," she said.

"You needn't have said that!" Jean was defiant. She wanted the glory of her iniquity.

The last days of school piled up with hectic speed. Mr. Turner stopped one morning, to tell Jean confidentially that she better pass all the children.

"Eddie and Tola and Lloyd!" Jean looked at him, incredulous. "They haven't learned a thing!"

"But they've been in those grades several years. Their mothers will take them out of school. Just give them a certificate—if you feel you can, honestly, of course. I advise it."

Jean was stubborn about that. Tola's noisy weeping did not move her. If certificates meant anything, she'd give them where she thought she should!

Final exercises, with recitations and songs, mothers in their best shirt waists, a crowding around of the children, with good-bys gruff or shy. Jean threw the last of the papers from her desk into the wastebasket, left the textbooks in a neat pile in the drawer, said good-by to Miss Porter— Mr. Miller still had a few parents in his room—and walked slowly along the village street for the last time on the return trip from school.

Mrs. Collins cried softly, poked a jar of sweet pickles into Jean's bag, and begged her to come over sometime to see her.

"I can't tell you"—the tip of her nose quivered—"what this year has meant. My mind is better. You gave it something to think about."

As the car ran through the fields with their stretches of pale flat leaves of corn, Jean tried to think over the year. She felt a dim glimmer of her early reverent enthusiasm. Had she done all she could? A part of the life—she hadn't been much of a part. What was there to be a part of? Mr. Turner rolled that phrase out between his neat mustaches—what did he mean? He wasn't part—nor his family. The children had liked her. Mrs. Collins liked her. Over and done with. Curious melancholy of the end of anything. Who would have her room next year? Summer ahead of her. What should she do all summer? Dorothy wanted her to visit at her home.

At the corner as she stepped from the car, her father met her.

"Wanted to see you a minute." He looked at her with sharp defiance. "Everything go all right?"

"Yes. Glad it's over." What did he want?

"Here, step out of the way." He moved her suitcase in to the grating over the drugstore basement. "You know the row your mother kicks up over signing deeds? Well, I wanted to tell you—I've had some lots made over to you. Business proposition. I got them just to sell, you understand. You can sign instead of her. That's all. Don't say anything to her."

Jean moved away from his jerking elbow.

"Can't you do it some other way?"

"You don't have to do a thing but write your name." Danger signals in her father's quickened speech. "You aren't such a fool as your mother about things—balling up deals."

"I don't like the idea," said Jean.

"You don't like fracases, either, do you? Well, then! This is a simple way out. Here." He pulled a folded paper from his pocket, spread it out, screwed up his fountain pen. "Right there! Your full name. That's all there is to it."

"Hm." An obscure alignment with her mother urged Jean into her next question. "What do I get out of it?"

"Hell and damnation!" Her father roared so loudly that she glanced up in distress. People would hear them! "Get out of it! Are you as bad as your mother? Sign it!"

Jean's fingers shook as she signed her name. She couldn't argue about it on the street.

She watched him hurry down the street, his stocky figure plunging in jerky haste among the passers. An ominous discomfort filled her. She didn't want to be mixed up in things. She remembered the devastating scenes. Just business. Mother wouldn't understand it that way. She shrugged. Maybe it would smooth things out, her signing. She had done it, anyway. Let him bully her.

XIV

The first weeks of the summer Jean was busy. She had to take county examinations for a teacher's license. She sniffed over the dull books. A letter from Miss McNealy, who was in northern Michigan. "If your mother can spare you, I should be delighted to have you with me for a fortnight. I can obtain a room at the house which we are occupying in part. As I shall not see you next year, having taken another position, I should be especially glad to have you with me this summer." Jean thought, "I'd like to go away somewhere. That would cost a lot, though."

The examinations at the county seat. Hot, still days, when the smell of foolscap and the faint acridness of ink floated in the large room; examiners stalking about, fluttering palm-leaf fans. Jean wished the plump girl ahead of her would perspire less visibly! Easy questions, except the awful "Parse: To be or not to be——" Jean's mind insisted upon finishing the soliloquy, wandering off into a debate as to Hamlet's madness. Parse it! Arithmetic. She caught sidelong beseeching glances from the spectacled anemic girl across the aisle. Would teachers cheat? She watched. They certainly would.

She finished in a passion of distaste for the whole business, smells, heat, stupid faces, bustling, sweaty little examiners. What could those papers show about her?

She came home wearily the late afternoon of the third day. Her mother was sitting on the porch, the daily paper on her knees. Jean felt foreboding at the first glimpse of her rigid figure. What now? When she reached the steps and her mother turned her head, Jean stopped, her feet lead. What had she done? Terrible white lips, eyes wide, the pupils pin-points of contracted fury.

Her mother struck the paper with a clenched fist.

"You wicked, deceitful——" Her voice picked at Jean's nerves. "You know how I struggle to protect you and the boys—and you aid your father—in his wantonness, in his evil, selfish ways!"

Jean knew! She had found out about the signature. Culpability netted her, speechless, cold. Betrayal! Her mother seemed to grow huge above her, possessed of demoniac rage.

"You're a woman yourself! You can do this—with all you know of his wickedness, his selfish, headstrong—— Oh!"

"Mother——" Jean struggled into words, to escape this terrible guilt. "I did it, only to save trouble——"

"Trouble! You let him do as he pleases. Trouble! Go your ways. I'm done with you all! I've tried as long as I can! Follow him down to his hell——"

"I thought"—Jean forced herself into speech—"that I could save just such a scene as this. I see I was wrong——"

"Ah-h!" Her mother's cry was thin and white. She flung more words at Jean, scarifying, flaming words. Then suddenly she wheeled, and Jean heard her stumbling up the stairs.

She sat down on the steps. Thought stopped in her for a time. Her father came down the street.

"You'd better not go in," said Jean, laconically. "She's found out about the deeds."

"How the hell?"

"I don't know. Would they be in the paper?" The sheets lay on the porch floor.

"Um. Recorded, I suppose. Well, I put the deal through, anyway." He looked at Jean curiously, but she did not speak again. Then he went hurriedly away. Roger came home from work. Jean told him briefly.

"Gee!" He whistled. "So you caught it!"

"I did."

"He had no business to use you."

"I signed my own name, of course."

"Did you tell her you did it to save a mess?"

"She didn't hear anything I said."

Roger sat down beside her.

"Poor old girl! Say, and you just came back from those exams, didn't you? How'd they go?"

Jean's eyes filled with tears.

"All right, I guess." She patted Roger's hand. "You're an old brick! Come on, I'll hunt up some fodder for us. I'm glad James went to see Mamie last week."

No sound from her mother's room that night. None the next morning. After breakfast, Jean opened the sewing machine. She was glad she had some cambric. Nightgowns were good hard sewing!

As she stopped at the end of a seam, she heard feet overhead. She listened, the white stuff trailing from her fingers. The sound of something heavy being dragged over the floor. Silence. Soft feet. What was she doing? Sick with dread, Jean tiptoed through the kitchen to the rear stairs. Up she crawled, each step with caution. Would she—— Jean had a ghastly vision of a dangling body. The door at the top was ajar. Her mother bent over a small trunk, lifting out the tray. She spun around.

"Take your deceitful spying face out of here!"

All through the dragging hours of that day Jean sat at the machine, stitching, listening to those feet above her, stitching, listening—locusts in the trees, tiny heat waves over the dusty road, feet, padding above her.

The next morning she followed Roger out to the street, and spoke in a hushed voice, glancing at the upper windows.

"I'm going away," she said. "I can't stand it."

"Where?"

"Miss McNealy asked me. She's up north. I'll have to get some clothes. There's a train to-night, I think."

"I'll look it up, Jean." Roger nodded. "Good stuff! You aren't a criminal!"

"I'll come into the store this noon."

In recklessness Jean drew out of the bank fifty dollars. The largest sum she had ever held in her hands! She shopped, unaware of the heat, almost losing her fear of the aggressive shop women. A coat. A gingham dress. A white skirt.

"There's a train at midnight," said Roger, rather anxiously. "It gets to Traverse City at six. Then you change."

"I'll pack my suitcase and you take it down for me. Then I'll sneak out."

Midnight at the station. Roger and Jean were the only people beside the sleepy telegraph operator.

"He doesn't think they have a parlor car," said Roger. Jean had decided on that parlor car seat as part of the recklessness of the journey. "You're sure you'll be all right?"

"Of course! And, Roger, don't you tell her where I am! Not till she asks!"

"Does father know?"

"Haven't seen him. He's lying low."

The train, a length of darkened coaches, a conductor on the step of a rear coach.

"Any parlor cars?" shouted Roger, valiantly.

"Sleepers ahead! Day coach here."

Sleepers! She hadn't thought of that.

"Never mind, Roger! I'll be all right. I'll send you a note——"

They clung together for a frantic moment, kissing; Jean's lips were salt. "Oh, I wish you were coming!"

She swayed down the aisle of the dimly lighted car, as the train gathered speed. Seats full of sprawling, sleeping men. She found one seat empty. Something dismal, strange, forbidding, in the close air, the hoarse throat sounds of the sleepers, the black night outside. She couldn't raise the window. Her fingers were gritty from the dirty sill. She folded her new gray coat carefully into a pillow and leaned against the arm of the seat.

Perhaps she slept a little. When she looked out of the window again, the train had slowed for water, and just outside lay a shining creek. Astonishingly, through the trees, brilliant over the water, hung the constellation of Orion! She had never seen those stars save in the winter. They had swung over the edge of the world during the night. She lost her forlornness, and sat erect to watch their glitter. She had escaped!

Breakfast in a little bakeshop, a floury fat woman slapping the coffee and rolls on the counter in front of Jean. Two hours to wait. At the end of a narrow side street a glitter of light, like a reflection from a mirror. Could it be——Jean ran down the street, her suitcase banging against her. The lake! She reached the grassy margin. For a long time she stood, her hands gripped about the suitcase handle, her eyes on the calm, subtly changing water. She had not known she could see the lake here! As the sun moved up the sky, the white metallic expanse drew soft blue across its calm, blue from the far northern horizon. A gull swooped near her. She saw a dory put out from shore, the oars moving like tiny legs. Where had she seen this before? There should be a wall, with stones rough and cool under her hands, and roses. Like the vibration of a distant bell—— She sighed. She could not remember. But nothing was strange. She brushed through the silver-beaded grass down to the narrow, white, sandy rim. Across to the east she

could see another shore; north, to the horizon, nothing but
smooth blue water. She sat down, touching the round white
pebbles with her finger tips. She thought: yesterday and the
day before, this was here, as beautiful as now, while I——
She shivered as she felt herself crawl up the back stairs,
slowly. She was drawn out of a musty prison, malodorous
of bitterness and hate, into this.

The town behind her woke. Voices, the sound of horses'
hoofs, the slap, slap of rugs being shaken. Was it time
to go back to the dirty little station? First she would write
to Roger. He might be worried about her trip.

Jean sat on the lake side of the train. Perhaps the track
would run near the bay. No, it dipped inland, through
farming country. She felt tired, empty, like a vessel scrubbed
clean. She would not think of anything that had ever happened! For two weeks she could stay where she could see
that water!

Two more stations. She curled against the arm of her
seat. Then she heard her name and turned to see Miss
McNealy swinging down the aisle, people following her,
laughing, talking.

"Well, Jean! Isn't it nice to see you!" Miss McNealy
sat beside her. "We walked down to meet you. Five miles.
The morning was so lovely. Professor Small, this is my
friend, Jean Winthrop. Professor Small lives next door
and is a wonderful neighbor!"

"You came on the sleeper. Comfortable way to travel."
Professor Small sat on the arm of the seat ahead, lean, gray,
fine nose, gentle dark eyes, little gray mustache and pointed
beard hiding his mouth.

Jean liked him. She started to say, "I didn't have a
sleeper," but a woman ahead called to him, and Jean was
left with a guilty sense of deception. She didn't want to
explain that she hadn't known enough to do anything but
sit up all night!

She watched them all, wistfully, feeling their holiday
spirit, awkwardly conscious that she was an outsider.

They were all nice to her, because they liked Miss Mc-

Nealy. Jean could feel the pressure of a firm arm against hers. She loved her! She glanced shyly at the deep-set eyes, the coronet of braided silvering hair. If she could only do something to show her!

Beautiful days. Nights in the little bare room, with the night breath off the lake moving the white curtains. Breakfasts in the dining hall down near the wharves. Jean had never heard people have such fun as they ate together! Walks along the white shore, or back into the stretch of forest, dimly green even at noonday. Jean did not know that her delight flowered in her almost to tangible form, her face lost the slightly haggard pallor and flushed into color; her eyes lost their wistful caution and grew like the lake in sunshine.

"Miss Jean's enthusiasm makes this place seem even more desirable than I have always thought it," Professor Small said one day, as Jean came back to the camp fire, tugging breathlessly at a gnarled trunk she had found on the beach. "Wouldn't she make a good advertisement for a summer resort?"

Miss McNealy smiled at her. "You do have a good time, don't you?"

Jean wondered a little. Did she act too like a child? She couldn't help it! She wanted to run and leap and shout, she wanted to lie motionless in the sun, staring at the water, she wanted to sit in the forest while the green light dripped through the pines about her. Beautiful, beautiful!

She couldn't bear to go to bed because the days were so short, and yet she slept the minute her head touched the pillow.

Finally the last evening came. She sat on the steps, Miss McNealy beside her, silent. The stars over the hill were incredibly brilliant. Tears in her eyes. To-morrow it would be over. She had not known people could live like this, with nothing but peace, peace and beauty. Suddenly like a murky curtain across the stars rose the recollection of her last days at home. Her mother and her father had never played. Perhaps, if they had known how to play—— Still, if there were children, and not much money, maybe you couldn't play. Professor Small and his wife: Jean had watched them. The friendly peace of their days in the little cottage next door enclosed them securely.

"What are you thinking about?" Miss McNealy was looking at her.

"Oh——" Feeling flowed over Jean like a crested wave. "I—I wish I could tell you!"

"You have had a pleasant visit, haven't you?"

"I never had such a wonderful time, never!" Jean's face was solemn. "If you knew——" But how tell her! She would be horrified, wouldn't believe it. To her all people were good. Jean could see her shrinking, horrified. That would be a poor return.

"Do you know," Miss McNealy spoke slowly, as if she debated the wisdom of her words, "do you know, dear, what a gift you have? You have made everyone here like you. Your enjoyment—— You *are* a dear child!" She bent to kiss Jean's cheek.

Jean was as still as if someone had placed a sacrament in her hands. If she moved she might spill a drop! Quickly she burrowed her face into Miss McNealy's shoulder for an instant, and ran into the house.

Her farewell the next morning left her subdued almost to tragedy. Miss McNealy, waving to her on the platform, was a surrogate for the clean, sweeping beauty, the peace, the delight of days past. She might not see her again for years. Why hadn't she told her more of the things she had thought, more of the depths from which she had been lifted? Too late.

A last glimmer of the lake at Traverse City, steel gray under windy clouds.

Jean had written Roger that she didn't want to come home yet. She would stop at Caledonia to visit Dorothy Tiverton. She regained her sense of recklessness in this journeying. Money did this for her. She couldn't have escaped from that dreadful house, if she hadn't had her own money in the bank.

Dorothy met her.

"Why, Jean! I hardly knew you! What have you been doing? You look fine!"

"I'm glad to see you!" Jean hugged her. Always the first moment after a separation, that scar on Dorothy's lip challenged her. Then she forgot it.

"Come along. Father's waiting for us."

Father, round, bald, with blue eyes and broad, smiling mouth, leaned from the front seat of the surrey to shake hands.

"Hop right in. If you're as hungry as we are, it's time we got home to supper!"

"I'm hungrier!" Jean liked him. She thought of Miss McNealy's words: a gift, she could make him like her!

Mrs. Tiverton came to the door to meet them. Tall, graceful, with dark eyes and lovely curving mouth, lines from her nostrils, skin like Dorothy's except for fine wrinkles. She looked as Dorothy might have!

"I think your mother and father are awfully nice." The girls were in Dorothy's room, Jean curled on the bed in her nightgown, Dorothy brushing her long hair.

"Um." Dorothy took a hairpin from her mouth. "They're all right."

"Your father's so jolly."

Dorothy laughed.

"You've made a hit with him, appreciating his jokes!"

"And your mother is beautiful."

Jean felt a withdrawal in Dorothy's face. She ran the brush down her hair, and held out a dark strand.

"If she didn't have neuralgic headaches! They take it out of her looks," she said, cooly.

Jean watched in silence. Poor Dorothy! Was she jealous, of her mother?

"Wonderful hair," she murmured. "You've got the loveliest skin, too."

"Yours isn't bad." Dorothy braided her hair slowly. "Sunburn's becoming."

Dorothy snuggled into Jean's arms.

"Jean!" Her lips were close to the girl's ear. "John's coming. Thursday. On his way to Grand Rapids. Promise me something!"

"What?"

"Don't you leave me alone with him. You stick to me! Will you?"

"He won't want me around."

"I do. If you care anything for me!"

"I'll try, Doro."

Pleasant idle days. Cooking. New things to eat. Funny, how different families ate different things. Jean watched Mr. Tiverton and his wife. They liked each other! She laughed at his jokes, and he called her Elise, quite as if they hadn't been married for years.

John came, very like his picture. Tall, thin, eager, dark, with a deprecatory shyness in his voice and eyes when he was near Dorothy.

"Jean! Come here a minute!" Mrs. Tiverton called, and Jean thankfully escaped from the sitting room. "Let poor John have a chance! Dorothy treats him like a worm."

Jean peered doubtfully back at the sitting room. Should she desert Dorothy? Presently Dorothy herself appeared, John behind her, flushed.

"John would much rather help you get supper, mother. You're really his girl!"

"Well, I'll have John for a beau any day I can get him!" Sparks in Mrs. Tiverton's handsome eyes.

"I'm going to marry him this fall," said Dorothy that night.

"Doro!"

"Might as well. But till I do—— He can't have everything he wants." She was crying in the dark, her cheeks wet on Jean's throat.

Jean, distressed, hunted up Mrs. Tiverton in the tiny dairy pantry the next morning.

"Is Dorothy going to marry John this fall?"

"I hope so." Mrs. Tiverton moved near Jean, laid an arm over her shoulders. "Why?"

"Do you think——" Jean looked shyly at the older woman. She liked her! "Do you think she'll be happy?"

"Of course. Has she been talking?"

"No. I just wondered."

"There's not a finer boy in the world than John! Dorothy has notions. She'll settle down. You see! Don't you trouble that sober little head of yours. Run along and cheer her up!"

The last day of that week came. It had been different. Not so stirring as the previous week, but pleasant; revealing, too. Jean thought: are they happy because they have enough money? They are so nice to each other. Mrs. Tiverton looks—well, sort of hungry, sometimes.

Mrs. Tiverton called her.

"I've wondered, Jean. You seem to think—about life. Would you care to read a book? It's meant a lot to me." She laid in the girl's hands a small volume, "Power and Healing." "Dorothy doesn't care for it, but she's not intellectual." Crimson spots in the woman's cheeks. "Read it! Good-by, dear. I hope you'll come again. You are not like the other girls." She kissed Jean's lips, a firm, warm kiss. Jean's heart sang, "Oh, you are lovely, lovely!" She could say nothing but, "I've had a beautiful week, Mrs. Tiverton."

"What did mother want?" Dorothy's question had suspicion.

"She gave me a book to read."

"Oh, Lordy! Don't bother with it. She's always after some kind of religion or cult or something. We let her go, dad and I."

"I'm going to read it." Jean wanted to add, "And I think she's wonderful!" But instead she gave Dorothy's arm a gentle squeeze.

Roger met her at the station.

"Gee, you look some different!" He stood off to view her. "You look fat! Some sunburn!"

"I had the most glorious time!" Jean sighed. "If you'd only been along! Let's go north some time together." Then,

nonchalantly, "How's everything at the house?" She felt
encased in new armor.

"Pretty good. About the third day after you went, mother
came around. Wanted to know where you were. Didn't
say much, but I guess she worried about your telling Miss
McNealy why you went."

"She needn't have worried about that!" flared Jean.

"I know it. Here's a car."

Roger looked white and tir

"Don't you get any vacation?" asked Jean, with sudden
guilt at her own shining weeks.

"I've got a new job. Express agent at the railroad. So
I can't have one, not right off. This job's more outdoors,
though."

"Everybody ought to go away and have some fun," declared Jean. "It turns you into a different person."

"You look it, all right." Roger gazed at her admiringly.
"Some kid!"

Jean slipped into life at home, externally, as if she had
never gone away. Her mother looked at her almost beseech-
ingly as she came in, and Jean said "Hello" casually. Mother
never asked about the visit, and Jean retained her feeling
that it had equipped her in shining armor against future
wounds. Professor Small sent her a package of snapshots.
Jean left them on her dresser, and knew that mother had
looked at them. Secretly she recognized her mother's silence
as a mixture of defeat and apology.

Going carelessly about the ordinary tasks, Jean felt a difference. The walls of the house were no longer the walls
about the world. There was sky above the roof. Within
she might still hear the crumbling of dissolution, but she
knew now that even if the walls fell, the world stood unchanged. Unchanged? No, changing. But the haunting
fear of her childhood, as inclusive as a fear lest the whole
world rock to a horrid end some judgment day, that fear
was done. No matter what happened here, something
would go on. She, Jean, would shake off the dust from
ruined walls, and walk forth. Outside people lived and

thought and loved; they lived in peace, in beauty, some of them.

She wondered, watching her mother, whether she had lost her fear of her. Suppose she did something which angered her mother. Would her heart contract with that clutching tightness? Would she escape, scotfree? She was not sure. When she had walked out of the house that night, to go away, she had cut through a maze of binding threads. Since the earliest days she could remember she had struggled to prevent scenes. Could she be adamant thus overnight?

She thought about her father. Did he have that shrinking, that craven guilt, when mother turned on him? He went ahead, his own ways. Perhaps at first—— She remembered that once he had said, "I cried." Perhaps—the thought played along the horizon of her mind, heat lightning—perhaps he had chosen his ways in defiance of that very feeling!

And yet, poor mother. Jean saw her hysteria unexpectedly as a weapon, futile, but still a weapon of impotence. A house was small to hold two people so different. All houses were small. Some felt less crowded—— She thought of Professor Small's cottage, sunlight streaking the birch-bark bookcases and tables.

Mamie wrote that she wanted to keep James for the winter. He could go to school, he was old enough to run errands for her, and it was so lonesome alone with Grandfather all winter.

"He's better off there," said mother.

"He belongs here!" declared father.

"Maybe"—mother's voice iced over—"maybe he won't be so ashamed of his father if he doesn't see so much of him!"

Jean left them hastily. James stayed with Mamie. Father refused to send any money for his shoes or books. "I'll support him in the home where he belongs! Nowhere else!"

"You call it supporting!"

Roger gave mother ten dollars to send, and Jean promised part of her first check.

That was Jean Winthrop at twenty-one. For four years she had struggled to shape herself in patterns offered her, and always the pain of the effort had been more intense than any pleasure in the result. Full of rebellions still inarticulate and unexpressed, she concealed them almost from herself. The shell of her childhood had long been discarded. The shell she had built of docile response to the demands around her, was brittle, cracked, still clinging in fragments which hid her from casual eyes. Because her failures were those of her response to outer expectations, never failures of her identity, they had not touched her curious, unfaltering inner confidence.

PART IV
EMERGENCE

PART IV

EMERGENCE

I

School opened. The first day had the shadowy turmoil of
a nightmare. The new building was unfinished, and the
first seven grades were packed into a shed at the edge of
the grounds. The primary teacher, Helen Michael, a dark-
haired, stocky Greek girl, with the calm blue eyes of a
madonna except for a gleam of humor, laughed at Jean's
nervous, white distress.

"We can't do a thing but try to amuse them, of course."

"The awful racket outside!" Jean pressed her hands
against her ears. "If they'd pounded all summer as much
as they have to-day, that building would be done!"

"I hope it gets done before winter."

"How can we have recitations, both at once?"

"Duets!" Miss Michael laughed again. "If I speak softly
on my side of the room, perhaps you won't hear me."

"Nothing to do but grin, I suppose! Are the children
always so smarty?"

"Some of them. They aren't like country children. Faculty children seem nervous or something."

On Friday of the first week Jean went to Professor
Eldrich's office.

"I might as well give up my job," she told him. "I can't
teach. The children won't study—and you can't blame them,
with the noise."

"Oh, Miss Winthrop!" Mr. Eldrich was fat and smooth.
His face with its small features looked absurdly young.
Just like his little girl, thought Jean, smiling in spite of her

desperation. "My girl says you're a beautiful teacher. A few weeks and things will be better. Don't be downhearted."

"I feel like a failure!" Jean sat upright, her face stern. "And I don't want to be."

"Everyone knows the difficulties under which you teachers are working. Allowances——"

"I hate having to be allowed for!"

"Don't worry, my dear Miss Winthrop." He followed her rotundly to the door. "Keep a stiff upper lip. You'll do as well as last year."

Jean continued to wake with a feeling of oppression, as if she knew ahead of time that she could not lift the weight of the hours. She longed for the quiet of her room at Perry. The children, too—the difference there irked her. For several weeks she did not face the origin of that feeling. Then one day in geography, when Spencer, the son of the president of the college, rose to his well-shined feet and told about his trip last summer through Yellowstone Park, she knew. Last year she had been easily on top. She knew more than the children; she had done more than they had done. She had more than their fathers and mothers. These children had seen things she had never seen. They had at home more of wisdom, of pleasant life, of easy, satisfying things, than she had ever known. That night she tried, stormily, to think it out. "I won't let them shove me down!—— You can't dazzle them with superior knowledge," mocked an inner self.

Like a wrestling match. She had to stay on top, somehow! They were trying to pin her shoulders to the mat. She wouldn't stay down! Last year she had fought dullness, indifference, with a sparkling eagerness. This year— smartiness! She'd show them! She sat at her desk, her muscles tensed as if she were about to spring at a tangible enemy.

Living at home was not easy. After all, Mrs. Collins had helped puff her up. Perhaps she wasn't a good teacher. She rammed her way through that fear. She would be! One

Saturday she rode over to Perry to see Mrs. Collins, out of an unrecognized need for bolstering. Mrs. Collins cried with pleasure.

"Jim hates this teacher," she said. "And she is a light-headed, silly piece! The children all wish you were back."

Jean began the next week with more serenity.

At home, instead of storms with clearing, affairs had settled into a continuous fog. Nothing right. Jean felt through the fog a strong premonition, as if they bore swiftly down upon ragged, unseen rocks. Father waited at night for Roger and walked home to supper with him. They entered the house with the air of discussion abruptly ended. Jean, coming home from school, would find her mother crying, or sitting, her hands limp, her eyes staring emptily. She would begin to talk. Stories about father. He had gone driving with a student, back in the days of his first college position. He had never listened to mother's advice about anything. He would say, "That's none of your business! Tend to your business and let me tend to mine!"

"Mine!" Mother beat her hand against her breast. "What is a woman's business? I was trying to make him see what he ought to do. What can a woman do? She is helpless. Stubborn, selfish——"

"That's all past, mother," Jean would say. "Why think about it?"

"It isn't past. Something dreadful will happen before he is through. What is he doing this winter? Nothing good. Did you know that he was with those men the time the police raided that barn—cock fighting! You didn't know that, did you? They hushed it up. That's what those chickens are for. Think of that!"

Some stories Jean remembered vaguely, as part of her past life, with the emphasis altered, subtly. A story of one Christmas, with a brazen-faced hussy brought into the house to insult mother! That must be Mrs. Thorpe. She remembered that day. Father hadn't brought her!

"Oh, what good does talking do?" cried Jean.

"He says you're on his side. He says he has the children

on his side. You've got to understand what he's done to me!"

"Do something instead of talking." Jean muttered that under her breath.

"What?" asked mother, sharply. Then, quickly, "I think he's taking something beside the booze. The way he drops asleep. You don't see him at noon. Lies down there and sleeps! Like a—like a stupor."

"There they come." Jean rose hastily and went into the kitchen.

That night she asked Roger what father talked about so hard as they came toward the house.

"Oh, shooting off steam," said Roger, carelessly. "All sorts of stuff. About his life, how much he's done, how much he's earned—I don't listen to more than half."

"Does he talk about mother?"

"Some."

Jean looked at Roger. Sharp animosity sprang between them, startling her. Was Roger opposed to her? He was a man, like father. Jean felt astoundingly that difference in sex. Antagonism.

"I don't think he'd better say much," she said. "With all he's done!"

"I must say he's got some excuse!" Then, as quickly as it had flashed between them, the antagonism died. "He makes me tired," Roger was saying, "talking about how much he's done for us and everything."

"Let 'em talk." Jean's affection flowed out softly toward Roger. "As long as they don't do anything worse. We'll be gone, soon."

Then one day, at the end of school, she found her father waiting for her.

"Let's walk home," he said. "Air'll be good for you."

He talked. Jean heard against his voice the tones of her mother, like a refrain, an antiphonal apologia. Some of the same stories, from the other side. She listened in silence, as she had to her mother.

"There's lots we could have done, you and I." A febrile

explosiveness in his speech. "Like this walk! I could have helped you with your teaching." He strode violently along. "But what happened whenever I tried to talk to you? You know how she looked at me. You know we didn't dare be seen talking! Why? Jealous, that's all. Jealous of her own daughter."

"We used to talk about all sorts of things." Jean felt as if she searched for cold water out of which to wring a cloth for this fever. "I can remember——"

"But lately!" insisted her father. "Why do we always shut up when we get to the door? Why?"

Jean fingered her way back through fine threads of memory. Was her mother jealous? She didn't like to have them talk—discuss—argue, she called it. Never had. Why not? Jean caught a distinct thread.

"Not quite jealousy," she ventured. "A feeling that you were beguiling me into forgetting your—wicked shortcomings!" She grinned a little. "You should be rushing off to earn a living—and you were slinging words!"

Her father brushed that aside. He didn't want to listen. He wanted to talk.

Her mother saw them coming together.

"What was he talking about?" she demanded.

"Oh, we were talking about teaching." They had spoken of that, a few words.

"What's he got to say about that? Did he go out to the school?"

"He had some business out that way."

"Business! A lot of business he has anywhere!"

That night Roger came in, a cigar defiantly poised between his lips. Mother looked at him, and a torrent of tragic weeping burst forth.

"Roger! You!"

"What's the matter?" Roger removed the cigar, self-consciously.

"Oh, not you! You wouldn't begin those evil ways!"

"Now see here." Roger stood firmly in front of her. "I'm twenty years old. Smoking's no sin. If you don't want me to do it here, I'll do it somewhere else. I'm no villain. Why such a fuss?"

Jean stared at him. Within her approval and distaste held conflict. She knew that she would have thrown away the cigar before she came in. Was she a coward? Or was that diplomacy?

"It's your father's doings. He wants you to be as bad as he is."

"What would you have left to say if I did something really bad?" Roger put his arm about her shoulders, dauntlessly. "Come, mother, cheer up! I have to grow up!"

Mother shook away from him and went upstairs. Jean found Roger looking at her, a little defiance in his eyes. She said nothing. This was his affair. But she knew she could never have done it as he had.

One Saturday, dusting her bookshelves, Jean found the red volume, "Power and Healing." She had forgotten it! Mrs. Tiverton must wonder.

She dropped the dustcloth and sat down on the foot of her bed.

She should write to Dorothy. Stray images—— Dorothy marching into the kitchen, John at her heels; Dorothy, her wet cheek on Jean's throat; Mrs. Tiverton—what was there about her? She made you feel her, somehow. Jean opened the book.

Strange phrases. The Cosmic Whole. Dynamic personality a current for the Cosmic Whole. They sounded like sorcery! You were to feel yourself a drop in the ocean of the Cosmos. When you had that feeling, the Cosmos flowed through you, giving you Power. The capital letters leaped out of the page. Perhaps it was true. Jean shut her eyes. She was a drop in the ocean of consciousness. She held her breath. Life around her, larger, all inclusive. She heard her own heart beating. How could you be a drop and a current at the same time? She wanted a dynamic personality. To make people feel her. Was that what Mrs. Tiverton had? A fine hair tickled her nostrils and she sneezed. She opened her eyes and caught a reflection of

herself in the tipped mirror. How funny she looked! All
screwed up!

"Where did you get that book?" asked her mother a few
days later. She pointed to it. Jean, brushing her hair before
the glass, saw the red cover.

"Mrs. Tiverton gave it to me." Secret triumph in that a
mother had presented it!

"It sounds foolish," said mother. "Did you read it?"

"Part of it." Jean pinned the soft knot of hair in place.
"It sounds fine if you can feel that way!"

"I hope you aren't going to take up any of those mind
cults."

"Wouldn't it be grand to believe that nothing mattered
outside your thoughts?" Jean felt her contrary streak rise
to the surface.

"That's all right for people who have things the way they
want them. There are more important things than thoughts
in this life."

"What?" stubbornly.

"Doing the right thing. Following the laws of good."

"How do you know what they are?"

"You know well enough. Your heart tells you."

II

November came with the new school still uncompleted. A
huge rusty wood stove was erected in the middle of the
room. That meant that some of the children had to sit
together, to make room for the stove, and that it was difficult to keep the air endurable. Jean settled into a steady
pushing of herself against the ponderous days. Some of
the children were swinging clearly her way. Some stood out.
She would win!

The Wednesday before Thanksgiving she went home early,
with a free week-end ahead of her. Her mother sat on the
stairs under the window, her coat and hat on, a terrifying
rigidity in her posture. The face she turned to Jean was
ashen.

"What is it?" Jean reached for her hands. "Are you sick?"

"I've found out at last." Her mother spoke in a low monotone. "I have proof now. I'm through."

"Proof of what?"

"I've known. Almost a year. I had no proof. Now I have. Read this!" From her pocket she drew a crumpled letter, pencil scrawls over two sheets. "From that woman! Read it!"

Jean pulled back her hand.

"No, I don't want to," she implored.

"It's proof. Judge Allen said so. I went to his office. He wants to see you Saturday. It's over. I have more proof." She was whispering things so horrible that Jean pressed her hands to her ears.

"Don't tell me! I can't bear it. I'll believe it without knowing." Her father! Those whispers were about her father!

"I am going to-morrow. The Judge says I must go at once if he is to do anything."

The crawling horror had gone. Jean felt cold and hard, as if she had dropped from the riven vessel into deep water, as if she were about to swim boldly away.

"Separate maintenance. Not divorce. Not that. He'd want that! I won't give it to him. I'm going to Mamie's to-morrow." She rose like a mechanical figure. "I'll go pack now. He's been unfaithful in spirit all his life," she said. "How long he's been unfaithful in deed I don't know."

The next morning Jean telephoned Judge Allen. Could she see him? It was Thanksgiving Day, but she wondered—— He said, "Oh, Jean Winthrop. I can go down to the office. Come in."

"She has ample evidence, I am afraid." How old and wrinkled he looked, the sunshine pale on his bald forehead, thought Jean. She stared at the coiled spring stuck full of pens. "But I wanted to see you. It's a dreadful thing, legal procedure. Can't you children dissuade her? After twenty and more years together, to break up, to destroy their home."

"The destruction came long ago," said Jean steadily. "If they can separate, legally, it will be better. Better for James, too."

"You are very young, Miss Jean. You can't see the years ahead of them. What will they do?"

"What could they do together after this?"

"Worse things than this have been patched up."

"There's nothing left to patch!"

Judge Allen shook his head.

"Youth is hard and swift, my dear child," he said. "Age can't speak so definitely about anything in the world."

"There's nothing I can do." Jean felt his eyes reproaching her, as if she were to blame! "You don't know—— I just wanted to be sure this wasn't all suspicion."

"It's more than that." The Judge poked a pen between the coils of wire. Jean watched them separate reluctantly. He thought her mother should go on, saying nothing, forgiving the unforgivable. He was a man. Men would think that.

"Then what ought she to do?"

"If her mind is really made up, she must leave him at once. She can't stay under his roof. Then legal action can follow."

"Can you make him support her?"

"I don't know. He—— His business isn't very thriving, is it?"

Jean was silent.

"I'll see what can be done. But my advice——"

Jean rose; a thin, brittle crust rested over her churning despair. She must go before the crust broke!

"Thank you," she said, and hurried away.

"If she only gets off before he turns up!" Roger stood beside the small trunk and suitcase at the edge of the porch. "That hack ought to be here."

"Thank Heaven! There it is! Mother!" Jean hurried her into the recess of the carriage. "There!" She watched

the driver back the trunk up to the seat. If her father did
come now, they could drive off at top speed. Or the driver
could protect them. From what she had no clear notion. But
if he came home and found out—— Jean did not examine
the fear that jumped at her with every slight sound. Violence, sullen, threatening. Disaster, ominous, formless, like
the dark, when you were a child; like escape from prison.

They had gained the station platform.

"You stay here with Jean and I'll check your baggage."
Roger looked at Jean and she nodded. He meant that they
could linger in that corner where the office window jutted
out, making a shelter. Mother watched Roger into the
baggage room, a white incredulity in her face.

"She's amazed that she is going," thought Jean. "She
might turn around and go back even now."

"What will become of us?" Her mother moaned softly,
"Oh, I've tried to do all I could. No one knows how I've
tried."

"We'll be all right, mother." Jean felt her mother's
fingers dig into her arm.

"Who's that?" she gasped.

"That's not father. Don't you worry about us, mother.
Roger's going to live at the Y., and I'll find a boarding house.
It will be much better for both of us, and everything will be
settled, and you won't have anything more to worry
about——"

"He won't give me any money——" How gray and
shaken her mother was, clinging to her!

"He'll have to." Jean's mouth was hard. "The law will
see to that. It won't be like your asking him." Jean had
lost her fears. Time for the train. Roger was coming, the
checks in his hand. A quiet jubilance rose within her. This
was an end, a clean cut.

"Here you are." Roger wrapped a bill about the checks
and poked them into his mother's fingers.

"You won't stay with him, at that house?"

"We're going to-morrow. There! The train!"

"She's gone. I wasn't sure, until I saw the caboose."

Jean's laugh was strained. She and Roger were at the corner.

"I told her I'd help her out, as long as she stayed away. If she'll only see this through!"

"If she hadn't seen the Judge yesterday, she wouldn't have gone."

"She did, though, and now all we've got to do is to get out."

They stared at each other. Down the street crawled the car.

"I tell you, Roger! Let's go celebrate. Thanksgiving turkey! We have something to be thankful for!"

The tension broke into laughter.

"Come on!" Roger caught her arm, and they swung rapidly toward the main street. "Funny reason for thanks, but I am glad of it."

Jean couldn't eat much. She heard her mother's pitiful, "Thanksgiving morning! All the turkeys I've stuffed— trying to make things nice——"

"Do you remember," she asked, "how we always said things seemed to happen on holidays?"

"Too much strain." Roger beckoned to the waiter. He had an easy, professional way of handling waiters, thought Jean. "Mince pie, coffee, cheese. Two orders. I never thought it would come to a showdown. Gee, what a relief!"

"He's going to be some furious," said Jean, soberly.

"Lot of good that will do now!"

On the street they paused a moment, the raw wind biting after the warm, steamy restaurant.

"Guess I'll go see about a room at once." Roger moved the gilt band along his cigar. "What are you going to do?"

"Go to the house and pack."

"You aren't afraid——"

"No. When you coming?"

"Well——" Roger looked disconcerted. "You see, Molly asked me to supper to-night. So many of their folks were coming to dinner. She said she'd save me a drumstick. I didn't know, of course——"

"That's all right." Jean smiled jauntily. "You aren't deserting me! Run along. I may look for a place to stay."

She walked slowly into the empty house. The walls had crumbled at last. She had to crawl among the ruins, after her things. The last time. She stopped abruptly. Someone upstairs, dragging drawers open, rushing about.

"Nothing to be scared of," she told herself, but her face had a strained, peaked look.

"Jean!" Her father clattered down the stairs, missing a step, almost falling, catching himself. His hair, thin on top, flew up wildly about his face. "Has she gone? You let her go! Without stopping her! It's a lie." His fingers clutched at Jean's wrist. "What she told that lawyer! A lie! You shouldn't have let her go."

"If it's a lie"—Jean was rock, hard and cold. "You'll have a chance to prove it."

"You believe it! You!" His face twitched. Jean looked away from him. Indecent! He was fumbling through dead years, trying to reach her old love. "Jean, it's a lie!"

Jean walked into the library, pulling off her coat. She wouldn't be moved. She wouldn't let that dreadful, piteous flutter come to the surface.

"She needn't think she can get money out of me! I won't give one damned cent! Things on my side, I guess! She didn't leave me, time after time, did she? Think she can get away with that! She hasn't let me sleep with her for months! The law will listen to that!"

Jean sat with hands clenched. Her heart would stifle her! He, too, stripping life down to nakedness. She was their daughter, born of them. She couldn't endure it. She couldn't listen. How long would his voice roar on—thick, husky, shooting up into shrill denunciations?

"I should think"—Jean lifted her head at last, "that you would be glad to have an end."

"End! I'll fight it! I'll get me a lawyer, too! Not one cent of money will she get! I'll lie in the gutter and rot. She'll come back, you see!"

"Why, don't you want all this stopped?"

Suddenly he was crying, thick, dreadful sobs.

"She's got to come back! She's got to."

Jean moved hastily past him, away from the fingers that clutched at her, up the stairs.

"I'll go crazy mad," she thought, "if I stay here. Let me get away!"

As she packed her suitcase, working in clumsy haste, she stopped often to listen. No sound below her. If she let herself think, she would break down. He was to blame! Was he? Oh, surely it was over, all the corroding strife. Was it? Nothing clear and simple, like an end. If it had been someone else, not that woman—snail thing!

A clatter on the stairs. Her father again, at the door.

"You're going, too?" He stared at her suitcase. "Rats off the sinking ship. She's tried all her life to separate us. You're letting her?"

"I can't keep house and teach too," said Jean gently. Why not speak out what she thought? No, soften the edges——

"I am just going to a boarding house."

"There never was a father cared more for a daughter——"

"I know." Jean stood in front of him. Under her heart pressed a faint flutter; was she going to faint? She gripped the iron rod at the foot of the bed, and its cool firmness entered her. A small satiric voice said, "You haven't cared very much for any of us, not very much!" Why not say that? Roger would say it, if he thought it. She couldn't.

"You know how she talks when she's mad. You know things she's said to you! They ain't true. This isn't true. Do you believe it?"

Jean turned away, pulling open a drawer. Her departure must speak for her. She heard his feet, loud, defiant, on the stairs.

III

Jean did not see her father again before she left the house. Roger nailed up her box of books and pictures, and they carried it to the porch, where the expressman could find it.

She found a room in a boarding house not far from
Lora Tate's. Seven dollars a week for room and meals.
That would not leave much out of her monthly check. She
didn't care! Roger came in on Sunday night, to find her
arranging her books on the shelf.

"I had one peach of a row this afternoon." He threw
himself on her couch. "Good thing you got off yesterday."

"Roger!" Jean stood above him, agitated by his white,
drawn cheeks, the blustering snarl in his voice.

"I told him a thing or two! He started to lay me out,
and I told him if he touched me, I'd——"

"He struck you!"

"No. He just yelled around. Crazy. Drinking, I guess.
He didn't touch me."

"What did you tell him?"

"I spoke to him like one loving son, believe me! I touched
up a few of his actions, all right. Several he didn't know
I was wise to."

Jean saw him suddenly as a little boy again, hiding his
hurt under loud words. Poor Roger!

"I never said a word," she confessed. "Didn't want to
make a fuss."

"Oh, well." Roger sat up, a pleased flash in his eyes.
Jean saw it. The hint that he was a man, and she was only
a girl. She sighed. Let him feel that way if he wanted to.
But under her surface thoughts she was wondering: was
she a coward? Never speaking out? Was that weakness?

"Got a nice room?" she asked.

"Fair. Clean. Do to sleep in. I've got to be going along."

"Molly waiting for you?" Jean grinned at him.

"Sure she is. She's a good waiter, that girl!"

The next month moved slowly. Jean ate breakfast hastily,
trying between gulps to make conversation with the other
boarders: an old man who worked in the bank, two plump
women from offices, an anemic drawing teacher. School had
the same thick resistance to her efforts. Dinner, like breakfast. Papers to correct, lessons to plan. Bed. She saw
Lora occasionally, but a slight awkwardness hung between

them, since Lora was working on her trousseau, and Jean couldn't talk about Percy.

Letters from mother, frequent, tragic. Jean answered them, and then pushed resolutely away the thought of her mother and father. She envied Roger his absorption in Molly. She wanted a lover. If Luther had been at the college—she flushed at the half-articulate wish for him. She thought, "There's the principal—captivate him!" But when she saw him, she shivered away from her earlier thought. Unconsciously, however, it gave a tinge of coquetry to the brief conversations. He was heavy, tall, with pudgy hands and plump face, always scarlet during school hours, a slight twitching of his round cheeks, of the eyelids over his small eyes; heavy curling hair, astonishing clusters of it on his fingers. A country boy, with several years of teaching and a year at a small normal school. Jean sensed his struggles against intimidation by the pupils, or the faculty members of the board.

"You're the first teacher I ever had that I could really get on with," he said to her one night, after a conference about the new building. "I haven't had one scrap with you!"

"Can't scrap with me, ever," said Jean.

To herself she thought, resentfully, "They pay that boob more than me! Thirty dollars a month more!"

She looked reflectively at men on the streetcars. Would I like him? Would I—— Then she struggled away from such thoughts. No decent girl would have them, she mourned.

She was a ship on a windless ocean, sails empty, no motion but the empty swell of inert waters.

Perhaps a letter to Miss McNealy carried a flavor of that stagnation. Miss McNealy sent her a catalogue from a correspondence department of the university, suggesting that she go on with college work. Jean read the catalogue; a faint puff into her sails. She might—— She hadn't the sixteen dollars, but Roger lent her ten. She enrolled for a course in writing. "Write whatever you like," came the official instructions. "This is a course in criticism."

She went to Mamie's for Christmas. Mother was hectic, strained, nervous. Mamie tried to whisper to Jean, but somehow mother always appeared at the door. Mamie looked smaller, grayer, more bent. James seemed chiefly thin legs and arms sticking out from his clothes. He hung about Jean in a delight which made her want to cry. Poor Jamesie! Probably mother talked to him—and Mamie, too. She made a snowman with him, and a fort. He begged for the old stories.

Roger came down for Christmas day. Jean walked to the station with him that evening.

> Gray dawn behind the tamarisks,
> The sky is saffron yellow,
> And the women—dum-de, dum-de—grind the corn,
> As the day, the ghastly eastern day, is born,

she chanted.

"What's that?"

"Christmas in India," said Jean. She went on with the poem. "Feels like that, doesn't it?"

"How much longer do you have to stay?"

"Till Sunday."

"Do you think she will stay here till things are settled?" His face peered at her anxiously through the dusk.

"Don't know. She says Allen isn't doing anything. He probably doesn't see any money for himself."

"She hinted she'd been thinking she ought to go back, sacrifice herself to save us disgrace! I just told her right out that divorce seemed polite and decent compared to some things!"

"Oh, Roger! That's what she was crying about, then."

"Well, doesn't it? Maybe I'd better see Allen."

"She says she's written to him again. She's got to have more money. Says Mamie fusses over the bills. I gave her what I had."

"Tell her I'll send some next week. *He* ought to have to fork up!"

James cried when Jean packed her suitcase.

"Don't, Jamesie!" Jean felt near tears herself. "Don't, little kid brother!" Her arms were tight about him.

"Can't you get a job teaching here? I'd like you for my teacher."

"Some day you can come and live with me. How'd you like that?"

"Fine." James sniffed.

"You write to me, and I'll write you long letters just for your very own."

Mother came in.

"I can't bear to let you go!"

"Have to earn my living." Jean strapped her bag vigorously.

"Be thankful that you can."

"Mother! Why don't you get a position, teaching——" Jean was sorry she had spoken. Her mother turned away, her face quivering.

"How can I? I'm ruined—health, spirit——"

"There!" Jean spoke loudly. "You don't need to!"

On the train she sat erect, the brim of her hat poked into the dusty green plush of the seat. At least she didn't have to stay there!

No one met her. Roger had said he was going to take Molly to a New Year party that night. She hesitated, then walked past the waiting hacks. Only a few blocks, if she took a car. She better save her nickels.

She hadn't known how cold it was. Her fingers ached under the drag of the suitcase. The wind buffeted her hat. Black despair folded over her, partly physical discomfort, partly emotional fatigue, product of the week just past. Mamie was ashamed. "If your mother would only go out and act different! She hides here, and people think it's queer. We Stevens never had to hang our heads! What's she going to do?" And mother—"I can't stay here much longer. Your aunt doesn't want me here. She's ashamed." What were they to do? Poor Jamesie, in the midst of that coil of feeling!

"Oh, what's the use?" Jean stopped, shifting her bag to the other hand, thrusting her numbed fingers between the buttons of her coat. "Just going on—— I wish I was dead!"

She slipped on a bit of ice, and the bag flew from her hand.

"Stop being a fool!" she cried to herself. "Take a brace!"

She went on gingerly. One more block. What was her father doing? How covertly her mother had asked, "Haven't you seen anything of him? You must have seen him!"

She reached the boarding house and fumbled with stiff fingers at the doorknob. The door swung open.

"Oh, Miss Winthrop!" Miss Sargent, the landlady, stepped back. A black bow pinned on one side of her streaked, sandy hair, announced festivities. "How nice you've got back. I wanted all my little family here. Come right in. Cold, isn't it?"

Jean saw the parlor jammed with people. She darted for the stairs.

"I'm frozen and tired," she began.

"Just a little New Year party." Miss Sargent was dolorous, her pale eyes widening. "You must come in. To get us all better acquainted. There's a new man——"

"I'll have to scrub off the train dirt," Jean conceded, unwillingly.

She couldn't go down! Chatter, buzz! She took off her coat and hat. Rumpled waist, untidy hair, a kind of purple gray color on her cheeks and nose. With a sigh she picked up her towel and started to the bathroom. Perhaps if she went down she would lose the awful gone feeling in her stomach. She would put on the new silk waist she had made at Mamie's.

When she came into the parlor, old Mr. Jessup, the bank clerk, rose to meet her, smiling, the yellowed folds of his throat expanding amiably. He liked her. Old people always liked her.

"Well, Happy New Year, Miss Winthrop! I'm glad you got back. Pleasant Christmas? Santa bring you just what you wanted? We're just going to have some music. Miss Lester's going to play. Here, meet Mr.——What was your name, sir?"

Jean turned to meet the cool gray eyes of the new man. Tall, lackadaisical, sardonic, he was laughing at them! She had a quick impulse to stand in front of doddering, kindly old Jessup, to protect him.

"Fletcher," he was saying. "Hard name to remember. Miss Winthrop." He bowed easily over her hand. How different his voice was, low, distinct, slipping over his words.

Jean watched him resentfully through the evening. What was he doing here? He didn't belong. He was laughing at them all. Miss Lester, the anemic drawing teacher, was fluttering at him!

Miss Sargent served the refreshments in the dining room. Grape juice and welsh rarebit. Jean found Mr. Fletcher beside her, plate in thin hand.

"Food like this repays one for much," he said, under his breath. Jean felt a distinct challenge, as if she heard him add, "You aren't like these others——"

Mr. Jessup had wound up the phonograph and put on his favorite record, "The Palms." Miss Biddle, round and pink, was murmuring, "Wonderful, I call it. I was saying to my sister yesterday, you can't tell it from real voices if you shut your eyes." Across the room Miss Lester broke out, "They say cheese isn't digestible, but I never mind it any time of day or night." Mr. Fletcher waited, and suddenly he smiled, a strange lighting of his lean, sardonic face.

"They mean well," said Jean, hostilely.

"I thought so," he said. "I drink to your delicacy of perception."

Jean felt a quickening of pulse. Who was he, this gray-eyed stranger, saying things like that?

She moved away from him in answer to a question from Miss Biddle, but she was acutely aware of him, of the subtle grace of his walk, of his ease of manner, of the light behind his eyes.

As she started up the stairs, she found him just below, his hand on the railing.

"Good night, Oh ox-eyed Juno—no, not Juno, Minerva, rather."

"Are you living here now?" she asked abruptly, her eyes on his hand, with its long, restless fingers.

"For a time. Between rough voyages."

Radiance drifted through her. She lifted her eyes; was there gray in his short dark hair, brushed so straight back from his high forehead?

"Then—" she laughed. "I may hear your winged words again! Good night, Ulysses." And she ran up to her room.

He was not at breakfast the next morning, and Jean discreetly asked no questions. But through the hours of school she saw him, looking up at her, smiling. Would he be there at night? He had noticed her. That was only her eager conceit, and his nonchalant, easy manner. Ah, no, he had seen her!

IV

She reached the boarding house early. For a moment she stood in the upper hall, looking at the closed doors. Which was his—that at the end? On the floor above were two rooms, too. She closed her own door softly, and gazed at her reflection. Why had he called her Minerva? She brushed her hair, leaning forward to peer at her image. The glass gave her back seriousness, wind-flushed cheeks, intent eyes. She wished she were pretty! Should she try curling her hair? She shrugged and brushed the soft, dark, flying mass up to the crown of her head, in a single broad knot. It was too fine to stay in curl. Too fine to do anything but limpse down! She buttoned her fresh white blouse. She couldn't wear her silk waist every night. Linen collar and blue Windsor tie. Did she look school-ma'amish?

Supper at last. There he was, at the round table in the corner, with Miss Lester and Miss Biddle. He smiled at her. Never had old Mr. Jessup a more animated listener to

his old anecdotes. No mirror there to show Jean the exqui-
site deepening of color, the ecstasy of eyes, the softening of
the curve of her lips. Her sails were filled at last, with the
swift dominant wind of romance.

She lingered on the stairs after supper. Would he stay
in the parlor? Would he come up to his room? He was
beside her on the stairs.

"Do you always let that poor antique find himself so fascinating?" Confusion under his clear gray glance. "Would
that I might find such an audience!"

"Come in and try," Jean held her door ajar.

"Is it done?" He looked into her small room. "The cot
lends respectability?"

"It's my sitting room," said Jean. Was it done? She
didn't care.

"Have you read nothing later than Meredith, Oh Minerva?" He turned from the shelves of books beside the
window. "Or does the Sargent furnish your books, too?"

"They are mine." Jean looked at the books. "They're
not all I've read," she said, and then flushed, as if caught in
a childish boast.

"No?" Mr. Fletcher dropped to her couch, sprawling
against the pillows. "Well, tell us about it. What do you
do? What are you like?"

Jean sat in the little rocker. She wanted to keep him
there, where she could look at him, hear him, see his long,
supple fingers clasp about his knees.

"I teach school. I don't know what I'm like." She
smiled. "Who are you?"

"The short and simple flannels of the poor!" He mocked
at something—himself? Her?

But when he rose, much later, and said, "You are flatter-
ing, with your attention," Jean knew many things. That
he had been at Yale. That he had been ill, very ill, and in
a sanatorium for months. That he meant to study at the
college, forestry or sheep raising or apple growing, something out of doors. That G. B. Shaw was the greatest
modern writer. That she should read Marx. And Kautsky.

That he would live under this roof with her. That his father was an eastern lawyer, brilliant, erratic. "He begot me with brains and no body," the man had said lightly.

When he had gone, she listened to the sound of his door closing. Her hands clasped against her breast, she stood and listened. And she heard the great sweep of wings, lifting her, carrying her out of herself, out of her own life.

"He has seen so much, and done so much—he can't like me," she thought. And then, "But he will be here! I can see him!"

In her dreams he walked, shining and wonderful, clothed in the radiance of all her desires, possessed of the glamour of strange lands and experiences she had never touched.

She never saw him in the morning. School had faded into an immaterial filling of hours. Strange how easy tasks there became, once they were no longer important! As if the children felt they could not touch her inner self, and so laid aside their attempts, growing docile, eager. She liked them. She found them lovable, or pitiful, or amusing. Strange metamorphosis! When she no longer needed their yielding to her as a source for her strength, they gave it to her willingly. The new building was finished, and she had a shining new room, with model seats and blackboards. Grand indifference to these glories! A deep spring within her, from which energy bubbled up, unending.

At night she left her door ajar, pretending to read papers from school, or books. Waiting. For a step, a voice.

"Too busy for Ulysses, O Minerva?"

He liked to sprawl on the couch while she read aloud. Shaw at first. Candida. Jean thought, "Can people ever say just what they think, like Candida! I couldn't——" She kept cruel guard over her tongue, lest she utter some banality and see the sardonic glint in those cold eyes.

"Amusing duffer, isn't he?"

"He's exciting." Jean laid the book aside.

"You react through your mind first, don't you?" That speculative gaze, as if she were a specimen! "He excites only the intelligent."

One night he came in with two photographs.

"What do you see in these, O Ox-eyed?" He laid them on her table.

"They're the same girl." Jean looked from the cardboard faces up at him, disturbed.

"Before and after. Look on this face, then on this. Ah, what a change is there! She's going to marry me." He pointed to one. "She's the girl I wanted to marry. I went to a sick-coop, and when I escaped, this!"

Evening dress, with curved shoulders, soft braids of hair, great dark eyes, conscious of their beauty, of their length of eyelash. Fire trembling at Jean's finger tips. She hid her hands in her lap lest they tear the face across.

"Before and after what?" She pushed her voice out. He mustn't see! He was watching her!

"Three years. The alchemy of time. What would you think of her, I wonder? Only daughter, wealthy banker father. Lap of luxury. Petted darling, parasite, trained to the last shade in the subtle art of being beautiful and pleasing males. That's the only thing she can do. Loessa French. She is rich. I shall still marry her."

"What would she think of me?" Jean sat very still and heard frantic little thoughts dart at her. He doesn't love her, or he could never talk that way! How do you know? He talks that way of anything. He's testing you! Look out! No, he's warning you. This is his warning.

"Of you, Minerva?" She could never be sure what he thought. Other people thought of themselves first, as they talked, and Jean could guess, often, what rested in their eyes. But this man—he was terribly aware of other people first. Not in any kindly fashion. As a mocking onlooker. "Can't you see that Loessa never sees the toilers of the world?"

"When are you going to get married?"

"Oh, literal-minded one!" He stared at Jean until she rose and moved to the window. What could he see? "As soon as Loessa will. I think she is even now persuading her father that she must have me. He has sent her to the coast to find some other plaything. My value is thus enhanced. No, Minerva, it isn't love. Who are you to ask me if I marry for that fond illusion?"

She heard Roger's voice in the hall. She had asked him to come in for supper. As she introduced him, she waited. Would Mr. Fletcher make fun of him? But he was discreet.

"What's that fellow do?" asked Roger abruptly, when he had settled himself in the armchair, after supper.

"He's studying to be an expert farmer or something. He's been to Yale. Then he was sick."

"Funny farmer!" Roger's expression was that of a scarcely restrained sniff.

"Don't you like him?"

"Seems to like himself well enough, so that wouldn't matter! Guess he's all right. You think so, that's easy!"

"It's interesting to have someone to read with and talk to"—Jean made her reply elaborately casual. At which Roger grinned.

"Go ahead!" he said. "I'm having some fun, too! Say, it is one fine relief, not to have to listen to family thunder."

"Mother doesn't sound any more contented." Jean came reluctantly back to family affairs. "Her letters get worse all the time."

"She's got to wait a while till things are settled. Then we can see——"

Roger went early.

"You look tired. Better go to bed." As he stood at the door, Jean felt sharply his personal flavor, as if she looked at him through alien eyes. His staunchnes, his integrity, his reliability. Like a tree, she thought. And the other— like fire, or quicksilver, or acid. Nothing staunch.

"Good night, old dear. Don't work too hard." She kissed him, in a momentary renewal of their old pledge to each other.

With his departure they were at her with a pounce, the thoughts she had pushed under. That pictured face! Smug, useless thing! She hated it. That was being jealous. It felt like that, sullen, wild rage, impotent. Jean couldn't sit still. Her thoughts seemed to pull at the nerves in her legs, twitching them. She walked back and forth, ten steps each way. Why had he shown her those pictures? What had he meant? Illusion of love? She could make him care. Could she? That mocking, thin, sophisticated, Mephistophelian face! What was he thinking of her, as he watched her? Thoughts of her mother whirled up in the flotsam. Her mother had been jealous. She had walked back and forth. Jean stopped abruptly. What had she to offer—any man? Disgrace behind her. Indefinitely she felt the delicate, sensuous appeal of that photograph. She had none of that. Nothing. Her feet on the floor, ten steps each way. Perhaps he might hear her, in his room. He would think she was disturbed. Suffering. Terrible tragedy. She could hint at it. If he was engaged, what then? She should decide. What?

Later she stood at the window, looking out at the dark wall of the next house. Tired, ashamed. She had been play acting, walking back and forth. She needn't have done that. Her thought, half formed, ran thus: He will be here, all winter. I don't care what happens. I mean to take every second! Every tiny, small drop of time. It is mine! In a vague, distorted phantasy, which bridged the void between waking and sleeping, she saw him towering above her, his face a mask of glittering steel, his hands full of strange gifts, while she, a little, awe-filled figure, reached her hands up vainly toward him.

She had lost the radiant delight of the first days. The hours ran flushed and hectic, and Jean gathered them in breathless fear.

The books they read threw added light about him, as if he had made them. "Penguin Island." The brilliant, weary satire was part of Ulysses and his searching, unrevealing eyes. "The New Word." The vague, elusive, romantic philosophy seemed to expand the world itself, and all through the man who brought the book into her room.

"Do you know Henley's poems?" he asked one night.

" 'Out of the night that covers me,' " Jean's pleasure as she quoted was self-conscious. She knew so little!

"Lord, not that rot! That's not Henley. Oh, he wrote it, but only for school books. Hunt him up at your library. 'Where forlorn sunsets flare and die'—— 'My head is bloody but unbowed!' He knew better than that!"

Jean found a volume at the college library.

"You read poetry much worse than you do other things." Stuart scoffed at her from the couch. "Don't chew it like nails! Read it!"

Jean flung the book to the floor.

"Read it yourself!" Her cheeks flamed. After a moment, Stuart rose and strolled out of her room. She stared at the blue cover, one hand against her lips, pushing back the angry tears. She had read abominably! She was afraid, afraid of those singing, betraying lines! She was afraid he would think her sentimental, if she let them sing. She hated him, treating her like a naughty child! Slowly her hand crept out to the book, and she turned the pages, the poems beating into her mood. Passionate, despairing, youth seizing at the one golden hour, intense, fragile—— She couldn't bear them! She wanted him to come back, wanted to grovel, abjectly, for her flare.

An apple rolled across the floor to her feet. He was standing negligently in the doorway.

"My apology, Oh Minerva! Let us fare forth, you and I, in quest of mundane amusement. A hot chocolate at the town drugstore——"

Jean hesitated. She wanted to sulk. To stay there—— She rose swiftly.

"In a minute," she said, running for her coat and hat. What was the matter with her? Touchy!

She couldn't stop to analyze her outbreaks. The days were too swift, too heady. She wondered whether the self-control she had labored for, all these years, was only a delusion. She had so much to hide! Nothing broke through but these quick, childish flares of anger; never any of the hungry longing for his step outside her door; never any hint of her shy, subtle, outreaching for the things he would have her say or do; never any of the constant delicate plumbing of the man—what was he, underneath? What did he think or feel? If Jean had tried to understand those spits of fire, she would have failed. The tension of the vortex in which she dwelt, whirling passion implicit but hidden, humility, the old child-impulse toward submission, toward pain, the secret, dominant quest for herself—out of that tension shot up at times stray bits of self-pride, of assertiveness latent but unstifled. Her submission was no passive kneeling; it was the negation poised in contrary impulses. So much that she desired! To gain a whit of all that desire, this kneeling must come first.

V

One February afternoon as she crossed the street to the corner where she waited for the car, her heart tightened. Stuart! Ah, she saw him everywhere! No, it was he, this time.

"Hello, Minerva." He looked at her, the quick, surprisingly gentle smile on his lips. "I thought I might catch you, winning back from Erasmus. Come, let us dine in state at the corner beanery. Then we can walk beneath the stars."

"Too cloudy for stars." Jean shed her weariness like a garment. "But I am hungry!"

They sat on a stool in the basement lunch room. Jean laughed at the waiter's distrust of Stuart's wordy elegance. The dinner, the dingy, common place, the counter—— Stuart was laying out a farm with the catsup bottle for a silo, toothpicks for the pasture fence—a shining, infrangible bubble of delight enclosed the hour, each slightest gesture large, potent with secret beauty.

"Leave your books, here. Serf, do you draw the bridge before eleven?" Stuart beckoned to the waiter, who eyed him suspiciously over his spotted apron.

"How late are you open?" asked Jean. The boy would

think they were laughing at him! She didn't want him hurt, not to-night! Not anyone!

"Twelve."

"We may return. Shelter these." Stuart flipped a coin across the counter, and swept Jean out of the dim room.

"There's wind in the twilight—" whispered Jean. They had taken a road which led into open country beyond the college. The snow lay packed into frozen ruts, with jagged piles along the ditches. The clouds had blown away; there were a few sharp stars.

Silence, save for the high little note of snow under their shoes. Jean's hush was that at the edge of beauty; she knelt, gathering into her heart all that her eager fingers could reach of this perfect hour.

"Enviable Minerva!" His voice startled her. "Do you know how enviable you are?"

"I don't think I am, particularly." Jean turned a key against the tremulous beauty in which she had walked, and stood guard at a locked door. Had he guessed? Would he pry that open?

"Strong, a stride like a man's. No, like an Amazon. Wonderful body, Minerva. A mind. Like a man's. Women don't have them. Yet yours is distinct, not male. A heart, tender, soft. That makes an irreducible conflict. Then there's something more. You keep it hidden. What is it?"

"I hide less than you." Again that tension within her, shrinking and an urge forward. What did he mean? "And you are more enviable."

"Kind words and flattery, but untrue. No dog would envy me. Useless. A tool on the workshop floor, worn to the butt—— Imitative, empty. I warn you, Minerva, a sepulcher walks here."

"Sepulchers are interesting—for their past!"

"Bah! Inscriptions on a mummy case. Now you, what *will* you do?"

Jean felt his face bend toward hers in the white dusk, grim, sardonic.

"That vigor, you don't know what that's worth! And the rest, with the something you still hide——"

The tranquil delight was gone. Jean was a specimen, quivering under instruments. The shining bubble had vanished. He was no longer with her; he stood off, mockingly, inspecting her.

"Don't you wish you were a man?"

"No. Never."

"You'll have trouble, getting all you want."

"No matter." Vague words, full of omen.

The road came to a corner, another country road crossing it, nothing beyond but snow-covered fields. They stood a moment, Stuart looking down at Jean. Her heart began to beat in a slow, terrible rhythm, in her breast, in her throat, at her wrists. She felt that he drew her spirit out, in a fine white thread, glistening there like starlight, held it taut between his fingers. If it snapped, she would be lost! She could never find it. She would throw herself at his feet, begging him to take her. She was mad, a white, cold madness, like the snow. No, not a thread! A fine, steel spring! It had coiled back from his fingers, resilient, strong! She turned away, scuffing her foot along a rut.

"That lunch place will be closed. I'm going back," she said, marveling to herself at the clear firmness of her voice.

Jean's swift walk back was flight, flight from the great stretch of empty, white, untenanted places. She craved walls and lights and warmth and people! They saw the shaft of light from the streetcar sway around a distant corner.

"Missed it," said Stuart.

"No, we haven't!" Jean ran, thumping over the hard ruts. She must catch it!

In triumph she glanced up at Stuart as he settled beside her. A queer purple line on his lips, under his eyes; he was breathing in gasps.

"Oh, did I go too fast?"

"Must you taunt me with my weakness, O Amazon?" His eyes with dilated pupils looked black in his pale face.

Jean turned hastily away. She had been malicious! He knew it! But no small triumph!

She remembered her schoolbooks.

"Can you live till morning without them?" Stuart stretched his legs under the seat ahead, and pulled off his soft hat. The purple shadows had gone and his breath came evenly again.

"I might." Jean's glance had entreaty in it. She had not meant to flaunt her vigor.

They parted in silence at Jean's door, with a fleeting, strange exchange of glances. He knew she had escaped him! Just as he had almost vanquished her! He was reaching out subtly, quietly, to win her back to that complete subjection.

A letter from her mother on the table. Judge Allen hadn't even bothered to answer her letters, she wrote. No one would do anything for her. What was she to do, which way could she turn for help?

Restlessness, black, disturbing. Jean paced her floor. Stage play! No, she couldn't sleep.

The next night she closed her door. When Stuart whistled, she said, "I'm busy. I've got the black devils. I don't want to see you."

She heard him on the stairs, on the porch, down the street. She clung to her chair lest she run after him, calling him back. What perverse demon had spoken, leaving her the long, dragging hours of the evening?

As she poked listlessly among the school papers on her table, she saw the folder from the university. She hadn't thought of that correspondence course since she had sent the money! She hunted up the box of paper she had bought to use. Fresh, smooth sheets. That story she had thought out last summer, on the lake. The clear peace of those days returned to her, faint, like a song she had heard long ago. A story of an obscure Mormon colony on an island—someone had pointed to an isolated dead pine, and told the legend. Dead, because it stood above an altar where human beings had been slain to appease an angry god.

Jean brushed the school papers to the floor and began to

write. A long time later she looked up, stretched her cramped arms, gathered the scattered sheets. From her window she could see the patch of light Stuart's lamp threw on the next wall. His head moved across it, grotesquely enlarged. She had not heard him come in! She watched an instant. The shadow threw no tendrils out to enmesh her. Lightness filled her, a strange freedom. She had emptied herself upon these papers. Good? How could she know? She folded them, sealed them, addressed them, all with a wondering excitement.

But the next evening that mood had gone, and she waited, her door wide.

"Storm over?" Stuart lounged against the door frame. "Is it safe to enter?"

"No danger signals to-night." Jean's smile was fleetly deprecatory.

"Did you stay up all night with devils?" He dropped to the couch.

"Last night? I worked."

"You sounded black."

"I got over that."

"You know, Minerva, you'd be a perfect companion, if you had no moods."

Jean looked away. She didn't want to lose her temper, not to-night. There lay the letter from her mother.

"You don't know—what makes them." What would he think, she wondered, if she told him—about home?

"Ah, Minerva! I know! You may find some external cause. That's found for explanation. Look deeper. Such a pity, spoiling perfection."

The room was very still. Jean saw herself, pacing its length, wringing her hands, entertaining her demons. A small, derisive voice shouted within her: you thought it made you interesting! It wasn't that you feel so bad about them! Appallingly she linked herself with her mother. Like her hysterics. A dull weapon, futile, impotent. She was frightened. He had twisted a cudgel from her grasp, and looking at it, she saw it for a reed.

She moved hastily in her chair, turning to glance at Stuart. He was lying back against the pillows, eyes closed. How thin he was! The harshness was gone. Only a rush of tenderness toward him.

"Personal devils hang around, always." He opened his eyes suddenly, smiling at her. "The damned things lurk—— That's all! Here's more food, Minerva. The laborers' Bible." He tossed a fat volume across to her. Marx. "Capital. Don't read it to me. Try it alone."

"Head ache?" Jean drew her chair nearer the couch.

"Beastly." He held out his hand and Jean laid hers in his.

Eyes closed, he lay there. Scarcely breathing, Jean watched him. Could he feel in her cold finger tips the strange, rhythmic ecstasy that flooded her? Some thoughts he read obscurely in her face; would touch betray her further? Deeper than thought? She had a queer fancy, a story of blood transfusion she had once heard. Was he draining vitality from her, clinging thus? She dreamed, ineffably tender, over his face, the planes of forehead, hollows under the cheekbones, jutting chin, thin eyelids, faintly dark over the eyeballs. She it was who possessed virility, strength. Could she pour it into him?

Suddenly the eyelids folded back, and his eyes held her, hushed, quiescent. Only an instant, and she had sought covert in words.

"Sleepy head," she said, quietly, "you'd better go to bed."

"You cured my head." Stuart probed at her, but she was safely hidden. "Good night, Minerva."

He turned at the door.

"I'm off to Chicago this week-end," he said, casually.

That night Jean dreamed. Walking, she came to a cliff down which led precipitous stairs. She could not see what lay in the darkness far beneath her, but she knew she had to climb down the stairs. Stone, slippery wet, cold. She dared not walk down them. She slipped on hands and knees, clinging with bruised fingers, fighting against terrific panic. Down and down. Her foot struck cinders, and she turned. She stood on a mound, like the dump heap along the railroads, cinders, tin cans, rubbish. The stone steps were forgotten. Then she saw, dimly, for the light was like the gray before dawn, two figures. A child, deformed, gnome-like, running, crying, stumbling over rusty iron, holding up bleeding hands, sobbing, "Look! I am hurt!" And after the child, in mad gyrating pursuit, another figure, neither man nor woman, one hand hidden in the folds of a gray cloak. The child stumbled, and the second figure was upon it. In uplifted hand shone a sword, flashing like water. Jean tried to cry aloud. She tore at bandages swathed over mouth and throat, struggling to scream. The flashing knife descended, the child's scream broke abruptly, and Jean rent the bandages in a great cry. She woke, hearing that cry echoed ridiculously as a guttural noise from her lips. She sat up in the darkness, the terror of that struggle still resting over her. Vaguely she felt the dream as part of her, the waste place, the figures, all herself. She reached a hand out to the cord of the lamp, and as the light snapped on, the dream receded in mist.

When she woke in the morning, she could not remember the dream. Something had died. No use. Like grasping at wisps of fog. But as she dressed, she thought, "I feel as if I had lost something. Queer——" And later, "Stuart was right. About the demons. I let them in. I liked to feel bad. I'm done with that!" And a kind of exaltation filled her, as if she had sloughed off an old garment, tight and constricting, and could stand erect, breathe freely.

VI

A letter from Dorothy that morning, enclosing a note from Eva Jennings, one of the old Agora girls. Eva was to be married on Saturday. She wanted Dorothy and Jean to come over. They could stay all night. She lived in the country outside a small town not far away. Dorothy wrote that unless Jean wired her, she would come early Saturday and they could go together.

Jean thought: Good. Now I won't have time to miss him.

Dorothy was excited. When they had poked their bags into the rack and settled in the seat, she said,

"Weren't you amazed?"

"No. What at?" Jean was watching the town fly past them, thinking: Stuart must have reached Chicago by now.

"Why, at Eva! At Christmas she swore she'd never marry Tom!"

"I didn't know anything about it." Jean pulled her attention back to Dorothy. How sweet she looked, with the soft dark fur of her collar against her cream skin.

"Didn't you ever hear of Eva's Tom? Well! She's gone with him almost since she was born. Lived on the next farm. She was engaged to him when she came to college. Then he went off—he runs a drygoods store somewhere in Indiana. Messes with women—oh, he was awful! Married women, too! Eva broke off with him. He promised to reform, and she got engaged again. Then he went off. Eva wouldn't tell me what happened, but her folks wouldn't let him come into the house. Drink, I guess, and any sort of woman. And here she is, marrying him! I don't see how she dares!"

"Maybe she can't help herself."

"Jean!" Dorothy stared. "What's happened to *you?* Who is he?"

"I just meant she probably loves him." Jean pulled bravado over her embarrassment. Dorothy's eyes were close to hers, searching.

"Never you mind! You'll tell me to-night!"

Jean watched with a kind of fervent curiosity Eva dressing for her wedding, joking with the girls—there were six of them—talking with her mother about the wedding supper. Plump-bosomed, fresh color, rather bold, large features; Eva had always stayed outside Jean's horizon of interest. But this—she saw in the prominent blue eyes a devout glow, a hastening toward immolation. Tom. Jean peered at him, through the haze of the legend of his desperate career. Tall, hooked nose, white teeth, black eyes and hair. She guessed that Eva wanted him, no matter what the cost. Dorothy and Rachel were whispering. Rachel had married her Everett two years before, and bore an added dignity in this upper chamber as a matron. Jean heard Rachel's, "I don't see how she dares risk it! If it was just one affair—but how does she know——" Vague, veiled accusations. Eva came in then, the stiff white silk of her wedding gown rustling.

Then it was all over, and the carriage had driven away, with Eva in a new snugly fitting blue suit, and Tom beside her, Eva's mother sobbing in the doorway, waving a damp handkerchief, her stout bosom agitated, her features astonishingly like Eva's with the flush of weeping over them.

"Let's get out," whispered Dorothy, drawing Jean toward the stairs. "Eva said we could have her room. Rachel's got to sleep down here."

The girls undressed in silence, not looking at each other. Jean raised the window, shivering as the raw, thawing wind of March pushed through the curtains.

They lay side by side, still without speech. The sheets were clammy. Jean felt the small area of warmth increase to comfort. Suddenly Dorothy flung out a hand against her arm.

"Jean!" She twisted her arm under Jean's shoulders, and the two girls clung together, the tension loosening under the touch of soft bodies. "I hate weddings!"

"My first."

"Think—Eva—will never sleep here again——"

"Where is she, to-night?"

"At the hotel in town. They go on to-morrow to Ashley."

Silence. Jean felt Dorothy shivering. Her own thoughts glanced off from Eva, followed her no further than the carriage, smiling back as they drove away.

"Jean!" A little snuggling motion, quick, warm. "Tell me about him! Who is he?"

"Nothing to tell." Jean was rigid. "Nothing!"

"You're different! Something—— Oh, you can't fool me!

Jean, dear!" Warm lips on her throat, coaxing. "Jean, it's not that Luther?"

"Luther! Him!"

"Who is it?"

"You don't know him." The dark, the warmth of cling-ing arms, the soft, urging voice all worked on Jean, break-ing down her long loneliness. Tell her! Faint trickle through the dam—tell her! "There is nothing to tell," she said faintly.

"You are in love!" Dorothy leaned on an elbow, nearer Jean. "I knew it when I saw you! Does he love you?"

"He does not and he never will. That's why there's nothing to tell."

"He's made love to you!" Dorothy eagerly fitted the pattern she knew in bitterness over Jean's reluctant con-fidence.

"Never. He's played openly. Square."

"Whoever is he?"

"A man at the boarding house. Easterner. He's going soon. He's engaged. I saw her pictures."

"What's he done, Jean? Tell your Doro—kissed you?"

"No! Oh, no!" Jean twisted away from Dorothy, her face hidden in her arm. "No! Oh, if he had! If he had only taken my body and left *me!* He doesn't want me. If he had——" She stopped, stifled under the rush of her outburst.

"Jean——" Dorothy touched her shoulder. In her voice was fear. "I didn't know——"

"It's all right." Jean sat up, pushing her hair back from her forehead. "That's all there is. I didn't mean—to fuss. Doro, don't you think I'm sorry! Or broken-hearted! I wouldn't lose a minute I've had. Not a second! I know what I'm doing." Her fingers moved along Dorothy's silken braid, spread on the pillow.

"Can't you make him love you?" In Dorothy's strained voice Jean heard a faint, "I tried and couldn't, but you——"

"No. I can't even try." Poor Dorothy!

"He never kissed you." Dorothy paused. "Usually that's what a man's after, if he plays with a girl."

Jean lay down, silently. How explain what Stuart had wanted! Had taken!

"What's he like, anyhow?"

Jean built a picture of him, her phrases slow, liturgical. Happiness possessed her that she could phrase him thus, in candor, unreserved. When at last she was silent, Dorothy reached for her hand, pressed it against her cheek.

"He sounds to me like a highbrow flirt!" she said. "No, don't be cross!" As Jean squirmed away. "That's just what you'd fall for. The men you've known—they weren't up to you. But this one—you probably hold him off. Soften him up! If he's not even in love with that other girl—he's human, isn't he?"

Jean was silent. Human!

"They say any woman can get a man—you know——"

"He's different."

"Sounds like a fish!"

Jean sat up, fever in her racing blood. A strange compulsion rode her, to explain, to bring forth in words something she had not yet thought.

"No, Dorothy. It's that he knows about things—like love —instinct—— He'd see what you were doing—and laugh. He's thought about love."

"Thought!" Dorothy flounced in derision. "That doesn't change feelings!"

"It does something"——Jean thrust herself through a mist of bewilderment. "It's like"—— Suddenly, quite clearly, she saw. "Doro, I'll tell you. When I was little, I used to read fairy stories. Loved them. But there was one I couldn't ever finish. I tried to, and I always was frightened. I never read it through. The Snow Queen. About two children, and a mirror that broke. A piece flew into the boy's heart, changing him—he was like ice, and quite different. The girl loved him, and tried to get the bit of glass out of his heart. I never read it through. I couldn't!"

Jean had forgotten Dorothy. The strange, possessive terror

of that old story wrapped about her again, clogging, stifling.
It had been her story!

"I don't know what you're talking about," said Dorothy
plaintively.

"That's Stuart." Jean's hands moved along the quilt,
pulling at the tufts of wool. "And I can't do anything. I'm
afraid."

"Is that the way he talks?" Dorothy pulled at Jean's
arm. "Lie down or you'll catch cold and be your old snow
queen yourself!"

"Oh, Doro!" Jean dropped suddenly into the warm
hollow of Dorothy's arm again. "You're funny!" Her
mind had a new lightness, orderliness, as if she had an
amazing discovery. Later she could look at it. Queer, the
release which came from words. The dark, and Dorothy,
so close! She was floating, weights lifted from her. "I've
got more out of it than he has!" she cried. "I'm glad I told
you."

Silence. Then Dorothy's voice, dragging Jean back from
a deep pool of sleep.

"I saw John last week. I'm going to marry him this
summer."

"What for?" Jean was still half sleeping.

"I've got to marry someone. There's nothing else to do.
And he wants me."

"Why don't you do something else?" Jean was wide
awake, goaded into attention by the defiance in Dorothy's
voice.

"You can, if you want to. You've got brains. You can
do anything. I don't want to teach—nor just stay home."
Then, in a whisper through the dark, "Jean! They say girls
—women—don't have a hard time with their feelings—like
men. It's not true! Maybe it's wicked. Rachel said she
didn't care about loving. She lied! She was ashamed to
speak out." A taut vibration through Dorothy's body. "I
care! We all want it!"

"I don't think it's wicked. It's beautiful—loving."
Strange, how the dark was like night in the woods, when

secret wild things dare stir from hiding. "Beautiful! I'm not ashamed."

"Not even of your—feelings?"

"No. If we're made with feelings, I want them all!"

"Oh, Jean!" A long, choking sigh. "I never dared talk to you—you seemed cold."

Jean hugged her in a quick little passion of sympathy.

"That's why I'm marrying." Dorothy spoke austerely. "I ought to be thankful John doesn't mind—this——" She drew Jean's fingers against her scarred lip. "The other man——"

"That doesn't matter!" Jean flared up, pity like fire in her swift words. "It doesn't! You are lovely, Doro!"

"It mattered to him. But John—— Sometimes it frightens me, the way his heart beats, when he holds me—— Maybe afterwards—I'll love him. They say women do——"

They slept then; Jean would stir, half waking, and hear Dorothy's soft breathing. Then she slept again, in sweet peaceful emptiness, as if the words in the night had shriven them both.

She woke early. Scarcely light, but the house seemed full of sounds. Water being pumped, wood chopped, doors banged. She slipped out of bed and dressed, while Dorothy still slept.

Mrs. Jennings looked up from the stove, her round face rosy above her fresh print dress.

"Well, you're up early! Make a good farmer's wife!"

"Is there anything I can do?"

"Land sakes, no. Breakfast's most ready. He's doing the chores."

"May I watch him?" Jean went eagerly through the gray morning to the huge barn, an oblong of yellow light at its door.

She stood at the entrance to the narrow cow-stalls, sniffing the pungent, ammoniac warmth, watching the round, soft eyes of the cattle glimmer in the light from the lantern.

"Want to milk?" Mr. Jennings moved his stool to the next cow. "Hist there!"

"I don't know how. I like to watch."

Something steadfast and enduring and continuous. Their daughter married, gone, and they went on, just the same. Animals had to be cared for. Fires built, breakfast. No matter if they didn't like Eva's Tom.

Suddenly Jean laughed. How absurd, to think of Stuart squatting there, close to that tawny flank! A farmer! He wouldn't do it. And that girl, Loessa, building a fire before dawn!

The other girls had come downstairs. A quick glance at Dorothy, a tacit closing of the night together. Breakfast, the drive along the roads hard with the night's freezing, the warmth of the streetcar. They tossed jokes at each other, and laughed; something amusing in this morning ride. The fields looked black and moist under the rising sun, with patches of dirty snow in fence corners. Spring soon. The streets of the town had a Sunday emptiness. The car stopped, and Dorothy exclaimed,

"There's Eva! And Tom! That's the hotel——"

They sat down in the front of the car, scarcely looking back at the girls.

"Too bad," whispered Rachel. "Didn't she blush, though!"

"Why should she?" demanded Jean.

Rachel nudged the girl beside her, her eyebrows high. Jean hated her significant little smile.

VII

As Jean opened the door of the boarding house, she met Miss Biddle, off for church.

"Oh, Miss Winthrop!" Miss Biddle smirked. "We thought you must have eloped!"

"I've been to a wedding," began Jean, defensively.

"Your own?"

"Certainly not!" Jean hurried past her up the stairs. Horrid old snoop! Because Stuart was away, too.

The house was an empty shell. Jean moved about her

room, restive. The whole day. She picked up the bulky
volume of Marx. She would read that.

Dull. Pages of thick paper, filled with fine print. Lots
of words. Maybe they meant something. She couldn't read
it quickly, as she liked to read, and when she read slowly,
she found herself wandering far from the page. One phrase
thrust itself at her. About "Lambs of God." A good label,
because people let themselves be sheared and slaughtered like
lambs. Finally she closed the book. She ought to be interested in it. People—the Manifesto had stirred her. Land
belonging to all the people. Perhaps trouble would stop,
once everyone had what he wanted. What did they all want,
though? The theories sounded remote, foreign.

A black notebook just under the edge of her couch. That
was Stuart's. He must have dropped it, Friday night. She
picked it up and opened it. He had shown her, mockingly,
his diagrams of stock barns. His fine black writing, like
print, sung in her—an echo of him. Chemical formulas.
Unintelligible, stray words. Suddenly between the pages, a
letter. Open. A slanting, rippling hand. "Stuart Darling,"
she read. In a leap her eyes devoured it. From his Loessa.

You can't make me jealous, man, by your talk of a new,
adoring Jean, even if she's a school teacher this time instead
of a nurse. The nurse was more to be dreaded, for you
were helpless then! Let her adore you. For you belong to
me. You can't frighten me. But Stuart, you'd better come
soon or I may forget you. We shall be in Chicago the end
of the month for a few days. Monty is coming on
with us—he's been a dear all winter. Your letters—they
are delicious—when I can make them out—I shut my eyes
to remember that last kiss——

Jean laid the letter between the notebook pages and closed
the book. Her first thought was a darting, ugly suspicion.
He left that for me to find! Then, he's there! That's where
he is, to-day! Her mouth was dry, bitter, as if corroded brass
touched her tongue. He had lain there, on her couch, knowing he was going there—to her!

"You've known about her, all the time!" How loud her

thoughts sounded, dozens of them crying all at once! "Never like this, never! You might have known! You wouldn't face it!"

She knew, with sharp coldness, that she had never admitted that girl to full belief. She had accepted her and then had thrust her into a limbo of things not to be approached. "Let her adore you!" Oh, what had he said of her? Dorothy's phrase came back—highbrow flirt! Her thoughts shrieked at each other until she sank, deafened, in confusion. Finally she rose, brushing her hands against her temples as if thoughts were tangible, external things to be wiped away.

"I can't help it," she said, under her breath. "What's done, is done! But I'm not sorry! I'm not——"

A knock at her door. He couldn't be back! Roger pushed open the door.

"Well, where've you been?" He came in, and Jean saw some obscure agitation in his face. "I was here this morning and last night——"

"I went over to Eva Jennings' wedding. At Tremont. I tried to 'phone you, but you weren't in."

"Well." He sat on the couch, his shoulders sagging. "Just as well, I guess."

"Why? What's happened, Roger?"

An old fear, dormant, leaped at her. Her father had done some terrible thing! Her mother had killed herself!

"She's back." Roger looked up, his mouth grim. "Came back Friday. Said father wrote her. Putting on that he was sick and needed her. She said if anybody on earth needed her, even him——"

Jean sank down on the edge of the couch, close beside Roger.

"You've been out there?"

"She sent for me. Yesterday."

"I suppose——" Jean looked steadily at Roger. "I suppose we knew all the time it would come out this way."

"It felt awful queer. The house was a mess—— You know, father there alone. Then mother—they acted as if they were both holding their breath."

"Does she—do they want me to come there?"

"Uh-huh. Mother's worried because I didn't know where you were. Something about your running wild. I told her you were old enough to look out for yourself."

"What did you say to them?" Jean felt that she and Roger walked gingerly about the edges of an abyss, pretending it wasn't there. Why couldn't they shout out their thoughts!

"I didn't say much at first. Then he went off. He had a cold, I guess, but he wasn't much sicker than I am. Then she began—how Mamie was ugly and she couldn't stay and no one was doing anything for her and all."

Jean waited. The line of Roger's jaw looked ominous.

"I stood up on my feet and said I was through. Through! I wasn't coming back. I'd have helped if she'd gone through what she started. I was sick of shilly-shallying." His glance at Jean was beseeching; he needed assurance. "I am, too!" he added fiercely. "I'm going to get a job in some other town. Cleveland, maybe. A fellow I know told me about one."

"How did mother take it?" Jean had a queer feeling that she had known all this before, some way. That it was like an old play, read again long after its power to wring her heart had vanished.

"Oh, she didn't like it. She said we were heartless. We didn't care what happened to her. What could she do? No one wanted her!"

"Poor mother. I don't believe Mamie was really ugly. She was bothered. If that Allen had only known enough to do something quick!"

"I guess he knew how it would turn out. What are you going to do?"

Jean stared at Roger, her eyes remote, unmoved. He looked sick, gray hollows about his eyes.

"Are you going back there to live?" he insisted.

"No. I can't. Any more than you can." The sense of the desolate house, the afternoon she had packed to leave it, blew over her like bits of rotten timber, falling beams. "No,

Roger, I'm going away, too. Somewhere. I'm going to stay right here in this room till June." Nothing impassioned in her speech. Cold, definite words.

"Where're you going?"

"College. I've got to have more training."

"You haven't got the money, have you?"

"I'll get it, somehow."

"I've got a little saved. You're welcome to it."

"Roger! I could borrow it, and then return it and some more for you to go to college, later——"

"My college days look kind of thin. But you ought to go."

"Do you think I ought to go out there, to-night?"

"I don't know. I'll go along with you."

The house was dark. Jean and Roger stood in front, looking at the blank windows. Dim light appeared, as if a door had opened.

"I thought maybe they'd gone to bed," Jean sighed. "Well, here goes!" At the door she paused. "Did you ring the bell or walk in? We need a book of instructions on how to act on such an occasion."

"Walked in, of course."

But Jean pressed the bell before she opened the door.

The light came from the kitchen. Her father rushed toward her, stopped short.

"Oh, you! Come in, come in. Just getting supper. Fatted calf all ready. Here's some more of our family, Kitty!" His voice was hoarse and he coughed as he reached for the cord of the dining-room light.

He did look sick! Thin, gaunt, feverish excitement in his eyes.

"Jean!" Mother flying at her, arms straining about her, tears, kisses, half-articulate phrases. "Where have you been? We didn't even know where to look for you!"

"Over at Tremont at a wedding." Jean stood docilely under the flurry, but her heart pounded slowly, as if it moved sluggish blood with great labor.

"Roger didn't know where you were!" Entreaty in her mother's brimming eyes. "Have you had your supper?"

"Yes. But go on with yours. I'll come out——"

"I don't want any."

"Come on, Kitty. This rare chicken can't be wasted." Father had her arm, drawing her into the kitchen.

Her father must have brought the food from town—jelly, a garish bakery cake, pickles, all spread out on the kitchen table.

Jean sat near the door. It was like a marionette scene. Little figures jerked about by invisible wires. Some meaning in their gestures, some unseen hand manipulating them. What did it mean? At any moment the wires might break, the unseen hand lift, and all the figures would tumble down, motionless.

Piteous! Twisting at her heart. Fear there, in the kitchen; delight all too hectic in her father's animation. In her mother latent hostility, apology mingled with resentment.

"Want to come back here and board?" Her father assailed her.

Jean shivered, and glanced at Roger, standing near the door.

"I can't," she said. "I engaged my room for the year."

"We'll show our revered children how well we can get on without them, eh, Kitty?" His eyes sought mother's face, uneasily. She had turned away.

"Why not act pleasant?" Her father glared around at them. "You spoil my appetite!" He pushed the plate away and rose. "Got to see to the chickens."

Jean heard him stamping through the shed.

"I suppose you feel like Roger!" Her mother whirled on her. Roger slipped out of sight. Jean hoped he wouldn't desert her! "That I shouldn't have come back! That I should have stayed, while you all forgot and neglected me——"

"Mother, that's for you to decide." Jean thought, "I can't tell her what I think. It's too cruel!"

"I never thought Roger would say such things to me!"

Jean was silent.

"What else could I do? You wouldn't lift a finger to help me—Mamie wanted to get rid of me——"

"I don't know what we could have done——" Jean broke off. She hadn't, she knew, even thought about it lately. Perhaps that was a failure on her part. Treachery.

"Now you won't come back home. I thought if you boarded here, I could manage. He's promised to behave——"

"If we aren't here, you'll have less work." Jean tried to make her voice sound natural, easy. "If you'll be happier here, mother——"

"Happier! Where can I be happy?" Her mother wrung her hands in an old, familiar gesture. "I don't ask that! But go on your way. When you are as old as I am, you may understand better. When a woman gives her life to her family, there's no place for her. Unless they make one."

What use to say, "We meant to make one, when things were settled. We can't stand it here!" Perhaps secretly, profoundly, they hadn't meant to do anything. Jean said,

"I know, mother. But if father has promised——"

"Promises! I know what they mean!"

"You have to believe in them to get them to mean anything." Jean spoke half to herself, but her mother's face grew hard, as if Jean accused her.

"Who's the fellow you're running around with?" she flung out.

Jean was alert, defensive in an instant.

"You mean Mr. Fletcher?" What had she heard, and where?

"I don't care what his name is. Who is he? Is he going to marry you? Is that why you have no heart for me?"

"He is not. What do I want of marriage?"

"You won't leave that boarding house because he's there."

Jean rose quietly, white, stubborn silence settling over her.

"You don't understand, Jean." Her mother was close beside her, pleading again. "You can't afford to run with a man that way, unless you want to marry him. You lose your chances—and your name——" Then, as Jean kept her silence, "I hope—" her hands moved in a pitiful ges-

ture—"I hope things here—my life—your father—haven't
set you against marrying. It's a woman's only sphere."

"Oh, mother!" Quick fluctuation into tenderness again.
"Don't you worry! I'll marry if I want to."

"It can be the best thing in the world, if people do what
is right. If they are selfish and don't think of others——But
you don't want to be an old maid! Look at your aunt, set
and queer and full of notions."

"What chance has she had at anything? Staying there and
taking care of two old folks!" Jean stopped, hastily. "I'm
going to do things, I tell you. I'm going to college this fall.
Marry! Not yet!"

"You think you know more than your poor old mother,
Jean."

"Are you coming pretty soon, Jean?" Roger stood in the
doorway. "I have to get up at six, you know."

"I'll come now. Good night, mother." Jean hesitated,
then kissed her quickly. "I'll drop in some day soon."

It was a long time before Jean or Roger spoke. Then
Roger said, "Smells like spring, doesn't it?"

"Some." Jean sniffed. It did! A faint, damp, earthy
smell through the cold night. She hugged his arm. "Spring!
And we'll go away! Oh, Roger! I'm glad you stayed. It
was hard enough——"

"Was she telling you to get married?"

"Um. Where did she hear about Stuart? You never told
her?"

"Not a word. She asked me. I guess father picked it up.
You aren't going to marry him, are you?"

"I am not."

"That's good."

"Why?"

"He's too much for me." Roger peered at her, slyly.
"Don't want that for a brother-in-law!"

"I'm in no hurry to end my happy days." Jean felt flip-
pant, full of grotesque images, ideas. "Imagine me, 'Dear
husband, can I have a nickel please? I spent that other nickel
for soap last week!'"

"Do you think they'll stick, this time?"

"Maybe. With us gone."

"I suppose she didn't have anything to do but think about him."

"That's the trouble with women! I told her to get a job, and she didn't like it. Too late."

"Being married is usually quite a job."

"You talk like a man, Roger!" Silence for a time, as if Jean had advanced some unanswerable accusation. "I've got to do things! I couldn't bear sweeping and cooking——"

"You're smarter than most girls. That's the trouble with you. Some of them like it."

"Does your Molly?" Jean grinned at him.

"If I get married," Roger spoke grandly, "my wife's never going to lick my boots for money! I'll divide it up."

"You're a nice old thing." They had reached the boarding house. "You know, I couldn't open up and say what I thought, the way you did."

"Had to get it out of my system."

"You don't think we ought to go back?"

"You can, if you think so."

"Oh, I don't! I couldn't live, Roger!"

"Well, there you are, then! So long!"

VIII

On the floor lay Stuart's notebook. Jean thrust it under the couch. She was too tired to think. She fell asleep almost at once. Two strong floods of emotion, opposing, held her between them, unmoved, neutral.

The next morning as she dressed, the scene at home hung vividly about her. Sharply she was aware of an undercurrent she had failed to grasp the night before. She and Roger had thought they summed up that homecoming. They hadn't. There was something more, an indefinable element. As if those two, her father and mother, couldn't escape each other. Perhaps because they had lived together so long.

Perhaps—her curious plumbing failed to touch bottom. In spite of dissension, trouble, faithlessness, something held them.

When she came in that evening from school, she found a fat envelope with the university stamp. Her story! She ran upstairs, tearing it open. A long penciled comment. Emotional power, vividness, amazing ability, no sense of form, need to learn the artistic pleasure in form, and so on. Jean sat down, trembling. It had been good, then! She could do something!

After dinner she flew again to her room. Stuart had not yet come back. She would write Miss McNealy. She had to talk to someone! As she wrote, she remembered that last night on the steps of the cottage; the sense of the woman beside her, strong, friendly, tender—why had she been so inarticulate? She would tell her everything. The compulsion drove her swiftly into the letter, as it had driven her into confession to Dorothy.

"My mother is back," she wrote, "but I am not going home." She had written earlier that her mother was away for the winter. She need say nothing more about that. But her plan for next year. "Do you think I could work my way, if Roger lent me a little to start on? I've got to get away—to have more training——Maybe I can learn to be something more than a country school teacher." And then—it was like the darkness of night, with someone close and warm, listening—she emptied the passion of her heart. "He doesn't care a rap for me," she wrote, shamelessly—"but if he wanted me for anything, I'd have to go. No matter what. If I were different, I could reach him. I didn't know love was like this. No pride left——Yes, a little, for I don't tell him any of this. Or is that cowardice? It's like a terrible wind blowing——"

When she had sealed the letter, she sat with it in her hand. Strange, how quiet and content she felt. Almost as if she had poured her love at Stuart's feet. Release—— She went to the corner and dropped the letter into the box. As the lid clicked, panic seized her, and she poked her fingers under the cold metal. No use, it was gone. What had she thought of, writing all that!

A long, dreary week, with drizzling rains and uneasy children by day, and empty hours at night. She stopped one afternoon at the house, for an awkward, distant hour.

Friday she went to dinner with Roger, at a new restaurant. She pulled herself up to a companionable decency. Roger was going to Cleveland on Sunday, to look up the new job. When she came to her own room, she found two letters under her door. One from Miss McNealy. The other—as she stood erect, she heard Stuart's lazy, soft voice, closing about her heart like a vise. Then Miss Lester's tinkling laugh. He was upstairs, in her room! She closed her door, and slowly opened the letters. Miss McNealy was quietly aghast. She felt that.

Dear Jean, You frighten me by your wild words. I think you must mean less than you write.

And then, down the page, with a curious tightening in her throat, Jean read,

I shall be more than glad to lend you money for a year at the University. I am sending you a catalogue, and suggest that you send your credits to the office. Read the instructions.

The other envelope held the catalogue. Faintly through the door came those voices. Jean pushed them away, and read the thin leaves, one by one. Stronger than the voices rose their glamour. Anything she wanted! Courses about things she had never heard of. Wonderful, alluring——Why was Stuart up there? What was he talking about? She wanted to creep to the stairs, to listen.

Instead she began to undress, in feverish haste. She couldn't see him! He was showing off again. To a new audience. He had grown tired of her; perhaps his bag of tricks was empty!

She slipped through the hall to the bathroom. A hot bath, then she might sleep. How green the water looked, with rippled light! She let herself down with a sigh. Comfort-

ing to lie there, long and white, while all her blood grew
drowsy, warm. As she pulled her nightdress over her head,
she heard his feet on the stairs, in a heedless scuffle. Did
he go down to her door? She wasn't sure. She heard him
shut himself into his room.

She stared an instant at the yellow crack under his door.
Then she went softly to her own room and without a glance
at the wall where his shadow might fall, crept into bed.

The breakfast gong woke her. As she fumbled with her
foot for a slipper, she saw, just inside her door, a triangle
of paper. She opened it.

"Ave valeque, O Minerva." The fine script enkindled
her. "Morituri, we entreat a last boon. A day."

What did he mean? Something quite simple, no doubt.
She hurried down to breakfast. The dining room was
empty. Miss Sargent served her hastily. Jean saw that for
her, breakfast was over, and her mind was full of dinner
thoughts.

"Will you be here this noon, Miss Winthrop?" She
whisked Jean's fruit plate away.

"I don't know." Jean was thinking, she doesn't like me,
any more. "It's Saturday," she added, placatingly. "I have
to see what I am going to do. I'll let you know."

Back in her own room she fidgeted while the plump maid
spread fresh linen on her couch. Stuart might come in!
Why couldn't she hurry? There, she was through!

"Never mind that basket. I'll empty it." Jean almost
pushed the girl out of the door. She could hear Stuart
stalking about, whistling. What was he doing, slamming
around? Suddenly she knew. Packing. That was what
his note meant. He was going away.

She saw his notebook on the table. The maid had picked
it up. Should she say, "I read your letter!" She couldn't.
Clearly she saw why she couldn't. Not that he would care.
But she should resent it, what it revealed of him—no, not so
much of him as of his attitude toward her. Something
ignoble in it. If he knew she guessed that, had tasted that
bitter flavor, and still made no motion to reject—— His

mocking acceptance of that would degrade her. If she hid her knowledge, she might still salvage an hour. Where was he going? Back to that girl? Strange. You found something wrong, unworthy, *caddish,* that was it! and you kept it as a wound, hidden, instead of making a weapon of it. She heard his door fly open, his feet clatter along the hall, and with a swift breath she gathered herself tensely up, all her secret thoughts seeking swift covert.

"Yes, come in."

His glance was a hawk, seeking her out!

"I don't know just what your cryptic message means," she said; any words were safety.

"Just this. I'm going, to-night. I can no longer pursue agriculture, Minerva." He lounged in the doorway. "The doctors, holding inquest, disapprove. I have no stuff for a farmer, they assure me."

Time enough later to realize all that meant!

"What are you going to do?" Jean settled herself in a chair. "Where are you going?"

"Literal and practical, as ever!" Stuart sprawled on the couch. "I have a distinguished offer. My august father complains that I exhaust his finances. But a gilded youth wishes me for companion, tutor, friend. He has worn out his latest victim. A hundred a month, Minerva, and they feed the dog."

"Stuart! You're not fooling—they aren't sending you to a sanitarium again!"

"Not yet. I shall be governess select to this scion of the rich. That's all of that. Will you play with me to-day?"

"Where are you going?"

"Canada, the mountains, Florida. Who knows? I am to travel with him. Come, what shall we do with this handful of limpid hours?"

"You've given up all your plans?"

"Ah, Minerva!" Stuart looked at her steadily. "You have yet to learn the futility of plans." It was to Jean as if she held a lantern for an instant close to the surface of dark, deep water, and saw, far below, strange, weary fish glide

among jagged rocks. Only an instant. Then Stuart closed
his eyes. "My father refused to finance me until he had
assurance I could stick it out. That I can't furnish. So——"

"I should think you could get money somewhere!" In
Jean's feeling ran anger, sorrow, pity. "Instead of wasting
a year being tutor to a silly boy!" She had helped build
that farm, fences, stock, the tractor, even to apples wrapped
by hand in green paper, to sell for five cents apiece! Something was tottering, slipping, and she strove to keep it erect.

"You should! Try it." Stuart sat up, the sardonic glint
in his eyes. "Try it, Minerva."

"I am." She was stubborn. "I have borrowed enough to
go to the University next year."

"Yes?" That swift, gentle smile! "Fine! I thought you
couldn't stay a small-town teacher." He rose, stretching
wearily. "But you're a good investment, O Ox-eyed. Sound
wind, good chest expansion, amazing brain. No risk there.
You know——" He stood above her, his fingers touching
her shoulders. "You have an indomitable combination. I
think you may never know how failure tastes, unless your
heart betrays you. Think of that! Wonderful woman!"

Jean besought him, under that light, mocking tone. Where
was he? Was he jesting, mocking her?

"Do you mean that?" she whispered, her upturned face
palely irradiated.

That was her old feeling, deep at the core of self, clear,
effulgent, inflexible, in spite of ignominy, love, anything!
Submerged of late by the hectic, feverish flood of love. But
still alive!

"I mean it." He dropped his hands and turned to the
door. "Spring is somewhere outside," he said. "Let's go
hunt for it."

The day was like a wild bird, caught, held for a moment,
with strong, disturbing flutter of wings against the palm,
and then gone.

There was a new river road, built the previous fall, out
toward the park where Jean and Roger had danced that
summer, years ago. They walked there; the trees were

black, the mud of the road sucked at their feet, but spring rushed with the flood of the river, rose in strong, bright spikes of the skunk cabbage, hung in the fresh, cool wind. Gay, random talk. Jean thought: I may never see him again. Time enough to think of that to-night, to-morrow. The strong steel spring of her being was set, firm, resilient, against mawkishness, against revelation.

They had dinner, late, at a tiny restaurant. Stuart had said, "How about a banquet at the hotel, a final splurge?" But Jean shook her head.

"Let's go in here. Ham and eggs."

"For peace comes dripping slow—and a skillet full of chickens' wings!"

"Don't spoil that!" Jean flared at him.

"Apologies, Minerva."

They sat at an oilcloth-covered table, the small room with fly-specked lithographs and steaming coffee urn behind the counter empty save for them. The proprietor, thin, with heavy solemn jowls, waited on them.

"The home of the humble," said Stuart. "Often the humble feed well. That ham has savor. Did you read Marx, Minerva, since we speak of the humble?"

"Marx? Oh, yes. Some."

"You didn't care for the workingman's Bible?"

"It was interesting."

"Don't lie! You didn't like it, did you?"

"No, I didn't." Jean lifted her head. How tensely she had struggled to say the thing he expected, to discover that thing to say! Vain, silly endeavor. She straightened her shoulders boldly. "I thought it was dull."

"Women have no sense of the class struggle."

"It isn't human." Jean waited, slowly, for her thoughts to rise to the surface. "I like things about people."

"What else is it about?"

"Ideas. I think what folks feel—what they want—what they are like—those things are more important."

"A female, personal point of view."

Jean glowed with the inner excitation of something, part

thought, part feeling, emerging from the matrix of her own experience.

"Maybe it's female. But it's so. Take your materialistic conception of history. Partly true! It sounds so. But people's needs aren't just food. Women——" She felt vaguely her mother's life, the life of other women, Dorothy, Lora, Miss Pennington the artist—shadowy wholes of their lives—— "Women have a hard time," she went on slowly, "but it's because they don't know what they want. Not because they haven't money—although that's part of it. It's more. People need to know more about themselves. What they're like. They always say you're morbid, introspective, if you try to find out. What I want to do is to find out! About folks, me and other folks. So I'll know——" She stopped as the proprietor stalked toward them, his hands full of pie and coffee cups.

"You'd better hurry," he said ominously. "Place closes at eight sharp."

"We'll lock up for you if you're in a hurry." Stuart grinned at him. "Go on, Minerva."

"That's all." Jean stirred her coffee, her cheeks flushed.

"What are you going to do when you find out all you want to know about people?"

"Write. Or do something—with people."

"You'll fall in love."

Jean's eyes rose suspiciously to his. Was he ridiculing her? Or hinting that he knew?

"That isn't enough," she said quietly.

"By Jove, you're right!" Stuart rose and held her coat. "You are wiser than your namesake, O Minerva. You'll do it, too. What you want."

"Let's ride home. I'm tired." The long street climbed through the dark ahead of them, a double string of blurred lights.

"As you like."

They waited in silence for the car and then rode, still silent. Jean's thoughts drifted, bits of leaves in an eddy of air. Funny to burst out like that. That's what I want,

though. Never thought of it before, that way. It's true.
I'm going after that. Get it, too. An hour, now, and he
will be gone. Mustn't think of that! Is that the first time
I ever really thought, myself? Feels that way. Strange.
An hour—— That strong, lean curve of his cheek. I
never dared say what was in me, before. Why? Then a
composite, humiliating image of herself, all tentacles, delicate tipped, seeking for approval. I'm done with that.
Myself now! Why was I afraid of him? As if I loved
him in fear. And he's no better than I am. He's going.
He wears a mask, glittering. He's pushed his thoughts into
his feelings—until he's cruel. I can't get out to help him.
Like the Snow Queen.

They went quietly up the stairs of the boarding house.
At Jean's door they stopped.

"Just time to get my train." Stuart snapped his watch
shut.

"That's good," said Jean slowly. "No time for obsequies."
She backed against the door, hands outspread to touch the
solid wood.

"You've been a rare find in this dreary little town,
Minerva."

"Oh, don't!" she whispered, her eyes shrinking from his
steady gaze.

"You think I don't mean it!" His mask was off, for a
wistful, downright instant. "I do! But no matter. So long,
camerado, I give you my hand!"

IX

Jean crept into bed. She wouldn't think. She fought off
thinking, feeling, stubbornly, doggedly. She would go to
sleep. To-morrow——

Just at dawn she had a strange dream, vivid, clinging for a
brief time when she woke. She stood at the feet of a huge
figure, towering into the clouds, its face invisible above her.
She threw herself down on the enormous, dusty shoes,
abasing herself in agony and ecstasy. She was a child, too

young to stand alone or walk. Then she knew that she must stand, must try to walk, alone, and fear possessed her completely, so that she beat her hands on the rough shoes and wept. Safe there, in the dust—at whose feet? Her father's? Compulsion, like a mighty external force, dragging her away from safety, up, up, while she staggered, unable to balance her abject, frightened body. Up, until her head whirled among the clouds. She could stand! She thrust a foot forward. She could walk, alone! Where was that figure? She peered among the clouds into empty space. She walked mightily as if she strode from mountain peak to mountain peak. And then, in a valley below her, through a rift in the clouds, she saw a tiny figure, turning to wave a hand. Her father, with books under his arm. No, Stuart, with his suitcase.

A queer dream. It released a host of shadowy, distant impressions—Jean lay, half awake, while they drifted about her. She was very small, for the walk from the porch to the street seemed long; she waited for her father to come home, she was running to meet him, being whirled up in strong arms, away from the earth, up and up! Pounding her fists in delight against a broad shoulder. Jean, still smaller this time, for the square chin thrust above her seemed a great rock to shelter her, safe and warm in the crook of an arm, while her father walked slowly back and forth. A book in his other hand; the sharp corner prodded her as a finger flipped a page. The rustle frightened her, she didn't like the tickling smell. She kicked at the book and screamed. Did she remember that, or had someone told her?

It must be late. Mr. Jessup's Sunday morning concert had begun. Jerusalem the Golden, by a male quartet. The metallic vibrations floated up the stairs. Time to get up. They'll think I'm mourning—not that I care! I'll go out to the house. Perhaps things are going better there. A wistful, unanalyzed desire to find some trace of that misty past. To escape a heavy, threatening present in terms of an old safety.

In the hall she stood for a moment, staring at Stuart's

door. Open; the floor about the desk was littered with torn papers. Miss Sargent bustled up the stairs, her arms full of broom, dustcloths, linen.

"Well!" she turned to Jean. "Whatever your friend was, he wasn't very tidy! I got to red this room up myself to-day. Another gentleman is coming right in."

Jean made some light rejoinder; she couldn't recall later what she had said. She was thinking: it is true, he has gone.

She ate a hurried breakfast while Mr. Jessup stood near the whirring machine, beating time to "Hosannah, in the highest, Hosannah to our King!"

The house seemed empty. Jean called, and her mother hurried down from her room.

"Jean!" Her arms clung about the girl's neck. "I thought you were never coming to see your poor mother." The echo of recent sobs in her distraught voice.

"Here I am," said Jean.

"I went down to see you yesterday. They said you were off with that fellow."

Jean sensed a new caution in her mother's eyes, as if she tested the ground before she ventured far.

"I was." Jean withdrew from the clasping arms. The wistfulness of the morning had stiffened into coldness.

"You don't listen to what I say."

"No?" Antagonism leaped in Jean, an animal eager to spring. She gripped both hands about its neck. No use to say things! "You needn't worry about that, mother," she said calmly. She had the beast down! "Mr. Fletcher has gone. For good. I shall never see him again. We had a farewell party yesterday, that's all."

She had to meet her mother's searching eyes. Did she suspect? She couldn't say anything!

"Well, I'm glad to hear that." A long sigh. "He had no business taking so much of your time. Where's he gone?"

"Traveling with a rich family. Did you want something yesterday?"

She could see her mother's slow release of the discussion,

her slightly acrimonious reproach as she turned to her own affairs.

"I wanted to see you. I don't know what I'm going to do." Her voice dropped. "He's driving me crazy. Stays around here all the time. I think he's drinking again. He may even be seeing that woman."

Jean listened, her mind leaping about the two in grim, sardonic thoughts. One, from which she retreated: they haven't changed, they have started ahead just where they stopped—that terrible violation——

"Roger says he's going to get a Cleveland job. If you would get a school there I could come and keep house for you both."

"Oh, I can't." Jean fled from that suggestion, in panic. "I couldn't teach in the city, without a state certificate." Safe there! "I'm going to the University, anyway!" To herself she added fiercely: "You've come back. Now stay! I'm through! I won't be sorry——"

"You don't seem like yourself," her mother said, piteously. "You used to have some feeling."

"Feeling!" Jean trembled. "I've had nothing but feeling! I can't go on just teaching in little schools. I've got brains enough to do something. This is my chance. Later I can help you, more."

"You don't want me."

Jean looked away, about the familiar walls. Part of her was crying, "You are wicked, cruel, selfish!" But that lay like a soft, pliable streak along a hard steel band. The voice of that, like sparks of flying steel, said, "She has come back of her own will. This is her choice."

"I'm afraid of him, sometimes," her mother went on. "I don't know what he will do!"

"He wanted you to come back," said Jean, gently, "and you came."

"Because I had no one to help me! I couldn't see what to do!"

"Well——" Jean lifted her hands, palms upwards, in a gesture of helplessness.

Her mother made a swift detour, as if she felt the failure of that attack.

"You're tying a millstone round your neck, going in debt. Your father's furious about that."

"It's my neck and my millstone!" cried Jean. "I guess I can manage that."

"You haven't saved anything this year, have you? That's a new suit you're wearing."

"I haven't earned much." Jean retreated into hostility. "I have to have some clothes. I'll earn more, after——"

"You are stubborn, just like him! You'll go off to that city—I don't like it."

"Oh, come, mother!" Jean laughed. "A city's no worse than a town. I'm old enough to look out for myself."

"You may be old enough, but you don't know as much as you think you do."

"Learn more every day." Jean let her flippancy out deliberately. "Think how much I'll know after a year there!"

"Book learning isn't what I mean. It isn't that I don't want you to have a chance, Jean. If you weren't so headstrong——I wanted you to go to college. When you were a little girl, I planned it."

"I know it, mother. Don't worry! Worry killed a cat!"

"But I'd rather you never looked at a book, if it made you less a good, true woman."

Her father came in then, a kind of defiant tension in his jesting remarks. Jean, watching him, thought: I was sentimental this morning. That is all done with. I am not a child, now. Nor do I wish to be.

She stayed for dinner, suppressing a faint guilt at breaking bread with them. Silly to feel that way, she thought. I'm not a traitor to them. I am only separate, an individual. If I stayed, though, they could pull me under again. All that network, built for years. Perhaps fathers and mothers never can let go. They get such an early start! They want to possess you forever. You have to wrench loose, to clear out!

She stopped on her way back to the boarding house to

telephone Roger. He was out of town, the clerk told her. Back to-morrow.

Before she slept she thought: one day gone. I suppose I've got a broken heart. Funny phrase, broken heart. Ladies used to die of them. Mine beats just as steadily. I wonder —is there anything you can't bear, if you look at it, face to face? She turned uneasily on her pillow as a wave of desolation mounted, threatened to break over her. I won't moon about it, she whispered. I won't!

Tuesday evening Roger came in, jubilant.

"I've got it! A hundred a month to start! Going Monday!"

"Hooray for you!" Jean was glad. "Why, that's probably as much as I'll make after I have a degree and all."

"That's only a start, too!" Roger clapped a hand on her shoulder. "We'll show 'em a thing or two, won't we!"

"We will." Jean looked at him, quizzically. "Have you told Molly?"

"She's glad I got it and sorry I'm going. I told her I'd look the Cleveland girls over and if I didn't find one I liked better, I'd send for her some day."

"Roger! You want to marry her?"

"Well——" Roger puffed his chest out. "I might."

Jean laughed. "You look like a rooster!" she said. "I thought you wanted to go to college first."

"If I climb up fast enough, why bother?"

"You're sure you don't mind lending me money?"

"What I can spare you're welcome to, old Jean."

"I'll miss you this spring."

"Oh, you're so busy with that gink you won't know I'm gone!"

"He's gone."

Roger stared a moment, and Jean felt in quick resentment that between them lay a gulf neither of them could cross. What he felt, intimately, she could only guess. What she felt she could never show him. Why? A hangover of caution, because they were brother and sister? Protection against the old, possessive, moral interest of family? Or just a difference—fundamentally they couldn't meet? No, a gulf between any two human beings; you never quite touched another! She didn't know.

"Sorry. Thought you'd have him to amuse you till you left town."

At any rate, Roger had a fine loyalty. No suggestion that she might be left doleful, deserted.

"I guess I'll have enough to do," she said gratefully. "I've been collecting my credits to send. Have to collect a wardrobe, too."

"I've ordered me a new suit. Tailor made! Some style, eh, Jean!"

X

April moved sluggishly. Jean drew herself down to school work with a nervous absorption which left her tired, heavy of body. The first days she felt soft pushes of curiosity from the boarders. She didn't care! She was through trying to explore the ground, to place her feet just where other people wished. She had a callous, gay exterior for the dining room. When she was safe in her own room, she worked doggedly. School work. Writing. More penciled comments from the university instructor—latent power, no sense of form.

Her mother said, "You're dreadfully thin! Don't they give you any food at that place?"

"It's just spring." Jean brushed away her solicitude. "I'm working hard at school." She rubbed her cheeks with her handkerchief, bringing color into the hollows. "See my rosiness!"

Such foolish, easy things lay in wait to trip you up—the glimpse of a tall figure, down the street! Not like him, when you finally passed him. The tone of a voice in the distance. A phrase—on your own lips, echo of some ridiculous moment. The sound of feet in Stuart's old room, giving the empty space the phantom of habitation, so that your heart leaped unbidden before your mind could say, "Only that old

doctor who's taken the room." Sudden, twisting her breath
out of her; faint jerks on the cord he had woven to bind her.
"I won't have it!" Jean raged against herself. Sentimental,
silly nonsense!

Late in May Jean walked slowly from her school toward
town. The sky had a tender, ineffable blue behind the tiny
pale leaves of the elms. Red-winged blackbirds called over
the swamp near the road. A streetcar whanged past her,
and she had a glimpse of a figure rising, waving at her. She
wheeled and watched till the car stopped at a remote crossing.
Not Stuart. She throttled the quickly born hope. It hadn't
even looked like him. But some man was running back
toward her. Luther! His cap off, his fair curly hair
gleaming in the sun.

"Isn't this luck?" He held her hand an instant. "I
wanted to see you!"

"Just pining away for a sight?"

"You said it! You walking to town? Let me take your
books."

How easy to pick up that old, provocative, silly chatter!
Like thrusting a hand into a closet to drag out a discarded
garment. Jean watched him, as they walked. He was telling, eagerly, of his new position, forester, in the far west.

"You look in splendid shape," she said, suddenly.

"Tough as nails! Feel that muscle! Can't dent it."

He was heavier; broader. His neck had thickened, his
skin had a ruddy tan. His mouth had lost its boyish un-
certainty. Aggressive, obvious, male. Jean knew he was
appraising her, warily, awaiting a sign. Memory in his eyes,
a faint smoulder of resentment. That was for last year,
when she had sent him away, that night at Perry. Memory
of a night, a morning, more distant. She felt him like a
hunter, tramping with noisy boots through thickets. If she
lay, hidden, he would go away. If she stirred in flight, even
in recognition—all this swiftly, in a clear instant.

What did she want of him, simple, uncouth? Ah, but he
was strong. If he held her, kissed her, would it ease the
dreadful ache? Suddenly, without her conscious volition,

she felt a dark, swift thing rise in her, beating up on bare feet, running, running, with wild, mad face turned backward toward the hunter. As they talked, the chase was on, taunting, sudden lurking in stray thickets, flight again.

"You'd better come along," Luther said, his face bent toward her. "A woman's fine and useful, I hear."

"I always thought I'd like the west."

"I'm starting next week. Could you get ready in time?"

Finally at the edge of town, Luther stopped.

"I've got to get back to college. Promised to see some of the fellows at dinner." Then, after a pause—the hunter was close on the flying wild thing—"You going to be home to-night?"

"I'm not at home now." Then, hurriedly, "I'm at Sargent's boarding house. On Buxton Street. I'll be in—to-night."

What did she want of Luther? She hurried as if she might thus escape a grinning satyr face, peering over the edge of her being. It had been another self, bidding him come. She was crazy—nothing significant in those brief words. Just that she was going away, next week, and Luther was part of the past she left.

From the wicker chair at the window of her room rose a familiar, thickened figure. Mrs. Collins! Months since Jean had seen her.

"Aren't you dressed up?" Jean bent for the woman's quick kiss. "A new suit!"

"I made it myself." Mrs. Collins looked down at the gores of the skirt. "Tweed mixture, they call it. Do you like it?"

"I don't see how you ever made a jacket!" Jean saw the wistfulness in the pleased, subdued lines of her face.

"I suppose you wonder why I am here." Mrs. Collins sat down, gravely inspecting Jean. "At this time of day and all."

"Hadn't wondered yet, I was so glad to see you." Jean relaxed in a corner of her couch, knees crossed, thoughts jumping: if she stays, the evening's settled; queer how I'm

another person, now—last year's person, earnest young
school teacher. "I see you look important."

"I am. No joking, either. I have been sent by the board
at Perry. They thought it would come best from me. I
think they hoped I could persuade you, as we were friends,
last year." She paused, portentously, her fingers busy
smoothing her gray cotton gloves. "Miss Winthrop, the
board wishes to call you as principal of the school. At the
same salary they have paid a man. It is a great honor, Jean."
She lost the serious regard for her position as delegate in
quick pleading. "Oh, we hope you'll come back! We all
think there never was a teacher like you! Children and all.
You can have the same room you had with me. Jim sends
his best to teacher."

Unexpected tears in Jean's eyes and a rush of tenderness
toward the woman who sat there, waiting. Mrs. Collins
cared enough for her to feel this as her own intimate triumph! A flame through the dead ashes of her own life. In
a panoramic instant Jean lived through a year—principal of
Perry's school, the first woman, herself behind the desk in
the large assembly room upstairs.

"I think it was beautiful of you to come," she said, unsteadily.

"Jean, you won't refuse!"

"I'm going away next week, to the University."

"You might never get a chance like this again. Lots of
people don't, even if they go to college."

"Have to risk that."

"I hate to say it, but look at me! I took a risk——"

Jean brushed the tears from her eyes. She couldn't say,
"I'm not like you——" That would be cruel.

"Don't decide hastily. Think it over."

"I have. Tell them, the board, that I do appreciate the
offer. But I can't come back. I must go on——"

She was afraid for a moment that Mrs. Collins would
cry. She was hurt, as if the dignity of her mission suffered.

"Don't you see," explained Jean, "if I can make them
want me, now, there's no telling what I can do later?"

Mrs. Collins pressed her thin lips together. Her courage had been nibbled away.

"If you change your mind——"

"I won't. I'm sorry."

Mrs. Collins rose, shaking out her full skirt.

If I ask her to stay—Jean's thoughts leaped to Luther——

"Stay to dinner with me, Mrs. Collins. I can just tell Miss Sargent."

"I'd like to. But Jim isn't very well. I've been here quite a while. I'd better go."

"I'd like you to stay."

"Not this time, I guess."

Jean went down to the door with her.

"I don't want to seem—persistent." The conflict in her face made Jean's throat tighten. "But you are young. This is an unusual chance. You are so sure——"

"Don't feel so bad!" Jean patted her arm. "I have to be sure. No one else is—about what I want to do, I mean. But some day you'll see."

She dressed for dinner in a soft green mull, a new dress she had bought. A little frill of lace about the square low neck and sleeves, a girdle of black ribbon. She peered at herself in the mirror. How different she looked in that, after the stiff linen collar and tie. The spring mist softened her hair; her lips, faintly crimson, parted in a little jeering smile. She wasn't pale and wan to-night! Hard brilliance in her eyes; how green they looked!

Dinner. Endless, chattering; thick, floating odors—sweetish powder on Miss Biddle's face, gravy, vinegar for the greens like a shriek through the other odors. Some exterior self chattering, eating, smiling. Mr. Jessup had seen a robin. Once Miss Biddle had seen a bluebird in January. And so on—would it never end!

Against the clink of spoons in thin small coffee cups came the ring of the doorbell. Jean heard her name. The maid beckoned to her from the hall.

She went ahead of Luther up the stairs. Here he is,

send him away! What do you want of him? A fugitive glance over her shoulder. He was breathing quickly; the slight swerve of his long nose looked like a beak, a hawk face. Again the wild, unruly thing within her, in taunting flight.

He closed the door and flung aside his hat. For a long moment they stared at each other, something loud, jeering in Jean's ears.

"I couldn't wait," he said, and Jean retreated before him.

He caught her, drew her down beside him on the couch, his lips seeking her throat, her eyelids, her mouth. Jean lay quiescent, lost in rhythmic, whirling darkness.

"Jean, open your eyes," he whispered, his mouth warm on hers. "Look at me."

Slowly her eyelids lifted, dropped again. Great staring eyes, close to hers; she couldn't bear them! She wanted nothing, nothing but the darkness, the soft insidious tremors that ran through her.

"Jean, you wanted me, too! You did, Jean?" His hands crept along her arms, her shoulders, up to the white pillar of her throat. "Jean!" She could feel his heart beating under her shoulder. She moved and his hands grew hard. "Don't, Jean. Kiss me! Jean——"

She opened her eyes. Dusk filled the room, and close to her loomed his face, enormous, flushed, demanding. Luther! With a swift motion she pushed herself free; under her straining hand his heart pounded. His hand sprang out for her, and in a flurry of panic she slipped away. He thought she was in flight again, craving pursuit. She jerked at the chain of the lamp, and the light seemed to burst into the room like thunder.

The soft languor of her flesh was lost in a sudden bitter contraction, as if she tensed her body against attack. For a still instant she stood, looking at Luther. Dimly she felt that wild fleeing thing within her stand, with bright, mocking, unrepentant eyes, and then dive silently into its old hiding, far beneath the level she could touch in thought.

"I didn't mean to scare you." Luther moved uneasily.

Then, under her intent, white gaze, "I thought you wanted
me——"

"It's not your fault." Jean's hand was at her throat, still
roughened, burning, from his lips. "It's mine."

"Come back. I won't be rough——" He rose, slowly.

"No. I can't." Small penance to be honest! "I thought
I wanted that. I don't." She saw him shrink, puzzled. He
was only a boy! That aggressiveness, that dominance, had
existed only in her desire. "I was lonely," she added quietly.
"I'm sorry."

"You're trying to tease me." His face flushed, his lips
moving uncertainly. "Honest, I'm crazy about you, never
forgot you." She saw his male pride ridden down by her
steady, unmoved gaze. "You're the funniest I ever saw!"
He moved his head angrily, threateningly. "Leading a fellow on——"

"Luther——" Jean smiled faintly. "I said I was sorry."

"You don't care——"

"No. You'll get over it. Don't be so cross."

"There's plenty of girls——"

"Of course." Jean turned away, to lean against the window. He wasn't hurt; just his conceit. If he would go!
She heard a sort of inarticulate splutter behind her, and the
door closed.

For a long time she stood at the window. Thought moved
in slow, incomplete circles within her. I ought to be ashamed.
Am I? Not very much. That's my evil nature, mother
would say. Touch, wiping out every thing else. Hunger
for that—for that betraying touch. That's sex. Part of it.
It isn't enough, alone. Even Luther—silly Luther—he
wanted me to look at him. To know that he kissed me.
And when I opened my eyes, it was the wrong face!

A savage, waiting to jump into your skin. Does everyone
have that? Dorothy meant that by her feelings. That's
why she's marrying. Then, a flicker of lightning through
murk: that's what I've wanted, all winter! Love—Stuart!
When I thought—I was so noble. She struggled through

the cloud of abasement which threatened. Nothing to be ashamed of! That's part of me. Now I know.

She knelt at the window, her cheek against the sill, the soft spring night flowing in about her, dark, warm, pregnant.

"I want love!" Part of spring, that rush of joy, seeking out secret, waiting nerves. Love and all the rest! Real love. Not Luther—child's game—he did not know.

She laughed to herself. Things seemed so ponderous, so impenetrable. If you wanted something else, beyond them, you walked straight at the barriers, to find them paper, fluttering torn away. Her father and mother, winding ropes of old love and duty to hold her—ropes of sand! She saw them clearly, a little piteously, rounding their old circle, over and over, bound by the tethers of themselves. Of that circle she was no longer a part. Stuart—she shivered. That, too, she had walked through, but so lately that she could not look back.

She felt her strength, her youth, unutterably potent. This is I, she cried to herself. All these things together! I'm off now, away from all the old years, in quest of—what? Love, work, myself!

AFTERWORD

ORIGINALLY PUBLISHED in 1922, *Quest* was the first of seventeen novels Helen Hull published during her lifetime (1888–1971).[1] A prolific and respected writer, Hull also published some sixty-five short stories and several books about writing. She wrote chiefly during her summer holidays away from Columbia University, where she was a full-time member of the faculty from 1916 to 1956.

By the time *Quest* was released, at least twenty-five of Hull's short stories had already appeared in magazines ranging from the radical to the mainstream, including *The Masses, Seven Arts, Touchstone, Century,* and *Harper's*. Beginning in 1914, Hull's stories in *The Masses* addressed such topics as illegitimate birth, economic disparity, spousal abuse, racism, family dynamics, and the oppression of women. Even in her more mainstream pieces, Hull was concerned with issues raised by the women's movement in the first two decades of the century. For example, in a 1915 story in *Harper's* called "The Soul-Maker," Hull examines the effects of poverty on older women, choosing as her protagonist an older woman who claims a measure of autonomy at the end of a life of dependence and meekness.[2]

Over half of these early stories were—like *Quest*—concerned with adolescence, with the growth of a young female character into maturity.

Quest is part of the literary tradition called the *Bildungsroman*, or the novel of development. As a *Bildungsheld*, or the hero of such a novel, Jean Winthrop is preoccupied with her striving for growth, what Catharine Stimpson calls "that old and aching promise of the *Bildungsroman*." [3] Until recently this genre has been defined by critics mostly in male terms that have excluded the possibility of female heroes, but feminist scholars have begun to identify a distinct female tradition of *Bildung*. For the most part, we find that nineteenth and early twentieth century female *Bildungshelden* awaken to a sense of socially imposed barriers to their full development as mature adults. [4] When Helen Hull wrote about her young female heroes in the 1910s and 1920s, however, she portrayed them awakening not to a set of limitations, like their literary forebears, but to a sense of their own strength and potential. Hull created Jean Winthrop deliberately as an atypical literary female in that, as Hull put it in some notes she wrote on the novel, she "possesses intelligence, subtlety, personality—characteristics not always possessed by the women of fiction." [5]

Hull posited a feminist model for growth in a world of newly enlarged possibilities for women. Her early fiction presents adolescent female characters discovering that they must defy a whole set of gender-based prescriptions for their behavior if they are to become fully adult, if they are to become what in the 1920s were called "New Women." She describes the development of these young "New Women" essentially as a process of empowerment.

Jean Winthrop was not Hull's first *Bildungsheld*. While many of Hull's early stories focus on adolescence, of particular interest to us in relation to *Quest* is a series of six stories she published between 1917 and 1920 which feature an adolescent protagonist named Cynthia. [6] Each story presents the climax of some aspect of growth; taken together, the Cynthia stories provide a prescription for individual growth and offer testimony to the need for social change. In these stories the adolescent heroine recognizes the necessity of separating herself from her family and all of their expectations for her; she also develops a rudimentary social conscience, abandons romantic posturing and daydreaming, comes to respect her own abilities and her sexual energy, and learns how to secure some power over her life.

In the Cynthia stories, Hull worked out much of her concept of female development. In these stories and in *Quest* she maintains that strength and autonomy must be central to the new definition of adulthood for bourgeois females. Hull portrays the Cynthias and Jean Winthrop as isolated young heroes who learn how to survive: they practice wariness, cleverness, determination, disobedience, silence, and independence—hardly the set of characteristics usually associated with "good" turn-of-the-century daughters, mothers, or wives.

Hull drew a substantial amount of the material in *Quest* from the Cynthia stories. Jean is not only the same sort of developing young hero as the Cynthias, but her relationships with Luther Wallace, Stuart Fletcher, Mrs. Pratt, and Dorothy Tiverton are only slightly altered versions of the Cynthias' interactions with Clark Walton, Richard Daggart, Mrs. Moore, and Mona. When Hull reshaped this material in *Quest*, she incorporated it into a much larger body of material so that we see the full context of the young hero's life, especially the family matrix in which she functions. While the Cynthia stories each present a vignette that encapsulates the climax of a stage of growth, in *Quest* such episodes gather cumulative force. We follow Jean's slow progress through what Hull delineates as her four major developmental stages, each summarized at the conclusion of Parts I to IV of the novel. Although some of the political sharpness of the Cynthia stories is blunted in the novel, in

Quest, more than in the stories, we become particularly aware of potential barriers to the heroine's success. Jean studies, one after the other, the attempts that other women have made to survive and to flourish, and the compromises they have made with a culture that, as Jean begins to understand, does not have their welfare at heart.

Hull's use of an adolescent protagonist allows her to examine social structures through the eyes of the semi-initiated, a heroine who is at the same time both an "insider" and an "outsider." As Jean Winthrop struggles to understand social rules or social constructs that, the text implies, do not in fact make sense, Hull criticizes prevailing attitudes toward women, the institution of the middle-class family, and the economic and social status of women in the United States in the 1910s and early 1920s.

Jean Winthrop's growth takes place partly through books—perhaps a substitute for the geographical travels of a more traditional *Bildungsheld*. Hull is careful to record her young hero's bibliophilic journeys. Since Jean has little personal freedom, Hull indicates her changing mental environment in part through the books and authors she reads.[7] They include novels of Dickens and George Eliot, *Thorns and Briars* (a story set in the Civil War in which an old black woman drowns after being whipped, beaten, and raped by white men), Guizot's French history, Tennyson, historical novels, Edwin Caskoden's *When Knighthood Was in Flower*, *Les Miserables*, Matthew Arnold, Rabelais, *Leaves of Grass*, William Ernest Henley's poetry, and Marx. Her mother confiscates Kant, Hegel, and Olive Schreiner, but not before Jean has already consumed *The Story of an African Farm*. In part, Kitty identifies Jean's interest in books as a lamentable genetic inheritance from the husband she has grown to detest, and she goes to extraordinary lengths to crush any symptoms in Jean of her father's philosophical tendencies, actually snatching books from her daughter's hands rather than risk an infection of like-mindedness.

In addition to reading, Jean also seeks appropriate "real-life" models in her mother's generation and among her contemporaries after whom she might pattern her own rather confused life. Instructed from childhood to consider marriage her happy fate, Jean examines and rejects nearly every marital model she finds, particularly her parents' union, but also her friend Dorothy Tiverton's loveless marriage and her friend Eva's marriage to the disreputable Tom, which Jean views as a "hastening toward immolation" prompted by sexual fascination (318). Jean's landlady in Perry discomfits her by confiding that her husband abuses her, and both Jean's mother and her friend Daisy maintain that men are "brutes"(148), especially in marriage, an idea that the young Jean finds dismaying but intriguing. The pleasing example of Professor and Mrs. Small presents the possibility of happiness in marriage, but when Jean tries to envision her own parents happy together, her imagination fails her. "Perhaps," she surmises, "if they had known how to play—Still, if there were children, and not much money, maybe you couldn't play" (275–76).

Jean's mother Kitty clings to the bottom rungs of the middle-class ladder by virtue of her husband's professions but not his income, and a good portion of her unhappiness derives from the disparity between her expectations and reality. Jean's growing recognition of the importance of economic factors in family dynamics is reinforced by her working-class schoolmate Daisy, who reports that her sister Bessie has left her husband to go back to work as a book-keeper at the factory: "She says it's a cinch after being married. She says not having to ask anybody for money if she wants a pair of rubbers is worth the price of admission. Say, men have it easy, don't they?" (92–93). When Jean tries to imagine herself married, she, too, is repelled by the thought of economic dependence. "I'm in no hurry to end my happy days," she says to her brother. "Imagine me, 'Dear husband, can I have a nickel please? I spent that other nickel for soap last week!' " (331).[8]

From her friend Lora Tate, however, Jean also learns that marriage is not necessarily worse economically for women than the kinds of jobs usually open to them, since clerical or department store work is boring, tedious, exhausting, and poorly paid. She resolves to find a vocation that will enable her to support herself and that will also provide meaningful occupation. When she gets a teaching job that seems to promise independence from her family and some measure of significance, she soon realizes that female teachers like her colleague Rosa Porter are ground into near extinction and that male teachers who are less talented—even ones who are "boobs"—are paid much more than their female counterparts (299). Jean resolves to get more education so that she is not relegated for the rest of her life to the invisibility and poverty of female elementary school teachers.

Jean also studies the example of her unmarried art teacher, Miss Pennington, who has given up a promising career to care for her crippled mother. Jean recognizes Miss Pennington's carefully copied poems and sketches as a retreat into an inner life, "something within her, more real than life itself" (211). Seeing her teacher's pain, frustration, and despair, Jean rejects both sacrifice and retreat from the world as useful or appealing models for her own life.

Of all the models Jean examines, it is her mother's life that she most thoroughly rejects, and her mother bitterly feels Jean's increasing separation from her as a betrayal. On the other hand, Jean in turn feels betrayed by her mother, who, it seems to Jean, willingly condemns her daughter to a life of echoing unhappiness, of dependence and resentment. Among the many aspects of her mother's behavior that Jean does not wish to repeat, Jean rejects her martyrdom and withdrawal, especially once she recognizes herself falling

into a pattern established by both her mother and grandmother. Jean also dislikes her mother's intrusiveness and
manipulation. She describes her mother's attitude as "in-
tensely personal," and she speculates that this approach is
not necessarily idiosyncratic: "Perhaps mothers had to feel
that way" (216). Jean, in fact, frequently tries to understand what in her mother's behavior is individual choice and
what simply comes with the job. Eventually she identifies
her mother's emotional manipulation of the family as a
"futile . . . weapon of impotence" (281). Once she understands that her mother's sense of powerlessness underlies her
unfortunate patterns of behavior, Jean decides to search for
a partner or relationship that will not require her to be
powerless and a vocation that will secure her economic independence.

While Jean frequently dislikes and suffers from her
mother's behavior, she does feel some compassion for Kitty,
especially when she is aware of their shared experiences or
oppression as women. Although this identification between
mother and daughter causes Jean to feel some loyalty to her
mother, it serves chiefly to harden her resolve not to follow
her mother's footsteps into traditional female activities. She
concludes, for example, that one might accept housekeeping
grudgingly as a duty, but that no one in her right mind
would willingly choose it (and its attendant martyrdom,
dependence, and manipulation) as the center of her life.

While Jean's relationship with her mother is on the surface just another example of generational conflict, Hull
presents them also as two women on either side of the great
divide of the women's movement. Historian Carroll Smith-
Rosenberg points to the development of a marked mother/
daughter conflict in the United States at the conclusion of
the nineteenth century as daughters began to perceive their
mothers' lives as oppressive. Mothers, she says, "ignorant of
the new world their daughters wished to enter," offered inappropriate advice and sought control where earlier they
had "gently aided" their daughters. "Many mothers ex-

perienced as personal rejection their daughters' repudiation of the domestic role they . . . had so faithfully followed. Harsh generational conflict broke forth as psychological factors compounded institutional change."[9]

In *Quest*, Hull maintains that adolescent females must develop a sense of themselves as individuals, separate from their parents, but in this novel of development, the hero's separation from the family is more than a moment in her individual psychological development. Hull also points to the need for changes in the social construction of the family, especially women's role in it. The Winthrop family becomes a metaphor for a decaying social institution and for the restricted lives women were expected to lead within it. Jean grows steadily stronger as she removes herself, first, from her own relentlessly dissolving family unit, and, second, from her socially prescribed, family-based role as a middle-class female.

Quest, in fact, is concerned as much with the dissolution of the Winthrop family—and with it, the institution of the middle-class family—as it is with the development of its adolescent hero. The Winthrops are, in modern terms, a dysfunctional family. James and Kitty are truly ill-suited to each other. Hull portrays Kitty as a woman totally dependent economically upon a man whose judgment she does not trust (sometimes rightly so) and as someone whose very limited power is restricted to the emotional sphere. These restraints transform Kitty's considerable energies into a force destructive to herself and to the family she thinks she is serving—a theme Hull sounds in many of her novels. Much more conventional and practical than her husband, Kitty settles into a pattern of angry, desperate outbursts followed by periods of sullen, miserable, and spiteful withdrawal. As their marriage deteriorates, James becomes as wayward as Kitty has suspected him of being earlier: he turns to shady business deals, gambling, alcohol, other women, and a bitter, lethargic despair over his failures in business and in his family. James's economic control over the family ultimately works not only to his wife's disadvantage but also to his own.

The structure of the patriarchal nuclear family exacerbates Kitty and James's incompatibility, with disastrous results for everyone involved. Kathleen Field of the *New York Tribune* described *Quest* as

> the portrayal of a young girl's development in the unhappy atmosphere created by two unlike, unsympathetic individuals whose only moral right to live together was the fact that in some unreasoned moment they had married. This menagerie of two adult beings and their offspring bound together by marriage and birth constituted what Jean's father called home.[10]

While their desire to keep this miserable family unit together may seem like individual pathology in James and Kitty, Hull suggests that what we really have here is a case of a larger social psychosis, reinforced by the economic and legal systems. When Kitty tries to initiate a divorce suit, the judge balks at proceeding with the case because he is dedicated to preserving the "sanctity" of the family unit regardless of the pain being suffered by everyone involved, including the children. After a series of separations over the years, Kitty gives up and goes back to James because her legal recourse is illusory, because she is economically dependent upon him, and because she cannot think of anything else to do.

Quest was part of a continuing and frequently heated public discussion of divorce. Hull believed that, as she remarked in some notes on the novel, "There is a common American fallacy that so long as the home has been maintained something has been accomplished, no matter what takes place behind its closed doors." As Roger puts it, "divorce seemed polite and decent compared to some things," that is, compared to the way the Winthrops were living (300).[11]

Because she is so sensitive to the emotional atmosphere of her family, Jean makes a good observer of their family relations; because this emotional turmoil directly affects her well-being, Jean's experience also provides sharp commentary on the conventional wisdom that the family is inherently a safe harbor for its members. Katharine Anthony, Hull's sister member of the feminist club Heterodoxy, characterized *Quest* in *The Freeman* as a "defiant adventure in realism" in which "the conventional view of the family as a unit receives devastating treatment." Roger puts it more succinctly: "Families are bunk" (215).[12]

In the intense emotional atmosphere of the Winthrop home, Jean develops a keen awareness of emotional nuance very early in her life. She is told as a small child, for example, that her "badness" makes her mother unhappy and even ill. When Mrs. Winthrop also achieves these states without any inappropriate behavior on her daughter's part, little Jean quickly learns to feel guilty and responsible anyway. Like the child of alcoholic parents Jean quickly becomes a household arbiter, and she tries anything she can think of to smooth out difficult, tense, or potentially violent situations.

Hull titled this novel *Quest*, but the victory for Jean does not lie in actually seeking and finding the grail of more traditional tales, but rather in her decision to escape from her female restrictions—to leave her troubled family and to cast aside the family unit as her destiny. It is her departure from the family (both physical and metaphorical) that marks the climax of the novel. With Hull's female hero, then, the suspense of the plot (what little plot there is) revolves around her beginning a quest rather than completing one.

Hull defines Jean's maturing as that process during which she rejects alternatives that both older women and her contemporaries have adopted to survive within a culture that is so inhospitable to their growth, including marriage, martyrdom, retreat, resignation, religion, and an overriding concern with making oneself attractive to men. This rejection of traditional resolutions is essential to her emergence both as an adult and as a "New Woman." As Jean Winthrop steps out of her adolescence at the conclusion of *Quest,* she pledges herself to finding what Hull saw as the three crucial ingredients of the life of the New Woman: love, work, and self.

The term "love," as used by Jean and other characters, refers to a variety of things: marriage, a love relationship, sexuality, emotion, or a conflation of these meanings. Love in all its many meanings is the chief source of adolescent confusion for Jean, and in this confusion she is a typical adolescent hero. Her attempts to learn about sexuality, which she refers to as "this terrible mess" (257), are generally frustrated, and her response to sexual knowledge, especially in her early teens, resembles that of many literary adolescents, among them Lallie Rush in *Ordinary Families* and Mary Olivier in May Sinclair's novel of the same name—a combination of fear, shame, and curiosity.[13] Her most detailed information comes from books she discovers under the counter at a store where she works: *The Heptameron, The Decameron,* Rabelais. Totally caught up in reading this material, she becomes at times "ashamed of being ashamed. Something robust and vigorous stood out, reaching for her with cleansing power. But shame had tentacled roots of habit." When she tries a more genteel source of knowledge—*What a Young Girl Should Know*—it seems to her "mawkish and pale after Queen Margaret" (240). Eventually, Jean learns to respect and cherish her own body recognizing at the same time that its erotic demands can undermine her determination to be independent of the emotional chains that keep women subservient and ultimately unhappy.

As she grows up, Jean finds herself attracted to both females and males.[14] The intensity of her mother's anger over Jean's attachment to her classmate Esme Maurey reflects the growing social awareness, fear, and condemnation of women's passionate friendships in the early part of this century, fueled by the popularizing of work by men such as Sigmund Freud, Richard von Krafft-Ebing, and Havelock Ellis.[15] Hull's Cynthia stories and *Quest* mark an interesting transition in the process Lillian Faderman describes in her book *Surpassing the Love of Men*. Around the time of World War I, she says, magazine fiction shifted from unselfconscious portrayal of passionate friendships between women to silence or outright condemnation (297–313). In "The Fire," Hull presents Miss Egert (a woman suspected of what had by then come to be considered perverse or unhealthy behavior) as the responsible, unselfish, and admirable adult worthy of emulation; on the other hand, Hull portrays the socially sanctioned, "healthy" mother who voices the growing popular and professional hysteria about lesbianism as childish, unloving, and cruel. The adolescent girl, meanwhile, remains oblivious to the nature of the suspicion underlying her mother's anger. Far from condemning this relationship between Cynthia and Miss Egert, Hull instead presents Cynthia's love for her as a saving grace; the girl's maturing means that she will leave behind the restricted world of her mother, taking with her Miss Egert's values and the memory of her love.

Perhaps because of growing social pressure, Hull's criticism of the new attitudes toward homophilic attachments is less pointed in *Quest* than it is in the earlier Cynthia stories, and the description of Jean's responses is not as explicitly erotic. Instead, in *Quest* Hull emphasizes Jean's unconventional conviction that her physical strength and her sexual energy should be sources of pleasure and pride rather than shame. Kitty Winthrop still becomes hysterical over Jean's attractions to women, but Hull's portrayal of Kitty does not, like her portrayal of Mrs. Bates in the Cynthia stories, verge on parody. Miss McNealy, the older woman in *Quest* reminiscent of Miss Egert in "The Fire," is similarly important to Jean as an inspiration in her quest, but she is not, like Miss Egert, a source of ecstasy to Jean. Instead, Jean finds that "The decorum, the serenity, the assurance of Miss McNealy's thoughts stood before [her] in a curious mixture of barrier and ideal. The unattached tendrils of her affection pushed out around the woman. Perhaps some day they could be friends. Equal" (213). Although her feelings for Miss McNealy are at times intense, the relationship is not as highly charged as that between Cynthia and Miss Egert, nor is there the added confusion of conflict with her mother over this attachment.

Miss Pennington is the "older woman" to whose acquaintance Jean's mother does object because, as Jean's father explains, Kitty does not like Jean to keep company with "older women like that [who] sort of take a fancy for young girls, strong, healthy girls like you" (210). This reference to the lesbian menace is clearer than the veiled allusions in the Cynthia stories, but it makes no particular impression on Jean, who like the Cynthias, remains naive about the supposed dangers of same-sex attractions.

Jean's relationships with men are never really satisfying either. Her mild interest in David Sterrill has mostly to do with poetry, and she draws back quickly when she realizes that he wants a more physical relationship. With Luther Wallace Jean learns that it is possible to respond sexually to a person one neither loves nor intends to marry, for he represents the unwelcome prospect of a wholly conventional marriage in which she would be dependent and subordinate. Stuart Fletcher inspires apparently unrequited sexual longing in Jean, but he also opens a new view of the world to her and gives her more confidence in herself and in her ability to leave the confines of her parents' world. Although Stuart's encouragement is crucial to Jean, he also is not free of stereotypical responses to a woman with energy, talent, and intelligence. Stuart calls her an "Amazon" and insists that she would really like to be a man. "No.

Never," she says. But he rightly observes that she will "have trouble getting all you want" (313). He also describes her as a Minerva with a wonderful body, a mind like a man's ("yet distinct, not male," he adds), and a tender heart (312), but when she finally stands up to him in an argument about Marx, he dismisses her view as "female, personal" (338).

In Jean's world, Stuart seems about the best she can hope for in someone who recognizes her "real" self, and even he is lacking. At the end of their relationship, Jean dreams that she literally outgrows (i.e., becomes much larger than) both her father and Stuart—and, presumably, her respect for, fear of, and dependence upon the male authority and approval they represent. She pledges herself to finding a partner who could participate in a truly equitable union.

One of the central things Jean learns about finding an appropriate mate is that she must not simply turn off her mind and let herself be led by her heart or body. Jean discovers to her dismay that her mother was quite "in love" with her father before their disastrous marriage. Kitty becomes to Jean a prime illustration of the cost to women of refusing to use their minds, either in choosing their mates or in other kinds of observations or decisions. When her mother insists that it is more important to "Follow . . . the laws of good" than think, Jean asks, reasonably enough, how her mother knows what those laws are without thinking about them. Kitty replies, "You know well enough. Your heart tells you" (291). But Jean already knows the cost of allowing feeling to dominate one's judgment and one's life, in the form of her mother's jealous rages, her constant sense of betrayal. Jean determines to replace this heart-twang response with a more reasoned approach not only to moral judgment but also to questions of love.

When Jean thinks about her relationship with Stuart, she likens her helplessness in the face of his failure to love her to that of the girl in "The Snow Queen" who does not know how to melt the ice in the heart of her friend and playmate

Kay. Jean remembers that, when she was a child, the implications of this story (to find love and then have it withdrawn for reasons one does not understand and cannot control) were always so painful for her that she could never finish reading it. Gerda's story, in fact, ends happily, but it is an ending that would have helped Jean only in part had she read it. When Gerda finds her friend Kay, her open expression of joy—her tears—melt his heart, and his responding tears clear his vision. For Jean, however, simple expression of emotion will not solve anything in her relationship with Stuart; in fact, her emotion and her erotic response only blur, not clarify, her vision. What she must learn is to see him and her relationship to him more clearly. Even Stuart points out to Jean that she is indomitable "unless your heart betrays you" (337). After Stuart has left, Jean is relieved to find "her old feeling, deep at the core of self, clear, effulgent, inflexible, in spite of ignominy, love, anything! Submerged of late by the hectic, feverish flood of love. But still alive!" (337).[16]

While Gerda's resolution of her dilemma through the unfettered expression of feeling is inappropriate for Jean, it *is* important for Jean to have the equivalent of Gerda's robber girl and old woman—people like Miss McNealy—who recognize her strength and ability and who can offer her just enough practical help (e.g., information about how to apply to a university) so that she can discover and exercise her own strength. Like "The Snow Queen," *Quest* is a story of empowerment. Jean's growth is a process that results in her becoming strong enough to venture out into a potentially hostile world, knowing some of the dangers that await her.

At the end of the novel Jean sets out on a quest that she knows will be isolating but exciting. Even when she was still fairly young, Jean was drawn to the idea of a quest, inspired, for example, by the courage of her friend Anne Bishop who "dared to rush out on her quest," breaking through the false "wall" of rules and restrictions. Anne's death in childbirth makes Jean feel her own strength, "secret, indomitable . . . push[ing] up from depths as a living spring; it moved in her as antagonism, a secret rebellion upon which her strength might feed until she too broke through the wall" of restriction (137–38). By the end of the novel, Jean realizes that she has indeed become "strong, young, unutterably potent" (353).

Jean Winthrop adds a third term to the definition of the quest for new womanhood, one implicit but unstated in the Cynthia stories. Determined to find both love and work, she also swears to find "myself" (353). *Quest* ends not with a traditional closure of marriage or engagement but with Jean's challenge to a social order that demands that she live, in a sense, without a self. Jean pledges herself to this quest for self not in the more modern, hackneyed sense of "I need to find myself" or "I have to be me"; rather, she learns to identify and nurture a "curious, unfaltering inner confidence" (282). What Hull meant by the self in these tales of *Bildung* is an inner sense of integrity and confidence, a solid core at the center of the self that cannot be fractured no matter what forces are brought to bear against it. This development into strength, honesty, and wholeness was for Hull the real point of growth; it was central to her definition of maturity, and, as the essence of adulthood, it became the standard against which she measured her characters, both male and female, for the rest of her career.

When *Quest* first appeared in 1922, it was well received. The *New York Times* claimed that Hull's "admirable restraint adds immeasurably to the charm and reality" of the novel. This story of "the spectacle of a disintegrating family," the reviewer went on to say,

> must be bracketed as a realistic novel, and nothing but praise can be accorded its careful handling. Plot there is none in the accepted sense of plot. But the book achieves what it sets out to do—to draw a full-length figure of a growing girl in regrettable surroundings and to do it with a psychological veracity.[17]

The *Boston Transcript* described Hull's study of young Jean Winthrop as "keen and searching," while the *New York Tribune*'s Kathleen Field claimed that *Quest* "breathes the very essence of drama. It is a book to pick up the second time." Charles Trueblood in *The Nation* said that *Quest* is "in a word admirable, . . . a novel full of life, and full of a feeling that grows in a crescendo to an excellent climax." The *New York Evening Post* described the record of Jean Winthrop's struggles as "an absorbing story as well as a valuable study in child psychology." [18]

Reviewers were not entirely without reservations, however. One accused Hull of indulging in a slavish imitation of May Sinclair's *Mary Olivier*, early chapters of which are, like the beginning of *Quest*, written from a child's perspective with adult language and interpretation.[19] It is unclear whether Hull had read *Mary Olivier*, which explores over a period of forty-five years the "psychological history" of a central character who struggles to achieve a satisfactory relationship to her family and to men. Probably the resemblance of the two novels was more a result of the authors' similar psychological and political analyses than a matter of direct imitation.

The same reviewer who criticized Hull for imitating May Sinclair also forgave her for this fault on the grounds that she was an inexperienced writer who took herself and her material too seriously. "One feels," s/he remarked, "that the author has known her heroine very intimately indeed and has taken her too much to heart." Although this reviewer stood alone in being condescending about the subject of *Quest*,[20] it does seem to be true, judging from everything we know about Hull, that *Quest* is indeed a highly autobiographical novel, perhaps the obligatory first novel in which the author writes fairly directly from her own experience. Hull's later books, in addition to being more polished, draw less obviously from her personal life.

Helen Rose Hull was born in Albion, Michigan, on March 28, 1888, the oldest of four children and the only female. Her father, Warren C. Hull, earned a B.S. from Albion College when Helen was five, and in 1896 he received an M.S. from the same school. From 1884 to 1901 he served as the superintendent of schools in three Michigan communities: Birmingham, Albion, and Flint. In 1901 he went into the real estate business in Lansing and then into permanent unemployment following World War I, when he was in his late fifties. Hull's mother, Minnie Louise McGill Hull, was a schoolteacher before she married, but she left paid employment for a life centered on her family. For many years she was afflicted with poor health. Hull and her brother Frederick M. Hull shared the responsibility for supporting both their parents until their mother's death in 1933; they continued to support their father until his death at ninety-six in 1956, but Frederick, who stayed in Michigan, shouldered the main part of the burden. The Hull marriage was apparently a stormy one, with Minnie decamping to Plymouth frequently to stay with her sister Annie, but she and Warren were never permanently separated.[21]

Helen Hull's paternal grandfather, Levi T. Hull, was a printer and the owner and editor of the Constantine *Mercury* in Michigan. He encouraged Hull's childhood literary ambitions by publishing some of her earliest efforts in his paper; when Hull was eight, her grandfather also printed one of her stories in the form of a little book for family consumption called *Four Wishes*. An avid reader from as early as she could remember, Hull said that her childhood reading included anything she could get her hands on, including

> supplementary readers, lessons in hygiene, models of rhetoric, anything! The ceiling-high bookcases in the study had sets of Dickens, fat and gray, of George Eliot, fat and red, Guizot's History of France in many volumes, Les Miserables, The Hoosier Schoolmaster, Andersen's fairy tales.[22]

"I still have a scar under my chin," she recalled in 1942, "the result of a fall when I climbed up the shelves to reach a book on the top. Books and printing were so much the background of those early years that I do not remember when I did not intend to write."[23]

Hull graduated from Lansing High School with the class of 1905 and then commuted for two years from the family home on Baker Street in Lansing to attend Michigan Agricultural College (now Michigan State University). In her later years, she emphasized the fact that she studied a regular liberal arts curriculum, not home economics, as did many female students at the college.[24] Apparently Hull, like Jean Winthrop, suffered from awkwardness and social isolation. Around 1906 she wrote to an unidentified friend called "My dearest lady" while she was waiting for some of her classmates to return from a party. Explaining that she had never even owned a party dress, she confessed,

> I do feel just now as if I would like to be a pretty popular girl, instead of *me*. I feel as if I were being cheated out of something which really belongs to me. Suppose that I may come out as well as the rest in the end, but I do feel ornery tonight.

Hull never posted this letter, writing at the end that she was "ashamed of myself," but she preserved it among her personal papers.[25]

Like many other young women who sought employment at that time,[26] Hull became an elementary school teacher, first in the public schools of Dewitt (where like Jean Winthrop she roomed with the custodian and his wife) and then in East Lansing, for a total of three years. She then returned to college, financed partly by a loan from a former teacher, Janet White. In 1912 Hull completed a Ph.B. and some graduate work in English at the University of Chicago, and that fall she was hired to teach English composition at Wellesley College in Massachusetts.

At Wellesley Hull lived and worked in the company of other lively, independent, professional women, many of whom lived in "Wellesley marriages" with each other. There she met the woman with whom she would spend the next fifty years: Mabel Louise Robinson, an instructor in zoology who, within two years of Hull's arrival, left Wellesley to become, first, a researcher for an educational foundation in New York and then a specialist in writing for children.

In 1914 Hull and Robinson began their lifelong pattern of summering in the coastal village of North Brooklin, Maine, where they rented and eventually bought Bayberry Farm. There they did most of their writing, each in her own small building separate from the main house. Several other women from New York with artistic or literary interests also purchased or rented houses in North Brooklin, and they formed a small and unpretentious but lively summer community whose principal interests were writing, gardening, dog-walking, sailing, eating potluck dinners on the beach, bicycling, and sleeping outdoors in Gloucester hammocks.

In 1914, about the same time that Hull published a one-act play in the suffrage magazine *The Woman's Journal*, Carrie Chapman Catt offered her a position as a writer, speaker, and organizer for the New York State Suffrage Association. Under considerable pressure from her mother to avoid such women, Hull regretfully turned down the offer.[27] Still determined to leave what she saw as the artificially affluent and politically sterile environment of Wellesley, Hull resisted parental attempts to draw her into high school teaching in the midwest. In 1915, when she was twenty-seven, Hull moved to New York City, grateful for the offer of an appointment as lecturer at Barnard, and in 1916 she took her teaching across the street to Columbia University. Mabel L. Robinson, too, was hired by Columbia, where she completed a Ph.D. in Education (1916) with a dissertation on the curricula of women's colleges. Both

Hull and Robinson remained at Columbia for the rest of their professional lives and were central to the university's writing program for adult students in the Department of English and in the School of General Studies.

Although her mother may have thought she rescued Hull from the clutches of feminism by diverting her from the 1914 suffrage association job, Hull had already committed herself to the feminist movement at Wellesley and in Boston, where she lived during her last year of teaching at Wellesley. She became even more active once she moved to New York City. As she described these early years in a letter she wrote to her brother at the end of her life,

> I planned to join the Socialist Party, but after a few visits to their meetings, changed my mind. But I was asked to join a Saturday luncheon club called Heterodoxy, which channelled my rebellion into work to improve the status of women. I marched in the front line of a long parade of women of all ages, and I carried a banner saying Votes for Women all the long way up Fifth Avenue.[28]

Especially for someone who was both a writer and a feminist, the late 'teens was an exciting time to be in New York, when Greenwich Village was the scene of Cooper Union debates on feminism, endless talk in clubs, and a very active leftist publishing community. As a member of Heterodoxy, Hull met regularly with women from a wide variety of backgrounds and professions who were politically active, especially in the suffrage movement. Her sister Heterodites included, for example, Inez Milholland, Charlotte Perkins Gilman, Marie Jenny Howe, Inez Haynes Irwin, Doris Stevens, Crystal Eastman, Rose Pastor Stokes, Mary Ware Dennett, Elizabeth Gurley Flynn, Susan Glaspell, Fola La Follette, Alice Duer Miller, and Mary Heaton Vorse. Through Heterodoxy Hull participated in extended discussions not only of suffrage but also of the new field of psychology, for Freudian phrases were on the tip of everyone's tongue and a number of Heterodoxy members were particularly concerned with new theories of human development.

The 1920s were a heady time for Hull: in addition to the publication of her first four novels—*Quest* (1922), *Labyrinth* (1923), *The Surry Family* (1925), and *Islanders* (1927)—Hull's short fiction appeared regularly in major magazines, and she went overseas for the first time in 1926 to Turkey and Italy, where she wrote most of *Islanders*.[29] Nineteen thirty marked the publication of *The Asking Price*, the beginning of Hull's long association with Coward-McCann (Macmillan had published her first four novels), and the launching of a very prolific and successful decade, including the publication of six novels and a collection of short stories.

Hull's feminism, vigorous and overt in the 1920s, became more muted in her fiction of the 1930s as the climate of opinion in the United States became more conservative and as Hull herself grew disheartened at the ever diminishing returns from her generation's tremendous investment in the women's movement. She continued to record inequities and misery in middle-class marriage as well as the unfortunate effects of women's economic dependence, but in the 1930s she began to employ more conventionally "happy" endings in which estranged couples reunite—returning to the safety of known social forms rather than experimenting with new ones. These endings, however, usually did not really resolve the marital dilemmas she described in her fiction with great care. Although Hull bowed at times to certain literary and social conventions, she also retained a level of feminist analysis or observation that disrupted those seemingly more complacent or uncritical resolutions.[30]

Although the 1940s began well for Hull, her literary output slowed significantly by the end of the decade. Between 1940 and 1946, Hull published a collection of four novellas called *Experiment*, three more novels, and a biographical sketch of Madame Chiang Kai-Shek. In the late 1940s, however, Hull channelled most of her creative energies into professional activity, especially in the Author's Guild. A member of its council from 1935 to 1965, she served as its president from 1948 to 1951. In 1950, in collaboration with Elizabeth Janeway, Hull edited an Author's Guild publication, *The Writer's Book*, and in 1959 she co-edited a companion volume. Her own literary output in the 1950s included only two novels; they elicited relatively little critical notice.

Hull's last publications were two mysteries. The first, a rather unconventional example of the genre called *A Tapping on the Wall* (1960), won a Dodd, Mead prize for the best mystery written that year by a college teacher. The writing of this book, which Hull undertook as something of a joke, provided only slight distraction from the terminal illness of Mabel Louise Robinson, who died in February 1962, and the book's success offered Hull small consolation for the waning popularity of her more serious fiction. In order to fulfill her contract with Dodd, Mead she struggled to complete a second mystery, *Close Her Pale Blue Eyes*, during what were for her the bleak days of the summer of 1962. An account of the helplessness and slow death of a once-spirited older woman, the book is particularly poignant in light of Robinson's final illness. The 1960s was a time of poor health and discouragement for Hull, and although she worked intermittently on the manuscript of a novel called "Sibling," it was rejected by publishers [31]; for the most part she preferred to read and enjoy visits from her former students. Helen Rose Hull died on July 15, 1971, greatly disappointed that her fiction had disappeared almost entirely from both literary and popular view.

The most notable change in critical reaction to Hull's work was the increasing tendency to classify her as a "woman's" novelist, a term that became pejorative in the 1930s. Reviewers grew more critical of her fiction because they considered her subject matter—especially the nuances of family interaction—boring or too "lightweight" a topic for "serious" fiction. Ironically, Hull wrote about family life chiefly because she thought it mirrored, influenced, and was affected by social, political, and economic interaction in larger, more public spheres of activity. She believed that studying the dynamics of human relations on a microcosmic scale where they are easily observable, could enable us to function more successfully in our personal, communal, and international relations.

Principally, however, Hull's novels are studies of character: she portrays humans as creatures who have the potential to change through learning, and she presents them at moments of discovery which are crucial to their development. Her work is concerned, above all, with development, with *Bildung*. As we have seen, Hull's early fiction often featured vigorous young heroes pitting themselves against the social order. As Hull herself grew older and as the women's movement lost momentum, she wrote about women who no longer look to an exciting and limitless future. Recognizing that women's opportunities for employment were narrowing again and that the institution of marriage remained essentially unchanged in the 1930s (and 1940s and 1950s), Hull showed her middle-aged female characters demonstrating their maturity through patience and what she called "imaginative endurance." They do the best they can under difficult circumstances, learning to preserve their own integrity in situations in which it is easily undermined.

Throughout her career, Hull criticized gender-based prescriptions for behavior. Both her male and female protagonists learn that typically "masculine" and "feminine" traits or behavior must be tempered, whether in individual people or in social, economic, and political institutions. In a sense, then, Hull defines maturity as the achievement of a kind of personal or social androgyny. Even as early as *Quest*, Hull conveyed Jean's strength, energy, and promise in an interesting combination of male and female sexual imagery; for example, Jean feels her "potency" as "the soft spring night flow[s] in about her, dark, warm, pregnant" (353).

Helen Hull believed that people feel a "secret and devouring hunger for what we once called things of the spirit, an inner dignity, self-respect, fearlessness, tolerance, a discipline of the self."[32] Her characters struggle to achieve these "things of the spirit," all the while caught in a net of "their own follies, their madnesses, their weaknesses, their despairs, their futile, hidden impulses," and a whole set of external forces over which they have little control.[33] It is this struggle of her characters towards maturity that dominates her fiction, and it is her relentless and yet essentially generous portrayal of that struggle that draws us back to her work today.

Patricia McClelland Miller
Windham Center, Connecticut

NOTES

1. This edition of *Quest* has been photographically reproduced from the original edition, published in New York in 1922 by Macmillan. References to the book are cited parenthetically in the text.

2. "The Soul-Maker," *Harper's* 130 (Mar. 1915): 589–97. Hull's stories in *The Masses* include "Mothers Still," 6 (Oct. 1914): 14–15; "Yellow Hair," 8 (Feb. 1916): 15; "Unclaimed," 8 (May 1916): 10; "Usury," 8 (Sept. 1916): 7–10; "Till Death—," 9 (Jan. 1917): 5–6.

3. "Doris Lessing and the Parables of Growth," in Elizabeth Abel, Marianne Hirsch, and Elizabeth Langland, *The Voyage In: Fictions of Female Development* (Hanover, N.H.: University Press of New England, 1983), 205.

4. Jerome S. Buckley's *Season of Youth: The Bildungsroman from Dickens to Golding* (Cambridge, Mass.: Harvard University Press, 1974) provides the standard male-centered definition of the *Bildungsroman*. Abel, Hirsch, and Langland's *The Voyage In* is an

excellent volume of feminist scholarship on the genre. See also Annis Pratt, Barbara White, Andrea Loewenstein, and Mary Wyer, *Archetypal Patterns in Women's Fiction* (Bloomington, Ind.: Indiana University Press, 1981) and Patricia Myer Spacks, *The Adolescent Idea: Myths of Youth and the Adult Imagination* (New York: Basic, 1981). For a discussion of female characters' awakening to the limitations of their lives, see Susan J. Rosowski, "The Novel of Awakening" in Abel, 49.

5. Publicity notes for *Quest*, Helen Hull file, Macmillan Archives, New York Public Library.

6. These stories include "The Fire" (*Century*, Nov. 1917), "Separation" (*Touchstone*, Mar. 1920), "Alley Ways" (*Century*, Feb. 1918), "Groping" (*Seven Arts*, Feb. 1917), "Discovery" (*Touchstone*, Aug. 1918), and "The Fusing" (*Touchstone*, July 1919). They have been reprinted in a collection of Hull's short fiction, *Last September*, ed. Patricia M. Miller (Tallahassee, Fla.: Naiad, 1988), 1–111.

7. May Sinclair is also careful to note the reading habits of her adolescent heroine in *Mary Olivier* (New York: Macmillan, 1919).

8. Even though Roger is fairly traditional in fantasizing for himself a wife who will want to stay at home to minister to his needs, he also has learned enough from his parents' unhappiness that he swears he will divide his income evenly with his mate, that she will "never . . . lick my boots for money" (332).

9. *Disorderly Conduct: Visions of Gender in Victorian America* (New York: Oxford University Press, 1985), 33.

10. "Quest," *New York Tribune* Books Sec., 21 Jan. 1923: 23.

11. Helen Hull, notes on *Quest*, Helen Hull file, Macmillan Archives, New York Public Library. See also Ruth Hale's article published five years after *Quest*, "Why I Believe in Divorce," *Woman Citizen* (Mar. 1927): 10–11. For a discussion of the portrayal of divorce in some American novels of this period, see James Harwood Barnett, *Divorce and the American Divorce Novel, 1858–1937: A Study in Literary Reflections of Social Influences* (Philadelphia: University of Pennsylvania dissertation, 1939).

12. Katharine Anthony, "Sweeping Cobwebs," *Freeman* 7 (30 May 1923): 283–84. In *Ordinary Families* (1933), Arnot Robertson also argues against the middle-class family. Examining the deleterious effects of a "model" English family rather than one torn by conflict like Hull's American Winthrops, Robertson traces the in-

tellectual, emotional, and sexual development of adolescent heroine Lallie Rush.

13. Cf. also the Cynthias, Marjy Surry in Hull's third novel, *The Surry Family* (New York: Macmillan, 1925), and Ruth in Hull's story "Summer Storms," *Collier's* 76 (22 Aug. 1925): 19–20, 30–31. These characters continue to be confused about sexuality well into their twenties.

14. Jean's youthful battle of wills with her mother over "inappropriate" relationships is analogous to the mother/daughter struggles in three Cynthia stories: "The Fire," "Separation," and "Alley Ways."

15. Twentieth-century "sexologists" drew most heavily on Sigmund Freud's *Three Contributions to the Theory of Sex* (1905), in *The Basic Writings of Sigmund Freud*, trans. A. A. Brill (New York: Modern Library, 1938); Freud's "The Psychogenesis of a Case of Homosexuality in a Woman" (1920), in *The Standard Edition of the Complete Psychological Works of Sigmund Freud*, vol. 18 (London: Hogarth, 1955); Havelock Ellis's *Studies in the Psychology of Sex: Sexual Inversion* (1897; reprint, Philadelphia: F. A. Davis, 1911); and Richard von Krafft-Ebing, *Psychopathia Sexualis* (1882; reprint, New York: Surgeons Book Co., 1925). See Lillian Faderman, *Surpassing the Love of Men: Romantic Friendship and Love between Women from the Renaissance to the Present* (New York: William Morrow, 1981), 239–53. See also Carroll Smith-Rosenberg, "The Female World of Love and Ritual," *Disorderly Conduct: Visions of Gender in Victorian America* (New York: Oxford University Press, 1985): 53–76.

16. Cf. Hull's one-scene drama, "The Idealists," *Touchstone* 1 (Sept. 1917): 457–63. The heroine, Mary Lake, rejects two suitors; one cannot accept her eroticism and the other cannot accept her intelligence. She sees herself "wrenched . . . out of chains" by her decision to have neither of them.

17. *New York Times* Book Rev., 12 Nov. 1922: 24–25.

18. D. L. M., "*Quest:* A Study in Fiction of the Growth of a Woman," *Boston Transcript* Books, 18 Nov. 1922: 5; Kathleen Field, "Quest," *New York Tribune* Books Sec., 21 Jan. 1923: 23; Charles Trueblood, "Some Looks at Life," *Nation* 116 (7 Feb. 1923): 152–53; *New York Evening Post* Lit. Rev., 30 Dec. 1922: 355.

19. "Briefer Mention," *Dial* 74 (Feb. 1923): 210. Whether Hull knew Sinclair's work or not, she certainly was writing in the age of fascination with stream of consciousness narration: *Quest* was published the same year as James Joyce's *Ulysses* and Virginia Woolf's *Jacob's Room*, and six volumes of Dorothy Richardson's *Pilgrimage* had appeared between 1915 and 1922. Hull used the technique in a relatively unadulterated form only in the first few pages of *Quest* and not again in any highly stylized way until her last novel, *Close Her Pale Blue Eyes* (1963), which in several lyrical passages bears a striking resemblance to *To the Lighthouse*. *Hawk's Flight* (1946) contains several chapters in the first person, but they are presented as Carey Moore's attempt to *write* about her past.

20. Kathleen Field, for example, described *Quest* in the *New York Tribune* as "a remarkable study of feminine psychology in immaturity . . . a work of real distinction" (23).

21. Letter, Frederick C. Hull to author, 26 July 1989.

22. *Saturday Evening Post*, 1 June 1935: 87.

23. "Helen Hull," Stanley J. Kunitz and Howard Haycraft, eds. *Twentieth Century Authors: A Biographical Dictionary of Modern Literature* (New York: H. W. Wilson, 1942), 687.

24. Autobiographical notes, Collection of Frederick C. Hull.

25. Collection of Frederick C. Hull. Cf. the college experiences of other young heroines in Arnot Robertson's *Ordinary Families* (1933; reprint, New York: Dial, 1982); May Sinclair's *Mary Olivier;* Dorothy Canfield Fisher's *The Bent Twig* (1915; reprint, New York: Holt, 1942); Honore Willsie Morrow's *Lydia of the Pines* (New York: A. L. Burt, 1917); Olive Deane Hormel's *Co-ed* (New York: Scribner, 1926); Bess Streeter Aldrich's *A White Bird Flying* (New York: Appleton, 1931); Warner Fabian's *Unforbidden Fruit* (New York: Boni & Liveright, 1928); Kathleen Millay's *Against the Wall* (New York: Macaulay, 1929); Mary Lapsley Guest's *The Parable of the Virgins* (New York: Richard R. Smith, 1931); and Helen Hooven Santmyer's *Herbs and Apples* (Boston: Houghton Mifflin, 1925). See also John O. Lyons, *The College Novel* (Carbondale, Ill.: Southern Illinois University Press, 1962).

26. See Joanne Meyerowitz's study of women workers in the midwest during this period, *Women Adrift: Independent Wage Earners in Chicago, 1880–1930* (Chicago: University of Chicago Press, 1988).

27. Letters, Helen R. Hull to Minnie Louise McGill Hull, 30 April and 6 May 1914, Collection of Frederick C. Hull.

28. Helen R. Hull to Frederick M. Hull, 2 Jan. 1970, Collection of Frederick C. Hull.

29. *Islanders* was reissued by The Feminist Press in 1988.

30. For a discussion of women's "palimpsestic" writing, see Sandra Gilbert and Susan Gubar, *Madwoman in the Attic: The Woman Writer and the Nineteenth Century Literary Imagination* (New Haven: Yale University Press, 1979), especially 73.

31. Both Coward-McCann and Dodd, Mead refused to publish this novel, which reworks some of the material from *Quest*.

32. Typescript of 1939 WABC broadcast, Collection of Frederick C. Hull.

33. *Through the House Door* (New York: Coward-McCann, 1940), 99.

ACKNOWLEDGMENTS

I would like especially to recognize the generosity and assistance of Frederick C. and Eileen Hull. I also gratefully acknowledge the help of the Rare Book and Manuscript Division of the Library of Columbia University, the Special Collections and Interlibrary Loan Departments of the University of Connecticut Library, Wyn Hackmann of the College Archives at Albion College, the Periodicals Department of the Central Connecticut State University Library, Judith Schwarz, Alden Waitt, Joanne O'Hare and Florence Howe at The Feminist Press, Barbara D. Wright, Jennifer Brown, Susan Goranson, and my parents, Jane and Donald Miller.

The Feminist Press at The City University of New York offers alternatives in education and in literature. Founded in 1970, this nonprofit, tax-exempt educational and publishing organization works to eliminate sexual stereotypes in books and schools and to provide literature with a broad vision of human potential.

OTHER TWENTIETH CENTURY NOVELS FROM
THE FEMINIST PRESS

Brown Girl, Brownstones, by Paule Marshall. Afterword by Mary Helen Washington. $8.95 paper.

The Changelings, by Jo Sinclair. Afterwords by Nellie McKay, Johnnetta B. Cole and Elizabeth H. Oakes; biographical note by Elisabeth Sandberg. $8.95 paper.

Daddy Was a Number Runner, by Louise Meriwether. Foreword by James Baldwin and afterword by Nellie McKay. $$8.95 paper.

Daughter of Earth, by Agnes Smedley. Foreword by Alice Walker. Afterword by Nancy Hoffman. $9.95 paper.

The End of This Day's Business, by Katharine Burdekin. Afterword by Daphne Patai. $35.00 cloth, $8.95 paper.

Islanders, by Helen R. Hull. Afterword by Patricia McClelland Miller. $10.95 paper.

Leaving Home, by Elizabeth Janeway. New foreword by the author. Afterword by Rachel M. Brownstein. $8.95 paper.

The Living Is Easy, by Dorothy West. Afterword by Adelaide M. Cromwell. $9.95 paper.

Now in November, a novel by Josephine W. Johnson. Afterword by Nancy Hoffman. $35.00 cloth, $9.95 paper.

Quest, by Helen R. Hull. Afterword by Patricia McClelland Miller. $11.95 paper.

Sister Gin, by June Arnold. Afterword by Jane Marcus. $8.95 paper.

This Child's Gonna Live, by Sarah E. Wright. Appreciation by John Oliver Killens. $9.95 paper.

The Unpossessed, by Tess Slesinger. Introduction by Alice Kessler-Harris and Paul Lauter. Afterword by Janet Sharistanian. $9.95 paper.

Weeds, by Edith Summers Kelley. Afterword by Charlotte Goodman. $9.95 paper.

For a free catalog, write to The Feminist Press at The City University of New York, 311 East 94 Street, New York, NY 10128. Send individual book orders to The Talman Company, Inc., 150 Fifth Avenue, New York, NY 10011. Please include $2.00 for postage and handling for one book, $.75 for each additional. *Prices subject to change without notice.*